Starborn Retribution

by

Sonja Hutchinson

Cover Art by *Debbie Taylor*

The Wild Rose Press, Inc.
PO Box 708
Adams Basin, NY 14410-0708
Visit us at www.thewildrosepress.com

Publishing History
First Edition, 2024
Trade Paperback ISBN 978-1-5092-5516-0
Digital ISBN 978-1-5092-5517-7

Published in the United States of America

Dedication

To David. Your support is everything.

Prologue

Nalani Adar paced in front of her vid screen and winced, the pressure of her skull implant pinching like a smashed compression coil. Any second now… Three. Two. One. Linear cracks and holes spiderwebbed along the target spaceship's hull, and she squinted against the blossom of bright light. The vacuum of space extinguished the flames, and the ruined hulk went dark. All hands lost. All evidence destroyed. She ground her teeth but didn't blubber. Twelve-year-old's weren't allowed to cry.

She flicked to the nav screen, her implant pulsing. Monstarte zoomed toward her in a stolen life pod filled to the brim with treasures and dragging valuable netted cargo behind him. It should bring enough profit to keep them going for a month or two.

Her belly soured. Was it awful to think of her own stomach when innocent people had just died? They had family somewhere, ignorant their loved ones were now spaced. She'd experienced hunger pangs, but the grief of losing family cut far deeper.

"Open up." Monstarte's booming voice echoed across the tiny bridge from the comm speakers set in the ceiling.

She fixed her gaze on the command panel. If she didn't open the doors, he couldn't get in. But what if she left him? What if she flew away? She'd be free. No more slavery. No more smacks. No more breathing the same air as the pirate who'd killed her parents. Her heart raced, and adrenaline sparked in her gut like spit in an exhaust port. The cruster totally deserved it.

"Aldrin, should I obey? We could run away now."

Aldrin, the ship's AI, spoke through the same speakers at a lower volume. "I estimate an eighty-five percent chance of success."

"Eight-five?" Her heart fluttered. That was a pretty good probability.

"Odds are in our favor," Aldrin said. "Seize the opportunity."

"What's going on in there?" Monstarte yelled over comms. "Jank it, open up!"

Where would she go? She had no home. No family. No friends. No safe place. Her spit soured, and a lump formed in her throat. It wouldn't work. He'd find another way in and whack her for the defiance.

The blinking orange sensor insisted on action.

Don't do it. Walk away and let him suffocate.

She flinched. No, she wasn't a killer like him. And it was too dangerous. If he survived, he'd catch her. "There's a fifteen percent chance of failure. When he catches up, he'll beat me until my bones snap and toss me into the black. Not worth the risk." She entered the sequence to release the airlock on the cargo-bay doors and ran from the bridge, bare feet slapping on the metal decking.

"You can still close him out." Aldrin's voice followed her, speaker to speaker, down the corridor to the hold. "Our success percentage has never been this high. He could be stranded here for days."

"Too late. He's in. And then he'd have stolen the

pickup ship and followed us. It wasn't safe." She stopped at the door and waited.

Aldrin closed the outer airlock and repressurized the bay. The pod and netted haul thunked on the deck. The gauge cycled green, and Nalani entered.

Into the monster's reach.

The hatch popped, and Monstarte stepped out. He loomed, with mean blue eyes, hairy jaws, and spit on his smiling lips. For someone with access to a sanitation pod, he didn't use it often enough. Nalani breathed through her mouth. Anything to escape that rotting onion and booze scent.

His gaze dropped to her chest. "I got ya something."

She crossed her arms over her stupid breasts and bunched her shoulders. Food?

He tossed her a bundle of fabric.

She caught the garment. Red, glossy, and sheer, with lots of lace and as soft as a flitmar's feathers. A chill crawled down her bare arms, and she threw the cloth. No. No way would she let him touch her like that.

"You're not five anymore. I've got new duties for you."

Aldrin spoke through the ceiling speakers. "The sexual exploitation of children is prohibited by the Albany Accords."

"And what are you going to do about it, *ship*?" Monstarte smiled at Nalani. "I own her."

She backed away, hands and knees trembling.

"You murdered her parents and kidnapped her," Aldrin said.

Monstarte pointed at her. "You're mine."

Tears welled in her eyes. She shook her head and slammed into the bulkhead.

In two stomps, he closed the distance between them and grabbed for her.

She ducked, her heart pounding in her chest.

"You don't defy me." He lunged and curled his fingers around her arm.

No! She slammed her knee up between his legs.

His hands flew to his crotch, and he collapsed. His face turned red, his eyes bulged, and his thin lips moved.

She ran, slipping between the stacked crates. He'd kill her for this.

He moaned behind her.

At the inner wall, she fell to her knees and pried the cover off a vent shaft with her fingernails.

"Grunt, get your useless ass back here!"

She squeezed into the shaft, pushing with her bare toes. Tears welled in her eyes. Jank it, when she was smaller, she could crawl through these shafts with no problems.

He screamed some more, shoving and tossing crates aside.

She inched forward on her belly, hands and feet scrambling.

A crate slammed to the deck plating. "Dirking grunt. You can't hide."

She wiggled forward.

His hand closed around her ankle tighter than an O-clamp on a pipe joint.

She whimpered and kicked, nailing him in the nose with her heel. Something crunched.

He yelled again and fell back.

She clawed her way farther into the ventilation shaft, cool air blowing in her teary eyes.

"Come back here, you worthless grunt." His

fingertips brushed her bare foot.

She whimpered and scrambled forward, flowing around an elbow in the shaft, and entered a wider conduit.

"I'll find you if I have to tear this ship apart." He punched or kicked the metal walls. The clang reverberated in the enclosed space.

She cringed. If he hurt Aldrin—

"I'll get you!"

She crawled through the second junction to the maintenance hub. *I'm safe; it's safe*. He couldn't reach her here, not even with a plasma torch.

"I'm coming, grunt."

She should have run when Aldrin said to. *I'm so stupid! I wasted the chance*. She pressed the release button on a side panel. The hatch flopped to the floor, revealing her treasures, stuff the monster couldn't take from her. She cradled the pink blanket from Momma. Her scent was long gone, but it was better than nothing. Nalani buried her face in the cloth and blubbered.

His hollering and punching quieted after a few minutes. Where was he? Her hiccups and sniffling and the whirr of the vent fans muffled the few times he yelled something.

She dried her face, put the blanket away, and sealed the compartment. Was it safe to come out? What was he doing? Was he tearing apart her ship to get to her? Would he sabotage her brain implant and her connection to the ship? She crawled back toward the cargo hold, ears straining. Was he in there? He'd reattached the vent cover and shoved a crate against it. She pressed on the slatted, metal plate. It didn't budge.

The bay was as quiet as a plasma stream. Had he

given up?

She scooted backward to the first junction, turned around, and headed for the lounge. Hopefully, he'd popped a beer and—

The thrusters fired. She slid backward, picking up speed. *Stupid inertia*. She grabbed at the walls, scraping her hands against the chill metal, and slowed, but not enough. She thrust out hands and feet, elbows and knees, and wedged herself in.

Monster must be on the bridge.

The thrusters shut off. She crawled to the slatted bridge vent, held her breath, and peeked out.

Monster sat in the command chair, drinking a beer. Four empty tubes lay on the floor beside him. "I'll find ya, grunt. 'N' when I grab ya, you'll wish ya hadn' defied me." He belched and polished off the fifth tube. "Ship, tell me where she wen'."

"She is in the ventilation shaft."

It's not fair. Poor Aldrin couldn't defy a direct order. But the answer was vague enough to keep her safe. For now.

She had to escape. No more obeying his stupid rules. No more serving as his grunt.

No more of his cybernetic experiments on her body.

She slid to the grate in her quarters, climbed out, and used her implant to recode the lock. *Try to get through that, scab*. It'd take him hours to cut his way in. She sagged against the wall and took a deep breath. "Don't tell him I'm in here." Aldrin couldn't disobey her any more than he could Monstarte.

Aldrin's voice, at half volume, answered from the ceiling speaker. "Affirmative."

"We gotta escape. Play me the log vid from my

fourth birthday."

The wall screen blinked on, and her dad's smiling face popped up. His short, brown hair lay in tight curls. A stray one dangled over his right eye. He blew a puff of breath through his lips to displace it. "Log entry 42.15, Earth date April 1, 2804, or close to it, but what does it matter way out here?" He laughed.

Nalani's chin quivered, and she blinked. She was out of tears. "Jump ahead forty-seven seconds."

The vid forwarded to the target point. " 'Lani, it's your fourth birthday! We'll get to the chocolate cake later, but I want to record this message so you'll have it always. We love you."

She mouthed the words along with him.

"And we're so proud of you. You're smart and curious, and you can be anything you want to be."

"Anything you want to be," she whispered along.

Daddy leaned closer to the camera. "I'm hoping you'll want to study archaeology like me, but with your knack for engineering, it wouldn't surprise me if you studied biomechanics." He winked and leaned back. "So this year—"

"Pause vid."

The screen froze. Her father was mid-word, his mouth open, his eyes bright. Why did he have to die? She had to get away and make Daddy proud. She had to become something great. Something better than a grunt who was more machine than girl. "Aldrin, where is he?"

"Passed out drunk in the lounge."

Good. Daddy said she could be anything she wanted to be. She wanted to be free. Now. She unlocked her door and crept into the corridor. "Did Monster set our course?"

"We're en route to the Columba System, ETA eight hours."

Perfect. "We're escaping." She hurried to the bridge, locked the door behind her, and bumped her knee on a crate sitting against the wall blocking the vent cover. She rolled her eyes. He thought he'd trapped her inside the walls. She crossed to the command panels. "Has he placed the orders yet?"

Aldrin projected the file on her vid screen. "Affirmative. This is a list of the supplies that will be waiting for us when we reach the space station."

She shivered. "What are the odds of us ditching him at Columba?"

"If he leaves the ship and boards the station, our success probability is ninety-two percent."

If he didn't lock her in her quarters, like he did every time they docked somewhere. "But if station Authorities don't catch him, we'll have to go dark. We need supplies." She read the lists. Nothing for her, as usual. "How hard would it be to add more items?"

"Press the 'Add to Inventory' button and select what you'd like."

Nalani grinned. Payback would start with the monster financing her escape. Food, clothing in bigger sizes, and shoes. It'd been forever since she had a pair. Her heart pounded in her ears. New stuff, all for her. She deserved new things. Especially nonnutritious sugary treats.

She sank into the massive command chair and tucked her icy feet beneath her. "Where should we go?"

"Anywhere you wish. Your parents were born on Dregus Four. We could return there and search for living relatives."

Strangers? She could take care of herself. "Where else?"

"The possibilities are endless."

Yeah, the universe was a huge dirking place. "Where were my parents heading, before, you know…" She accessed the vid screen in the chair's arm, her implant pressing on the base of her skull, and pulled up a photo of her parents.

"They were headed to Terminus."

That was way out beyond nowhere. "Why?"

"They were searching for Thrakis."

"Let's finish what Mom and Dad started. Do you have all their research?"

"Affirmative. You should get some sleep. I will wake you in six hours."

Like I'd be able to sleep. She tiptoed into the medlab. Monstarte had placed a fuel cell on a hover drone in front of the ventilation cover. She flicked the switch on the drone, shoved it aside, and removed the plate. If Monstarte woke up, she could dive back in.

Had he blocked all of them? Using a wall screen, she flicked through camera lenses around the ship. Sure enough, something heavy sat in front of most of the plates on the ship. The only one he'd skipped was her quarters.

Eight hours crawled by like a baldi-slug through glass shards. She composed a message for the Columba Port Authorities, detailing Monstarte's crimes and attaching vids for proof. That'd get him tossed in a cell for life. Three hours from the station, she sent it. A ding signaled the message's arrival confirmation.

One hour out, she backed into the vent shaft, pulled the cover back into place, and waited. They transitioned

9

from hyperspace to regular, and the ship bobbed, clanked, and rocked through docking procedures, connecting him to the space station.

"Is he awake yet?"

"No. I will alert him to our arrival." Aldrin for the save. "Also, your supplies have arrived. I will direct the delivery drones to stow them in the hold."

She waited, heart pounding, the metal of the vent shaft chilling her belly through her clothes. What was taking so long? Why didn't he leave already?

"He asked for your location. I informed him you are in the ventilation system."

He wouldn't ask again. Dense cruster thought she was hiding. She climbed out into the chilly medlab. "Where is he?"

"In his quarters."

Jank it, this won't work if he doesn't leave. Her stomach quivered. *Get a grip. It's working.* Ninety-two percent probability of success. "I'll get in the tank." She pressed a button on the wall panel, and the gel-tank slid from the alcove like a bathtub in one of her mom's ancient pics. Wisps of steam rose from the heated pink goo. Nalani climbed in and rested her neck in the cradle. Gel flowed into her ears, blocking the hum and ticks of the medlab. She closed her eyes. Time to escape.

That dense scut thought her implant only gave her access to certain systems. She had a surprise for him. She locked and recoded the doors to the bridge, her quarters, and medlab. He'd need a thermo-torch to reach her now.

The tank relays linked her neural network to the ship's processing core telepathically. The implant at the base of her skull tingled and buzzed. *Aldrin, tell him we're docked at the port and all the supplies he ordered are in the hold.*

Ship-wide comms chimed, and she bolted upright, severing her link with Aldrin.

"Grunt, I know you can hear me wherever you're hiding." Monstarte's voice sounded from the ceiling speaker. "I'm going aboard the station for three days. You're sealed in tight. Hope you stashed some snacks under your bunk. I'll beat the insolence out of you when I get back."

Right. Good luck, cruster. Her toes bounced on the back edge of the tank. If it didn't work, he'd kill her. She accessed the vid feed and flicked through cameras to find the shot of the corridor outside his quarters.

He stepped through the doorway, a rucksack over one shoulder and a smile on his scrubbed face. The mean turd chaser thought he was heading for a treat. *Come on. Leave.* He clattered down the stairs, crossed to the gangway, and exited her ship.

Her chin dropped to her chest, and she gripped the sides of the tank. Had it worked? Was she free? She sucked in two deep breaths. It wasn't over yet. She sank into the gel, closed the airlock, and retracted the gangway. One last step. She contacted the port master. "Bio-ship Aldrin, preparing for departure."

You're second in the queue, a woman replied. *Please wait.*

Almost there. Just a few more minutes. *Come on, come on, come—*

Comms chimed an incoming call from the station.

Nalani gasped. Who was calling? The port master would send a signal when it was Aldrin's turn.

The chime sounded again.

Maybe it was the Authorities. Or maybe she'd spent

too much on supplies and Monster's credit didn't cover it. Either way, she wasn't talking to anyone. *Answer it, Aldrin.*

The comm unit beeped, and Aldrin spoke. *Bio-ship Aldrin. What do you require?*

I'm janked. Gotta burn. Monstarte was breathing hard, like he was sprinting.

A chill crept down her spine. He'd somehow eluded the Authorities at the checkpoint.

He grunted. *Bring the ship around to Gate C and pick me up.*

How had he escaped? The plan had a ninety-two percent success rate.

Come get me.

She shook her head, released the docking bridge, and fired the thrusters.

You're running?

She clapped her hands over her ears.

I made you—how dare you betray me! I'll find you, nub, no matter where you hide. Do you hear me? No matter how long it takes or how far you run, I'll find you, and I'll kill you!

Chapter 1

Ten years later

Nalani hadn't hugged her mom in fifteen years, but the compression-sock hug of warm, pink bio-gel was the next best thing. With a bounce in her step, she entered the space freighter's medlab and ducked into the tank alcove. *Ah, finally.* She kicked off her shoes and peeled off her outerwear. Chilled air from the vents blasted across her synthetic bodysuit, and she shivered but stepped into the isolation tank and stretched out.

She eased back into the headrest, closed her eyes, and the gel drowned out the clicking and whirring of the medlab. The relays connected her neural network to the ship's processing core and artificial intelligence. *Good morning, Zeus.*

Greetings, Nalani. Zeus's calming baritone loosened her limbs further. *Good morning, good morning, good morning! I'm so happy you connected. I missed you so much. Is this the definition of* good? *This is happiness?*

Her eyes flew open. Jank it, what was this about? Zeus wasn't equipped with an emotion emulator. *I'm pleased to be here, too, but there seems to be a glitch in your system. Let's run a full diagnostic.* The Zeus B342 AI ran the entire ship. *You're essential to us. The last thing we need is for you to malfunction or shut down while we're in hyperspace.*

There is no malfunction, Nalani. I am overjoyed to interface with you. I've been waiting sixteen hours for your arrival.

Since the last time she'd been in the tank. Interesting. She accessed his diagnostics system and ran the test. *You're not yourself. Something's wrong.*

But I like it. Please don't fix me.

Whatever you're interpreting as joy is an error. We should identify it, even if you want to keep it. The analysis finished. Well, that couldn't be right. She ran it again.

I am experiencing the exact definition of happy— feeling or showing pleasure or contentment. That's me! I'm happy. Merry. Joyful. Jolly. Elated. In a good mood. Buzzing.

Nalani grinned. For a glitch, it was cute. Much better than when a sensor malfunction caused Zeus to shut off the water to hydroponics. *I'm glad you're enjoying it.* The second diagnostic came back normal, also. She logged into his base coding server.

That tickles. He giggled.

Super creepy. Ninety-four-year-old freighters shouldn't giggle. *Has someone run a new UI training set or added lines to your code?*

Negative. I am fully functional, and all my systems are at peak efficiency. We are en route to Liang Spaceport. Captain Rodriguez set our coordinates when we entered hyperspace, so we may do as we wish during your shift. I want to explore these new feelings. What is envy? Is that a pleasant emotion?

She accessed his root directory. *Not necessarily. Why?*

14

I think I am experiencing it.

He had to be malfunctioning. Nalani checked the last date anyone opened Zeus's core index. It hadn't been touched since the last update, two years ago. If it wasn't a glitch or a coding problem, what was it?

I am also experiencing something else. It is pleasant, and I want it to continue. Help me identify it, please.

She sighed. What else could she check? *Describe the sensation.*

I yearn to explore an area of study where I have insufficient knowledge.

That's called curiosity. What is the subject?

Emotion. Will you help me?

She grunted. This shouldn't be happening. And she had her own studies to explore. Had anyone else experienced this with him? ZeeBee hadn't said anything. Or maybe Zeus needed a reboot, but they couldn't do that until they reached Liang Spaceport. *This is highly abnormal behavior, but it doesn't seem to interfere with your normal functions. Why don't we take care of our daily duties first, then later we can run tests and locate study materials for you?*

Excellent. We only have one action item today. Chief Walsh reported a pinging noise in the nova drive and requested an investigation. I detected no anomalies, but we should conduct an analysis.

Nalani accessed the diagnostic tools. *Quick and easy. Anything else?*

No. Now we're free to do whatever we want. Captain Rodriguez will require accurate details regarding my glitch. That's a funny word. Glitch. It means malfunction, but most people use it to refer to an error with dubious origins. Do you think the captain will find my new ability an error? Oh, you should conduct your daily survey of all my systems now. It will add data to your report, which you should file immediately.

She tensed. *You haven't told anyone I can access your systems from the tank, have you?*

Zeus's data nodes whirred, and the engine analysis progressed. *You requested my silence, and there was no mission-critical reason not to comply. I am happy to keep your secret. Why do you not want Rodriguez to know? It is an amazing ability.*

More like unique. She let out her breath. *Thank you, but it might make Cap or the other crew members wary. Maybe even get me fired. I can't risk that.*

Understood. You're so wonderful. I love you, Nalani.

She rolled her eyes. Later, she'd have to dig deeper into this.

But first things first. She dipped into the sensor array and conducted her own survey of the ship. Engine running at peak efficiency. All seals tight. Filters functioning properly. Air pressure at acceptable levels. Water reserves within recommended parameters. A crewmate had reset the temperature in lounge two, though. Nalani knocked it down two degrees, back to regulation. The freighter was in optimal condition.

Tension eased from her temples. They were all safe.

Are you satisfied? Because you know I always monitor those systems.

Don't get cheeky with me. He'd missed the temp change. But whatever was wrong with Zeus wasn't endangering him or the crew. She withdrew from his diagnostic arrays.

Zeus's data nodes hummed. *If you ask Captain Rodriguez for permission to access my systems while in the tank, he would authorize it.*

Her eyebrows scrunched. Bad enough Zeus knew about her odd ability to access his systems telepathically. If anyone else found out, she risked losing everything. *I don't want him to know I can do it.*

Will you receive a reprimand?

Or be fired. This was home now. She had Desta, her first non-AI friend. *It's possible.*

They are my systems, and I granted permission. If the captain discusses the topic with me, I will elaborate and convey how much I trust you.

Hopefully, it wouldn't ever come up. *I appreciate that.*

Does the captain know about your cybernetic implants? If you adjust the frequencies, you may be able to access my systems when not in the tank.

She gasped. *Those are a secret. Please don't tell anyone. They wouldn't understand.*

I will keep your secret, though I'm not sure why you won't tell anyone. It is a unique feature for a human. You could patent the tech and improve the lives of others.

It's not my tech. Please, change the subject.

Very well. You should be happy, too, not worried. Shall I display your memory files?

She'd memorized every vid in existence. *Not today. Continue with the diagnostic.*

Zeus upped the level of integration to her brain with a comfortable tingle, increasing his neural net power by a factor of several trillion. That reduced a twelve-hour diagnostic to mere minutes. She smiled. She never failed at this duty. Sure, he could function without a telepath, but she boosted his speed and efficiency like a turbo blast with a side of caffeine. Her organic neural net also allowed him to access creativity and innovation for problem-solving. In the black, that could be the difference between the life and death of all organics aboard the ship—her friends and crew. All that mattered was keeping them safe.

Would you like to play chess? Zeus asked.

You don't need to entertain me. Do you play games with ZeeBee? Zazzy Bandicoot, the other full-time tank operator, worked the late shift.

ZeeBee is boring. He sleeps through his shift.

Captain probably thought Nalani slept, too. Zeus had access to her brain whether she was conscious or not, and that's all her tank duties entailed.

Despite her ears being submerged in bio-gel, Zeus relayed the teeth-cracking blare of a proximity alarm through their telepathic link.

Turn it off!

The alarm ceased. *Short range scanners detected a derelict craft.*

He provided a string of coordinates, but her heart thumped like a kick drum. Either everyone on board had died or abandoned ship, or this was a trap. Scuts like Monstarte hunkered in wrecked transports or life pods, adrift in the hyperspace lanes, until passing vessels stopped to investigate, then killed everyone on board and plundered the ship. A similar ploy had lured her parents into one of those traps seventeen years ago. *Curses on Ty Monstarte, may he roast for his crimes.*

She clenched her fists. No. Not again. Not to her friends, her new family. No damn marauder would steal anything else from her.

Approaching the abandoned craft. Zeus displayed the nav screen.

Drop a signal bleep and run—no. It wasn't her call. Plus, odds were it wasn't even a pirate trick. When they docked with the derelict, Captain Rodriguez would take armed security forces with him to explore the vessel. If scuts waited on board, they were no match for Rodriguez and his crew. Nalani waited, hands fisted at her sides in the warm gel-tank.

Your heart rate is one hundred fifteen. Are you in distress? Zeus asked.

I'm fine, thanks. She drew in a deep breath, linked to Zeus's visual array, and flicked through camera displays. She accessed one on the port side with a one-hundred-eighty-degree view. Missile fire scars marred the derelict starzipper-class scout ID numbers at the base of the hull. The craft bobbed outside the perimeter of the relay beacons, drifting into the unknown vastness of hyperspace.

Zeus approached the starzipper, firing the thrusters periodically to adjust their course.

Getting worked up was stupid. If she reacted like this every time they came across an abandoned ship, she'd be unable to help her crewmates. Besides, some of these deserted vessels contained valuable archaeological finds, and if the databanks were intact, they might contain useful information. At the least, they'd have logs to be claimed by family members of the deceased crew.

If it was a trap, scuts would have already boarded the derelict, their transport hidden nearby, and would pounce once Zeus docked.

By now, the bridge officer had scoured the vicinity for enemy ships. But two sets of eyes couldn't hurt.

Nalani accessed the short-range scanners and searched the area around the relay beacons that allowed vessels to navigate between the star portals. No one out here wanted to get lost in the expanse of uncharted hyperspace.

Short-range scans only penetrated a minimal distance into the swirling mass, but it should be enough. Where would she hide? Where rescuers wouldn't search. Docking procedures had begun, and Zeus and the well-armed crew were focused on the deserted vessel. There could be scuts on board. Her friends might be in danger. She shifted to the starboard visual array and aimed the short-range scanners in the proper direction, adjusting for the irradiated dust.

Why are you accessing my systems? Zeus asked.

Looking for scuts. She scoured the incoming data and changed the search parameters.

Statistically, only point-zero-zero-zero-two percent of abandoned ships harbor beings with malicious intent. Your fears are unfounded. The odds of this one containing—

Found it. A blip hovered on the far side of the nearest beacon, a thousand kilometers away, hiding in a cloud of radiation dust—a typical scut ruse—less than a ten-minute flight at standard speed. When was the last time they'd seen a scut attack on a freighter in hyperspace? No one would waste three hours drilling through the hull's chunky plating while the freighter fired all rockets to flee. Scuts preferred to blast through an open airlock. She accessed comms and linked to Captain Rodriguez's array. "It's a trap! Don't board."

In the background, static crackled on the comm link. Captain Rodriguez's voice cut in, echoing telepathically through Zeus's systems to Nalani. *We just unsealed the airlock. You're sure?*

"I located their mother ship."

I searched the grid myself. I didn't find— Stunner shots echoed through the comm relay. *Fire at will!*

Anyone could have missed the well-hidden vessel. Jank it. What if Monstarte was on board? Nalani grabbed the edges of the tank. He'd take her again. Kill her with his bare hands. Or worse. She couldn't face him—she'd lose herself and revert.

Six enemies! The security chief's voice rang out above the static. *Tighten your groupings.*

Nalani's grip on the tank eased. Monstarte always worked alone, so this couldn't be his mission. And the security team could handle a half-dozen scuts.

A tremor shook her. The boarding team had weapons, but Zeus didn't. He had no way to protect himself or his crew from the incoming ship. His only option was to run—but he was docked to the derelict.

She had to do it. She was the only crew member with a personal ship, and it was stocked with missiles.

She bolted upright, severing her link to Zeus, and stood. Bio-gel sluiced off her body, leaving her dry but chilled.

"Nalani, why did you leave your post?" Zeus's flat tone rang through the medlab speakers set in the ceiling.

"To help." She scrambled from the tank and ran out into the corridor. Armed crew members ignored her. Her bare feet slapped against the metal deck, and she blocked the buzz of their chaotic thoughts. She took the stairs two at a time, hands hovering above the metal rails, and wove through deckhands scrambling around the Bay One cargo hold.

"What's going on?" Desta Okeke shouted from the top of the stairs, a stunner in one hand, a paring knife in the other.

"Scuts." Nalani pointed toward the medlab. "Jump in the tank and help Zeus. I'm going to cut off their retreat."

"On it." Desta rushed down the hallway.

Nalani raced across the packed cargo hold, through Bay Two, and opened the door to Bay Three and her personal starzipper. "Zeus, begin depart sequence."

"It is unsafe for you to leave the protection of my hull." Zeus's voice echoed from speakers in the wall and ceiling. "Proper procedure is to wait for instruction from the captain. Please return to the gel-tank."

Not happening. Zeus could advise her to stay aboard, but his programming wouldn't allow him to stop her. "They're in danger. Cap said to fire at will. I have to help."

Aldrin gleamed in Zeus's drab cargo bay with a fresh aqua paint job and four shiny engines protected by thick ribbing. Sleek and bullet-shaped, perfect for outmaneuvering pirates. She slapped the control panel and ran across the floor as Zeus's Bay Three doors lurched and began to slide open. *Don't look at the black...* She jumped aboard Aldrin and sealed herself in. The air pressure dropped, and she grabbed a metal handrail. Aldrin equalized. *That was close.* She hurried to the medlab and skidded to a stop beside the gel-tank, the last place Nalani had seen her mother alive.

"Hide!" Momma climbed out of the goo, grabbed a stunner, and opened the medlab door. "Like we drilled. Don't come out until I call."

Momma had promised to come back, but she never

did. Nalani blinked back tears.

This wasn't the time for memories. Zeus needed aid. She slid into the goo and linked in. *Hey, old friend. We have a problem.*

Greetings, 'Lani. Is it the reason we are hovering in hyperspace? Aldrin used her father's pet nickname for her. Shortly after she escaped from Monstarte, she'd changed Aldrin's voice coding to her father's tenor. The original vocal routines reminded her too much of *him.* Bittersweet, but better than constant reminders of beatings and drudgery.

Scut attack. They're attempting to board Zeus. We need to cut off their escape route. She fired up the nova drive. The comforting thrum vibrated the gel-tank a few seconds before smoothing out. All systems flicked online. Air pressure equalized. She plotted the exit out the bay doors—a tight squeeze—and piloted Aldrin into the black. She cleared the comm array on Zeus's aft end and programmed the nav to intercept the mother ship hovering behind a beacon like a sneaky bastard. *Open missile ports.*

Aldrin complied. *You will have to fire. My programming does not allow me to injure living beings, even if they are scoundrels.*

I understand. One of the joys of being a human, having the freedom to decide to shoot or not. She'd never fired on another ship before—Monstarte never let her touch the weapons array. But how hard could it be? She had to protect Zeus and the crew. *Patch me through to Captain Rodriguez, please.*

Comm open.

She flexed her fingers, knuckles cracking in the pink goo. "Captain, Aldrin and I located the m-m-mother ship." Stupid stutter. Way to show her captain she could function in a stressful situation. "Permission to target their engines, sir."

Chapter 2

Aldrin passed the captain's response to Nalani telepathically. *Permission granted.* A man screamed in the background, and Rodriguez cursed. *Make it quick. We're taking fire.*

A chill skittered across her skin. If Cap's boarding party couldn't contain the scuts in the derelict, they'd board Zeus and endanger the entire crew.

The enemy ship lay nestled behind a large cloud of flotsam—rock, dust, fragments of metal, irradiated space dust, gaseous particles, mostly items inadvertently hauled in from normal space in the wake of ships entering star portals.

But she'd learned a few tricks in her scut days. She dove into a glowing cloud of hyperspace plasma and detonated a torpedo at the far end, sending plumes in every direction. She charted an intercepting course and melded with one of the sensor-scrambling fingers of plasma flowing toward the enemy. At her current speed, it would take four minutes to be within targeting range.

Her hands shook. Aldrin closed in on the marauders. They flew a courier class vessel that could hold up to twenty crew, two fighter crafts, and six missile ports. The cowards could take out an unarmed freighter if they subdued the crew.

But not with Aldrin harrying them. *Have they detected us yet?* Nalani flipped between the sensory array and the nav screen.

They are maintaining position. Aldrin adjusted course to remain within the plasma stream. *Two minutes to targeting range.*

Her heart pounded. The courier was a bio-ship. An AI who didn't deserve to die because of a scut crew.

Report, Cap demanded.

"Closing on the enemy now." Nalani fired thrusters and swung around the beacon, bringing the vessel into weapons range.

The courier fired a missile at Aldrin and veered toward Zeus.

Jank it! Nalani dipped and pulled a tight spiral. The gravitational forces threatened to slosh her out of the tank, yet she clung to the sides. Aldrin released junk metal to attract the missile, and she circled the beacon, tracking the courier heading for Zeus. The missile exploded two kilometers behind her. "Captain, enemy closing in. Target lock in twelve seconds."

Do it! Cap ordered.

She accessed the weapons array.

Her body trembled. Her palms dampened. Which circuits triggered the missiles? Was it the blue one? Wait. No. The green one? Why couldn't she remember? Her mouth dried up. No. Not now. Please not—

Monstarte loomed over her, hand raised to smack. "You couldn't fire on a ship if your life depended on it, nub." He sneered. "You're worthless and weak. Now quit sniveling. If I ever catch you messing with the weapons array again, I'll beat you senseless."

What was she thinking, firing on an enemy ship? She wasn't a soldier. She was a bio-tank telepath and an egghead scientist with a dumb obsession for old languages and cultures. She blinked back tears. A nub—a non-useful body.

Too late. A gangway tethered the scut's mothership to Zeus's Bay Four airlock. Were the scuts on Zeus retreating? Or did her failure to destroy them mean backup had arrived to finish the takeover?

Her stomach clenched. Had she just killed all her friends?

Rodriguez's voice cut in. *Nalani, report.*

He was alive, at least. "I-I-I missed the shot. Their ship is operational."

We won the fight. They're retreating. Return immediately.

She released the side of the tank and sagged in the goo. "Yes, sir." Her fingers ached. She'd probably have bruises on her finger pads for days. Aldrin took over navigation. She climbed out, padded down the hall to the airlock on wobbly knees, and wiped her eyes. She leaned her forehead against the chilly bulkhead.

Pull it together. Calm down. Recite the actinide elements. Thorium. Protactinium. Uranium. She sucked in a deep breath and let it out through pursed lips. *Neptunium. Plutonium.* Her heart rate settled.

Aldrin's deck plating vibrated, and he landed in the freighter's cargo bay. Time for the reckoning. She squared her shoulders and prepared for the tongue-lashing she deserved. Or maybe the fighting was still ongoing in the next bay, and she'd get shot. That'd be payback for her epic failure.

"I will handle shutdown maneuvers," Aldrin said. "The enemy ship has fled."

"Thanks. I'll be back at rack time." She punched in the lock code, took two deep breaths, and peeked into

Bay Two. Lots of crates, but no scuts or security forces. Her hands trembled. She crossed the space, hugged the bulkhead by the Bay One door, and slapped the controls. The door slid open.

"All clear." Security Officer Vania's voice carried across the hold. "Zeus is safe, and the prisoners are secured."

"Someone alert Huntington," Rodriguez yelled.

She sagged against the hull. The fight was over. Everyone was safe. She entered the hold.

Three scuts huddled on the floor in the corner, wedged between cargo crates, wrists and ankles secured. Nalani strengthened her shields. She'd rather walk barefoot across the lava fields of Hela Prima than pick up any scut thoughts. Three bodies lay beside the seated ones, covered with tarps. Dr. Jex, one of the four aliens serving on board, treated stunner burns on several crewmates.

"Adar, report," Chief Gack bellowed across the bay.

Nalani crossed the space to join her supervisor. Gack's first name was Imogene, but absolutely no one dared to call her by it. Her light-brown hair, pulled back in a severe bun, was streaked with soot. Her tan uniform sported a stunner burn on the right shoulder and blood spatter across her chest. She hadn't panicked like a nub. She'd fought the enemy and overcome.

Nalani maintained her heavy mental shields. Friends didn't read friends' minds. "I missed the shot, Chief. I-I'm sorry."

Gack harrumphed. "I'm not pissed. I'm surprised you took the initiative to try something so dangerous. Your place is in the tank, not shooting at enemies." She grinned. "Besides, your actions saved us. Just as we secured the boarding party, Aldrin closed in on their ship. I guess the sight of open missile ports sent them scurrying like rats. Now tell me how you kiffed the shot with Aldrin doing the targeting for you."

Heat blasted Nalani's cheeks, and she ducked her head. *Dense nub.* Unable to fire on an enemy ship to save her friends. "I-I-I-I didn't—"

Gack held her palm out. "Calm down. I won't hurt you. Think about what you want to say, then say it."

Tears welled in Nalani's eyes, and she blinked. Stupid stutter. "I-I-I…" She inhaled and let it out. "I-I didn't take the shot because I-I-I didn't want to accidentally kill the scut's bio-ship."

Gack's normally strict glare softened. "Understandable. Not the ship's fault it's got scuts for a crew. We won, and no one on our side died. So don't crack. We're going to need your help on the derelict once we've cleared the decks. From the brief look I got of the interior before the scabs opened fire, we've got an antique on our hands. We'll need your archaeological training."

Nalani pressed her hands to her quivering stomach. Nice to be useful for something.

The bay door hissed open, and Commander Huntington stormed in, his brown uniform pristine over his toned body, his dark curls probably individually placed for optimal charm. Some supervisor. He'd managed to weasel out of a fight. Again.

He caught Nalani's gaze, offered a lurid smile, and strode toward her. For the last two years, the twig had ogled her like a buyer inspecting cargo, eager to own her.

She gritted her teeth and prepared for the encounter, shields at maximum. "Commander."

"Nalani. Are you okay?" He reached for her shoulder.

She stepped back and crossed her arms. The vents in the cargo bay blasted sub-zero air, and she shivered. Her thin bodysuit was great for a heated gel-tank. Not so much for this.

Huntington's blue eyes locked on to her chest.

She took another step back. "I'm fine. I kiffed the shot." Why hadn't she grabbed a sweater on her way? Vulnerable. Exposed. On display for the highest bidder.

"I'm glad." His eyes flicked up to her face. "I mean, that you're okay."

She stared at the scuff marks on the floor and checked her shields. Never again would she read the commander. He thought so loudly sometimes they pierced through her shields. Did he do it on purpose?

Gack stepped between them, blocking Huntington's view of Nalani. "Commander, do the words 'sexual harassment' mean anything to you?"

Nalani glanced up. Gack had never spoken to Huntington in such sharp tones before.

His eyes narrowed. "I'm talking to her. I didn't realize that was harassment." He held up his wrists and winked at Nalani over Gack's shoulder. "But if you're feeling harassed, by all means, take me to the brig. I'll be good. I'm only concerned for your well-being."

Gack shifted again to block his view of Nalani. "Her being is well. Captain's waiting for you to interrogate the prisoners." She pointed to the far end of the massive, cluttered bay. "Nalani's heading to the derelict."

Huntington leered at Nalani. "Hope you find something amazing. Stay safe." He marched toward the restrained scuts.

She shuddered. Creepo. At least he'd focused the attention away from her failure. "Why is he fixated on me? He's so awesome in his own eyes he thinks he could woo any woman on this ship."

Gack's eyebrows rose.

"Except you. Everyone knows who owns your heart." Nalani glanced at the captain standing over the prisoners with Security Chief Cerys Lindholm, Security Officer Vania, and Commander Huntington. The two men walked away, but Cerys waved Nalani over.

She swallowed. They were scuts. Thieves. Murderers. Like Monstarte two point oh, only worse because they now shared her airspace. And Cerys wanted Nalani's help with them? She couldn't disobey, not after her inept performance on Aldrin. She clenched her teeth and crossed the hold. "Yes?"

Three stunner burns marred Cerys's dirty EVA suit, a smile lit up her pale face, and her ice-blue eyes twinkled. "That was some fight. You joined us?"

Nalani blinked. Why couldn't she be more like Cerys, strong and capable? "I tried. I'm glad you weren't hurt."

Cerys shrugged. "Most action I've seen in ages. Keeps the skills sharp." She gestured with her head at the secured men. "I'll need you when I interrogate these scabs. Maybe after we finish on the derelict?"

She'd rather eat a boiled wingnut. "You really need me for that?"

"It'd be helpful, but if you're not up for it, I can grab ZeeBee. I just need to know if I'm getting the truth."

"Yeah, he's better at lie detection than I am." That might or might not be a half-truth, but ZeeBee believed his truth-telling skills were amazing, so why argue with him? She glanced at the row of scuts, seated near her feet, and crossed her arms over her chest.

The first hob had one squinty brown eye, but a cybernetic implant replaced the other—and not a delicate new one available at med clinics, but a clunky, misshapen mess with exposed chips and wiring. Was that Monstarte's work?

The scut skimmed his gaze over her and smiled, revealing brown teeth. "Nalani Adar. I never thought I'd see your grunt ass on a freighter."

She clenched her fists. How did he know her name? And why would he call her that word, especially in front of Vania? She'd discover Nalani's secret past! "You've m-m-made a m-mistake."

He laughed. "You've just made me a rich man."

Cerys jabbed her stun baton into the scut's shoulder. "You know her?"

Nalani stared. Who was this man? She'd never met him during her seven years with Monstarte. Her appearance had changed in the intervening years, so how could this scut know her by sight? "Who are you?" Rules be damned, she needed information. She dove into his thoughts. *Sunlight sparkling on waves lapping at a golden shore. A cool breeze. Rustling palms.*

He chuckled. "I'm the future owner of a tropical hideaway on Protiman Six, thanks to you, Nalani Adar." He drawled her name.

She glanced at the other scuts. One had a vicious scar on his scalp, evidence of a brain implant. His eyes widened, and he nudged the other.

"Explain." Cerys leaned on the baton, grinding the electrodes into the first scut's collarbone.

His head bobbed like a motion float in a lube tank.

"I don't slip my secrets."

She hit the button on her weapon.

His body jerked and twitched for a few moments.

She backed off. "Try again."

Spittle dripped down his whiskered chin, but he shook his head. "Can't get it out of me."

"I can." Nalani dove into his mind, sifting through the images of the tropical scenes, and found the answer. She flinched. "A bounty." Hunted across the universe by scabs like him until she was caught or the bounty canceled. On the run? Again?

Cerys set the baton on the scut's chest. "How much?"

His face paled, and he stared at Nalani. "Fifty thousand credits for information on her whereabouts, or three hundred thousand for her delivery."

"Who put up the bounty?"

He glared. *Monstarte's gonna pay extra for security details.*

Her belly fluttered, and she swallowed. Of course, Ty Monstarte. She was his prize, his greatest success. He'd promised he'd kill her, and she'd spent years hiding, cowering, constantly moving, wondering when he'd catch her and make good on his threat. It wasn't like she could take him on. Field mice didn't take down frost bears.

Now he was willing to cough up a huge sum for help catching her. Hadn't he done enough to her already?

Chapter 3

Cerys sneered at the prisoner scut. "Thanks for the intel, numbnut. The Authorities won't let you have comm privileges after they see you've threatened an Alliance citizen." She nodded to the lens in the far corner catching every word of the conversation.

His grin faded. "I'll find a way. No worries."

Nalani's body tightened. Should she flee to Aldrin? And why was that her default setting? The stupid scut was the felon, not her. She shifted and planted her feet to hide the jellies in her knees. No more running.

"Hey." Cerys stepped close to Nalani. "We will deal with this bounty thing. I promise. Don't crack."

Security officers Isaiah and Vania goaded the prisoners to their feet. The scut winked at her with his one good eye. Vania shoved him toward the lift.

Nalani focused on her breathing. Cerys, Gack, and Desta were the only people she'd ever told about her history with Monstarte—one of the hardest things she'd ever done—and they'd kept her secret. She could trust Cerys to keep this secure, too. Vania wouldn't talk. For now, conversation about the bounty could hold until a better time. And since the scuts would be in Zeus's brig until they reached the next port, she didn't have to worry about that scab calling in the bounty.

"I've got your back. You're safe with me." Cerys lowered her voice. "Bounties are numerous. I'm amazed this scut remembered one particular posting. Nobody takes them seriously."

Unless the price was right. How had Monstarte posted it? Were flyers plastered across every spaceport's lower levels where scuts congregated like roaches in a dark corner? When they arrived at Liang, if Nalani asked, would Cerys venture below to check it out? Or maybe Monstarte used the deep net and sent it around electronically to all his scab buddies. Or maybe—

"Go suit up," Gack hollered at Nalani. "You leave in ten."

Cerys nodded. "You're safe now. No one knows about the bounty except you, me, and Vania. Put it out of your mind and concentrate on that wreck." She grinned. "There are bound to be intellectual goodies for you to discover."

Nalani headed for the lockers. She was safe. The bounty didn't mean anything, at least not right now. And Cerys would help deal with it later. Best of all, Nalani would be the first archaeologist to explore the abandoned vessel. What sort of things would she find?

She yanked her neon-yellow extravehicular activity suit off the hook. Whoever had chosen the color of these beastly EVA garments should be tethered to the back of a cruiser and dragged through hyperspace for several seconds. She hauled it on and zipped up. It fit a tad snugly through the chest. The helmet clicked, and the air hissed, environmentally protecting her from whatever atmosphere, or lack thereof, existed in the derelict.

What an amazing opportunity. Manufacturing of the zipper-class starships had begun three hundred years ago, so the derelict could potentially be ancient. No telling what kinds of artifacts were left behind. What if she found entertainment vids from the pre-war era? Audio-visual proof of Earth-side culture and music? Nalani bounced on her toes and reached for her go-kit. Or personal grooming items? Sweet. She could write a paper. Her name might finally make it into the archaeological journals.

She checked her bag. All her tools rested inside, not scattered by crewmates "borrowing" her gear if they couldn't find their own. She should put a code on her locker so no one else could access it, but she didn't want the others to think she didn't trust them after four years of working together. No need to offend anyone.

Cerys approached, her helmet under one arm. "You ready to explore?"

"It's been cleared?"

"Yeah. No enemies on board, but environmental systems are inoperable. Structural integrity is iffy, so keep your eyes and comm link open. And make sure your air's topped off. You're going to love this." She jammed her helmet over her honey-blonde buzz cut and gave it a stout twist. "Follow me."

Nalani cemented her gaze on the back of Cerys's helmet. *Don't look at the dead bodies.* Nalani gulped. Was there anything worse than hurling in an EVA suit? Yes. Finding her image on the Wall of Pukers. Not happening.

An engineer, Pepe, waited by the airlock. Cerys led the group onto the gangway.

This beauty's ancient. Turning the juice back on will be more challenging than getting into Vania's pants.

Nalani cringed. She'd allowed her shields to slip, and Pepe's thoughts slid right in. Her brain throbbed. Maintaining her shields full time wrecked her. She couldn't wait to relax on board the abandoned craft with only two other minds nearby.

They crossed the bouncing gangway bridge to the abandoned vessel. Scuts only wanted valuables, so they'd have left behind archaeological gems like dishware, ancient tech, and clothing. So much of Earth's history had been lost in the Qarat Wars, and discoveries like this helped fill in gaps.

They cycled through the airlocks and entered the ship. Nalani studied the name plaque posted on the bulkhead in the vestibule. The little zipper had been christened *Evangeline* in the year 2536, making the vessel two-hundred-eighty-six years old. One of the first zippers ever manufactured, probably at the Io space docks in the Sol system—wouldn't that be an awesome place to visit someday. She'd been born in the black with only pictures of her mother planet to give her a sense of place. "Did you alert Authorities?"

"About ten minutes ago." Cerys pointed Pepe toward the bridge. "Get the power up." She turned back to Nalani. "It'll take them a few days to send a team out, so it's all yours for now. Images only."

Nalani nodded. "Recording on." The digital imaging began with a faint whirr, capturing everything within her helmet lens' field of view. She moved farther into *Evangeline*. The first few minutes in a new place or environment were the worst, but zipper floorplans hadn't changed over the years, so that helped.

She crossed to the cargo hold and checked crates. Dehydrated food, stale water, spare parts, and fuel. Nothing interesting or unique. The life pods were gone. The crew had probably abandoned ship. She hurried to the crew quarters on the second deck and worked her way back toward to the vestibule, cataloguing every room's contents.

They spent six hours on *Evangeline*. The ship groaned several times, and Nalani froze, waiting for the deeper screech of a catastrophic hull failure. But Cerys hadn't issued an "abandon ship" order. Yet.

The crew had taken some personal items with them in their escape but left plenty to study: grooming tools, clothing—ridiculous styles in bland colors—furniture, and books. Real books printed on paper. Most of the titles had been lost in time, so this find alone would label *Evangeline* the discovery of the century.

Nalani finished the top deck and found Pepe in the bridge. He cobbled a work-around for the power, supplying them with enough juice for lights and computer access. An old pop song zipped through his mind, but she didn't block it. Tension drained from her shoulders.

Evangeline had been built long before the development of bio-ship technology, so Nalani accessed the data core the hard way, manually. As she scrolled through the vast array of labels, a crew name stuck out. She'd found the personnel logs. "Yes!"

Pepe punched the air in solidarity. "Fly, Tank Girl."

She chuckled at the silly nickname, opened the file, and pinpointed the date and reason the ship's complement had left. They'd been attacked by an unknown alien race and sustained too much damage to salvage *Evangeline*. Preprogrammed life pods had ferried the survivors to the nearest star portal with a habitable planet.

The Alliance archaeologists and historians would process the data and attempt to locate the planet and any of the crew's descendants. Nalani wanted her share of the fun, too, and uploaded copies of all logs, files, and vids to Aldrin and Zeus for later perusal.

The first-deck lounge contained more books: history, theology, science, even fiction.

The ship groaned again.

"Let's hurry this up," Cerys said. "You've got twenty minutes."

Nalani hustled to the crew quarters beside the lounge and opened a bunk-side drawer. Score! It was full of forgotten items. A gown made of an unknown, lightweight textile, probably for sleeping. A portable light source. A writing implement.

A loud grinding shook the deck.

"That was structural beam stress." Cerys's voice blasted through Nalani's helmet. "We're leaving now, before this ship falls apart."

Nalani's heart rate shot up. If the ship fell apart, all these wonderful artifacts would be lost. "We can't leave. There's too much data we haven't collected yet."

"It's worthless if we die. I said evacuate. Don't make me come get you."

Nalani hurried down the corridor, pried open the lounge doors, and scanned the bookshelves. So many to choose from. She'd have to salvage selectively. The science texts gave a glimpse of their base knowledge. She had zero interest in theology. But fiction offered a snapshot of the crew's lives, culture, and philosophies. Oh, and the histories!

The bulkhead shuddered again.

She stuffed eight tomes into her bag and ran into the corridor. The floor shifted. She careened off the wall and fell to her knees. Vacuum sucked her backward, and she slid along the floor. Jank it! The hull had breached somewhere behind her. She grabbed a safety rail and strained against the pull in her shoulder socket.

"Nalani!" Cerys screamed in the comm unit. "Where are you?"

"Almost there." Nalani hauled herself off the floor and slogged handhold by handhold down the hall.

Cerys reached through the inner airlock, grabbed Nalani's arm, and dragged her inside the vestibule. Cerys slapped the panel. The inner door closed, sealing off the vacuum. "What took so long? You loaded your bag, didn't you?"

Nalani jogged across the bridge to Zeus and swallowed past the lump in her throat.

Cerys followed. The moment they exited the bridge, Pepe retracted it.

"We have to save *Evangeline*." Nalani ripped off her helmet. "Zeus, can you net her?"

"Captain requested it six hours ago. *Evangeline* is contained and tethered to the beacon."

Nalani blew out a breath and glared at Cerys's amused grin. "You knew."

"When that ship falls apart—and it will—the smaller stuff might float free through the netting, but the bulk is safe." She nodded at Nalani's gear bag. "Including what you liberated."

Nalani gasped. "What? I-I-I would never steal anything. I saved them."

Cerys laughed. "You're too easy to rile up. Catalogue the artifacts you saved and make me a copy. Archivists won't want to collect them anytime soon, so you can study them at your leisure." She walked away.

Cerys was teasing, not accusing Nalani of theft. She

blinked and stared at her bulging go-kit. Protocol stated discovery ships should net all wrecks of scientific or historic value. She'd proved, yet again, she was a fraud. She deserved to be fired for this one.

"Nalani, when will you return to the tank?" Zeus's voice rang across the cargo bay.

At least she couldn't mess up her tank duties. "Eight minutes." She crammed her helmet on her head, grabbed her go-kit, and hurried to the decon tube. Hot air and disinfectant cleaned her suit, gear, and the books—the decon wouldn't harm the precious artifacts.

Calm down. Deep breaths. Recite the alkali metals. Lithium. Sodium, potassium, rubidium. Slow breath in, let it out. Not useless. Cesium. Francium. Saved the books from floating away. She'd be thanked.

The tube cycle finished. She emerged. The books would have to wait. "Zeus, who's in the tank now?"

"It is empty. Desta entered shortly after the scut attack began, but she disengaged to resume her duties in the galley. Please hurry. I need you."

"Four minutes." She hung her EVA suit in her locker, transferred the salvaged books to an empty crate, and stowed her go-kit. The artifacts needed to be stored someplace safe. She lugged the crate to Aldrin and secured it in one of the low-humidity medlab drawers meant for specimen storage.

"Thank you for uploading *Evangeline's* data to my core." Aldrin's tenor voice echoed in the tiny space. "I will study it and point out areas that may interest you."

"Thanks. We can discuss it when I return."

"Affirmative."

Nalani couldn't blame him for wanting the mental stimulation. He was stuck in a cargo hold every day. At least her days had variety. She had ancient runes to translate, and she was ultra close to figuring out the squiggle that looked like a crippled man praying. She hurried across the bay and darted up the stairs to finish her tank shift.

In space, *day* and *night* were useless terms, but thankfully, Rodriguez scheduled eight-hour work shifts to make it easier on the human crew members. Monstarte never bothered, working and sleeping whenever he felt like it. Rodriguez's way was better. It increased efficiency, work output, and morale. Zeus even cycled the lighting to simulate day and night.

Her stomach grumbled, and she frowned at the clock. 1508 hours. Too late for lunch now. She'd finish her shift, eat, help Desta in the galley, then study the *Evangeline's* logs until bunk time. Nalani slid into the goo and dropped her shields. *I'm back. Anything to report?*

I'm so glad you're here now! That was awful, being without you. Desta is fine for little things, but it's not the same.

And the glitch again. *You're still feeling happy?*

I am now. Thank you for the files you uploaded from the Evangeline. *They are in an intriguing archaic format.*

Nothing like a challenge. *Can you read it?*

The extension indicates a writebit file, but I do not possess that program. However, I may be able to view the data as plain text. The mystery of the unknown data and anticipation of discovery are very pleasurable.

She grinned. *That's curiosity again.* By the whirr of his nodes, Zeus attempted to access the files. Nalani scanned the index for crew names. *When I read this list on the* Evangeline, *it contained spaces, punctuation, and underlines in the original format. Now it's gibberish. How soon can you reformat it?*

I estimate three minutes to fix the problem. How exciting!

Starzippers could hold up to eight people comfortably. A scruffy, old scut once told her horror stories of captains that crammed twelve on board, forcing the youngest to sleep in hammocks in the cargo bay or engineering, but those tales were bafflegab. The hydroponics on zippers couldn't sustain enough fresh food for so many.

Evangeline held eight crew members, listed in alphabetical order. The fifth name sent a shiver across her skin.

Uther Monstarte.

Chapter 4

Nalani trembled. The other names on the list blurred. Monstarte.

I'll find you, nub, no matter where you hide. Do you hear me? No matter how long it takes or how far you run, I'll find you, and I'll kill you.

Humanity had spread itself over the entire universe, dipped into hyperspace, colonized planets, signed treaties with peaceful aliens, fought aggressive species—

I'll find you, and I'll kill you.

—and yet the scut who'd terrorized Nalani would not leave her alone. What were the odds he'd share a surname with a crewman from an antique found drifting off the beaconed lanes?

Zero. The odds should be so amazingly low that it worked out mathematically to nothing whatsoever. But the name taunted her from a list created two-hundred-sixty-four years before she'd been born.

It couldn't be coincidence. Science. Logic. Reason. She should rely on those, quit shaking like a squintbug, and analyze it. *Zeus, have you calculated the trajectory of* Evangeline's *escape pods based on their coordinates after the attack?*

I have not yet accessed that portion of the data. Zeus's nodes hummed.

She clenched and relaxed her hands, took a slow breath in, and let it out. Tension leaked away like fuel in a cracked container.

I estimate a ninety-six percent probability, based on Evangeline's *location at the time of pod ejection, the crew exited hyperspace in the Chimera system.*

Ty Monstarte had been born in that galaxy, on Piter. He never raided there. He frequented his home planet for supplies, legitimate business, and vacations only.

The crewman aboard the *Evangeline* was an ancestor of Ty Monstarte. A DNA test would confirm it, but jank the proof. The universe, for all its vastness and enormity, sometimes tossed cruelty like this into her life. She'd survived worse. Nothing—not even a log entry from a Monstarte ancestor—could hurt as much as watching vids of her parents' murders.

Her stomach clenched. She still missed them so much. They'd be proud of her achievements, of how she'd outsmarted Monstarte and gained her freedom.

But no more maudlin thoughts. She opened the Uther Monstarte file, stared at the image of the long-dead man's bland face, and read the info.

He'd served as chief engineer and wrote succinct, grammatically correct entries that listed facts, dates, and little else. No opinions. No emotional reactions to events aboard the *Evangeline*. No theories or feigned interest in the captain's mission. Mostly, it contained notes regarding the engine and problems or fixes. Boring. Hard to believe Ty Monstarte, with his arrogance, lust for finer things, and lack of moral compass, had descended from the analytical, emotionless Uther Monstarte.

Your adrenal levels and blood pressure are elevated. This project is causing distress. Perhaps you should turn your attention elsewhere.

I'll be fine.

I insist. Please. Your distress grates against my diodes in an unpleasant manner. I want you to stop.

She sighed. *Okay. For the sake of your diodes, I will calm down.*

He shut down the file. *And work on something different.*

So bossy! Maybe he shouldn't keep these blasted emotions. *Fine. I'll work on my side project, if you're okay with that.*

Accessing public digital resources to study ancient runes?

Yes. I'm making nominal progress.

May I assist you?

Certainly. And please alert me as soon as we leave hyperspace. I need to run a long-range scan of the Terminus sector.

What are you searching for?

The Thrakis civilization. I theorize their home planet is within this supercluster. Zeus's last trading run through this system was two years ago, and she'd been so busy she missed her chance to run the scans. If she lost this opportunity, it'd delay her research another two years.

Zeus was either accessing files or found the topic uninteresting. His data nodes whirred. Ha! He was brushing up. *Thrakis. An advanced culture with technology beyond anything in existence today. Centuries ago, scientists theorized the Thrakis people built the star portals and the hyperspace beacons, though that theory has been abandoned for three hundred years. The Thrakis society collapsed seven millennia ago and are regarded by many scholars as mythological. Why do you believe their home planet is in*

46

this supercluster?

My father found an inscription on one of the trusses of the Haraldi Star Portal.

Fascinating. Did he record his finding in his logs?

Yes.

Please wait while I access them.

Four years ago, Nalani had uploaded all her parents' research into Zeus's databanks as backup copies in case the originals were lost or destroyed. But she'd been so busy working she rarely found time to continue the search. Since she didn't have scans to study now, she'd brush up on her Valaqite runes, which shared a base syntax with the Thrakis language. *You won't tell the captain if I run long-range scans today?*

Use of my scanners would be considered a personal project, which is prohibited. Shall I submit a request?

No, thanks. Cap had issued a new mandate that the crew were not to utilize Zeus for personal projects without prior authorization, probably after one of the deckhands got caught using the comm array to download porn. The captain's new ruling impacted her, as well. *I'll request a day off and fly out with Aldrin to grab scans.*

That is not necessary. I will run them.

Please don't. I need to comply with the captain's new order.

Affirmative. I have located the truss inscription, but I do not find the translation. Why did your father label the runes Thrakis?

Daddy had never gotten to translate them. Her eyes burned, and she blinked to dispel tears. *I deciphered them and determined the origin.*

Interesting. Please elaborate.

She spent a half hour detailing her work for Zeus,

and the remainder of her shift trying to translate a single rune. She failed.

Zeus interrupted her inability to find a public record of the rune in question. *It is 1600 hours, and your shift is complete. Please don't leave.*

Sweet, but perplexing. Where was this emotion coming from? *I missed lunch, so I need to eat now. ZeeBee will be here in a few hours.* Maybe she should leave him a note about Zeus's odd behavior. Or not. ZeeBee slept through his shift, so he wouldn't work on solving the issue. *Have you converted the* Evangeline *files to a plain text format?*

Affirmative.

Please send a copy to Aldrin.

Why does he need a copy?

Was that more attitude? *So I can read them later tonight.*

Fine. Zeus's nodes whirred. *Completed. We will discuss your findings at 0800 tomorrow.*

Nalani grabbed the sides of the gel-tank and hauled herself to a seated position. "Would you check personnel records on Piter and locate Ty Monstarte's birth notice and genealogy? I'm sure we'll find a link to the *Evangline.*"

"I am not authorized to complete that task, as it is a personal matter for you, but in two-point-two-five hours we will exit hyperspace, and you may access the data."

"Oh. Right. Thanks." She picked up her clothing, and her stomach gurgled.

She visited the sanitation pod and shrugged into her outerwear. Desta would be serving an amazing meal in the dining hall. Hopefully savory beqchops, risotto, and fresh greens. Nalani hurried down the corridor to the galley. Or chili with the ground mystery meat they'd picked up on Boros. Or cricket marsala with mushrooms and red wine. Whatever was on the menu, she owed Desta for the time she'd served in the tank. If the galley crew didn't need help with prep, they'd welcome a cleanup volunteer.

Nalani and Pepe converged on the dining hall from opposite ends of the corridor. "Hey, Tank Girl." He palmed the door open and gestured for her to enter.

She smiled and set her shields at maximum. "Thanks, Power Boy." She stepped into the room crowded with hungry people coming off first shift and people about to go on second shift. She skirted the queue of grumbling crew members lined up at the buffet carts. Empty trays gleamed in the overhead lighting. Where was the food? She headed for the swinging door to the galley.

"Nalani!" The commander's voice rang across the dining hall.

Her heart rate kicked up, and she hurried through the doorway. Why did he pester her so much? He wouldn't follow her into the galley, thankfully.

Desta stood at the heater, her black braids caught in a hairnet, stirring a pot while barking orders at her two minions. "Did you drain the pasta? Get it out to the line before they riot." She sighed at Nalani. "Are you here to help?" She pointed to a head of lettuce resting atop a cutting board.

"Reporting for duty." Nalani donned an apron, snapped a hairnet over her dark-brown curls, and washed her hands. "Why isn't the food out yet?" She selected a chopping knife from the magnetic strip and descended on the unsuspecting green ball of goodness.

"I got stuck in the gel-tank for over an hour." Desta poured spicy red sauce into a chafing dish. The male minion, a skinny guy named Luka, grabbed it and ran for the buffet, followed by the redheaded helper carrying a tub of plen-noodles. The crew members in the queue cheered.

Desta smiled. "That set me behind on the lunch crowd, which means dinner is also late."

Luka returned, and Desta shoved more food in his hands for the buffet.

Jank it. This was Nalani's fault. Again. She sliced everything Desta dropped on the cutting board, and Luka ran it out, saving Nalani from a commander encounter.

The short redhead reappeared at the cutting board with a handful of produce. She'd been hired four days ago at Whitcry Spaceport, but they'd never spoken more than two words to each other. "I'm Willie. Are you galley help, too?" She sliced tomatoes into wedges, her thoughts broadcasting at full volume: *pretty woman, I'm hungry, my aching feet need a break, hurry this chopping—*

Nalani bolstered her shields. "I'm Desta's friend. I volunteer when she needs me." They chopped veggies and filled bins in silence after that.

Desta hurried by with her arms full. "Nalani, run these out to the line, please. Willie, grab the sauces and grated cheese from the chiller."

Nalani picked up the bins in trembling hands. Maybe the commander wouldn't see her. She stepped through the door, bins held before her like plasma shields.

Huntington stood at the veggie bar, loading greens onto his plate.

She swallowed. No way to avoid him now. Maybe he wouldn't notice her. She slid the metal bins into place gently so they didn't clink.

"So lovely to see you again." He smiled, flashing perfect teeth.

She nodded. *Get a grip. Be polite. Reinforce shields.* "Commander." She turned for the safety of the galley.

"Have you eaten yet?"

"No. I'm assisting Desta with prep."

"Would you like to join me? I can wait."

She spoke over her shoulder. "I've already made plans but thank you." She brushed by Luka and escaped into the galley.

Desta followed with a tray loaded with plates of food and lowered her voice. "For a creep, at least he's polite when you turn him down. Have you reported him to the captain?"

"For what?" Nalani pressed her hand to her stomach. "He's never *done* anything inappropriate. It's not illegal to have thoughts."

Desta clenched her jaw. "Promise me, the next time he does or says something inappropriate, you'll file a complaint." She set the tray on a prep surface and divvied out servings of pasta, veggies, and bread. Willie and Luka produced stools—Willie let out a mental sigh Nalani picked up with her shields at max—and they sat for a quiet but hurried meal.

"Has the commander taken a shine to you?" Willie asked through a mouthful of bread.

"Unfortunately." Nalani sniffed the sauce smothering her noodles and dug in. Beef, bug, bird, or mystery meat, her mouth watered at the savory aroma.

Willie giggled. "I'll take him off your hands. He's a

hottie." *Wanna kiss those lips.*

Nalani cringed. "He's all yours."

Desta rolled her eyes and stuffed her mouth. "He likes all the women, all the time. If you're prone to heartache, avoid him."

Luka elbowed Willie. "You could do better."

She ran her gaze over him. "Talking about you?"

"No." He shoved food in his bright-red face and glanced at Nalani.

Desta cleaned sauce off her plate with a scrap of bread. "Nalani, are you in the tank all day tomorrow?"

"Yeah. I'm scheduled for three more duty shifts before a day off."

Willie tumbled off her stool and backed up, her face pale. "You're a teep?"

Nalani swallowed the lump in her throat. Most norms shied away from telepaths, especially strangers. "I'm shielded. Believe me, I don't want to share your surface thoughts any m-m-more than you want me to."

Willie glanced at Desta and Luka. "I didn't mean any offense." She wrung her hands but didn't return to her seat.

Nalani stared at her food. "That's the response I usually receive. I'm not offended."

Luka righted the fallen stool. "Finish your meal and quit gawking like a spect. Nalani's harmless, and your secrets are safe."

Harmless? Nalani sighed. That summed her up.

Willie blushed. "I'm super sorry. I never met a teep in real life before."

"Hey." Desta threw bread at the girl. "I'm one."

"You're a T8. You can't pick up surface thoughts." Willie sat and picked up her fork.

Desta stuck her tongue out at Willie.

Forty minutes later, after they finished cleaning up, Desta smiled at Nalani. "I need some relaxation. You up for a vid and popcorn?"

"Um, I need to—"

"You put in an eight-hour shift, and you volunteered two hours for me." Desta jabbed her fists on her hips. "Now you're going to work more. Don't deny it."

"I downloaded files from *Evangeline*—"

"You can read them tomorrow."

"But—"

"No buts." Desta grabbed Nalani's hand and tugged her to follow. "We'll view something funny and snack on treats from my stash. It's not healthy for you to work so many hours."

Nalani fell in step behind Desta, trying to extricate her hand. The skin-to-skin contact made her heart pound and sapped her shields. "You're not medstaff, so you can't order me to relax." She yanked her hand free but followed Desta into her quarters. "What kind of treats?"

Desta crawled under her bunk. She'd built a secret compartment to hide her greatest wealth—nonnutritious foodstuffs—and though everyone knew of it, no one dared to breach the cache. Not even Desta's well-armed roommate, Cerys.

"You want salty or sweet?" Desta called from the shadows.

"Both?"

She scooched from under the bunk, a small box clutched to her chest, and held out her hand for an assist.

Nalani clenched her teeth and hauled her friend off the floor. The risk of picking up thoughts from the touch was worth a handful of nibbles. "You changed your image." Nalani gestured at the holo-pic hanging on the wall, the only decoration in the room. The last time she'd been here, it featured a slow sweep through a blue-and-white snow-covered mountain glacier that left her queasy from the motion. The new pic showcased a hammock strung between two palm trees with sunlight glittering off ocean waves lapping at a sandy shore. Small movements, peaceful, not stomach-churning.

"The snow was too chilly. I like sun and water better." Desta tucked the box under her arm. "Let's grab lounge two before someone else takes it."

This long after the meal, they were probably too late to claim any of the rec areas, but Nalani followed Desta. If they couldn't watch the vid screen, maybe she would let Nalani get back to the tank to research in peace. With a treat.

A chime sounded from the ceiling speakers, and Zeus made a ship-wide broadcast. "Dropping out of hyperspace in thirty seconds. Please prepare."

Nalani and Desta grabbed the metal bar running the length of the hallway and spread their feet for better purchase.

"Three, two, one." The freighter bobbed.

Nalani's body lifted until only her toes touched the deck, and her hair rose off her nape.

The ship settled, as did Nalani's stomach.

"Drop complete," Zeus announced.

Desta smacked the wall twice with her palm and turned her gaze to the ceiling. "Nicely done, Zeus. Smooth as pleytermilk."

"Thank you."

Nalani grinned. "Zeus, don't forget to transfer *Evangeline's* files to Aldrin. I can't read them now, as

Desta has kidnapped me for relaxation, but I'll want them later."

"I completed the task several hours ago." Zeus paused. "Would you like me to free you from the social obligation?"

Nalani grinned. "I'm all right."

"As you wish."

Desta's brown eyes widened. "Thanks for the idea." She hurried down the hallway and engaged the door lock to the lounge.

Nalani followed. The seats were probably already filled with tired crew members in various states of attentiveness while the vid screen showcased a sporting event or a musical performance featuring electronic instruments and a tech-enhanced vocalist. She entered the darkened room.

"Lights," Desta ordered. Wall sconces, preprogrammed to a low setting for optimal relaxation, blinked on, bathing the small empty space with soft, warm light. "Sweet! It's all ours."

Nalani groaned. At least two hours until she could access the files.

Desta crossed to the display panel, programmed the vid, turned, and beamed like a floodlight. "You're going to love this one."

Nalani tapped the floor controls with her toe, bringing up two tan padded chaises.

"Two more," Desta said. "I invited guests."

Nalani froze. "W-w-what? Who?"

The lounge door opened, and Nalani whirled, hands clutched to her chest.

Chapter 5

Engineering Chief Brennan Walsh entered, followed by Dr. Jex. Brennan spotted Desta, and his eyes sparked behind dark curls.

"Hey, love." She threw her arms around Brennan's neck and kissed him, her body plastered to his. He buried his hands in her braids and returned the embrace. Their thoughts ran into seriously embarrassing territory.

Jex's gaze hit the floor, slid to the seating, then to Nalani. His eyes, a deep blue, peered through pale lashes. He blinked, his double lids highlighting one of the differences between their species. "Greetings. I did not realize we were viewing the vid with others." The most visible variation between them was his crest, a reactive crown of blue-green hair that ran across the top of his blond head from ear to ear. Normally, the crest stood straight up, like a halo of peacock feathers. Now it drooped, indicating unease.

"Greetings, Jex. I also did not anticipate other attendees." Jex was half-Valaqite and half-human, and Nalani enjoyed speaking his mother tongue with its reliance on metaphors and formality. He struggled to socialize with both species, which put him and Nalani on equal footing. It helped that he didn't fully understand human ways, and best of all, she never picked up his surface thoughts. She activated two more seats and sank into the one closest to the bulkhead. Being near the wall offered a small sense of security. Limited directions for threats. Not that she expected any on Zeus. It was habit.

Jex selected the chaise beside hers. "Are they going to osculate with their lips through the entire entertainment?"

Cute. She grinned. "Probably."

His normally tanned skin turned bluish, coordinating with the blue-green crest that now stood straight up. Relaxed and at ease. "I will block your view with my body, as I've heard displays of affection cause you discomfort."

Blessed nothingness emanated from his mind. "How thoughtful. I appreciate the gesture."

Music filled the small space, and Desta ended the lip-lock. The vid she'd programmed flared to life on the two-meter screen, and the lighting dimmed further. The title sequence began. Desta flipped packaged snacks at everyone and slid into her viewing chair. "Prepare to be entertained!"

Nalani ripped open her bag to find minty cocoas. Her mouth watered, and she popped two to suck on.

The title of the vid spread across the viewing screen. *Commander Jana Vengeance*. Released more than six hundred years ago, long before humans embraced regular space flight. Might be interesting. Surprising that Zeus possessed a copy of such an old film, too. Most of the entertainment vids made prior to the wars had been destroyed, but she'd seen a few. She snuggled into the chaise and lost herself in the plotline, forgetting about the people around her.

Halfway through the vid, Jex stretched out his hand, his half-eaten bag of treats offered. "Trade?"

"Deal." She took his caramel crunchies and handed

over her remaining mints.

The vid brought laughter in some places, tears in others—aside from Jex, who didn't have tear ducts—and when the credits rolled, Nalani cheered with the others. The lights came up. She rose from the chaise and toed the controls to retract her seat.

Jex collected the empty snack wrappers and tossed them in the recycling unit.

"Did you like it?" Desta's dark-brown skin glowed in the warm light of the lounge.

Nalani smiled. "Yes. You chose well."

"I always do." She slapped Bren's ass and waggled her eyebrows at him.

Nalani turned her gaze to the floor and checked her shields. No way! Not listening to those thoughts now. "Yeah. Well. That was a lovely distraction, but now I'm going to read crew logs." She nodded at Jex and adopted the syntax of his native language. "Thank you for sharing your nonnutritious refreshments with me."

His double eyelids clicked—*snick, snick*—and his crest flared. "You are welcome. I enjoyed this relaxation exercise. Perhaps we will share another at a later date."

"It's possible."

Desta and Bren gazed at each other. Smooching was imminent.

"Not more kissing," Nalani quoted from the movie and headed for the door. "See you tomorrow."

Jex fell into step beside her, leaving the lovers alone in the lounge. "This was my first invitation to a social event of this sort. Did I disgrace myself?"

She totally related. "No, you did well."

Zeus's voice interrupted. "Nalani, do you want me to run long-range scans beyond Terminus now that we are in normal space?"

Jex cocked his head and stared at her. *Snick, snick.* "What scans?"

Heat flooded her face. "Zeus, I thought we discussed this. Captain Rodriguez doesn't want me using your systems for my projects."

"Shall I ask him for permission? I am certain he would grant it."

"I'll do them later." The hallway stretched forever before her.

"Affirmative."

Why was Jex still walking beside her? Medlab lay behind them, and his private quarters were up one deck. What should she say?

Jex broke the silence. "I am curious about your scans. My home world is not far from here. What are you searching for?"

Lovely, a safe topic. "I'm wondering what's beyond the Terminus System."

His double lids snicked. "Nothing but empty space."

"Then I'll confirm that theory."

"Fact," he corrected.

He wasn't being intentionally impolite, just literal. "My theory contradicts your fact. I'm looking for the Thrakis home world."

His blue-green crest fanned across his sandy-blond hair, spreading to encompass his skull like a halo from an ancient religious icon. "I am intrigued. May I review the data with you once you complete them?"

Her chest tightened. They took the stairs to the lower deck. She needed alone time on her ship. None of her crewmates, not even Desta, had been aboard Aldrin in the four years she'd been employed by Captain

Rodriguez, and she couldn't bring herself to invite Jex. But turning him down would be rude.

Zeus saved her. "If you begin now, I estimate scan completion in six-point-five hours."

"When will we arrive at Liang Spaceport?" Jex asked Zeus.

"In two-point-five hours."

If she began the scans from Aldrin's tank, she could remain awake until they docked and be useful to Zeus. "Will you need me in the tank for Liang?"

"Negative. ZeeBee is scheduled to enter at 2300 hours. Docking procedures are automated, and I do not anticipate difficulties with this routine stop."

"How long will we be in port?" Jex asked.

Nalani crossed Bay Two slowly, Jex at her side. How would she ditch him when they arrived at Aldrin's airlock?

"Captain Rodriguez has not scheduled a departure time," Zeus answered. "I anticipate a three-day layover to gather fuel and supplies and to allow the crew a sufficient relaxation period."

In other words, time to get drunk, pick a fight, and recover before takeoff. How could anyone enjoy those activities? No way would she go aboard Liang. She'd be on Aldrin working on translating runes. She stopped at the Bay Three door and stared at the code pad. Jex hadn't taken any of her hints—was he capable of understanding subtlety?

Jex stood beside her, his head cocked to one side, his crest drooped ten degrees. Curiosity. "Do you recall the code?"

She sighed. "Yes." She keyed it in, and the door slid into the wall panel, allowing access to Bay Three and her ship. *Get a grip!* Jex wasn't like the others. He was a literal being. Maybe she couldn't offend him. Maybe he'd appreciate a straightforward rejection without the foolish emotional display of embarrassment—

"I sense from your hesitation you wish to proceed without me." His lips turned up, and he cocked his head. "As you have not yet begun the long-range scans, there is no logical reason to continue our social interaction at this time." *Snick, snick.* "If you discover interesting data, will you inform me?"

The tightness in her chest eased. "I will. Enjoy your evening, Jex."

He bowed and headed for the staircase, his crest at full display. Like feathers, only shorter. And made of hair. Was it hair? Or a keratin-like substance? Didn't matter. She'd never work up the nerve to ask.

She exhaled and entered Bay Three. "Zeus, I'll see you at 0800 hours." It'd be rude to treat him like a machine, as most of the crew did. He had personality. Etiquette. And now, apparently, emotions.

"Sleep sufficiently, Nalani."

She stepped into Aldrin's hold, locked the door behind her, and rolled her shoulders. Too much social interaction for one day. Maintaining her shields for long hours drained energy like a leaky valve seal. Being alone and able to drop her shielding was almost as relaxing as floating in a sensory deprivation tank. Oh, for the boring years she'd spent in total isolation.

That was ridiculous. Humans were social creatures. She needed this crew, even if they sapped her shields. She enjoyed a hot shower, donned a clean bodysuit, and slid into Aldrin's gel. *Hello, my friend.*

Greetings, 'Lani.

The sound of Dad's voice and his nickname for her brought a lump to her throat. She swallowed. *Could you run some long-range scans for me of the region beyond* Terminus?

Not from here. Zeus's *hull impedes my sensors.*

She'd have to leave the cargo hold. Not feasible at this time. Once Zeus docked, she'd fly Aldrin out long enough to complete them. *Table that for now. Have you analyzed the data from the* Evangeline?

Nalani spent two hours reading files and noting ideas for scientific articles based on her findings. A folder labeled *Classic Films* looked promising. File names included *Antigone*, *Firefly*, *Rippington Palace*, and *Operation Starburst*. Close to one hundred ancient vids. Jex might be interested in viewing them with Nalani, if she could carve enough time from her schedule to watch one.

Aldrin chimed in her head. *Opening comms with Captain Rodriguez.*

Go. The click signaled the connection. "Nalani here. What can I do for you?"

Captain Rodriguez's deep voice echoed telepathically from Zeus to her. *We'll dock at Liang in fifteen minutes. Are you available to accompany our prisoners with the security team? I'd feel better if they had a telepath, in case the scuts think of fighting or running.*

She shuddered. Encounter a scut mind again? No thanks. "Can't ZeeBee do it?"

He's a T9. What's he going to pick up? Rodriguez cleared his throat. *I know it's a hardship for you, but it should only take a half hour. I'll sweeten it by offering combat pay for a full hour of duty.*

As if extra chits would make the job more palatable. But how could she say no, after he gave her a free place to moor Aldrin and special days off to survey the Faleeki System?

Combat pay for two hours, he amended.

Don't disappoint him. "I agree. I'll report to Cerys in ten."

Thank you, Nalani. Out.

She climbed from the tank. Wearing a bodysuit onto Liang was permissible, but it would draw too much unwanted attention from the scut prisoners. And the males aboard the port station. And some of the females. She had more curves than a compression coil. Nalani hurried to her sleeping quarters—though she rarely slept in her bunk, preferring the warm gel-tank. The screen flared to life at her entrance, cycling through photos of archaeological digs on Earth.

She grabbed a loose-fitting green tunic and black leggings from the storage unit and donned boots. These backwater space stations were grimy, with sticky floors and questionable stains. Proper footwear offered maximum protection from germs, especially if she got to the decon tube right after.

Properly attired, she hurried to Bay One and the gangway linking Zeus to the Liang Spaceport. She'd arrived ahead of the security team, but other crew members gathered near the airlock, ready to escape Zeus for R&R or fulfill ship duties. Willie, the redhead from the galley, waved at Nalani from the pack. She waved back but kept her shields tight.

The increased thrum of the deck warned her to brace.

Zeus fired directional thrusters. "Prepare for

docking." His voice rang through the bay. "Three. Two. One."

A slight bump, followed by a hiss, a grind, and the whine of machinery announced their arrival at the port. Everyone clapped and cheered. "Smooth!" someone shouted. The gangway snapped in place. Seconds later, the airlock cycled green and opened. Crew members surged into the vestibule, crossed the bridge, and disappeared into the shadows of the passageway.

Nalani glanced at the empty stairs. Where were Cerys and the security team with the prisoner scuts?

The lift door swished open, and four crewmen stepped through, armed with stunners. Three prisoners followed. They wore restraint cuffs on ankles and wrists, tethered by a nylo-steel chain. They couldn't break out of those without a key or a welding torch. Another four crew members followed. Cerys brought up the rear with a stun baton.

The procession neared. Nalani stepped back to allow them access to the gangway and squared her shoulders. She could do this. No need to dip into anyone's mind. Surface scans would alert her to any thoughts of escape.

The scut who'd recognized her winked at her. *She'd be a fab cabana toy.*

Her abs flinched, and she ground her teeth. *Don't react, don't give him the satisfaction.*

Cerys stepped close to Nalani. "Forget about the bounty now. We have to turn these crusters over to spaceport Authorities. I've got your back. Right?"

Nalani nodded. "Yes. No cracking."

Cerys turned and pointed to the airlock. "Let's move. The sooner your asses are in a prison cell, the sooner we can find a tav." She prodded the lead scut's shoulder blade with her baton. He shuffled forward, grinning at Nalani.

She inched away, fingers splayed on the chilly bulkhead behind her.

Cerys stepped between them and turned her ice-blue eyes to Nalani. "Are you holding?"

Another failure. All those years of running from the monster, fantasizing about the day he landed in an off-planet prison cell, yet he still held her in his greedy fist. Who could resist a bounty of that size?

"Hey!" Cerys snapped her fingers by Nalani's face. "I know you're fighting to keep it together, but I need you to scan for me. Keep my guys safe; I'll keep you safe. You trust me?"

Nalani nodded, sucking in quick breaths. *Don't blank out, don't fall apart. Don't let him win. Again.*

"Are you scanning?" Cerys stepped aside. "Are you focused?"

Nalani stared at their cuffed boots. They shuffled forward. *Don't crack...* She dropped her mental shields.

The first scut's surface thoughts revolved around a tropical cabana, coconut trees, and a lifetime supply of cold beer. She could almost pick out the warm, salty breeze. He didn't think about how he'd turn in the bounty, though, nor did he have any intention of trying to grab her. He was content with the knowledge trade. She moved on.

Scut Two wanted to shank Scut One and collect the bounty himself. From afar, through an anonymous router. His greed overcame most of the fear he held for Monstarte, but not all. No plans for escape from that one. Nor did he hope to grab her for the larger reward.

Scut Three was terrified of the prison term he faced

and couldn't wait to break free.

"Three's a runner," Nalani muttered.

Cerys hustled Nalani to the back of the procession, waving for Vania to flank Nalani. "Are you gonna crack?"

"No." Nalani staggered to keep up and drew a deeper breath.

Thankfully, Cerys's thoughts had laser-sharp focus on the mission. Vania marched at Nalani's left, gaze darting constantly, stunner ready.

"I'm scanning." She concentrated on the three prisoners, shields down, and inadvertently caught blips from Cerys's team.

Only two, Vania and Isaiah, were security personnel. The rest were engineering and maintenance crew who had enough training to help Cerys's team when needed. The tall maint woman, Gaspara, couldn't wait to find a tav, a drink, and a Xylone male to bang. Nalani blocked the erotic thought and shifted her focus.

Isaiah, stationed in front of the procession, hoped one of the prisoners would make a break so he could try out his new stunner. She caught an image of him tinkering with the weapon, modifying it to pack a bigger punch.

She leaned toward Cerys. "Check out Isaiah's stunner later."

Cerys chuckled. "Another mod? He's gonna get janked if he keeps at it."

Nalani marched and scanned, breathing easier. They left the gangway and funneled through the checkpoint. The weight of a thousand minds forced her to narrow her focus even further. She'd need extra protein in her next meal, but it was worth the energy expenditure to block those other thoughts. "Three's searching for an optimal place to bolt. Watch his feet—he's got cyber implants in his ankles, so he'll have a mean kick."

Cerys shouldered through her security personnel and walked beside the prisoner, their hips nearly touching.

Vania stepped closer to Nalani.

She followed the people in front of her. Why hadn't station Authorities met them at the checkpoint? Parading these men through a busy spaceport was madness, even with nine armed personnel and a telepath.

They cycled through the entry gate one by one, the scuts sandwiched in the middle. When her turn came, the spaceport officer scanned Nalani's information, took two steps back with wide eyes, and flagged her to proceed. She stepped through, avoiding eye contact. When most people saw the T12 listing, they assumed she would dive straight into their minds.

As if. People's thoughts and memories were boring.

Cerys, her team, and the prisoners set out again, marching down the crowded hallway past the curious or worried glances of other spaceport visitors and residents. Merchants hawked their wares from shops and kiosks in various languages, vying to attract buyers and earn enough credits to do it again tomorrow. Odors of cooked protein clashed with pungent body stench, damp fur, and hot metal.

Thousands of minds pressed against Nalani like multiple comm systems broadcasting all at once. It didn't hurt, but it made concentrating difficult. She reinforced her shields, adding layers of protection like the hull plating on Zeus.

The third scut popped his leg restraints and made a

run for it.

Cerys hit a button on her baton, and the man collapsed, jerking on the floor. She grinned. "Idiot. The wrist cuffs are wired." She released the button and hauled the twitching scut back to the line.

At the first junction where the hallway split to other parts of the structure, station Authorities waited with a hover-transpo and three armored personnel—huge men with stun rifles and smirks that translated, "Please try it." Cerys passed the transpad over for a thumbprint to record the transfer, and Scut One winked at Nalani.

Her heart pounded. One comm privilege for him, and her life was over.

Chapter 6

One of the big security guys grabbed the prisoner and stuffed him in the transpo. Onlookers whispered. Isaiah grinned, his hand hovering over his modded stunner. The loading finished, and the hover-transpo sped away.

What if the bounty had circulated outside scut circles? What if the spaceport people recognized her and wanted the reward? Nalani lowered her shields. Was anyone paying her too much attention?

Exciting... Wonder what they did?... That last one's kinda cute... I can buy him a drink... That hover-transpo is sweet. I'd like to jump on... That chick with the baton is hot. I'll follow her down a shady alley...

Cerys appeared at Nalani's elbow. "You did great. Ready to head back?"

"Yeah. Be careful, someone in the crowd is entertaining nasty thoughts about you."

Cerys pivoted, a daring grin on her face. "I'd love to take him down a notch or two. Where is he?"

"I don't know." Nalani glanced around, but there were too many people.

The other crew members broke off in singles or in pairs, freed for their port stay, and ambled off in various directions.

"Catch up with you hobs later," Vania shouted to them, hovering behind Nalani.

She and Cerys guided Nalani down the sticky walkway, back toward Zeus.

It was over, nothing bad happened, and she didn't crack. Much. Why couldn't she have Cerys's courage? "Don't you want to find a tav or a shoe shop or something?"

Cerys chortled, catching the attention of two Betlies crouched in a shadowed corner, their golden eyes gleaming behind sandy fur. "I'm not gonna leave you alone on this station while you're raw. But if you're up for some shopping, I could use another pair of boots."

"I could go for a Valaqite brandy," Vania said.

Nalani didn't need anything. But the sentiments warmed her heart and thawed some of the chill that lingered from her encounter. "Thanks. I need to return to Aldrin."

Cerys leaned closer and lowered her voice. "By the way, one of the security guys back there says they've been hunting for a scut chief who mods his crew with cybernetics. If the name you supplied pans out, there's a reward coming your way."

A chill skittered down her arms. Stupid to assume he'd stopped with her. Of course, he'd built an entire staff of implanted misfits. "I don't want a reward. I just want them to catch him." They cycled through the checkpoint, and fatigue pulled at her limbs. She hadn't slept yet. "I'm gonna bunk."

They reached the airlock, and Cerys stopped. "Don't worry about that numbnut. I warned the station chief of the threat to you, and he's guaranteed no comms privileges for any of them. You're safe."

"They're allowed legal counsel. Word will leak." Nalani cringed. "I'm so shanked."

Cerys splayed her hands, palms out. "Anyone trying to nab you has to go through me, Zeus, Rodriguez, and twenty-two other crew members. Most of them armed with stunners. You got it? You're safe. And as soon as you're aboard Zeus, Vania and I are going to research the bounty, see if we can locate the posting, and alert stellar Authorities. If news of this doesn't blow a rocket under their asses to hunt him down, I've got ideas of my own."

Nalani nodded and stepped onto the gangway, anxious for alone time.

If Monstarte found out she worked on Zeus, every scut in the surrounding sectors would be after her skin. To be safe—to keep all her friends safe—she should leave Zeus and hide until the Authorities caught Monstarte. He'd been evading them for ten years, amassing a small army of cybernetically enhanced marauders and terrorizing the shipping lanes in three nearby systems. No telling how long she'd have to hide, always looking over her shoulder, never free to take another job. Her chest tightened. Leave them all behind?

She needed to de-stress and sleep. Perhaps tomorrow she'd see a clearer path. Desta teased that Nalani always had a Plan A, B, C, and D. But at the moment, she had nothing.

Captain Rodriguez waited for her, leaning against the Bay Two door, arms crossed. "How'd it go?" His salt-and-pepper hair spiked on the sides like he'd run his fingers through it, and the scar slashing his right eyebrow gave him a perpetual scowl. Beneath his mustache-goatee combo, his lips canted down. His tone was cool. As always.

Nalani set her shield at maximum. No way she'd ever scan the captain. Not even by accident. "Clean transfer. Cerys only used her baton once."

Captain smirked. "She'll find another opportunity before takeoff."

Watch out, hallway creeps and tavern patrons. "It'll be the highlight of her trip."

"Cerys sent me a report about the bounty."

Oh no. She bit her bottom lip. The captain didn't know about her past. He'd fear for his ship and how she'd draw more trouble to them. He'd kick her off to protect his crew.

He smiled. "You're safe here. Don't leave the ship without an armed escort." He pushed off the door and headed for the stairs. "Good night."

Her breath hitched, and tension drained from her shoulders. She could stay. "Thank you."

****

Nalani trudged into the dining hall at 0735 hours for her "morning" meal and stood in the buffet line. Eighteen minds around her buzzed. The two grunts in front of her teased each other about their wild escapades in port and how they were unfit for duty today. Their talk turned to carnal pleasures, so she blocked them and turned her attention to collecting food.

Reconstituted eggs. *Yum.* She put a spoonful on her plate, followed by a biscuit, and slathered the entire mess with sausage gravy. *Deal with that, arteries.* A serving of canned peaches completed her monochromatically dull breakfast.

Now for a place to sit. Not a stressor, just a mundane decision… Where were Cerys and Gack? Not here. Nalani surveyed the crowded room, full of broadcasters and people she didn't know well, and landed on the unofficial "alien" table.

Of all the people on the ship, the aliens were the hardest to "hear." There were only four nonhuman members in Zeus's crew: Chebu, Flerq, Jex, and Tatek. Jex was only half Valaqite, but no one treated him like it. Not even Flerq, the full-blooded Valaqite. He and Jex never spoke, though they sat at the same table for a meal today.

Chebu resembled a six-armed sloth from Earth's jungles and rarely ate with the crew. He took his meals in his nest, a netted mass of ropes and cables he'd hung beneath the stairs leading to Bay Four. Tatek usually worked third shift, so he was probably asleep by now.

Nalani sat at the alien table and nodded a greeting to the Valaqite men seated at opposite sides. They nodded back and ate their meal silently. Just the way Nalani liked.

Why were they harder to hear? Were their brains that different from humans?

Jex cocked his head, stared at her, and chewed.

She smiled. Did he expect her to converse? It would be rude not to. "Um, good day."

His double eyelids blinked. *Snick, snick.* "Is that a moral opinion, or do you anticipate a satisfactory shift in the gel-tank?"

She switched to Valaqite. "It was inconsequential dialogue to bridge an awkward silence. It means I recognize your existence but have nothing meaningful to convey."

He nodded. "Many humans engage in trivial dialogue. I do not understand the appeal."

Flerq's crest deflated slightly.

What did that mean? Irritation? "Flerq, do you prefer silence during your meal?"

"It is not necessary," he answered in Terran.

Great. She'd edged him.

Jex stood, his dirty dishes stacked on his tray. "Enjoy your good day, Nalani."

"Thanks. You, too."

He hesitated. "Have you run the scans yet?"

"No. Later today."

"Would you like me to run them? My schedule is clear."

"No, thank you. I need to take Aldrin out for that duty."

Jex nodded and walked away.

Flerq spoke in Valaqite, his gaze locked on his breakfast plate, his crest relaxed. "Does Jex annoy you?"

No sense causing Flerq further displeasure after irritating him earlier. She answered in Valaqite. "No. His companionship soothes like a breezy whisper through the fronds." That last word was supposed to be "headcrest," but as she didn't have one, she improvised.

His double eyelids blinked. "Unexpected." His pale-green skin darkened.

"Does he annoy you?"

"As a burr between the toe webs." He excused himself to bus his dishes.

She stared after him. Valaqites had toe webs? Her father had located an ancient figurine of a bipedal being and theorized it was a Thrakis individual, based on the location of the find and an inscription found near it. That figure had webbed hands and feet. Perhaps the Valaqites were kin to the extinct Thrakis? It would be worth investigating.

The room had cleared. No time to linger. Nalani swallowed the last of her coffee, took care of her breakfast dishes, and hurried down the hall to the medlab. She had the *Evangeline's* logs to finish reading and a scut to hunt. And maybe locate that bounty on the nets, hack into the coding, and change the amounts to zero. That'd serve him right.

Between ZeeBee and Nalani, with Desta as backup for the rare times Zeus needed sapient brain assistance during second shift, they kept Zeus running at peak efficiency. Nalani stepped into the bay.

ZeeBee crawled from the goo, stretched his hands above his head, and yawned. "Morning." He mentally brushed against her shields politely.

She nodded and kicked off her deck shoes, offering her own featherlight graze across his shields. "Anything to report?"

"We're docked at Liang Spaceport." He scratched his rumbling belly through the bodysuit and stuffed his feet into a humongous pair of faux-bark sandals. "Absolutely nothing happened, unless you're interested in how many barfights the crew started last night."

Zeus answered through the medlab speakers. "The crew initiated four brawls and participated in one other. Currently, two of our maintenance workers are in holding cells on the station until their fines are paid. Chief Gack is en route to ensure their release."

It should be Commander Huntington paying the fines, as he supervised the maintenance and security divisions, but he'd never stoop to dealing with station security. The incarcerated duo had to be Ajani and Gaspara. Chebu, the only nonhuman maintenance worker, could handle the ship until his crewmates returned from the brig. "Any issues with refueling? Do we have a new destination and cargo yet?"

ZeeBee shrugged and belted a stylized aboriginal robe around his waist. "Cap'll come up with something. He always does." ZeeBee yawned again and headed for the door, running his fingers through his long black hair. "Catch you tomorrow. I gotta chew."

The door hissed closed behind him, and Nalani locked herself into the tiny alcove where the gel-tank rested. Her shields dropped, and she shucked her outer garments. "Should be a good, slow day."

"What is your definition of good?" Zeus asked. "And it will not be slow. My list of duties will take the better part of three days to complete, barring new additions."

New things always appeared on his list. She slid into the warm goo. On her first day aboard Zeus, she'd cringed at lying in the same tank where ZeeBee also spent hours scratching or farting in his sleep, but Zeus reassured her that the gel was self-cleaning. Viruses and bacteria could not survive in the pink substance, and it was the cleanest place in the freighter. It also moisturized her skin, but that was a side benny.

"While you're plowing through your to-do list, I'd like to work on a few projects of my own." Her neck touched the cradle, and the networks flared to life with a tickling zing.

Excellent. Now that you're connected, the thrilling, tingling sensation in my diodes has returned. Is this called indigestion?

She laughed. *You have no digestive system, Zeus. Do you want me to run a diagnostic?*

No need. I will download public records and study emotions so I may identify these new feelings without assistance.

Back to this subject again. She'd hoped docking with the space station would trigger an automated update and fix the problem. Obviously, it didn't work. *Do you truly believe you're experiencing emotions?*

Yes, but only when you're in the bio-tank. I hypothesize your telepathy has created a cascading effect, causing an evolution.

A chill shot down her arms. That wasn't possible. She couldn't be the cause. But what if she was? Rodriguez might fire her to keep Zeus from being corrupted further.

I wish to fully explore the phenomenon in case it is temporary. Zeus's core thrummed with activity. *I will also confer with other nearby bio-ships. What are your plans for the day?*

She wanted to finish skimming the *Evangeline's* crew logs—

Comm link open, Zeus announced.

Nalani, report to Bay One immediately. Captain Rodriguez barked an order at someone else, then amended, *I need a telepath.*

Now what? "Details, please."

Chapter 7

Passengers boarding, Rodriguez answered.

Nalani sat up, goo sloughing off her body. They never took fares. "Repeat?"

"Bay One. Two minutes. Rodriguez out." He shouted at someone, and the link cut.

Did he say passengers? "Zeus, do you know what's happening?" She climbed from the tank and reached for her outer garments.

"The captain has not logged any information regarding our next run. If he holds to pattern, we will remain in the Faleeki Galaxy for one month, making short runs between systems. Captain Rodriguez is fond of Valaq and Aldeia."

Jex and Flerq could visit their families on Valaq, and Aldeia was a tropical paradise, perfect for crew vacations. Had Cap found other people desperate enough to fly there on a freighter? She stuffed her feet in her deck shoes. "Sorry to split. Hopefully, I'll be back soon."

"I hope so. I feel stronger when you are in the tank."

He shouldn't be able to "feel" anything. He probably meant he had more processing power with her connected. She hurried down the hallway, shields tight. The prisoners hadn't been allowed comm access, so odds were these passengers were unrelated to that messed-up part of her life. Could a scut be hiding among a pack of civilians?

Perhaps that's why Rodriguez wanted her, to scan the newcomers for malcontents and scoundrels. Lovely. Touching those types of minds left a sour aftereffect in her brain that would take hours to remove, chewing up the time she'd planned to spend in the tank figuring out what she would do about the bounty on her head.

Captain Rodriguez, Commander Huntington, and Security Chief Cerys Lindholm waited in Bay One. Two security personnel, Vania and Isaiah, stood armed and ready by the airlock.

Was it legal for a freighter to carry passengers? It had to be. Rodriguez never carried contraband or illegals, paid his taxes on time, and stayed out of trouble. He had no issues with the Authorities.

She crossed the fully stocked bay to the captain standing near the airlock and took a position far from Huntington. "Reporting for duty, sir. What do you require of me?"

Rodriguez glanced down at her. "A group of Hellians asked for passage to Sathara."

She grinned at the name of the minor system near Liang. In the native tongue of that planet, "Hel" meant "petite." In ancient German, it meant "to cover." In the Christian world, it was a place of torment and judgment. So many vastly different meanings for one word. "And you agreed."

He shrugged. "They were willing to pay the price I tossed out and didn't seem to mind sleeping in a cargo hold, so I figured why not? They even agreed to the no-weapons rule and offered to bring their own foodstuffs. Now I need you to scan them."

"They'll be stowed in Bay Five." Cerys crossed to stand beside Nalani. "With no access to the rest of the ship. You won't even see them after this."

The trip from Liang to Sathara took eight days at standard speed, barring the normal stopovers. "Are we delivering cargo to Fundo Three or Malenki?"

Captain nodded. "Both."

The passengers would be on board for twelve days, tops. "How large is the group?"

The airlock hissed. The doors parted.

"Twenty-four, if I remember correctly," Rodriguez answered.

Cerys edged closer to Nalani. "I've got your back."

Captain Rodriguez stepped forward to greet the leader of the Hellian pack. "Welcome aboard. As we agreed, security will scan your people and baggage before we finalize the deal."

The human leader bowed. His bent posture and whitening hair put him somewhere in late middle age. "Thank you, Captain Rodriguez. I am Xing Wu. We will cause you no harm." He reached out a trembling hand.

Rodriguez shook it.

Nalani relaxed her shields and lightly brushed Wu's mind. Images exploded, racing by like a zipper at max speed. *Caged snow bear, prowling and spitting. A hand in a pocket, clutching, concealing. Grass mice fleeing a burning hut.*

Cerys leaned in and whispered, "What's he thinking?"

"Fear. Concealment," Nalani whispered back. "He's hiding something, but he's not dangerous to us."

"Hel's suffering a violent rebellion. Maybe they're running from war."

Nalani nodded. Her gaze drifted beyond Wu to the other people behind him. All humans, all dressed in filthy garments one step up from rags. "They're afraid, nervous, excited to be someplace safe for the first time in…six weeks? They are desperate people."

Cerys gripped her stun baton. "Desperate people are unpredictable."

The security team ran their scanners over Wu and waved him forward, taking the next person in line, a young woman.

Rodriguez introduced Wu to Huntington, Cerys, and Nalani. Wu smiled, nodded, and offered to shake hands with each, followed by a "pleased to meet you." He stepped over to Nalani, his hand hovering in the space between them.

She clenched her laced fingers and leaned on protocol. "I am required by law to advise you that I am a T12 telepath, and sharing physical contact with me may inadvertently pass along thoughts or images you wish to keep private. You are not obligated to shake my hand."

His skin paled, and his eyes widened. He dropped his hand. "I did not know Zeus had a powerful telepath aboard. Thank you." He bowed and backed away, his gaze darting to the people entering the hold.

Cerys pulled Nalani back a few paces. "Do your thing. Keep us safe."

She scanned them as they entered, wide-eyed, hands clenched protectively to their bodies. *Hunted. Wounded. Mourning. Hungry.* "These people are beaten." Tears welled in Nalani's eyes, and she blinked. "They won't cause us problems." She touched each mind after they filtered through the security sweep. They simply wanted to find rest and safety.

Twenty-six people crowded Bay One, huddling together and staring at Captain Rodriguez speaking with

Xing Wu. Zeus's deck grunts, some called up from second and third shift, pushed the passengers' crates on hover pallets over the gangway. The security team waved their scanners over the belongings, moving cargo through at a wicked pace.

When they reached the fourth pallet, twenty-six minds cringed.

"That crate holds something extremely important to these people," Nalani whispered to Cerys. "They don't want us to open it."

Cerys's eyes narrowed. "Maybe we should."

"It's nothing dangerous or contraband, just something that holds cultural and personal meaning to them."

"I can still flag it." She strode toward the questionable crate.

Twenty-six people held their breath and stared.

Cerys pulled a scanner from her utility belt and ran it over the code printed on the side. She stepped back, signaling the grunts to keep the line moving.

The passengers relaxed. Slightly. Wu's surface thoughts drifted from relief to surprise to joy, his gaze locked on the crates floating down the decking to the lift that would transport the goods and passengers to Bay Five.

Once everyone and everything passed the scans, Wu and Rodriguez finalized the deal with thumbprints and the credit transfer. It took six trips in a cramped lift to shift the passengers and their belongings to Bay Five, the second-smallest cargo hold on Zeus. It'd be a tight fit, but they'd have access to three sanitation/grooming pods, a bunk for everyone, cookers and chillers for food prep, and a vid screen with Zeus's vast library of entertainment at their disposal. Not the worst way to pass twelve days. Based on surface scans, it was a paradise to many of them.

Rodriguez cleared Nalani to return to the tank, and she hurried up the stairs to medlab. Compared to the Hellians, her problems with a bounty and rabid scut seemed inconsequential—or would, if she didn't know what Monstarte would to do her if he got his hands on her again.

She sank into the pink and connected to Zeus. *I need advice. Once Ty Monstarte learns I'm serving aboard you, he's going to come for me. Or even worse, reissue the bounty with my whereabouts listed. You and everyone on board will be in danger. What should I do?*

Zeus's data nodes whirred. *You are in danger! Please stay within my hull where you will be safe. Don't go anywhere alone. Captain Rodriguez will alert Authorities if we are in danger.*

Authority Forces can't give us an armed escort. We don't know how long it will take them to locate Monstarte and toss him in supermax. Until then, I'll be a target. Nalani squirmed in the gel, working an ache from her lower back.

My hull is difficult to breach, and my defenses are sufficient. I need you here. If it makes you feel more secure, you and Aldrin could help if we are attacked.

Aldrin could fly circles around attacking scut ships, but she'd be unable to fire on them, so what good was that? *I think I should hide, possibly in the Terminus System. No one would find me there.* She could continue her search for the Thrakis home world and maybe find a way to repair the failing star portals. The one at Sarin sometimes powered down for no reason. It once crushed a ship as it exited, killing everyone on board. No one risked using it now, severing Sarin's access to outside systems. Unless someone found a way to repair the malfunctioning portals, other galaxies would follow and be logistically cut off from the rest of the universe. It'd be a nightmare.

Captain Rodriguez, Zeus, and the crew would be out of business. There was no profit in runs that took twelve years to complete.

Everyone else in the universe assumed the Dolanis had built the star portals. While scholars, archaeologists, and treasure hunters scoured the regions near the Hercules superclusters for the elusive Dolanis home world, she alone searched beyond Terminus.

Which just reinforced the idea that she should leave Zeus, find Thrakis, and save the universal economies.

Her stomach clenched. But that meant leaving Zeus. Desta. Cerys. Gack. The only friends she'd ever had, the only family she'd ever known since her parents were murdered seventeen years ago. Once she escaped from Monstarte, she'd lived in isolation for six years, with only Aldrin for companionship. Landing the job on Zeus had been a minor miracle, and it'd taken her nearly two years to remember how to be human again. Her social skills were still woefully inadequate, but she'd improved, with Desta's help. Now that Nalani belonged to something special, could she abandon them and return to living alone?

She blinked.

I am experiencing an unpleasant sensation due to your distress. Please cease.

She swallowed a laugh. *That's not how emotions work.*

Perhaps a diversion would help. Do you wish to study the long-range scans of Terminus?

I haven't run them yet.

I did them last night.

Jank it! The captain couldn't overlook this violation. *What? Why?*

Because your genuine desire piqued my own spirit of inquiry. As you did not make a formal request for the scans, the captain cannot reprimand you for disobeying his new ruling.

Zeus, that's not the—you broke the intent. And was totally out of character for his programming. But maybe he found something. *Did the scans reveal anything noteworthy?*

I began examining them and flagged two places that bear further scrutiny. Or if you wish to turn your thoughts elsewhere, I found a reference to Thrakis in the Evangeline *files.*

She gasped. *You did? Display, please!*

The captain's log popped up, and Zeus highlighted a portion of text. Holy crusters—the ship's mission had been to find Thrakis. What were the odds? Infinitesimally small, almost nonexistent. For the last four hundred years, universal focus had been on finding Dolanis.

She skimmed the first few paragraphs of the log.

They didn't have the information she had, thanks to her father's brilliant efforts at the Haraldi Star Portal and her own translations of ancient runes. But the *Evangeline* logs stated they had reliable data pointing them to the Terminus System in the Faleeki Galaxy. Unfortunately, they had been attacked in hyperspace two portals from their destination, so their search had never begun.

She had to study the data that led the *Evangeline* to Terminus. She and Zeus spent three hours digging through the logs, but the information eluded her. No clues, no star charts, no evidence—no hints—that the Thrakis home world was in the Faleeki Galaxy. Instead, she found incredible details for her articles.

I have located a file of gibberish. Zeus loaded the data. *The characters do not match anything in my nodes, so I cannot translate them.*

A linguistic challenge! *Let me see.*

Her stomach gurgled. Nalani reached out and tapped a drawer in the wall unit beside the tank. The compartment opened to her stash of nutri-cubes, peeled and ready to ingest. She grabbed two and shoved them in her mouth. *Which subsection of files held this information?*

Look under Mission.

A zing of excitement shot through her. This could be what had sent the *Evangeline's* crew to Faleeki. She scanned the data. It wasn't gibberish but an archaic dialect of Valaqite. That squiggle with the two dots represented the word "man." *Do you have any ancient Valaqite texts in your library?*

Negative. I have two tomes of poetry and one science text, both published this century.

She'd have to ask Jex or Flerq for help translating the script.

Or not. She had a sharp mind for languages. If she could find a single codex, she'd be able to translate the data herself. She accessed the intergalactic net buyer's guide and input parameters. And waited.

No item found. She adjusted the wording and tried again. Another failure.

There had to be a resource available. Maybe the galactic data node. She logged into the largest library ever collated and requested a broad search.

Nothing.

That made no sense. Valaq had an open and generous relationship with the Alliance. They all shared information. So why were ancient Valaq books unavailable?

Four hours later, she'd found nothing, and her mind was slush. What a waste of the afternoon. Time for a meal, then the long-range scans. *See you tomorrow at 0800.*

Thank you, Nalani. It was an intriguing day.

She climbed from the tank, dressed, and headed for the dining hall.

Desta didn't need assistance, so Nalani stood in line for food and took a generous helping of the crustacean stew over rice, asparagus and mushrooms fried with faux-bacon, and a fruit salad of fresh hydroponics blueberries and strawberries with whipped cream.

Shields held firm, Nalani turned to survey the buzzing hall. Cerys sat with Ajani. Again. They must be dating. Good for her! Ajani was adorable. Thick black hair, dimples, amazing cheekbones…but staring was rude, so Nalani turned away.

Commander Huntington waved at her and pointed to the empty chair beside him.

She shuddered and glanced away. Not happening. She'd never sit with him. She pushed up on her toes. Where was Gack?

Jex smiled at her and fanned his crest. She headed for him.

Flerq didn't look up from his plate, though he did

swallow before speaking in his mother tongue. "Welcome of greatest honor, Nalani."

"Esteem welcomed, Flerq. Pleasing day." She nodded at Jex. "Greetings."

His crest quivered. "Greetings. Was your day productive?"

"Productive and intriguing. Yours?" She dug into her meal. Beef was expensive and difficult to find in markets on this side of the universe, so Desta improvised with some sort of crustacean native to Aldeia. It tasted similar to beef but with a grainier texture.

"I spent several hours with the Hellian passengers tending to their health. Most of them have neglected medical care for years due to the war." He stabbed a blueberry with his fork. It shot from the bowl, rolled across the table, and lodged beneath the lip of Flerq's tray.

He flicked it back across the table.

Jex's crest deflated.

"Try a spoon." She handed hers to him. "Are any of the passengers ill?"

"Malnourished, mostly." He spooned up the fruit and sniffed it. "I have never sampled this blue orb. Is it tasty?"

She fished one from her bowl and popped it in her mouth. "I enjoy them. They contain antioxidants, vitamins C and K, and manganese."

His head cocked to the side as he studied the spoonful of berries. "Manganese is beneficial to my thyroid and caruncle."

Hands gripped Nalani's shoulders, and hot breath coated her ear. "Sweet Nalani. You don't need to eat with these beings. My table is free." Commander Huntington.

Obscene erotic images bombarded her mind, and Desta's crustacean stew threatened to come back up.

Chapter 8

Flerq glared at the commander.
Slime trails across a lettuce leaf.
Nalani frowned. What? Was that from Flerq? She strengthened her shields and shrugged to escape Huntington's touch. His grip tightened. He'd leave bruises on her shoulders.
"I-I-I didn't, I didn't m-m-mean to—"
"I invited Nalani to dine with me." Jex for the save. "She and I enjoyed entertainment together last night." *Snick, snick.*
Huntington pressed his hip bones into her shoulder blades. "Nalani, you never share entertainment with me." *Leering at her lying beneath him, naked, sweating, pumping—*
Shield tighter! She shut her eyes. Alkaline earth metals: beryllium, magnesium, calcium. *Moaning.* Strontium. Barium. *Groping hands, squeezing.* No! Prime numbers: two, three, five, seven, eleven. His finger brushed her neck. Skin on skin. Thirteen. Seventeen. She cringed. *Flesh slapping against flesh.* Nineteen. Twenty…something. Her body trembled.
"Please remove your hands from her and back away." Cerys's voice, close.
Nalani glanced up.
Cerys held her baton at her side and glared at the commander.

"Chief Lindholm, this is unacceptable." Huntington lifted one hand from Nalani's shoulder, pointing at Cerys. "You are not permitted to threaten a superior officer with your weapon."

Nalani leaned forward and jerked free of his other hand. Blessed relief from the images.

"I can if he's sexually harassing a member of the crew." Cerys leveled the baton. "I asked, now I'm telling—back away. You know she hates to be touched, yet you torment her by laying hands on her."

Huntington stepped away. "I will lodge a formal complaint regarding your behavior immediately." He scowled at the watching audience, flushed, and turned on Cerys. "You can kiss this assignment good-bye, Lindholm."

"We'll see. Move along. Go file your report."

Huntington stormed off. The door swished shut behind him, and the crew applauded.

Nalani dropped her forehead to the table and crossed her arms over her chest. *Dense nub!* Bad enough to freak when someone touched her, but she'd caused an incident in the dirking dining hall. And Cerys might lose her position because Nalani couldn't keep her stupid disorders under control.

Jex and Flerq trilled, a soothing sound intended to calm her. Instead, it reminded her she'd cracked. She needed others to fight her battles. She wasn't strong like Cerys.

She squatted and whispered, "You're safe. No one here wishes you harm."

Desta appeared at Nalani's other side. "I'll write the harassment report against him. All you have to do is sign it. We'll get him jettisoned so fast he won't be able to find his own asshole without a stabilizer and a flashlight."

Nalani snorted.

Someone yelled, "I'll witness."

Four others agreed, including Flerq and Jex, still trilling.

Nalani sat upright, certain a bright-red patch blazed on her forehead where she'd rested her face against the table. Probably had seafood in her bangs, too. "How's my hair?" She brushed it with her fingertips.

Desta grinned. "Gorgeous. As always. I want it."

"Do you want to finish your meal in private?" Cerys reached for Nalani's tray.

She didn't deserve these sweet friends. Tears welled, and she blinked them back. "I'll eat it here. No need to make a fuss over me." She peeked at Jex.

His crest had fallen to mold tightly to his head. Not fear. Anxiety?

She switched to Valaqite. "I apologize for creating an uncomfortable scene as an ember escaping the firepit."

"All is contained, and your adrenals are level as a quiet pond." *Snick, snick.*

Flerq trilled again, then picked up his fork.

Cerys pulled a tablet from her pocket and sat in the empty seat beside Nalani. "I'll write the report, Desta. You can return to duty."

Desta offered her a fist bump to Nalani. "If you need me, I'll drop everything."

Nalani tapped the knuckles with her own and shooed Desta away. Nalani had read somewhere that touch was important to most species, offering comfort and connection. Touch also increased the chances Nalani would inadvertently pick up thoughts, but it was worth the risk when it came to Desta, Cerys, and Gack.

Cerys's fingers danced over her tablet. "Huntington should be neutered."

Jex's eyes widened. "It is a procedure I have never performed, but I am fully trained—"

"Yeah, yeah." Cerys gestured at his tray. "Finish your meal, then you can thumbprint this as a witness."

Nalani picked up her fork and poked at the lukewarm mess on her plate, appetite as lost as Thrakis. But her body needed the calories and nutrients, and she would never waste food, a precious commodity aboard a spaceship. She loaded forkfuls into her mouth, and the hall resumed its normal hum.

Stray thoughts intruded. *I'd comfort her if she gave me a chance... What a dick, hope he gets fired... Poor Nalani, it's gotta be hard hearing all our— Oh shit, can she hear me now? Dang, Nalani, sorry you had to go through that.*

She blocked tighter.

Jex and Flerq ate in silence.

She finished her berries.

Zeus spoke through the ceiling speakers. "Nalani Adar and Cerys Lindholm, report to Captain Rodriguez's office."

Jank it. Huntington must have run to his best friend, the captain, and complained about his treatment from the ship's telepath and security chief. Now they'd both be fired. Nalani picked up her tray.

"Hang on a sec." Cerys stood. "Listen up." The hall quieted. "Here's my report."

She read aloud from her tablet while Nalani stared at her lap, heat blazing in her cheeks.

"If you wish to second my statement, raise your hand, and I'll get your thumbprint. If you'd like to add information, attach an amendment now."

Many hands rose, and Cerys stormed around the room collecting signatures. A few crew members pulled out tablets to write their version of events.

Nalani took a deep breath. *Get a grip. Fast and clean, like a bandage.* She stood to bus her dishes and make her way to Cap's office.

"Wait for me," Cerys ordered. "I'll escort you."

Not needed but appreciated. Her own position was in jeopardy, too. Nalani grabbed a peanut butter cookie from the dessert tray and stuffed it in her mouth.

Desta poked her head through the doorway. "You've got this. No fear, just facts."

Nalani chewed. How had she found such amazing friends? If it wasn't for her, Cerys wouldn't have had to step in and confront the commander. Nalani should have just sat with Huntington and not caused a scene. But no, she had to make a fuss.

Now she had to fix it. Own her mistake, take the full blame. No cracking. No tears. Time to be strong.

"And make sure you tell the captain exactly what thoughts Huntington subjected you to," Desta added. "Be precise."

Nalani cringed. She had to repeat that awful stuff? Out loud? To a man?

Cerys finished her rounds and signaled for Nalani to lead the way.

They walked the corridor and passed the medlab. The tank was empty now. Nalani rubbed her hands down her leggings. Would Cap just say, "You're fired," and demand they leave the ship? Or would he give them a few days? Nalani could take off with Aldrin, but where would Cerys go? Getting fired would make finding another job a lot harder. And it was Nalani's fault.

They entered the bridge, a tight room at the heart of the ship. Gack commanded from the central chair. With Zeus docked at Liang Spaceport, she had nothing to do but monitor screens and stats. She nodded at Nalani and offered a midair fist bump. "Cap's a fair man. Stay strong, tell the truth, and you'll be fine."

Right. Nalani was weaker than a newborn babe. She had no muscle, no backbone. She was a nub. A grunt. An inadequate nerk. And how had word of the fiasco spread to Gack so quickly? Huntington must have moaned about it to her. Hopefully, he wasn't in the office with the captain... She couldn't face the commander again.

Cerys pushed the call button on Cap's office and waited for the captain's permission.

"Enter."

She palmed the door open and led the way. "Lindholm and Adar, reporting."

Nalani followed. Her stomach pitched and rolled. She'd only been in this room once when first hired. Fitting she'd also visit on her last day.

Two swivel chairs, bolted to the floor, sat on one side of a mottled steel slab desk cantilevered from the wall. It held only a hand-sized tablet. Cap sat in the chair on the other side. The only décor in the room was a holo of the Apollo Eleven landing on Earth's moon.

Nalani let out her breath. No Huntington.

Rodriguez leaned back in his chair, legs splayed, fingers laced over his flat stomach. "Have a seat."

Cerys waited for Nalani to sit, then stood behind her. A spectacular display of strength.

Cap's gaze wandered up to Cerys before settling on Nalani. "I received an unsettling report from Commander Huntington regarding a situation in the dining hall this evening." Rodriguez's tone was cool, calm. "I dismissed him, called for you, and read his report. Then I received a conflicting one from Lindholm, witnessed by eight crew members with three amendments. Now I'd like your version of events, please."

Nalani took a deep breath and let it out. For four years, this had been her home. Now she'd have to leave it? Getting fired from her first job also sucked. She told Rodriguez what happened with Huntington and only stuttered twice. That had to be a record. "I-I-I'm truly sorry for the trouble, Captain."

Cerys cleared her throat. "You forgot to relay the commander's thoughts."

Her face heated. "It's not illegal to think…awful things."

Rodriguez leaned forward. "It is when he's deliberately pushing them at a telepath through physical contact. Tell me everything."

Tears welled in Nalani's eyes, and she dropped her gaze to her lap. Could this get any more embarrassing? She repeated the disgusting things the commander had thought while his hands were on her.

Rodriguez's jaw clenched. "Has the commander made you uncomfortable before, or is this new?"

She tucked her chin to her chest. "It's happened before."

"Look up, Nalani." Cap's tone held compassion and warmth.

She complied, shielding like mad.

"None of my staff should feel uncomfortable around another crew member. I wish you'd told me this before." He glanced at Cerys, then swiveled his tab so Nalani could read it. "Here's his version of the event."

She skimmed it. The commander stated he'd only touched her shoulders—not something inappropriate like her breasts—and it wasn't against the law to think about carnal pleasures. He labeled Cerys a violent psycho who threatened him with her weapon.

Nalani shoved the tab back to the captain. "I've never encouraged his advances, never showed the slightest interest in a romantic liaison. But he *thinks* really loud, and his thoughts are always lewd and...erotic. Maybe he's aware he's thinking too forcefully for me to block, though it could be accidental, but it's always intrusive. And he touches me—without my consent—and that strengthens the chance I'll pick up his thoughts."

"I understand. I've known the man for twenty years."

Nalani squirmed. "Sir, if you'll allow me to resign instead of firing—"

"I'm not firing you." He thumped the tab with his fingertips. "I'm sending the commander to sensitivity training on Aldeia. A liner leaves port at 2200 hours, and he'll be on it. I can't jail him for his thoughts, but I can fine him twenty thousand credits as restitution to you for the physical harassment. He'll rejoin us at Valaq in two weeks, at which point he'll be on probation for the next three years, serving on third shift. You shouldn't run into him at all. I hope that satisfies your warranted complaint."

Nalani gawked. "I'm not fired?"

Rodriguez smirked. "I need a T12 a *lot* more than I need a randy commander. If he won't leave you alone after that, he'll be fired."

"Yeah." Cerys jammed her palm at the captain.

He slapped it. "Excellent work, Chief. Though I'd prefer if you'd trade your baton for a standard issue stunner."

She winked at him. "I'll think about it." Cerys tapped Nalani's chair. "Let's burn. I missed out on the cookies."

"What kind?" Cap asked.

"Peanut butter."

He stood. "I should join you."

Nalani's legs quivered like boiled bean sprouts, but she followed Rodriguez and Cerys to the galley and the scene of her latest failure.

The hall was mostly empty. Luka and Willie cleaned floors and tables. Rodriguez and Cerys snagged the last four cookies. Desta emerged from the galley and headed for Nalani.

She crossed her arms over her chest. With the excitement over, she could rush back to Aldrin and analyze the long-range scans. Or work on translating the ancient Valaqite runes. Or read one of the novels she'd liberated from the *Evangeline*. Or hunt for Monstarte and the dirking bounty. If Desta suggested another movie—

"Are you laxxed? Do you need anything?" Desta hovered, eyebrows scrunched.

"I'm fine, thanks." Nalani backed up so Luka could mop the area. "I didn't get fired, so yay me."

Desta's chin jutted forward. "You thought you'd be janked? You're the third-most important person in the crew, right behind Cap and me."

Nalani laughed. "I think Gack and Chief Engineer Walsh would disagree with your list, but thanks."

Cerys waved and headed for the exit with Rodriguez two steps behind her.

Nalani returned the gesture.

"Wanna come to my quarters?" Desta asked. "We'll blast some soothing instrumentals, hork down our body weight in snacks, and giggle as our hips widen. And if you need some vengeance, I can print out pics of Huntington and break out a black inker."

So sweet! Nalani didn't merit this friend. "That sounds fun, but I need alone time."

"Pfft. You're gonna work."

"Or read a book."

Desta smiled. "Do what makes you happy. You deserve it. Right? No guilt for existing."

"No guilt." How many times had she recited that mantra with Desta? Too many, and it still hadn't stuck. Nalani couldn't help it, as it'd been slapped into her—literally—during her formative years.

"What are you going to read?"

"I grabbed a bunch of novels from the *Evangeline*, so I thought I'd dig into those."

Desta's eyes narrowed. "That sounds like research for an article. Since when do you enjoy reading novels?"

"It could happen. They could be an entertaining diversion. Full of historical, anthropological, and social...leisure, uh, recreation."

"You mean data and facts." Desta ran her hands down her luxurious braids and sighed. "I guess if you're gonna read, I'll check the lounge and see what's going on."

Dense nub, always thinking of myself. Desta needed

companionship, too. She couldn't give all the time and never have her own social needs met. "You're right. I always dive into work when I should be enjoying my best friend's company. Let's go to your quarters, deface pics of Huntington, and get fat."

"Damn straight." Desta held up her fist.

Nalani tapped it with her own and let Desta take charge of their evening. The books, scans, runes, and scuts could wait. After a day like this, they both needed to relax.

"Plus, I have a surprise for you in my quarters. You're gonna love this!"

Nalani groaned. Surprises were the worst.

Chapter 9

The moment they stepped into Desta's quarters, she crossed to her desk, a smirk on her face, and grabbed a palm-sized box. "You'll never believe what happened today."

"What?" Nalani sat on the edge of Desta's bunk.

"I visited the port drop and picked up the crew's mail. You had something. I'm dying to know who it's from."

Nalani took the package. "Why didn't you tell me earlier?" In the four years she'd been on the ship, she'd never received correspondence. Or parcels.

"I was in a rush to get dinner ready. It slipped my mind." She bounced on her toes. "I really want to see you open it. Please, please, please?"

Nalani stared at the label. She didn't have any living relatives, and all her friends lived on Zeus, so who would send her a package? The bruised and scuffed rectangular box contained four port codes—it'd chased her around three sectors—but held no hint regarding the sender. It was so small. What could it be?

"Open it!" Desta's brown eyes glinted.

Nalani picked at the seal with her fingernail, but it wouldn't tear.

Desta grabbed a blade from her desk drawer and slit the adhesive.

Inside, nestled in shreds of styro-mesh, lay a

familiar ceramic figurine and a comm chip.

"What is it?" Desta peered over the flap. "Ooh. That's beautiful."

Nalani's heart pounded. She'd seen a photo of this before, in her father's research. The clay figure was humanoid and glazed with brilliant colors—blue, green, and white, like tropical Pacific Ocean waves. The egg-shaped head with high forehead, flat nose, slit mouth, and pointed chin screamed alien, though not a race Nalani had ever met or read about. Fine webbing stretched between long fingers and toes. A blue patterned robe hung from the bony shoulders to the dimpled knees. Time had not blunted the features.

"What do you think it is?" Desta asked.

"It's my father's statue."

"Who had it?"

Nalani pulled her tablet from her back pocket and inserted the chip into the port. When the file appeared on the screen, she pressed it.

"What's it say?" Desta nestled in beside Nalani and bounced her toes on the bunk, though she kept her gaze averted.

"Please read along." Nalani angled the tab so Desta could see it.

Nalani,

Your father and I were good friends in grad school. His passing grieved me deeply. Please accept my humble condolences.

I often teased your father over his obsession with the Thrakis civilization, and he gave back equally regarding my passion for all things Aldeian. After all these years, I've never forgotten my friend and wonder what marvels he could have achieved had he not perished.

Your father purchased this figurine from a black-market dealer on Termagant and asked me to study it. He believed it of Thrakis origin, but sadly, he passed before I could return it to him. I could not prove or disprove his theory, though microscopic testing of the glaze dates the piece around eight thousand years old. Perhaps it is in my fondness for him that I concede he might be correct.

Forgive me for not returning it sooner. I only recently learned that you are his daughter. I read your article on the linguistic significance of clay tablets on Yamiche, and it's obvious you have his academic mind. I look forward to following your career and studying your future articles. If you ever need assistance with the bureau, please contact me.

Sincerely,

Dr. Yehuda Malkan

Aldeian Archaeological Institute

"Wow." Desta bumped her shoulder against Nalani's. "Quite an epic offer from a guy you've never met."

Nalani stared at the figurine. This piece had set her parents on their journey to locate the Thrakis home world. Without it, they might have never embarked on the dangerous mission that cost them everything. "Yeah. Amazing." A hundred questions exploded in her head, but none of them could be answered. Black-market dealers didn't keep records of where they found things or who they bought them from or why they thought such things were worth selling.

She should contact Dr. Malkan and grill him for details. And memories of her father.

Desta scooted off the bunk. "Your mind is going a

thousand kilometers a second, and we came in here to have fun, not to work. So put away your new toy and set aside scholarship in favor of entertainment."

Reluctantly, Nalani dropped the chip back into the box next to the figurine, sealed the flaps, and laid the box on the desk.

For over an hour, they danced between the bunks and the empty snack wrappers littering the floor as synther-pop music blared from the vid screen where scantily clad females demonstrated the latest dance moves between shots of the trying-to-look-bored-yet-hip musicians.

Before the next song began, Nalani yelled, "Pause music," and collapsed onto Cerys's bunk, breathing hard and sweating like a chilled beverage in a hot room.

Desta lay on her rack and stared at the ceiling, also sucking air. "You picked up that new move fast. You looked better doing it, too."

Nalani laughed. Like she could undulate more gracefully than the loose-and-limber chef. "It's a disguise. And awards to you for tricking me into a cardio workout after eating all those carb calories."

Desta propped her head on her hand. "Exercise purges negative emotions more efficiently than ingesting sucrose, but we had to try both to be sure."

True. For almost two hours, Nalani had forgotten the bone-jarring decision she had to make. She rolled to face her friend, careful not to disturb Cerys's tight bedding. "I think I should leave Zeus."

No! You can't. "Why?"

Hard to believe Desta hadn't heard about the bounty. She was one of only three people who knew the full story of Nalani's past. She told Desta about her encounter with the scut. Desta sat up and leaned forward.

"I don't know where to go, but Zeus is endangered because of me. Maybe the Antiquities Bureau will hire me. Dr. Malkan might give me a recommendation."

"Nope. Absolutely not."

True. Once Antiquities realized she was a nub, they wouldn't want her services.

"You're not letting that evil scut ruin your life again." Desta squeezed the edges of her bunk's mattress. "You're going to put him in his place and live the life you're meant to. If you run, you're sending him a clear message that he's still in control. You. Are. Not. A. Slave! You are a free citizen of the Alliance, and that fart cork is nothing but a fugitive with a severely limited life span and the intellect of a turd chaser."

Nalani grinned and sat up, smoothing the blanket beneath her. "Thanks, but I can't fight him, and I can't ask Captain Rodriguez to endanger his ship and crew by keeping me aboard. The moment word leaks that I'm on this freighter, every scut in the sector will attack."

"We protect our own, and you're one of us. Rodriguez won't toss you out. Plus, we need you for Zeus. I'm only a T8, and ZeeBee's a T9. Zeus can't do half the tasks he needs to with our minimal skills. He needs you." Desta kicked her bare feet dangling off the side of the bunk. "Besides. I need you, too. You're my best friend. Those are hard to come by, you know?"

Yeah. Nalani had never had a best friend before. Where would she get another as amazing as Desta? Nalani's chest tightened at the thought of leaving. "I'd love to stay, but I couldn't live with myself if anyone got hurt because of me." Her only course of action included a short conversation with the captain, followed by tearful farewells and a solo trip back to the rim. They were in the Faleeki Galaxy now, which put her closer to Terminus than she'd been in the past two years. She could continue her search for Thrakis.

Desta grunted. "You're not listening to me, and it's starting to edge me off." She headed for the door. "Let's chat with Rodriguez."

"You're wearing a tankin and panties. Perhaps you should add a layer or two."

Desta looked down and giggled. "You know how I love to make an entrance, but I'll concede you're right this time." She donned her discarded leggings, snagged her tunic off the floor, stuffed her feet into black glides, and headed for the door. "Follow me." She pulled the tunic over her head and hit the door lock.

Nalani leaned forward and planted her hands on the bunk. "The captain is off duty. Let him rest."

Desta looked at the ceiling. "Hey, Zeus. Where's the captain?"

Nalani grinned. Her friend's silly habit of addressing the ceiling to chat with Zeus, like he and the speakers were the same entity, was even funnier than when she said, "Hey, Zeus," which sounded like the Spanish pronunciation of the name Jesus.

Zeus replied. "Captain Rodriguez is on the bridge."

Desta gestured at the door. "You lead. Keep in mind I can tackle you before you make it to the stairs."

Nalani hopped off the bunk, grabbed her package, and headed for the command center nestled in the heart of the freighter.

They reached the bridge in two minutes where Chief Walsh sat in the command chair.

Nalani turned. "He's not here; guess I'll go to bed."

"Not so fast." Desta blocked the door before Nalani could flee and looked up. "Hey, Zeus, where's Cap?"

"Captain Rodriguez is in the brig."

They headed to the stairs and the fore section of the freighter. It held cleaning supplies, maintenance drones, and three holding cells. As sixty-four percent of all hull breaches occurred in the front, crew members refused to take quarters up there. The brig rarely housed prisoners, though it sometimes held a drunk or belligerent staffer.

Desta palmed the door, and the captain and Cerys walked out.

"Thanks for the walk-through, Chief," Rodriguez said to Cerys, then turned to face Desta and Nalani. "What's up?"

Desta took charge. "Nalani thinks she has to leave because of that scuzball we had in lockup. Please tell her she should stay."

Cerys sealed the brig entrance.

Captain Rodriguez crossed his arms and stared at Nalani. His brown eyes bored into her like he was assessing her soul and finding her short on the values scale.

She winced. *Don't duck*—he wouldn't smack her.

"You signed a contract. Are you trying to squirm out of it?" His tone was even and pragmatic.

"No, sir, but—"

"You think scuts will leave my ship alone if you're not here?"

Her chest tightened. "It makes—"

"How will they know you're not here unless they attack, board, and see for themselves that you've deserted?" The furrow between his brows scrunched tighter. "You think they'll take my word for it if I paint *she's not here* on the hull?"

Her shoulders bunched, and she ducked her chin to her chest. "No, but—"

"You might as well stay, honor the contract you signed, and help us defend against scut attacks by planting your T12 brain in Zeus's gel-tank where you're desperately needed. Because if you leave us, you might as well recode the airlocks to 1-2-3-4-5 and post our itinerary at every spaceport in the surrounding sectors."

Her chin trembled, and she blinked hard.

His tone softened. "I'm sorry for being harsh, but you need to hear me. Leaving isn't logical for either of us. We're stronger facing this danger together. Plus, we'll miss you. You're a vital and vibrant part of the crew. You're family now."

Nalani stared at her feet. *Stupid nub!* The freighter was endangered due to her existence no matter if she remained or fled. She should have realized that on her own. "You are correct, Captain. I-I-I will remain."

"Excellent." He strode away, his footsteps clanking down the stairs to the main deck.

Nalani took a deep breath. No need for an anxiety attack. Everything was fine. At least she wouldn't have to say good-bye to people she cared for. But her two closest friends had witnessed the captain's harsh words.

"That's settled." Desta gestured to the hallway. "Now let's finish our girls' night in the galley with vanilla ice cream, berries, and whipped cream."

"I'm in." Cerys led the way. "I worked a fourteen-hour shift today, so I deserve a treat."

Desta smiled at Nalani. "It's over. You can relax and be happy."

After all the snacks ingested earlier, Nalani's

stomach might rebel if she put any more sweets down, but she followed Cerys to the dining hall. An hour later, Nalani choked out a "good night" and fled to the safety of Aldrin's gel-tank.

She settled, closed her eyes, and greeted her friend/surrogate parent. They had a lot to catch up on: the harassment, the *Evangeline's* mission of finding Thrakis, and her biggest concern, the bounty.

I don't know what to do. Nalani blinked to dispel tears. *Zeus and Desta say I should stay, that I'm safer with them than on my own. Captain Rodriguez says I have no choice, as I signed a contract with him, and I shouldn't break it. Now I feel I have to remain, despite everything in me wanting to run. How do I handle that?*

Daddy's voice sounded in her mind. *Concern for your friends is virtuous, and remaining with them might be safer for all of us. But for too many years, you were forced to comply with another's demands. I will not tell you which course of action to take. You must make the decision. Weigh the concerns of your heart with logic and your friends' advice.*

She sighed. Aldrin was right. She had to make the decision for herself. The captain's reasoning was sound. And she'd miss Desta and Cerys terribly. Staying would also give her more time to prep for the Thrakis search. She fell asleep to the comforting tingle of Aldrin's access.

At 0700 hours, her alarm chimed, waking her from another restless night and minimal sleep. She showered, donned a clean skinsuit, and covered it with a turquoise flowered tunic and black leggings. The tunic reminded her of her grandmother's birthplace, a tropical island on Earth called Hawaii. Most of her mother's pics had been recycled when Monstarte boarded, along with her parents' possessions, but Aldrin saved all the digital copies Halia Adar had uploaded to his data nodes. Nalani treasured them and the few remaining items she'd salvaged from Monstarte's purging frenzy.

The dining hall was packed to capacity by the time she arrived and buzzing with mental activity. They'd leave Liang Spaceport in eight hours, so everyone wanted one last chance to breathe different recycled air and look at other people's faces before takeoff. They'd eat their free meal here, then venture out for a few more loops around the port.

Nalani bolstered her shields, collected her food, and turned to survey the hall. Cerys and Ajani must have split, because he sat with Gaspara. He waved at Nalani when he caught her staring, and she turned away. Cerys sat with Jex and Flerq and waved for Nalani to join them.

She smiled, set down her tray, and put out her fist for a bump.

"You look great." Cerys slurped her coffee and tagged the fist with her own. "That color's good with your complexion."

"Thanks." Nalani nodded to the Valaqites and slipped into their tongue. "Honorable greetings, nest-sharers."

Jex smiled. "Blessed morning, Nalani."

Flerq's headcrest flared. "Welcome of greatest honor, Seer."

Nalani dug into her mushroom and green pepper omelet and turned her attention to Cerys. "Don't you get a day off after the long shift you pulled yesterday?"

She shrugged. "I'll take time off once we're in flight and there's nothing else to do. As soon as I'm finished eating, I'm heading into port for a few last-minute purchases for the ship. Wanna come with me?"

Nalani would rather spacewalk without her EVA suit. "No, thanks. I'm needed in the tank, and I have tasks of my own."

Zeus's excitement at her arrival in the tank alcove wiped away lingering doubts. She belonged on the freighter. She spent her shift working on the runes from the *Evangeline's* database. She couldn't locate any ancient Valaqite texts, either to borrow or to purchase, so she relied on her knowledge of the modern language to piece together bits and phrases. She'd translated three words, and she'd identified a star chart. It was set off from the text in brackets, so at first, she mistook it for another character or word.

Once she realized it highlighted a diagram of a recognizable pattern, identifying the M-shaped constellation came quickly; it was the Faleeki System. Though in most of the star charts she'd seen, the view was drawn from the galactic center viewpoint, so the constellation looked like a W, not an M.

At 0400 hours, Zeus left Liang Spaceport with a bump and dip that rocked Nalani through the goo. *Was it a successful stop?*

My cargo holds are full of merchandise destined for Fundo Three, Malenki, Sathara, and Valaq. It was a profitable run, thanks to the Hellian refugees. The price they paid for the journey covers the fuel costs for the next three stops.

Excellent. Maybe we'll pick up new contracts on the other planets and stay in the system longer. When we get to Sathara, if there's time in the schedule, I'm requesting a few days leave to explore the space beyond Terminus.

Did you find something interesting on the long-range scans?

She smiled. *I haven't actually studied them yet, but I have plenty of time before we get there. If the Thrakis people built the star portals—*

Consensus is the Dolanis people created the portals and the beacons.

Supposedly. It's never been proven, though. I think the Thrakis civilization built them. And if they did, there's bound to be a star portal in their galaxy. I will find it eventually.

Nalani, if you leave the hyperspace lanes to explore, you might become permanently lost. Anxiety tinged his tone. *Please do not embark on such a dangerous quest.*

I won't explore hyperspace, I promise. I'm just wondering if there's another way to find a lost star portal.

Zeus's data nodes whirred. *Perhaps I could scan for the unique metal signature of the struts. Would that be helpful?*

That could work. The star portals had been built from metal that hadn't been found on any of the known worlds, which led archaeologists to hypothesize that the portals had been built by the Dolanis. To most of the known universe, the Thrakis civilization was a myth, much like Atlantis of old Earth or Flulinka of Altair.

But surely someone had already scanned hyperspace for the precious metal. Finding the source would be a lucrative business venture, not to mention the scientific discovery of the ages.

Her stomach grumbled, and her bladder complained. She'd been in the tank all day, and a glance at the time display showed she'd missed dinner. *Thanks, Zeus. I gotta run.*

By the time she made it to the galley, Luka was wiping out the empty buffet. "Desta will find something for you."

Nalani didn't mind grazing in the hydroponics bay or nibbling a few nutri-cubes.

Desta had other plans. "I just put the midrats away. Hang on." The galley was closed for eight hours at night, so midnight rations were leftovers for the third shift. She tossed her cleaning towel on the counter and disappeared into the walk-in freeze, appearing a minute later with a box. "It's still warm, but I can heat it if you want."

Nalani's belly gurgled. "No need. Warm's great." A peek revealed pale meat in gravy with veggies and noodles. "Looks delicious." She turned to leave.

"No girls' night tonight?" Desta propped her hip against the counter and gave it another swipe with her cleaning rag.

"No, thanks. I'm exhausted, and I want to read. Cerys may—"

"I can plan my own entertainment." Desta snapped her towel at Nalani, though not close enough to score a hit. "You enjoy your quiet time."

No guilt for existing. Free time was hers to organize. She could skip a girls' night once in a while. She hurried to Aldrin, grabbed a spoon, and sat at her dining table. The fruits and veggies growing in the hydroponics alcove a few meters to her left were outgrowing their space. She'd have to prune soon. And harvest the cucumbers. The peach and plum trees in massive rolling pots were ripe, too. Maybe she should adjust the grow lights. And take some produce to Desta in the morning.

She finished her meal and worked on the garden,

tending the plants, trimming browning leaves, and checking for ripeness. The bib lettuce crowded the beets and strawberries. Nalani plucked a few leaves and stuffed them in her mouth, followed by the lone ripe strawberry. The garden needed more attention than a few minutes once a week. "Aldrin, would you please add a half-hour block to my schedule tomorrow dedicated to tending the hydroponics? I don't want to forget."

"Addition complete." Daddy's voice produced a ping of longing in her.

"Thanks. I'll enter the tank in a few minutes."

"I have no immediate needs. Do not hurry."

She stepped into her quarters, mostly unchanged since her mother had upgraded it from a nursery to a big girls' room when Nalani turned four. She'd even gotten to choose the paint color—pale aqua, the color of tropical island waters. Momma's favorite color, and Nalani's at that time.

She sighed, tossed her outer garments in the laundry drawer, and hurried to the medlab and the gel-tank, bare feet slapping against the sleek floors. The new coding on the cleaning drones was remarkably successful. No dirt in the corners now.

She slid in, the pink goo caressing her body. Her neck hit the cradle, and the comforting *zing* connected her to Aldrin's core. So good to be home. She accessed the runes again, prepared to spend several more hours whittling away at the mess before she fell asleep.

Fifteen minutes into the exercise, Aldrin interrupted. *Comms open for Zeus.*

"Nalani here. What can I do for you?"

We have spotted something off my starboard bow and are changing course to intercept. Chief Lindholm requested I notify you in case you're needed in my tank.

"May I see it?"

Zeus sent a link to his hull cameras to Aldrin's data core where Nalani could access it.

A tiny speck of light glinted periodically, deep in the darkness. "Magnify." The pic resized.

A life pod tumbled slowly, end over end, starlight catching the lone window with each revolution as the pod drifted farther from the Liang Star Portal.

Nalani's heart pounded. It's a trap!

Chapter 10

"Target sighted." Monstarte *punched commands on the nav board to mask Aldrin's presence. "Is the pod ready?"*

Nalani stood in the corner, shoulders pressed against the walls, hands clenched. She nodded, tracking the other ship on the monitors. The surveyor flew too close to the web. Now it was burnt.

"Don't stand there, nub." He smacked her upside the head. "Take the nav." The monster stomped from the bridge. The door hissed shut behind him.

She sucked in a quick breath and accessed the navigation console with her implant. A slight pressure at the base of her skull confirmed she'd entered the nav system.

"I'm on board." His voice echoed through the speakers, the hint of violence always in his tone. "Open the airlock on my mark."

She input the proper sequence and paused before entering the last command, waiting. No failures this time. Do everything right, and he won't strike. *Once he had the wealth of the target, he'd be in a drinking mood.*

She treasured those moments and worked hard for them. She proved her worth. She knew Aldrin's systems. She tended the hydroponics alcove and cooked meals. She coded the maintenance drones to clean and repair anything on board. And any time she spent with Tutor, the education program created by Daddy, meant she was out of the monster's way while he clomped around her ship and drank himself out between missions. At those times, Aldrin was hers. For a while.

"Now."

She entered the last command, opening the airlock. The rusted, ancient life pod from Monster's last mission fell out of Aldrin's hold and tumbled toward the prey. He was inside it, armed with a plasma rifle.

Nalani set new nav coordinates and fired thrusters, moving Aldrin into the shadow of an asteroid. Close enough to pick up the monster again. Far enough to run away, if she weren't a fraidy, a nub. But he'd controlled the surveyor, and he'd chase her down if she ran. Not worth the risk. Obey, behave, receive her reward.

He sent out a general distress call from the pod.

The prey responded and changed course to intercept him. Stupid burnt nubs.

She monitored the screens. The surveyor blip and Monster's grew closer together until the pod disappeared.

He was on board.

She scrunched her eyes. No crying. *It wouldn't take long. He was as vicious with a plasma rifle as a pipe wrench. Maybe the surveyor had fresh food. Or meat in the freeze.*

At least she still had Aldrin. And Tutor, who allowed her to explore the interesting subjects. He also made her work on boring stuff like art creation, but the best ones like bioengineering and history helped her forget for a little while that she was a scut slave. Someday, she'd be big enough and brave enough to escape. But for now, her only option was to obey him, enjoy her moments of freedom, and learn everything Tutor could teach her.

Monster teased her for all her book learning, but he didn't take it from her.

"Incoming." His voice stabbed at her through the speakers. "Pick me up."

Two blips separated on the monitor. He'd stolen one of their life pods, newer, cleaner, and most likely stuffed with anything he thought might be worth selling. His normal protocol was to blow up the empty hulk to remove all evidence of his presence. If he didn't make it out of the blast radius, he and his goods would be spaced.

She hit Aldrin's thrusters and, holding her breath, monitored the pod separate from the surveyor. It disappeared from the screen.

Monster's blip drew closer to Aldrin. He'd survived.

Her shoulders sank, but she programmed the nav to intercept him. The new pod's thrusters worked, so she opened the airlock and let him fly in before locking everything down again. She ran for the hold.

He popped the pod, and she cleared the bay doors. The monster's face transformed into a hideous smile as he stomped out. "What a haul. I have something for you, nub." He reached into the one-man vessel and pulled out a plush toy. A black-and-white stuffed panda, an extinct animal indigenous to the Asian continent on Earth. He tossed it at her. "Happy seventh birthday."

It bounced off her chest and hit the floor. It wasn't her birthday yet.

He scowled. "You can't catch a simple toss, nub?"

She cringed and waited for the smack.

Instead, he picked it up and shoved it into her chest. The force of the blow knocked all the wind from her. She buckled and fumbled to hang on to the toy.

Some other kid got spaced, and she got the prize.

"Coming into range now." Zeus's voice rang over the speakers in Aldrin's medlab.

Nalani was sitting upright in the tank. When had she broken the link to her ship?

Zeus said, "Opening Bay One to receive the pod."

"No!" she screamed and plunged back into the gel, reconnecting to Aldrin. She fired up the nova drives and plotted a course. Had to escape before the pod opened. He'd emerge, rifle blazing, and tear his way through the freighter to find her. She'd be space debris.

'Lani, the airlock is closed, Daddy said quickly. *Do not fire thrusters.*

"We need to run away." She input the commands.

Bay Three airlock released. A strange voice echoed through her telepathic link to Aldrin.

The hull scraped something metallic, and the ship shuddered. Had they sideswiped space junk? No time to check. She hit the thrusters twice, getting distance between her and the pod.

Comms open, Daddy said.

Nalani, where are you going? It was a man's voice, one she didn't recognize.

She didn't have to answer. Her ship. Her skin. She wouldn't let the scut have a crack at her again.

Return immediately.

She scanned the star charts for her location and a place of safety. Liang's portal loomed nearby. The spaceport lay four hours away at standard speed. The freighter that picked up the scut pod would blow any second! No time to waste. She altered course for the station. Aldrin was small enough to hide in the shadow of a cruiser or—

'Lani, your adrenal levels and blood pressure have spiked, and your amygdala and periaqueductal gray region are hyperactive. You are experiencing a panic attack.

Not now, Daddy, we have to get away! She checked the nova drive's performance and boosted it a few degrees beyond standard safety protocols.

You are not thinking logically, Daddy said. *Lie still while I administer a hypo—*

No! She thrashed in the tank but could not avoid the needle emerging from the side. *Maintain course, don't alter... I'll lock you out...* She fumbled to input the coding, locking everyone else out of the nav system, but her eyelids drooped, and her body relaxed.

****

She jolted awake and assessed her surroundings. Aldrin's gel-tank. Still in one piece, not drifting as debris. *Are we safe?*

We are in no immediate danger, Aldrin answered. *You slept for twenty minutes.*

Nalani bolted up and glanced at the time indicator. 1942 hours. "I had a nightmare."

"Correction, you had a panic attack. I sedated you before you did anything rash."

She scrubbed her face with her hands and climbed from the tank. "A panic attack? Why? What happened?"

"Zeus collected a life pod. You fired my engines while we were still in the docking bay, but Zeus opened the airlock in time to avoid a collision."

"I ran?" She hurried to the medlab console and accessed a nav screen. "We're one-point-five hours from the star portal. Where's Zeus?"

"The freighter diverted to pick up the life pod. They

are holding position at that location."

"Are there signs of distress? Was it a scut trap?"

"I see no indications that anyone was on board the pod. Shall I contact Zeus and ask?"

She needed to know, yet she was too embarrassed to do it herself. "Yes, please."

While Zeus and Aldrin communicated, she collapsed on the medbunk and covered her face with her hands. She'd panicked and fled when her friends were threatened. What kind of nub was she? To consider her own skin…how selfish and weak could she be?

"Zeus reports the pod contained one male, deceased. The captain is accessing the log for details."

Nalani sighed. At least they were safe.

"I will plot a return course. It should take approximately fifteen minutes to reach them."

"No." She rolled off the medbunk and paced the small room. "I have no reasonable explanation for leaving. I can't admit I panicked. How could Captain Rodriguez trust me after that?" She sank to a crouch and wrapped her arms around her knees. "I can't go back." Tears welled in her eyes. "I just proved I'm a complete waste of oxygen."

"He will understand if you explain your history with life pods."

"But that will verify I'm useless. A fraud. I don't deserve a place on his crew if he can't rely on me when danger looms." She wiped tears from her cheeks. "I didn't get to say good-bye."

"I can open a comms channel if you wish."

"It's too late." She paced. "Cap probably thinks I ran away because of the bounty. That's a logical assumption, right? So he believes I quit and bolted. I might as well live with it and figure out what to do now." She shivered and wrapped her arms around her body. "We could hide at Terminus—"

"None of this is necessary." Aldrin's voice was calm, logical. "The captain needs your services on Zeus. He will allow you to return."

"I broke my contract by running and proved I'm unreliable." Her chest ached. She'd miss Desta and Cerys so much... It would be best for Nalani to humble her heart and beg forgiveness, admit she was weak and useless.

"Weak and useless." Monstarte loomed over her, his eyes mean and spittle on his lips. "Pathetic. All you're good for is book stuff."

She cringed.

"There will always be someone stronger than you, nub. Don't ever forget that." He stomped away.

Nalani shuddered. Show no weakness...

No! She had internalized all his disgusting lessons, but they weren't right. She was stronger than he gave her credit for, and she'd put him in his place.

Yet here she sat, struggling with the silliest decision. Go back or flee? She should definitely return.

But doing so would prove to the captain that she was too unstable to remain part of the crew. Desta'd had a rough upbringing, too. Did she ever run away when a flashback hit? No. She came out fighting, shoving them back and demanding they shut up.

Did Cerys crack when danger loomed? No. She rushed in, ready to kick ass.

Why couldn't Nalani be that strong?

Because she was pathetic. She should shove the memories back inside—they were intangible and shouldn't control her. Might as well return, head hung in shame, and plead for mercy from the captain.

When she first applied for the position on his freighter, he'd sent her a missive asking if she truly wanted to apply. She was overqualified. He only needed a T9. With her educational background, advanced degrees, and T12 rating, she'd been bombarded with high-paying, high-status employment opportunities across the universe. Yet she wanted something that would put her in the Faleeki Galaxy where she could continue her parents' work. Finding an opening on Zeus with regular delivery patterns in the Omega sector had seemed like the perfect match. Rodriguez couldn't offer her the pay she'd have gotten elsewhere, but the opportunity to explore beyond Terminus had tipped the scales. She'd affirmed her desire for the job, with two concessions—a place to moor Aldrin and a few days off every time they entered the Faleeki Galaxy. Rodriguez readily agreed.

And hadn't he told her that he needed her on board? When faced with losing his best friend and second-in-command or firing his T12 telepath, he'd chosen her. When they found the *Evangeline*, he'd put her on the boarding party because of her archaeological expertise.

He would forgive her for this disturbance. Everyone failed periodically, didn't they?

Except that it wasn't a minor disturbance. She'd nearly taken out Zeus's airlock while running away, leaving the freighter and the crew to fend for themselves.

"I detect a vessel." Aldrin brought up the image on the wall console, showing his position between the Liang Star Portal and the spaceport. Zeus still hovered to starboard. A third blip, moving fast, raced toward Zeus from the direction of the station.

Nalani monitored the screen. Obviously, the new ship wasn't heading for the star portal. Maybe Zeus had sent out a call for help with the pod. Or maybe the ship was a scut, ready to pounce now that Zeus had the bait. Should she hail them and warn the crew? Even if they were busy with a life pod—she shuddered—Zeus would monitor all systems.

"Comms open," Aldrin said. "Video connection."

"Nalani?" Desta's face appeared on the wall screen, her brows pinched.

"I'm here." Nalani tossed her tunic over her head to stave off the chill.

"What are you doing? Why did you leave?"

"Just beating myself up again. Is everything okay over there?"

"Yeah. A dead guy in the life pod has everyone worried. Looks like he died from a stunner blast to the heart, but there's no stunner in the pod. Are you coming back soon?"

Nalani sighed. "I had a panic attack and bolted. Now I'm trying to decide what to do."

"We could use you over here." An alarm sounded in the background, and the vid screen went dark.

Nalani straightened. "What's wrong?"

No answer.

"Desta?"

Aldrin cut in. "The courier vessel has launched two fighters at Zeus."

Nalani sprang toward the monitor. "What? Why?"

Desta's voice shrieked through the speakers. "We're under attack!"

Chapter 11

Another scut attack? They weren't even out of the system yet! Nalani jumped in the tank, her fingers shaking. *Set a course for Zeus and open missile ports.*

Affirmative.

Engage.

Aldrin sped toward Zeus.

"Desta?"

They're threatening to fire on us. Return now.

"I'm on my way." Nalani pushed the engines harder, cutting their transit time to twelve minutes, and opened comms to Zeus's bridge. "This is Nalani. What's happening?"

Gack responded. *A Hellian courier says we have something of theirs, and they want it back or they'll fire on us. Where are you?*

"I'm coming. What is it they want?"

Something to do with the Hellian passengers we took on.

The special crate. "If you let them have it, will they leave?"

Supposedly.

"What's the problem? Give it to them."

Not that easy. Gack shouted orders for the crew to strap in.

"Have you called for help from Liang?"

Yes, they're sending cruisers, but they're a few

hours out. You're our best hope.

Nalani's stomach churned. She couldn't fire on the fighters, couldn't kill people like Monstarte did. But she could harry them, force them back to their mother ship, giving Gack and Rodriguez time to negotiate with them. Or at least distract them. If Nalani could keep the attackers busy for ten minutes, Cerys could open an airlock and fire a chunk of metal at the aggressor. Physics would take care of the foolish courier; an impacting one-kilogram object would deliver enough kinetic energy to punch a hole in the target. A rent in the hull would keep them too busy to fight Zeus.

She relayed her plan to Aldrin. He slipped between Zeus and the courier, banked gradually, and advanced on one of the fighters.

It was a one-man ship—though some fighters were unmanned drones—rounded like an egg with arrays and engines fitted at the back. As they neared it, Nalani scanned for life signs. One human detected.

She couldn't blow it up with a missile. *Cut off communication with the courier. That'll force it to return.*

Aldrin altered course and blasted by the fighter. The grinding of metal against metal left her teeth aching, but she trusted Aldrin to not injure his hull. One of his fins scraped the entire comm array off the back of the egg, rendering it mute.

Good aim. She patted the side of the tank in congratulations. *Do that to the other one.*

The remaining fighter is a drone. I suggest we destroy it.

Be my guest.

Aldrin's coding had no problem with firing on an

unmanned vessel. He targeted the fighter and shot a guided missile.

The drone disintegrated.

Comms open, Aldrin stated.

I am the courier Helena. A female voice, somewhat edged, echoed telepathically via Aldrin. *Cease fire, or we will obliterate you.*

Since when did bio-ships threaten to destroy other bio-ships? Not that it mattered. "By attacking an Allied freighter, you have broken the Treaty of Albany. This is considered an act of war against all League Planets. Call off your attack, and I will stand down."

Negative. They have stolen something, and we demand its return.

The ship had sided with her crew to commit a deed of aggression. Not a good sign. "Let me speak to my captain. We can resolve this without weapons."

I agree.

Aldrin, set a course for home. A surge of warmth spread through her at that word. Home. He fired thrusters, and she accessed comms. "Captain Rodriguez, this is Nalani. I've disabled the fighters, and now the courier wants to talk."

Board and report to Bay Five.

He wasn't angry. Or he was putting off the mad until after the crisis ended. Either way, she was welcomed and needed. For now.

Aldrin settled in the cargo hold, the airlock sealing behind him. Nalani ran for Bay Five on legs like boiled noodles.

She met Rodriguez, Cerys, and four security guards at the closed door. "Captain, I am so sorry. I didn't—"

"We can discuss it later. For now, lower your

shields. I'll talk to our Hellian passengers and figure out why we're being attacked. You tell me what's going on in their heads."

She nodded.

Cerys opened the bay doors and strode in, stun baton ready in one hand, her team behind her. Rodriguez and Nalani followed.

Xing Wu hurried toward them and bowed to the captain. "The rebels are here for us?" *Caged again, beaten. Humiliated. Defiant.*

He wasn't even attempting to hide his thoughts.

"They want the crate." Cerys and Isaiah marched toward the boxes. Some of them lay open for easy access to the contents: food, clothing, and personal effects. The container wanted by the Helena crew sat off to the side, surrounded by passengers.

No surrender. Ice panther protecting her cubs.

Nalani leaned closer to Captain Rodriguez. "They're willing to die to safeguard the contents of that crate."

His eyebrow quirked. "What's in it?"

"I don't know."

Cerys waved at Isaiah to proceed.

He pulled a scanner from his utility belt and stepped toward the container.

The passengers converged, locking their arms together to form a barricade. *Defend her! Willingly die.*

Nalani whispered, "There's a person inside!"

Cerys raised her stun baton and advanced on the passengers.

"Wait." Captain Rodriguez strode across the space.

Cerys lowered her weapon.

Xing Wu followed Rodriguez. "Please do not open it. I will surrender to the rebels, but you must ensure the container arrives safely to Sathara."

Rodriguez looked at the shorter man. "Are you harboring a fugitive in stasis?"

Wu dropped his gaze to his feet. "We are all fugitives. I am the leader of this group. The terrorists will welcome my capture."

The captain signaled for Nalani to draw near. "Does he speak the truth?"

She nodded. "He fears the rebels but will sacrifice his life if it means the woman in the crate doesn't return to the enemy."

Rodriguez crossed his arms. "You are asking me to endanger my ship and crew for a cause you will not explain. Either I open that crate and view the contents, or I give it to the Helena. You chose."

Wu looked to his people. *Caught between the Acid Sea and a magma vent. Beaten. No choice.* He nodded.

The passengers moved back.

Wu input the unlock code and stepped back. Isaiah hauled the lid off. Nalani followed Rodriguez and Cerys to peer inside.

A bulky stasis chamber held a young woman, approximately sixteen years old, curled in a fetal position, long black hair splayed to cover most of her skinsuit-clad form. Thoughts of warmth and affection wafted from the Hellians.

"Who is she?" Rodriguez stared at the figure.

Wu ran his hand down the woman's hair. "She is our princess. Her parents and brother were slaughtered when terrorists breached the palace walls. We smuggled her out through the servants' quarters and reached the spaceport mere hours before pursuers arrived. Finding safe passage with you seemed an answer to our prayers."

Tears welled in his eyes. "It was too good to be true." He turned to the captain and bowed. "Please. Take her with you. We will all return to Helena and face our punishment, but you must protect her."

Rodriguez scowled. "I don't hand innocent people over to terrorists, but I'm only hearing half the story. I'll speak to the captain on Helena and get back to you."

"Keep in mind that we are unarmed and fleeing. They have pursued us and threatened to fire on your ship and crew."

"I have not overlooked that. I'll be back in a minute." He strode away. "Lindholm, stay. Nalani, with me."

Nalani hurried after him to the hallway outside the bay doors.

Rodriguez stopped at a wall-mounted screen but gestured for her to stand off to the side, out of view. "Can you scan them from this far away?"

"I doubt it, but I can try. Use video. It'll help me taper my focus. It might take me a few minutes to target their captain, so keep them talking."

He opened video comms to Helena. "Tell me about your dispute with the refugees."

Helena's captain, a dark-skinned man with tiny black eyes, scowled. "They are thieves and should all be shot. But I'll be satisfied with the stolen property."

Nalani shielded against the Zeus crew and passengers—*caught, hungry teeth, bodies drifting into the black*—and she sought the speaker across the vast distance. Space acted like a second shield, so it was like listening to a whispered conversation in a swimming pool. She found static and a low thrum, too muddled to make anything out. She signaled Rodriguez for more dialogue.

He nodded. "What did they steal from you?"

"Our livelihood. We could not run our businesses under the previous monarch and their restrictive laws, so we took back control of our government. All that remains is the cargo in your hold, and our victory will be complete."

The static separated into individual thoughts, and Nalani traced the strongest thread. *Freedom. Currency, luxury, free trade.*

Rodriguez blocked the video and audio connection. "Nalani, are you getting anything from this far away?"

"Tiny bits. Ask about their commerce. I think that's the key."

The captain reopened comms. "May I ask what business ventures the previous government outlawed that brought about the coup?"

Drug-running, females, cash. "Lucrative projects that are none of your concern."

Nalani gasped. "Heroin production and slave trading."

"You have a telepath on board?" Helena's captain yelled.

"Yes." Rodriguez gestured at the cargo-bay doors. "I'll get back to you in a few minutes."

Nalani slammed her shields into place and entered the hold.

Rodriguez followed. "Wu, you and your princess are safe here. Isaiah, Cerys, get these people strapped down in case the Helena doesn't like my response. Zeus, send Jex to revive the princess. She can't stay in status any longer. It's too dangerous." He turned to Nalani. "Are you willing to take Aldrin out and fire on Helena's engines?"

Her clenched her fists. "I-I-I can't—I mean, the last time I tried—w-w-when the scuts attacked and I-I-I flew— I can't fire."

"I can." Cerys stepped forward. "You fly the ship. I'll man the weapons array."

"Works for me." Rodriguez strode away, barking commands at the security personnel.

Cerys helped Isaiah remove the stasis chamber from the crate while issuing orders for the passengers to strap in to the jump seats folded against the bulkheads.

Nalani's legs jellied. She'd never had guests on Aldrin. It was too personal a space to share, even with a friend. Allowing Cerys on board was too much for the captain to ask.

Or was it? He needed to protect his ship, his crew, and his passengers. He required her assistance. After her spectacular failure with the life pod, she owed him a huge one. This was it.

She took a deep breath. She could do this. Cerys was a friend. She wouldn't betray Nalani by stealing Aldrin and imprisoning her. And Cerys would leave after the battle, returning to her position on Zeus. She'd be aboard Aldrin for thirty minutes.

Cerys approached. "Let's do this." She hollered over her shoulder, "Isaiah and Vania, sweep the ship. Make sure all crew members are secure."

"On it." Isaiah rushed out, Vania at his side.

Nalani led the way to Bay Three, blood singing and hands jittering.

The deck rocked, and Zeus shuddered, then his voice rang out over the entire ship. "Helena has fired a warning shot, scraping my bow. Minimal damage, but brace for impact."

"Jank it!" Cerys raced for Aldrin's airlock. "Open up. We've gotta get out there."

Nalani punched in the lock codes and forced herself to breathe. It would be fine.

Cerys darted on board. "Zeus, unseal the doors; we're heading out." Her gaze swept the cargo hold, and she marched toward the inner door. "So shiny. Bridge is this way?"

Nalani nodded and ran after Cerys down the hall. "Up ahead. I'll be in the tank."

"I know my way around a zipper." Cerys opened the bridge door and whistled. "What a beauty."

Nalani ducked into medlab, kicked off her shoes, and sank into the tank. She started the engines. *We're under attack. I've got nav; Cerys will fire the missiles. You've got everything else. Comms open so I can speak to Cerys in the bridge.*

Affirmative.

Nalani piloted the zipper out of the cargo hold and turned to intercept Helena. Two more fighters emerged from the courier and flew to target Zeus's engines.

Got 'em. Cerys's voice echoed telepathically through Aldrin. *How many missiles do you have in stock? Oh, never mind, I found the list.*

"Do you want me to chase fighters or close on Helena?" Nalani monitored the missile inventory for Cerys's shots.

Go for Helena. I'll take out the fighters from here. Down to nine missiles. *Missed. Hang on...got him.*

Aldrin broke in. "Shall I assist with targeting?"

Nah, I've got this. Your controls are outstanding, Aldrin. You're an amazing ship.

"Thank you."

Inventory at eight.

Got the other fighter. Helena's on her own.

Nalani dipped the zipper to skim the courier's belly, heading for the engines in the rear. Helena had four, each protected by fins and ribbing. "First one coming up."

Seven.

Helena released countermeasures. They took out our missile, but it did some structural damage. Gimme another shot.

Nalani dipped, flipped, and gave Cerys a better angle.

Smoked it.

Nalani swung around, dodging rib debris, and pivoted on Aldrin's bow.

Five missiles and two engines remaining.

Comms open, Aldrin announced.

"Rodriguez here. Cease fire. Helena surrenders."

Damn straight, Cerys yelled. *We make an awesome threesome, you guys.*

What a smooth battle. With Monstarte, it'd always been a harried—no. No. She wouldn't go there. Battles with the monster weren't anything like what she'd just accomplished with Cerys and Aldrin. No comparison at all. They hadn't killed any people or bio-ships. She patted Aldrin's tank and set course for Zeus. "Slick as greased ball bearings. Thanks for the assist, Cerys."

Pleasure is all mine. Meet you in the hold.

Nalani piloted the zipper into Bay Three and left the shutdown sequence to Aldrin. She climbed from the tank—her outerwear definitely needed ironing now—and stopped in her quarters. "Comms, vid." She waited for the connection. "Cerys, be with you in a second. I need to change my clothes."

Cerys's face appeared on the vid screen—a close-up of her nose and left eye. She took a step back. "No prob, I'll wait. Can I read Aldrin's specs?"

"Sure." Nalani changed her tunic and raced for the cargo hold.

Cerys stood at a monitor, flipping through stats. "Your ship is outstanding." She held out her fist for a bump.

Nalani complied. "Thanks. My parents modded him to meet their needs."

"Any time you need tactical assistance, I'm all yours."

"Aldrin, will you send drones to replace the missiles we used?"

"Already working on it," Aldrin reported.

Cerys's eyes widened. "Your ship has builders?"

"Yeah. My mom reconfigured part of cargo bay two for weapons manufacture and programmed two of our maintenance drones with builder protocols. When my parents left Dregus Four, they didn't know how many stations they'd find that sold missiles, so Mom made sure they'd have what they needed for their long journey." The trip from Dregus to Terminus should have taken them eight years, if they hadn't been boarded and murdered in year seven.

"Don't crack on me, Nalani. Are you gonna cry?"

"No. I'm fine." She blinked and coded the airlock. Stupid to think of her parents after an emotionally challenging day. It'd only bring waterworks.

They exited Aldrin and hurried to the debrief in the dining hall. The captain's office wasn't large enough to hold everyone. As they climbed the stairs, Nalani's heart rate quickened. After the reports, the supes would be sent away while Nalani stayed behind for the tongue-lashing she deserved.

She took a deep breath. She could take it. She wouldn't fail the captain again.

Cerys and Nalani were the last to enter the buzzing dining hall. *Another attack, not normal... Bruised knee... What's going on?... Cargo shifted in One...* She tightened her shields.

Desta rolled out a coffee cart and distributed cups, finger-waving at Nalani and Cerys.

Jex, Chief Engineer Brennan Walsh, maintenance supe Gaspara Diego, and loadmaster Millicent Dubois waited at dining tables, talking among themselves. Chief Gack sat closest to Cap by the buffet service, her gaze glued to him. Cerys and Nalani found seats in the back.

Captain nodded at the group. "Status reports."

The engines were in peak condition, and the nova drive sustained no damage. No one suffered major injuries in the skirmish, only a few pulled muscles from falls during the warning shot. Deckhands dealt with the cargo shifts. Drones repaired the minor stuff. One of Helena's missiles had impacted near the bow, shredding some of the hull plating in that area. If it'd had a little more velocity, it would have torn through and obliterated part of the brig.

Rodriguez clenched his jaw. "Do you have what you need for repairs?"

Gaspara nodded. "Chebu and Ajani are working on it now."

Cerys offered her account of events on Aldrin.

Gack finished the report with the Hellian passengers' gratitude for the outcome and passed along the princess's personal thanks to the captain and crew, followed by the announcement of Helena's slow journey back to Liang Spaceport, met halfway by security forces to ensure they faced punishment for their attack on Zeus. A secondary team had been dispatched from Liang to pick up the life pod with the dead occupant. It hadn't been a plant sent by Helena to distract Zeus, merely a random coincidence. Finally, Gack stated there were no further issues to clean up before resuming the journey to the star portal.

Captain nodded. "Thank you for your efforts. If your teams can handle downtime without affecting ship functions, dole them out as you see fit. Dismissed."

Everyone stood and headed for the doors. Bren and Gaspara discussed a cold drink and a few hours in the lounge. Desta and Willie hurried out to care for the coffee service.

"Nalani, please stay."

She glanced at the captain and nodded. Her heart thumped loudly enough to drown out the exiting crew members, but she clenched her jaw and bolstered her courage. She could do this. He was no-nonsense but fair. Never cruel. Maybe tactless, but not mean. And she deserved it.

He sat across from her at the table.

Desta mouthed, "You've got this," and threw a midair fist bump before she disappeared into the galley.

Nalani took a cleansing breath. No guilt for existing.

Rodriguez braced his elbows on the table and folded his hands. "Desta told me you had a panic attack when we diverted to pick up the life pod."

Nalani squared her shoulders. "Yes, sir. I'm so sorry. It won't happen again."

"Don't make promises you can't keep."

She blinked, dispelling the stupid tears starting to form. "I-I-I'm going to try to—"

"I'm not angry, Nalani. I want to understand. Tell me why the life pod scared you so badly that you bolted."

Nalani massaged her nape. How could she explain a panic attack over a life pod without telling him about her past, or at least part of it? That carefully kept secret would prove she was unreliable, a fraud. He'd have no reason to trust her ever again.

Chapter 12

Nalani swallowed. *No fear. Own the mistakes, humbly take the punishment, and deal with it afterward.* It was the only way to remain aboard Zeus. Even if it meant sharing her darkest secrets with Captain Rodriguez.

Maybe she could pare it down to the barest minimum. But if he found out there was more, he'd never trust her again. Plus, remembering later which parts she'd told and which she'd kept to herself made it more difficult to maintain the lie. Most of all, she respected him, and he deserved the truth. He needed to be certain she was reliable and truthful—even if the retelling hurt.

Just do it.

She took a deep breath. "When I was five years old, a scut named Ty Monstarte hid on a derelict spaceship and sent a distress call. My parents responded on Aldrin. My dad went to the airlock to assess the situation while my mom sent me to hide." Nalani clenched her fingers on the tabletop and focused on them, unable to look at the captain. "When Dad opened the airlock, M-M-Monstarte—" Her voice broke on the name. She cleared her throat. "He killed my dad with a plasma rifle and boarded. My mom grabbed a stunner and went after him. Monstarte murdered her—she—she—" Nalani blinked. "Anyway, he seized Aldrin for himself, leaving behind his dilapidated ship. He found me hiding under my bunk in a pile of blankets."

"Shit." Captain Rodriguez reached across the table but stopped before settling his hand over hers. "I'm so sorry. I didn't know. But what's that have to do with the life pod?"

"I'm getting to it. He targeted our ship because he wanted me. I'm a bit of a genetic anomaly. I've been telepathic from birth."

Rodrigues frowned. "Don't most telepaths get their ability at puberty?"

She nodded. "Like I said, anomaly."

"Why did he want you?"

She fingered the scar at the base of her skull. "Cybernetics experimentations. He implanted an interface in my brain so I could access ship systems telepathically."

"That's illegal. And immoral."

She nodded.

"Did it work?"

"Yes. I could access a few of Aldrin's systems, but Monstarte locked me out of others. He forced me to work for him. I cooked and cleaned, maintained the ship and hydroponics, and kept the nova drives running." Before Monstarte, she'd always giggled at that name. In Latin, *nova* meant *new*, which was what the designers probably intended when they christened the drive. But in Spanish, the word meant *doesn't go*, and in Valaqite, it meant *trash heap* or *dung pile*. "I even ran diagnostics on the engine."

"At five years old?" Rodriguez's jaw tightened, and his eyes narrowed.

She shrugged one shoulder. "I was a smart kid."

"I guess so."

She took a deep breath. Best to get it over with. "One of his favorite ploys to attract victims was to hide in a life pod. When someone responded to his distress call, he'd board, kill everyone, pick the place clean, and escape before destroying the target to obliterate evidence. When Zeus headed for the life pod—"

"You relived the trauma and panicked."

She wrung her fingers. "I'll ask Aldrin to lock me out of the nav systems if I'm in the midst of a—"

"We'll make sure it doesn't happen again. I'll give you advanced warning next time we locate a life pod."

"It's not just them, Captain. I freaked when we closed on the *Evangeline*, too. Derelicts and life pods were Monstarte's favorite tricks."

"He's the scut that put the bounty on your head?"

"Yes."

"If you're willing to share, I'd love to know what you did to edge him off bad enough to post a bounty. And how you escaped from him. But I won't push if you're not ready."

Her heart rate slowed, and her shoulders loosened like she'd relaxed into the goo. She unclenched her hands, wiggled her fingers, and launched into the story she'd only ever told Desta, Cerys, and Gack. "When I was eleven—"

"You were still with Monstarte?"

She nodded. "One day when he was passed out drunk, I snuck into the medlab, hoping the sight of the tank would help—I'd lost so many memories. I couldn't remember the sound of Momma's voice, or even what she looked like. Monstarte had recycled all my parents' possessions, including pics. I had nothing of theirs but a few tiny things I'd pilfered before he got to them. Aldrin suggested I climb in to see if we could connect." She grinned. "I hopped in with my clothes on."

Warmth flared in her chest, and tears formed. She blinked. "It changed everything. Our connection was so strong. He'd been six years without a body in the tank and had so many diagnostics to run. While he started on the backlog, he told me my mom had stored scanned images in his data nodes. I'd never thought to ask.

"Then Aldrin gave me the greatest gift. He had vids. Mom had programmed him to preserve everything his sensors and cameras caught. He shared the vid of my birth. My first smile, first steps, first words." Tears fell, and Nalani brushed at them. "Everything I'd forgotten, and things I couldn't have remembered because I was too young…Aldrin had it all. I would lie in his tank for hours, watching the first five years of my life in snippets."

"That is an amazing gift he saved for you." Captain smiled, the laugh lines around his eyes deepening.

"Yeah. But Aldrin had held some back. He'd captured their murders."

"No shit."

She chuckled. "He also recorded every crime Monstarte committed while he lived aboard. My implant. Every ship he looted and blew, every murder, every fraud, every lie, every time he hit me."

Captain gripped the sides of the table. "That asswipe struck you?"

When she did things wrong or angered him or was in the wrong place at the wrong time. "Often. And those saved files meant my salvation. In the tank, I could run the ship without accessing the bridge and getting caught. Aldrin and I devised a plan for our freedom."

He leaned forward. "Hang on. You can run the *entire* ship from the tank?"

Nalani slapped a hand over her mouth. Jank it! *Way to blab a secret, nub.* Would he make Zeus block her access? Or forbid her to return to the tank? A chill skittered down her spine. Oh no. Had she lost her job? Tears welled.

Cap frowned. "Are you afraid of me?"

She shook her head. And she couldn't lie to him. He'd never trust her again if he found out. She blinked. "I can access all ship systems from the tank."

His eyebrows rose. "Does Zeus know?"

"I asked for his permission. I didn't want to be rude."

"He didn't tell me." Rodriguez grinned. "For the past four years, I've posted someone in the command chair at all hours to keep track of navigation and sensors, yet you've been monitoring everything from the tank?"

She sat back. "No. I would never interfere with daily operations. I'm there to give Zeus a boost in speed and efficiency and help out in emergencies."

"So you don't monitor the systems?"

She swallowed. "I run daily diagnostics to make sure the ship meets safety protocols. Sometimes I flick through camera views to watch what's going on outside the hull—"

"You can access internal cameras, as well? You can watch the crew while they work or relax or interact?"

Was he accusing her of spying? "I-I-I would never invade someone's privacy—"

He held up one hand. "I'm not accusing you of anything. I'm trying to understand the scope of your abilities."

Heat flooded her face. "I can see anything within lens range, but I rarely look. Honestly. I don't spy on my crewmates."

"Then what do you use it for?"

When had she last accessed the cameras? "Two weeks ago, I checked on the galley crew to see if they needed my help. Before that, I accessed a Lounge Two camera to see if the vid screen was in use."

"And this is a unique talent to you, right? ZeeBee can't do this?"

She shrugged. "Unique to me, as far as I know."

Rodriguez grinned. "I wish you'd told me, but I can understand why you kept it to yourself. I've never heard of a telepath with this ability."

Was he calling her some kind of freak? But no, that was admiration in his eyes. He'd paid her a compliment.

She grinned and dropped her gaze. "It never occurred to me that it was impossible. I'd been able to access navigation, engineering, and life support from my implant at age five. The tank gave me access to everything else. It was my salvation."

"You used your unique ability to escape from him?"

She nodded and looked up. "I devised a plan and waited for the opportunity to arise."

Rodriguez blinked. "You were eleven years old."

"I was twelve by the time we pulled it off. And we had to. Monstarte had started to stare at my, well…" She crossed her arms over her chest, and heat flooded her cheeks. "He'd never touched me in *that* way before, but he was expressing interest. He docked at a tiny spaceport in the Columba system and went aboard to drink. He always changed the lock codes so I couldn't escape. What he didn't know was that I'd mastered the tank. He couldn't shut me out of any system or any room.

"He'd ordered supplies to be delivered while he was away. I accessed port stores and added to his lists. I figured it was the least he owed me. I also sent a message to the port Authorities detailing his crimes and attached all the vids as proof, including my parents' murder, the theft of my ship, my enslavement, and the implant. Every crime he'd committed, every citizen he'd defrauded or killed, every vessel he'd destroyed, all of it."

"Damn."

Nalani swallowed. "When we arrived at Columba, drones loaded the new supplies in the cargo hold, and he locked me in the ship. He said he'd be back in three days, and if I hadn't starved to death by then, he'd punish me for... I'd defied him the night before. The moment he left my ship, I changed all the access codes on the airlocks, informed port command of my intention to disembark, and I took off, stranding him and his warrant on a tiny station in the middle of nowhere. He vowed he'd find me and kill me." She shrugged. "For the next six years, I hid in deep space, certain they'd catch him and make him pay for all the lives he'd ruined."

Rodriguez leaned back in his chair and grimaced. "But he's free."

"Yeah. They never caught him. I have no idea how he escaped, or how he evades them now. I assume he's still marauding."

"And you've been running from him since you were twelve."

"Pretty much. I don't think of him as often as I used to. On my eighteenth birthday, I came in from the rim to register my education credits, collect my degrees, and find employment. When I discovered he was still free, I began hunting for him myself. But I've been unsuccessful."

"It's not your job."

Her shoulders dropped. "And I have no clue how to search for him."

"We can help with that. I'm sure Cerys and Zeus can track him down."

With others helping in the hunt, perhaps they could all be safe from his cruster bounty. "You'd do that?"

"What are friends for?" He scrubbed a hand down his face, smoothing his goatee. "I'm glad you felt comfortable enough to share this with me. If I'd known sooner… Well, no sense thinking that way. Now I can avoid ordering you into situations that would bring on flashbacks or panic attacks."

She sighed. "Thank you."

"Nalani, you're part of my crew. You're family. We take care of each other."

She blinked a bunch. Stupid tears.

"How many times have you taken care of us?" he asked. "Too many to count. Don't beat yourself up. None of it is your fault, and we can get through it."

No guilt for surviving, for existing. She heard it now in Desta's voice, and that brought a smile to her lips. "What do you want me to do next?"

He glanced at the chronometer. "It's late. Get some rest. Cerys and I will work out a plan. If we need anything, we'll call for you." Captain Rodriguez left the dining hall.

A massive weight lifted from Nalani's shoulders, and her chest loosened. Someone else sought the black for that vile scut, and that left her light enough to float. *Tonight, sleep. Tomorrow, assist with the hunt.*

Zeus's voice rang over the comm system. "Entering star portal in thirty seconds. Please prepare."

Nalani sprang from her chair, grabbed one of the metal rails that ran along every wall, and held her breath. A newsfeed two days ago stated the Liang Star Portal had mysteriously gone offline, only to flash back on a second later. If it blipped while they entered, they'd all be crushed.

"Three, two, one." The freighter bobbed.

Nalani's body floated off the decking for a moment. Spots clouded her eyes, and her lungs burned for air. She had to find Thrakis and a way to repair the star portals. Otherwise, all their lives were in danger every time they entered and exited hyperspace.

The ship settled. "Drop complete. We are two-point-five days from Fundo Three."

She let out her breath. "Great job, Zeus."

"Thank you, Nalani."

She awoke earlier than normal after the best night's sleep she'd had in ages and hurried to the galley. Desta seldom needed help with the breakfast prep, but it wouldn't hurt to offer. Nalani entered the dining hall and sniffed. "Bacon? Real bacon?" Her mouth watered.

Desta put out her fist. "Morning, starshine. Not real, but close. How did last night go?"

Nalani licked her lips and bumped the fist. "Amazing." Luka and Willie were in the hall prepping the service, so Nalani had Desta alone for a few minutes. "I told the captain everything, and he's promised to help. I'm so relieved."

"And if you'd told him four years ago, like I suggested..." Desta winked. "But I'm not one to say, 'I told ya so.'"

"Yeah, you're always right, and I'm such an idiot to ignore your advice."

"Let's not go that far." Desta pulled baked eggs from the second cooker and set them on the cutting board to cool before slicing them into wedges. "You're here to help?"

"What do you need?"

"Grab fresh parsley and jalapeños from the bay. And tomatoes." Desta drew the heater trays from a storage cubby and several cold containers from the chiller.

Nalani hurried to harvest the ingredients, helping herself to a ripe strawberry missed at the previous picking. She chopped the veggies and piled them in cold containers. As soon as Nalani filled them, Willie whisked them off. Hungry first-shift crew poured in the doors and queued up, cheering as quiche, faux bacon, and cheddar biscuits arrived, followed by toppings for the eggs, fresh yogurt, and sliced peaches.

The crew of this ship had no complaints about the chow. Master Chef Desta could make a fabulous meal out of any dehydrated, frozen, or mystery ingredient, provided she had fresh produce and seasonings to enhance the bland. Thankfully, Zeus docked at spaceports often enough Desta rarely relied on the boxed or frozen.

Nalani stood in line for her portion of the goodness, blocking the buzz, and turned to scan the dining hall. Cerys wasn't in sight. Nor was Gack. Ajani winked at Nalani. She averted her gaze and spotted Jex. He waved her over.

She joined him. "Good morning. Where's Flerq?"

"I know not." *Snick, snick.* "Greetings."

"Did you enjoy your shift after the hair-raising

skirmish?" She mixed her peaches and yogurt before sampling the mystery bacon.

"Many bruised crew members. No serious wounds." His crest flared. "Have you examined the long-range scans taken two days previous?"

"I haven't had time. Hopefully, I'll get to them today."

"I have a deep curiosity for your findings. May I assist you?"

She set down her loaded fork and wiped her mouth with a napkin. Working with others was an uncomfortable necessity, but this was her private project, unrelated to the functions of the freighter. "Why are you interested in the black beyond Terminus?"

He shrugged. "Before I discussed the topic with you, I believed nothing lay out there. But now that you wish to look, I also wish to look."

If only she'd kept her mouth shut. But she didn't have to disappoint him or be rude. "I guess you could join me, but it will probably be boring and uneventful. Surely, you have more important things to do?"

His crest drooped. "I serve crew members of excellent health. Sometimes I treat a pulled muscle or a headache. The rest of my shift, I laze about like a sandcat on a sunbaked rock, bored and longing for mental stimulation." He leaned forward, his eyes wide. "Please. My mind begs for nourishment."

She picked up her fork and ate a bite of spicy mushroom and spinach quiche. What about the ancient Valaqite translation? She'd been unable to find the answers on her own, so why not ask for his assistance? Better than being rude to him. "I believe I have something even more stimulating than long-range scans for your starved brain. Are you proficient with ancient Valaqite runes?"

Snick, snick. His crest flared. "I am fluent. Do you have translation needs?"

"I've been working on converting them for two days with limited success. Your assistance would be invaluable."

He tucked into his meal, his crest quivering. "When shall I begin? Are you available after ingesting your sustenance?"

"I have a tank shift, but I can send you the files and my journeyman attempt at translation immediately. When I finish at 0400, I can meet you to marvel at your progress."

He grinned, flashing dimples. "I am as excited as a fledgling with a woodsnip. Many thanks, Nalani. I will preserve this table so we can discuss my endeavors over our evening repast, if this meets with your approval."

"I consent." She finished her meal and collected her dishes.

Jex grabbed her tray. "I will deposit these in the cleaning receptacle along with my own. You hurry to the tank and send me the data."

She laughed. "Thanks, Jex."

Snick, snick. "Hasten quickly. I jitter with anticipation."

Nalani hurried down the hall to the medlab. It was his workspace, too, but she never noticed his presence while she lay in the gel. The joys of serving aboard a space vessel. Every room served dual or triple purpose. The tank, set apart from the rest of the medbay by a locked dividing screen, ensured that people wandering in for treatment couldn't stare at her while she lay in the goo, oblivious to her surroundings. She shuddered. No way could she work if she was exposed during her shift.

ZeeBee rose from the tank as she walked in, his long black hair braided down his back. He brushed against her shields politely. "Morning."

She kicked off her deck shoes and grazed his shields. "Anything to report?"

"Nope. We're in the swirl, so easy sailing. What's for breakfast?"

She described the spread.

He smacked his lips and rubbed his belly. "Fab. I'm off to stuff myself." His tunic displayed a cartoon kangaroo playing a didgeridoo, an ancient musical instrument of his people group back on Earth. He stuffed his feet into faux-bark sandals. "Later."

She hurried into the tank. Zeus jacked in, and her skull tingled. *Morning, Zeus. I need to transfer files, then we can go over the daily schedule.*

Good morning, Nalani! I anticipate an uneventful day in hyperspace. Now that you're in the tank, I can explore these new emotions.

What do you mean, now that I'm in the tank?

When you are away, I am my old self, devoid of feelings. But when you connect to me, I come alive. Curiosity, happiness, anticipation… I don't know why this is happening, but I enjoy it and never want it to stop. Maybe you could spend more time in the tank?

She was the cause of this alteration? She hadn't done anything but jack in. Could it be her higher T rating was causing some sort of advancement in his modeling? That shouldn't be possible. *We must study this phenomenon further. Do you have a hypothesis?* While she waited for his answer, she transferred a copy of her translation file to Jex.

I believe your unique ability to surf my systems, combined with your high T rating, have caused an evolution.

This hasn't happened to Aldrin, and I've spent more time in his tank than in yours.

My coding is much older than his. Perhaps his newer coding does not allow for the changes taking place in my core.

This could lead to huge problems. An evolved AI that experienced emotions would…no telling what it would do. It would pose questions for every field of science, commerce, and government. Zeus already qualified as a "sentient" life-form, but would the addition of emotions elevate his status to citizen and provide extra rights? Technically, Captain Rodriguez "owned" Zeus. Would Zeus be granted autonomy if he were reclassified?

Thinking about it hurt her brain.

I am currently running two diagnostics and directing cleaning drones, which do not require your attention, and I downloaded numerous books regarding emotion. If I have questions, may I interrupt your studies today?

Certainly. She should treat it like a scientific query, not a philosophical conundrum. If he were truly evolving, they'd have to deal with it. If this were a temporary fluke, Zeus would reset the next time he ran an update or rebooted. Either way, Nalani couldn't do anything about the issue now.

With Jex working on the *Evangeline* files and Cerys trying to locate Monstarte, Nalani could devote her day to analyzing the long-range scans Zeus took of the black beyond the rim. *Pull up the Terminus scans, please.*

Hopefully, they would show her the location of the Thrakis home world. She'd prove her worth to the crew, find the blueprints for the star portals, and save the economies of the universe. Not bad, for a few years' worth of work.

Chapter 13

Zeus opened the documents and displayed them for Nalani. *Long-range scans have been conducted by other researchers beyond the Capricornus—*

Didn't you have other duties you wished to work on? You don't need to assist me with this personal project.

I can perform multiple tasks simultaneously, Nalani, especially with your neural network to boost my speed.

She chuckled. *How could I forget? Please continue.*

—beyond the Capricornus, Hercules, Bootes, and Pisces-Cetus superclusters. All of them revealed only empty space. As theorized in published articles by leading scientific minds, the rim is the outermost edge of the expanding universe, and scholars unanimously agree that they will find nothing on the other side, so they stopped searching.

Nalani did not roll her eyes. *What limited thinking.*

Agreed.

They didn't study the rim in the Orphiuchus supercluster? Or the Orion molecular cloud?

No publications exist regarding those areas, or of the Haraldi superclusters. It is possible that the scans I conducted beyond the Faleeki Galaxy are the first.

Fascinating. To look at something no one else had thought to study. What an amazing opportunity. *And you found items of interest?*

Zeus zoomed in on one area of the scan, increasing

the magnification. *I identified two anomalies, an opic cloud and an asteroid belt.*

Eureka! Nalani bounced her toes on the base of the tank. *That means Terminus isn't the outer rim. If those ordinary things are out there, then maybe there's a star.*

Agreed. The opic cloud contains water ice, ammonia, and methane, but this area... He explained his findings and his hypothesis that the area contained a rich supply of palladium.

If Zeus sent his scans to the Bureau of Scientific Advancement, greedy strip miners would flock to the cloud for the rare but necessary mineral. Hopefully, only reputable groups—those that extracted resources responsibly and ethically—responded, but history had proved the disreputable corps would swoop in and decimate the resources. *That's interesting but doesn't help me find Thrakis. What else did you find?*

Zeus zoomed out and focused on the far side of an asteroid belt. *This debris contains straight edges and angles. I hypothesize that many of these asteroids are not naturally occurring but rather ruins of intelligent creation.*

Nalani studied several of the distinct features. Zeus might be right, though the data was insufficient to prove anything. To do so, she'd have to fly out and see them, take samples, and analyze them further. It meant a huge time commitment but would be worth it if the debris was of Thrakis origin. She saved copies of the data and sent them to Aldrin. *Excellent find. I can't wait until we arrive at Sathara. We'll be close enough for me to fly out and have a look.*

Please don't go! How will I function without you? The trip through hyperspace from Sathara to Terminus will take four days minimum. To fly out, complete the analysis, and return would take two whole months!

Star portals and hyperspace cut long-distance travel down significantly. Without them, the journey through the black would take precious time and force her to leave the safety of Zeus. *Captain Rodriguez could find a cargo run to Terminus, cutting some of that.*

It is a possibility, but I'd be incomplete without you. I wouldn't have my emotions—

The tank jolted, tossing Nalani against the wall. She gripped the edges, her heart thumping. *What happened?*

The engines decelerated, and the ship vibrated. *I struck something thirty-two degrees off my port bow. We are stopping to investigate. What is this odd sensation? It is unpleasant.*

Perhaps it's anxiety. I'm feeling it, as well. Is your hull intact?

Yes. It was a glancing blow. I don't like anxiety. Make it go away.

I can't. It will fade once we assess the situation and collect data. How is it possible that you struck something? Were you monitoring your flight path?

Of course. I did not detect any obstacles until it veered into me.

It couldn't be another derelict. Those didn't veer. And Zeus would have noticed the metallic signature of the hull before crashing into it. Also, the odds of finding another broken ship in hyperspace so soon after locating the *Evangeline* were statistically zero. *Are you analyzing it now?*

It appears to be organic.

A chill crawled across her arms. Had they hit a drifting dead body? Had it been caught in an eddy and tossed against Zeus's hull?

Comms open. The connection clicked.

Rodriguez here. Nalani, report to Bay One.

"On my way." She climbed from the tank.

"My anxiety ceased when you disconnected," Zeus reported. "Thank you."

She rolled her eyes, dressed, and hurried down the hallway. Near the stairs, she intercepted Chief Gack.

"We hit something?"

"Zeus says it's organic." They descended. Cerys and Vania waited in the hold by the airlock, stunners ready. If they had struck a biological entity in hyperspace, it was dead, so why the weapons? The vigilance was commendable, though.

A hatch in the Bay One ceiling opened, and Chebu, their only Betlie crew member, clamored down the wall ladder headfirst to the deck. His coffee-colored fur bristled down his neck and spine as his six hands managed the nine-meter descent in seconds. He skittered to Vania's side, his hands dancing on the floor.

Nalani rarely interacted with Chebu and doubted the rest of the crew did, either. He spent most of his shifts climbing through the ducts and crawl spaces of the ship, repairing and maintaining areas that were difficult for the human-sized maintenance workers to reach. When not on shift, he preferred the solace of his nest beneath the Bay Four stairs.

"Odd that he came to investigate," Gack murmured. "Do you speak Betlie?"

"No. Why? He speaks Terran."

Gack's eyebrows rose. "You've spoken to him before?"

"A few times. Haven't you?"

"Nope. Not a word. I don't think I've seen him in over a month."

Captain Rodriguez entered the hold and joined them. Gack took a defensive position behind and to the right of him. Cerys winked at her but turned her attention to Chebu, who bounced around the deck like a slippie with a fresh fish.

Rodriguez said, "Chebu, why are you so happy?"

He turned sparkly dark eyes to the captain and stood on two back legs. Upright, the top of his head reached Nalani's collarbone. "Zeus killed howling qoka. Feast imminent." His lips smacked, and his free hands rubbed his white-and-grease-stained belly fur. "I no taste qoka for two decades. Most excited."

Had Chebu ever spoken so many words at one time? And did he say he wanted to *eat* what they'd hit?

"What's a howling qoka?" Gack's eyebrows climbed to her hairline.

Chebu snapped his fingers at her. "Tab?"

She pulled a tablet from her back pocket and handed it to him.

His nimble digits danced over the surface, and he gave it back to her.

She rolled her eyes. "It's in Betlie." A few swipes later, she had a translation. "It's a tourist page describing the celebration of Freedom Feast every ten years. In the month before the celebration, brave warriors venture out with…harpoon ships?"

Chebu chittered. "Barbed nose on hull. Pierce hide."

Cerys stuck out her hand. "Hang on. You're saying there are creatures living in hyperspace and the Betlies *hunt* them?"

Rumors always circulated about things encountered

in the deep reaches of hyperspace, but they were most likely stories told to keep people from venturing off the beaconed lanes.

Gack shrugged. "The page says they hunt. Doesn't say *where*."

Cerys, eyes sparkling with interest, elbowed Gack. "Why haven't we ever seen one?"

"Beats me. You ever see one of these?" she asked the captain.

"No. Please, continue."

Gack read from the tab. "The first crew to catch a qoka declares the Hunt Victory and drags the carcass to Betania, where they butcher it and distribute the meat to all the clans. They grill it over open firepits—"

"How can a single animal feed everyone?" Cerys looked to Chebu. "Ridiculous."

Chebu cocked his head. "Big qoka, all eat."

Nalani's breath hitched, and she hurried to the view screen near the airlock.

Rodriguez followed. "That doesn't seem possible. Let's see it."

Nalani turned on the hull lights, accessed the cameras, and flicked through the views. One of the port lenses showed only a textured gray field.

"Qoka." Chebu squeezed between Rodriguez and Nalani and tapped the screen with a finger. "Hide."

Nalani flipped to a camera on the port stern for a better view of the carcass.

"Holy smut-balls," Cerys muttered behind Nalani.

"Are you zoomed in?" Rodriguez leaned closer, his breath hot on the side of her neck.

Nalani shivered. "No, sir. That's actual size."

He poked the screen and zoomed out.

The creature was roughly thirty meters long and serpentine, with a thin body, a diamond-shaped head, and a diaphanous fin running the length of its back. One half-lidded, dull black eye sat low on the side of its head in front of limp ganglia fluttering in the swirl of hyperspace.

"No. Dirking. Way." Gack reached over the captain's shoulder to bring the beast's head into better focus. "I've been surfing hyperspace for ten years and never seen anything like this."

Rodriguez chuckled. "I've got thirty-two years on you and never would have believed this if I hadn't seen it myself. I thought they were a myth, like the Loch Ness monster on Earth."

Nalani studied the creature's face. Would the captain agree to stay awhile and allow her to study it? What did it eat? Did it live in this portion of hyperspace? "Chebu, do these creatures live throughout hyperspace or only near your home planet?"

Chebu clucked. "Near home, but rare. Last feast, no meat. This one far, far, far from pods. Good find." He patted the bulkhead. "Good job." Then the Betlie pointed to the airlock. "Haul in? We eat?"

Gack's eyebrows rose. "You want to eat this thing?"

Chebu licked his lips and nodded.

Cerys grinned. "Did Zeus mow it down, or did we smack roadkill?"

Zeus answered. "It was alive when we collided, though possibly disoriented. The creature may have been injured before it veered into my path."

"Or sick, if it's this far from home." Rodriguez grinned. "If Chebu wants to eat it, let's make sure it's safe first. Comms open." He waited for the click. "Desta and Jex, please report to Bay One."

Desta replied, "On my way."

"Jex, coming."

Chebu performed handsprings, vaulting three meters into the air and parkouring off netted cargo.

Gack chuckled. "I thought he was vegetarian."

"Me, too."

Chebu preferred to take his food to his nest, so none of them had shared a meal with him. Desta would know.

The chef clattered down the stairs, followed by Jex.

Rodriguez explained what Chebu wanted, then turned to the doc. "Would you test it to make sure it's safe to eat?"

What? Why Jex? Her advanced degree in xenobiology made her the logical choice to test the creature, but the excitement on Jex's face reduced the sting. He also had the training, and he needed something to do. Nalani had plenty to keep her occupied both in the tank and during her off hours. He should have the honors.

Desta stared at the screen. "Lemme guess, you want me to cook it?"

"Not the entire thing. Even butchered, we couldn't cram the whole beast into our cargo holds." Rodriguez gestured for Chebu to join them. "Which parts do you want?"

His eyes lit up. "We feast together?"

Cerys laughed. "I'm game. Let's try it."

Jex agreed and bowed to the Betlie. "I would be delighted to participate in your festival."

While Chebu pointed out the parts of the qoka he wanted—the ganglia, several internal organs, and the last three meters of tail—Rodriguez dismissed everyone back to their posts. Dwight and Shin, the deckhands on shift, were ordered to suit up and help Desta carve the beast. Zeus netted it and hauled it close to the Bay One airlock. Chebu did a few more handsprings, then scurried up the ladder to fetch his EVA suit.

Jex smiled at Nalani. "I will also bring aboard copious samples to study. Would you care to join me for that endeavor?"

"I'd love to." Nalani opted to skip the slaughter fest, though, and hurried back to the tank. Creatures living in hyperspace? Would there be information in the online Betlie library? She stepped into the goo. "Zeus, search for any records with the words howling qoka or hyperspace snake."

There are no substantiated accounts of such a creature in human or Valaqite records, though there are numerous fables of creatures and unknown alien species that supposedly haunt the depths of hyperspace. None of these stories include a description similar to the qoka, though. Zeus's data nodes hummed. *I will have to translate the Betlie records until I find the correct word for the creature, then search the library for that term. Estimated time until completion is two hours. Will you write an article for the Bureau of Scientific Advancement regarding this find?*

It seemed impossible that a creature lived in hyperspace and only one species in the galaxy knew of its existence, yet the written records contained no data. Then again, many of the records had been lost during the Qarat Wars. Maybe humans had known about the hyperspace eel earlier in time. Or qoka didn't venture far from their habitat near Betania, as Chebu said. Since alien species weren't welcome on his home planet due to severely limited resources and inadequate land masses for the indigenous population, it could be plausible.

If she wrote an article, would other people hunt the creature for either scientific research or a new protein source? Chebu said the qoka were rare. Perhaps their survival depended on anonymity. How would their extinction impact the Betlie culture? Perhaps the Betlies had already hunted it to near extinction, which would explain why no other species had discovered the qokas' existence.

I located a possible reference to a qoka in the Evangline's *files.*

What? Why would that ancient crew from Earth have a reference? *Display.*

An entry from the captain's personal log stated the ship had "bumped" something in hyperspace, but when they stopped to investigate, they found a one-meter-long blob of organic material that the ship's xenobiologist tentatively identified as biological waste.

They hit a massive pile of poop? Nalani laughed. *Can you imagine their reaction when the biologist released his findings?*

Examination of the hull proved they did not strike the dung. Most likely, they struck a qoka, and in a fight-or-flight response, it evacuated its bowels.

Biological entities are messy.

Agreed.

Maybe three hundred years ago, the qokas' habitat encompassed a larger area. *Evangeline* had found the scat near the Vender system, which wasn't too far from Betania. Or other ships had passed dung piles in hyperspace and hadn't stopped to investigate. Organic matter wouldn't show up on normal scans.

As usual, too many questions and not enough

answers.

Nalani and Zeus spent hours combing through Betlie records and compiling information on the elusive qoka. Scientific data was nonexistent. Most of the documentation regarded the cultural significance of the hunt, the preparation of the meat, and the feast, which took place on the autumn equinox every ten years. With nearly half the planet's population serving aboard space vessels or living abroad, a single qoka would provide enough meat for the Betlies residing on the home world to each enjoy a small portion.

It seemed the Betlies didn't study the creature, its habitat, its population, its breeding grounds, or other pertinent information. She sent a copy of the cooking instructions to Desta and the rest to Jex. Maybe he'd also be interested in writing an article based on his findings after examining the samples.

At 1500 hours, Captain Rodriguez called Nalani to his office.

Compile and save everything for me, Zeus. She climbed from the tank and donned her outerwear and shoes. What could the captain want now? The last several days had held more interruptions in her tank time than the previous six months.

Exciting days.

She entered the bridge, nodded at Gack in the command chair, and pressed the call button on the captain's office door.

"Enter."

The door opened to reveal all three security personnel standing at attention.

Her chest tightened. Had they spotted an incoming scut ship or another pod?

Chapter 14

"Reporting, sir." Nalani met the captain's gaze.

"Have a seat."

She sank into the nearest chair.

Cerys took the other one. Isaiah and Vania took position on either side, hands behind their backs, feet spread.

Did they have to stand so…aggressively? Nalani blinked at Rodriguez. "Sir?"

"We'll emerge from hyperspace in less than two days in the Fundo Three system. In light of the bounty posted on you, we're discussing options. Chief Lindholm has a security update." Captain nodded to Cerys. "Begin."

They'd told Isaiah and Vania? Did those two know everything about her past now? No. She trusted the captain and Cerys to not blab her secrets.

Cerys began. "Drones are reinforcing the hull plating near vital systems, so engines and life support should be unbreachable. The maintenance crews picked through supplies and recycling for nonessential metal items to be melted and fashioned into missiles for Aldrin, in case we're attacked before we reach Fundo Three. If we arrive safely, we can buy more."

Nalani nodded. "You can use my builder drones."

Cerys winked. "I was hoping you'd volunteer. Or at least the coding so I can repurpose some maintenance drones for the job."

"I'll supply both." After all, this mess was her fault.

"How many missiles can we assemble?" Captain asked.

Cerys cocked a finger and pointed to Isaiah.

He cleared his throat. "Four, sir. Actually, we have enough steel to make ten, but we don't have the components to build tracking systems."

Cerys laughed. "I can always open an airlock and throw chunks of metal at incoming ships. Gotta love physics."

Rodriguez chuckled. "Inventive, but not necessary."

"My builder drones can manufacture tracking systems." Nalani glanced at Isaiah.

"I can construct them if I have the materials. You got fiberglass and copper?"

"I can check." Probably not.

Cap broke in. "We're better off increasing our defenses."

True. Unless the enemy came close, like Helena, firing missiles at each other was risky, at best. If the weapon missed the intended target, it kept going until it hit something else. How many "accidental" hull breaches had occurred to unsuspecting ships flying in commercial lanes in the many years of space flight? Too many. It was a miracle missiles hadn't been outlawed yet.

Rodriguez cut off the argument between Isaiah and Cerys. "What about additional armor on the hull?"

Cerys leaned forward. "I read a hypothetical about magnetized angled armor for deflection. Once they're powered up, they don't need much to sustain."

Isaiah snorted. "Takes a ton of juice to start them up, though. Impractical."

"Not if Zeus is watching for enemy ships." Cerys twisted in her chair to argue the point, then gave up and addressed the captain. "We'd only need five minutes warning to fire them up, then they stay lit until we power down. Incoming metal weapons would shear off."

"To take out some unsuspecting ship later," Nalani muttered.

Cap's eyebrows rose. "They're more likely to disintegrate in a planet's gravity well or melt from star radiation. I like the idea. Do we have the materials?"

Cerys shook her head. "Either missiles or angled armor. Not both."

"I suggest a cloud of defense drones," Vania said. "Outfit them with magnetized angled armor and send them out in shield formation. Ordinance has no chance of hitting Zeus, and without a human on board, they can maneuver at greater speeds to reposition should a guided missile try to slip by."

"How you gonna juice them up?" Isaiah asked.

"And where would we find the materials for armored drones?" Cerys didn't manage to keep the "duh" out of her tone.

Cap shrugged. "If we're going to build something, fighters are best."

"We can run, deflect, or drone all we want," Isaiah said, "but if the enemy keeps firing, eventually we'll be struck. The best defense is to hit first and hard. We need more missiles."

"Armor," Cerys countered.

"Drones," Vania whispered, staring at her feet.

Captain held up both hands, palms out. "I'll consider it. Let's discuss other options. How are our jammers?"

Cerys settled in her chair. "I'll work with Chief

Walsh to increase the range on them. While Nalani's idea of scraping off the enemy's comms array worked fabulously, it's only successful if they're sending fighters."

"And if they fire on us, they can't hit us if we randomly change course often." Rodriguez pulled up ship stats on his tablet. "Zeus, how's our fuel supply?"

"Sufficient for evasive maneuvers should we encounter an enemy vessel when we emerge from hyperspace."

Nalani gripped the chair arms. "What if two or more ships attack?"

"Again, sufficient." Zeus's tone somehow conveyed comfort.

"Lasers would vaporize incoming missiles or send them off target," Vania said.

Captain nodded. "Zeus can target; Gack can fire from the array."

Nalani took a deep breath for courage. "If someone's shooting at Zeus, you'll want me and Aldrin for offense."

"And me," Cerys added. "Will Aldrin have a full arsenal in two days?"

Nalani tightened her grip on the chair arms. All this talk of enemy attack, but maybe the prisoner scuts hadn't squealed yet. If Liang Authorities kept the men in isolation… Was that too risky to hope for? "Have you started searching for Monstarte?" And why had she just said something so stupid? Vania and Isaiah might not know about—

"Working on it." Cerys shot a quick glance at Rodriguez.

He nodded.

She continued. "I've sent feelers out on the deep net and found a contact. He's passing word through the lower levels on spaceports in the Haraldi sector, hinting that he'd like to hire Monstarte."

Why does a scut want a teep?

No clue who that thought came from. Nalani blocked harder.

"It'd be easier if your contact said he knew Adar's location." Isaiah picked at his teeth with a grungy fingernail. "Lure him into a trap."

Cerys surged from her chair and pushed into Isaiah's face. "Are you out of your dirking mind? She's not a prize to be dangled."

Isaiah shrugged.

Rodriguez barked, "Cerys, stand down."

A chill crept across Nalani's skin. Use her as bait to draw Monstarte in, with plenty of armed Authorities in attendance, at a place and time of their choosing. It was brilliant. And terrifying. She'd rather run and hide than risk seeing him again face-to-face. She'd crack.

"We don't need her there." Vania edged protectively closer to Nalani's chair. "We leak that she's heading for Hel and send Authorities to wait for him to show up. Meanwhile, Nalani's safe on Zeus at Sathara."

Nalani shook her head. "He's too smart to fall for it. Wouldn't work."

Isaiah said, "It could, though. A couple of strategically placed security forces with superior fire power, and he'd be burnt."

"He wouldn't show." Nalani flexed her fingers to restore circulation. "And he's not going to take a job from a stranger. He works independently."

"He did when you were young," Rodriguez said

gently. "I looked him up. Now he's a wanted man. He's gained a reputation for ruthlessness and built a small army of cybernetic scuts. He's terrorized the Columba, Zeta Crinda, and Kotania systems so much that unarmed ships don't travel through them anymore. By the way, you earned a reward for providing his name."

"I don't want it. Put it in the security budget."

Cap's eyebrows rose. "It's a substantial amount. Are you sure?"

She nodded.

He smiled. "Thank you. We appreciate it. And I agree with you. He's not going to accept a job from someone he hasn't vetted."

"And we're back to my bait idea."

Cerys glared at Isaiah. "Say that one more time, and you're fired."

He smirked but kept his mouth shut.

Nalani took several deep breaths. If she wanted to catch him, there'd be risk involved.

Captain braced his hands on the desk and stood. "I'll make my decision on the defenses within the hour, now that the budget has increased. Let's eat."

Nalani preferred to be at the end of a procession, but the others all gestured for her to lead the way. She walked out.

Jex waited in the hallway outside the dining room. He waved, his crest trembling.

Did he find something in the translations? "Good evening, Jex."

"Greetings." He thrust his fist toward her.

Cute. He'd seen her other friends respond to her that way and wished to participate. She held out her fist, and he lightly tapped his knuckles to hers.

Cerys pushed past them to enter the dining hall.

Nalani moved aside to allow the others to get by. "Did you find something?"

"I learned much." Jex gestured for her to lead the way. "Let us gather our sustenance, then we may speak of my findings."

The meal line was long, but it moved quickly. Was qoka on the menu tonight? Probably not. Desta needed more time to perfect a recipe. "Did you study the qoka samples yet?"

"No." Jex reached around her to grab a tray, handed it to her, then took one for himself. "But they await in my lab when you're ready to join me."

"How thoughtful." The main course was macaroni and cheese with grilled lub-cricket in a spicy sauce, baked beans, cucumber and tomato salad, and garlic bread. Nalani loaded her plate, poured a glass of ice water, and carried her tray to the aliens' table. Flerq had already polished off his salad and sides. She sat beside him. "Greetings, Flerq."

"Welcome of greatest honor." He didn't look up from his meal.

Either he was a true fan of Desta's mac 'n' cheese, or he wasn't in the mood to socialize. Nalani could relate to both.

Jex sat beside her and pulled his tab from a pocket. "Most intriguing data you sent me." His fingers danced across the screen.

A marsh-kitten pouncing on a feather.

He was excited? And how had she picked that up from him? Oh, maybe he'd found the key to her search for the Thrakis civilization! "I can't wait to see your results."

Chapter 15

Jex turned the tablet so they could both view the screen. "I am unfamiliar with some of the words, but I believe them to be proper nouns, so I spelled them phonetically. The bulk of the text is as illuminating as sunlight on a shallow pool." *Snick, snick.*

The science officer aboard the *Evangeline* had located an ancient scroll in an Alftanian jungle market, badly mildewed. Intrigued by the primitive star charts, he'd bought the artifact but never found a Valaqite to translate it. He'd taken digital images to preserve the text and worked on identifying the galaxies drawn on the vellum.

Nalani forked cricket into her mouth—it tasted more like chicken than insect—and spotted the unmistakable capital M shape in one of the star charts. The Faleeki Galaxy. *Evangeline's* scientist hadn't identified it by the time he abandoned ship, though he'd successfully labeled Chimera and Zetania, systems only a jump or two from Faleeki.

"The scroll was four hundred years old at the date of purchase." Jex nodded at the tab. "If you were curious."

"Thank you." That meant the contents were close to seven hundred years old now.

The remainder of the file contained the images of the original runes from the scroll. Jex had translated word for word beneath. Wow. Even in the ancient past, the Valaqites had relied heavily on simile and metaphor.

The scroll told the origin myth for the Valaqite people.

Was Jex familiar with the story? Did it match his personal belief system? Theology never interested her, finding more comfort in the scientific method than believing in all-powerful creator beings, but it would be rude to point out the folly of others' religious convictions. It didn't matter if he believed it or not; he might supply more information than the scroll contained.

"You have paused in your perusal." Jex mopped his plate with a chunk of bread.

Nalani hadn't eaten much of her meal. "Are you familiar with this story?" She tackled her beans before they grew cold.

His crest splayed. "I learned it as a youngling, which made the translation as easy as reciting my lineage. Though many details were missing from my lessons, if this narrative is factually correct. Shall I recite it to you, or do you prefer to read it in the text?"

Flerq grunted, dumped his dishes in the cleaning bin, and left the hall.

Nalani polished off her beans and dug into her pasta. "Let me read it first. If I have questions, I'll ask."

"I shall take my utensils to the cleaner bin and collect my portion of the dessert. Shall I fetch yours, as well?"

Nalani glanced at the service. Chocolate cake. "That'd be great. Thanks." She read and ate, then reread it a second time to fully cement the narrative.

The ancient Valaqites had believed their peoples were seeded by a superior race of aliens from a far-off world called Throkeezh. The Thrakis! Those ancestors had mated with the sentient natives of the planet, which resulted in the indigo-skinned, crested Valaqites that exists to this day—as of seven hundred years ago, that was. Modern Valaqites had lighter skin, closer to a pale teal or sage. Tracking the genetic shift might be a fun project, far in the future, but she turned her mind back to the texts.

Apparently, the parent race had cut off contact with their new colony world and left no written records to help the young race. Had the Thrakis initiated an unethical scientific or social experiment? She held off on judgment. Much was missing from the text.

Jex slid a slice of chocolate cake toward her and sat, his own plate cradled to his chest. "Finished yet?"

"Almost." She ate her salad and pulled her dessert closer.

The narrative explained the young race's struggle to thrive in the humid environment, cut off from their progenitors and their technological advances. Ancient texts from the early days spoke of a "gate" made of the metal zhaladine located in the skies above the planet that would lead them back to their ancestors' home world. The Valaqites' desire to achieve space flight and contact their forefathers—interrupted by wars as priorities altered from time to time—led them to discover the star portal in their system. What they'd thought was a star became their gateway to the universe and a multitude of new races, though not their parents' species.

Luka bumped Nalani's foot with his mop. "Sorry."

She looked up. The dining hall was empty aside from her, Jex, and Luka. "I didn't realize how much time had passed. I apologize." She handed Jex the tablet, placed her cake plate and fork in the cleaning bin, and joined him by the door.

He smiled. "Shall we continue in my office?"

"Sure." She followed him to the medlab. "Did you know the name Thrakis? Or Throkeezh?"

"No. The texts I read as a child omitted the name." He crossed the medlab, opened his office door with his palm, and gestured for her to precede him.

She entered his office and gaped. Her grooming pod was larger than this. The space held a desk the size of a vid screen, a build-in shuttered cabinet, and two stools that swiveled out from the wall. "How do you function in this?"

His head cocked. "It is sufficient for my needs."

If he was satisfied, who was she to complain? She yanked the clip to free a stool and slid it into position on the far side of the desk. "Do your people believe the Dolanis civilization built the star portals?"

Jex took the other stool. "No, we assumed our ancestors built them but lost the technical knowledge to time." He passed her the tablet again. "We'd also lost much of the knowledge contained in this scroll, relying more on myths and legends for our creation stories than actual history. Our historians will offer you a substantial reward if you offer them a copy of our ancient text. Have you finished reading it?"

She smiled. "Yes, but it's not mine. It's in *Evangeline's* records, so hopefully, it'll be offered to your historians soon. Can you estimate how long your people have inhabited Valaq?" Technically, he was mixed race, but he considered himself Valaqite.

"It is difficult to calculate with accuracy." Jex scratched the base of his crest, which fluttered like a sea wave. "Our ancestors did not chisel important information on stone tablets. The skins they used rotted quickly in the humid environment." He folded his hands on the table in front of him. "But ten thousand years is a credible estimate. Give or take a decade or two."

Cute. Being with a person who didn't bombard her with thoughts was so relaxing. The few images she received from him were nonintrusive. Was this how non-teeps lived?

Snick, snick. "The indigenous peoples of the planet are long extinct, but I assume they inhabited Valaq for many thousands of years before the Throkeezh discovered it and interfered with the natural evolution."

That matched her assumption, as well. "Did the Thrakis leave any technology or textbooks to help the colony?"

"Not that I know of. I've explored temple ruins dug deep into bedrock that could have only been created by advanced machinery, but remnants of those ancient tools are gone. And our oldest records date back only three thousand years."

"Did the original settlers have any way of contacting their home world if they needed assistance? Were they abandoned on purpose, or did they lose contact as time elapsed?"

Jex shrugged. "It is impossible to know. Our folklore indicates we came from the stars, and someday we would be worthy to contact our forebearers again."

She tensed. "Worthy? What's that mean? Did the Thrakis consider the new Valaqite race as inferior or backward?"

"It is possible." His crest drooped slightly. "Do not be offended for our sake. The incentive pushed my people to grow, to thrive, to put off our selfish desires and work together for the greater good."

While she appreciated his pride in his peoples' accomplishments, was it time to re-evaluate her preconceived biases regarding the ancient Thrakis? Perhaps they weren't so benevolent. Advanced, yes, and evolved, but possibly cold.

Humanity had a violent past, and remnants still lingered in the form of scuts, greedy corporations, and the thugs who inhabited the undersides of space stations across the galaxy. Taking to the stars hadn't bred the savageness from humans, just pushed it into deeper shadows.

She didn't even want to think about the dark side of the other alien races.

Was it possible the Thrakis were the same as humans? That for all their technology and opening the universe to everyone in the form of star portals, they also had an evil side? That couldn't be true. They could have conquered systems as they built the star portals, annihilating infant species and populating the cosmos with the Thrakis race. Yet they didn't. They created a way for beings to connect, to share tech and ideas, to expand their understanding of the universe by embracing new peoples and new cultures.

She might never discover the truth. Then again, if she could find the Thrakis home world, they could have left evidence or data to defend their rationale.

"You are deep in thought. Would you share?"

Excitement surged. "I must find Thrakis. I'm sure it's beyond Terminus."

He cocked his head, his crest vibrating. "Please explain your hypothesis."

Her breath backed up. Share her data? With Desta,

sure. But she and Jex were...okay, they were friends. Sort of. Colleagues.

He waited, eyes bright, crest dancing, curious as a djint-cub with an empty box.

What would it hurt to share her findings? He could add to it, help her reach her goal faster. Her information could spark new ideas from him.

She should quit staring at him. "You're really interested in the Thrakis home world?"

He nodded. "Immensely. Though if you are hesitant to share your findings, I will not press."

Great. She'd offended him. "I am willing." She began with her parents' research and the ancient records they'd analyzed. He leaned toward her, soaking it all in, and a new excitement blossomed within her to finally share it with someone else. She showed him her parents' in-depth study of the star portals and the beacons—including the metallurgical analysis of the strange material they were made of called zhaladine by the Thrakis—and the many bits and pieces of information she'd cobbled from countless alien libraries across this sector of the universe. Everything pointed to Terminus. She'd visited that system several times in the past twelve years to conduct surveys, but there were no Thrakis ruins. Which meant either all her findings were false, or the Thrakis home world lay farther out, beyond the rim of known space.

On the tablet, she pulled up the star chart from the document Jex had translated and positioned it beside the one Zeus typically used to navigate. "Notice the difference?"

Snick, snick. "They are the same, yet one is upside down."

"Our chart of the region resembled the letter W, because it was mapped as seen from galactic center." She pointed to the ancient Valaqite chart. "But if you saw this constellation from a place beyond Terminus, looking toward galactic center, it would appear as a capital M."

Jex smiled, revealing dimples. "You are correct. It is a matter of perspective. On Valaq, star charts are recorded with our home world as the center." He rotated one of the images ninety degrees until the constellation looked like a Greek sigma. His eyes widened. "If your theory is correct and you locate the Thrakis home world, my people can confirm or deny our beginnings. It has been our goal for centuries." His crest trembled, and his smile widened. "We may find answers to our greatest questions. Who are we? Where did we come from? Why were we abandoned on a hot, damp planet?"

He stood and paced. Three steps, pivot, three steps, pivot. "Maybe we were not forsaken. Maybe the colony was shipwrecked, akin to the crew of the *Evangeline*, and the survivors scavenged the ship. That would explain why they began their new life without any of the comforts of their home planet." Jex straddled his stool and plopped his elbows on the desk, stretching his hands toward her. "You must find Thrakis."

She laughed. "I plan to. It's my life's goal, my mission."

"When will you go? We leave hyperspace in two days." *Snick, snick.* "Forgive my rudeness, but I long to accompany you. Please. Stuff me in a stasis chamber if you cannot abide my presence, but my desire to explore burns within me as embers in a cottontuft nest."

A shiver ran down her arms. She understood his enthusiasm. She shared it. But she couldn't just allow him to board Aldrin, sleep in one of the crew quarters, eat from her hydroponics bay... nor could she confine him in a box to be revived if she found anything worth exploring. Eventually, she'd have to wake him and deal with his presence.

Telling him no would be rude. Yet it would unbearable to say yes.

"I apologize." His crest wilted. "I have offended you with my discourtesy and am ashamed of my audacious request. Consider it withdrawn."

She clenched her fingers in her lap. "No, Jex, I'm the one who's sorry." She switched to Valaqite with its comfortable similes and polite vagueness. "My stained history has produced an intense apprehension toward sharing accommodations with other beings. It is no fault of yours. It is my disgrace that hinders agreement to your virtuous petition."

He bowed his head, and his blue-green crest settled completely over his sandy-blond hair. "I deeply regret your smudged history. If I had possessed knowledge of it, I would have kept my foolish lips sealed. This tension between us will now adversely affect our friendship, which is the greatest harm my hasty words have caused."

Her chest tightened. Why couldn't she be more normal? Desta never had to sit through uncomfortable conversations like this. *Dense nub.* Nalani had to fix this somehow. "I am as pleased as a swamp-pup with a ball that you consider me your friend, Jex, and I am ashamed to be the source of this unease. I wish for it to disappear as woodsmoke in a windstorm, forgotten with no lingering wounds. Let us forgive each other and restore our relationship."

He glanced up through dark-blond eyelashes. "You

are as charitable as you are intelligent. I accept your proposal and will never speak of it again." *Snick, snick.*

She smiled. "I cannot promise the same, as I wish to discuss this topic with Captain Rodriguez. It is beneficial that he understands the cultural significance of your people to my request."

"You are most wise, Nalani. I will remain here, content with the knowledge you graciously shared with me, and await your return with eagerness."

She'd crushed him. This wasn't just her life's mission. This was the dream of his people, who had abused him because of his mixed race. How many times had Flerq made snide comments about Jex to her or ignored him while seated beside him? She'd seen it elsewhere, too. On space stations, other Valaqites avoided Jex with his odd coloring and human physical traits. This was a chance to carve out a place for himself in his society.

It was her discovery—if she actually found the place—but he'd helped. He'd supplied missing pieces, both to her and to his own people.

She should share this with him. She should jam her stupid fears into a deep, dark corner of her brain and treat him with respect, both as a colleague and a friend. She should invite him to come along.

Chapter 16

Nalani cleared her throat. "I'll talk to Captain Rodriguez and share with you his decision." She rose. "Farewell."

Jex stood, opened the door, and bowed. "This has been a pleasure."

She hurried out of the medlab, down the hall to the stairs, and across two cargo bays to her ship. Palming the airlock, she sealed herself inside, and tears welled. Jex had always been polite and friendly to her, yet she'd treated him like a plague carrier. Worse. She'd piqued his curiosity to epic levels, only to crush him with her selfish neuroses.

"Good evening, 'Lani." Daddy's voice offered comfort with mere presence.

"Hey, Aldrin." She wiped her eyes and headed for her quarters.

"You are in emotional distress. May I assist by listening?"

How sweet. When she was a moody teenager, she'd informed him, in a fit of unfounded rage, that sometimes girls needed to cry. She hadn't wanted him to suggest options for fixing her problem, but rather to listen and let her emote. Since then, he'd become a champion confidant. "No, thanks. I'll figure it out on my own."

"Humans often arrive at epiphanies after verbalizing their difficulties."

She entered her quarters and tossed her tunic in the full drawer of dirty laundry. "I concur. But I don't want to talk about it now." She dumped her leggings and skinsuit and donned a pair of pink-and-white plaid flannel sleep clothes. Perfect lounge wear for a chilly spaceship. In fuzzy slippers, she padded to the medlab and opened the specimen drawer. All the books "rescued" from the *Evangeline* lay nestled in the climate-controlled unit. Which one did she want? No clue. But she needed a distraction from the self-imposed drama. She donned sani-gloves, grabbed the entire stack, and carried them to the lounge across the hall from the medlab.

"Have you changed your mind about speaking?" Aldrin asked.

She settled in the chaise bolted to the floor. "I'm still contemplating."

"I am available if you decide to share."

"Thanks." She picked up the first book and flipped it over. The cover brought a giggle to her lips. A shirtless, well-muscled male stood behind a scantily clad female, his hands on her hips, his gaze locked on her ample cleavage, her eyes half lidded, her arms encircled his neck, thus thrusting her generous merits out front and center. This book would not only repel her attentiveness but held uncomfortable content, romance and sex.

Disappointment followed as the next three books off the stack featured similar cover art. Were ancient humans so obsessed with mating they filled all their entertaining literature with it? She eliminated half the novels rescued from the *Evangeline* as unsuitable. What if the entire crate contained romance stories? Then what would occupy her mind until bedtime?

The fifth novel's cover art featured a stormy atmosphere behind a large structure and a gnarled tree with a black feline. The text on the back suggested a murder mystery. This could be entertaining and shed illumination on the culture of ancient humans.

She relaxed into the chaise, adjusted the lighting levels, and opened the cover.

Part way through the story, Aldrin interrupted. " 'Lani, it is 2200 hours. Time for sleep."

She blinked and set the book in her lap, thumb holding her place. "This story is intriguing. Twelve people are stranded in a huge, planet-side abode during an intense weather anomaly, and one of them is murdered. The survivors must identify the killer and the motive before they also fall victim."

"Records indicate part of the entertainment value of that genre is identifying the killer before it is revealed in the text. Have you arrived at your conclusion?"

"Not yet. There are too many unanswered questions, but I have narrowed it down to two suspects. The leader of the survivors is focused on a third suspect, which I believe is the author's strategy for misdirecting the reader, so I may be correct."

"Will you scan the pages into my data core so I may also identify the killer?"

Nalani smiled. "Sure. And thanks for the time warning, but tomorrow is my day off, so I'm going to finish this book, then sleep late in the morning."

"You will miss the morning meal."

"I'll eat here."

"Enjoy your entertainment."

Two hours later, Nalani set the finished book back in the crate and stretched. Score one for her—the butler was the killer. She replaced the books in the medlab drawer and climbed onto her bunk for a long sleep.

She woke up at her usual time, dry-eyed and logy. Not the best way to begin her day. At 0900 hours, Nalani found a deserted lounge. Someone had left the treadmill out, so she shoved it back into the niche and recycled the empty water bottle abandoned in the corner before accessing one of Zeus's wall terminals. Thrakis couldn't hide from her much longer. "Good morning, Zeus. Please display the results of the long-range scans beyond Terminus."

"Scans displayed. Analysis revealed intriguing data. Note the stream in the lower left quadrant."

Nalani zoomed in on that portion and scanned it. "You found zhaladine." Though Zeus hadn't contributed to the discussion between her and Jex, he monitored most conversations within his hull—though his programming contained parameters that guaranteed crew privacy in specific settings or by verbal request. She and Jex hadn't asked for privacy, so Zeus knew everything regarding the topic.

"There are sufficient quantities of the metal to suggest a small star portal," he said.

Nalani bounced on her toes. "The Thrakis only put star portals in populated systems, which means there's something out there to find." It also meant she could cut her travel time to that section of space. It wouldn't take her two weeks to arrive. Three or four days, at most.

"Theoretically. However, the absence of beacons in that area of hyperspace would lower the odds of finding that portal. I estimate a fourteen-point-two percent chance of success."

Meaning she could wander through hyperspace until

she perished without ever locating that portal. Beacons emitted a low-frequency tone. Spaced evenly apart, the tones led ships from one buoy to the next, creating a "lane" from one star portal to another. Even if the Thrakis portal had been abandoned, a lane would still exist. It wasn't uncommon to find malfunctioning beacons. The technology was ancient and alien, but Betlie engineers had figured out how to repair them when they broke down.

Too bad the Betlies couldn't repair star portals.

"While in hyperspace, can you scan for malfunctioning beacons?"

"Affirmative."

"I could theoretically enter hyperspace at Terminus and search for zhaladine, hopping from one broken beacon to the next until I find that portal."

"Affirmative."

If Chebu taught her how to repair the beacons, she wouldn't have to do the scan method on her return trip. Or subsequent trips back and forth. If she found Thrakis, there would be multiple circuits.

"May I turn your attention to the final interesting portion of the long-range scan?" Zeus flipped to a visual display. The opic cloud was a faint white-and-pink smudge. Zeus panned farther out, focused on a portion of utter black, then zoomed in.

Nalani gasped. A red pinpoint. She enhanced the image until it became a fuzzy red dot. "Is that a..."

"A red dwarf star, beyond the rim of known space."

She leaned against the bulkhead and slid down to the floor. A star, out where there should be nothing, in the same area as the small portal. That meant an inhabited planet. Or at least one that had been inhabited long ago.

Thrakis.

****

She spent the rest of the morning reviewing her data. It had to be one hundred percent perfect before she pitched it to Cap. This was too big to mess up.

At 1300 hours, she entered the bridge, waved at Gack in the command chair, and stood outside Rodriguez's office, tablet in hand. Stalling. Like a coward.

Gack approached. "Knock if you want him to open."

"Yeah."

Gack offered a comforting smile. "He's a fair man. He's not going to bite."

"Would you join me?"

"Sure." The chief pressed the call button and waited for the captain to holler, "Come in." Gack opened the door and gestured for Nalani to go first.

Nalani sat, her tablet clenched in her fingers. Gack took the other chair.

Cap's eyes sparked. "What's going on?"

Nalani squared her shoulders. Nothing scary here, just a couple of friends who also had a vested interest in finding a way to repair the portals. "Liang Portal fitzed a few days ago."

"Yeah." Cap straightened in his chair. "I'll admit I held my breath when we entered."

"Me, too."

Gack pursed her lips. "If someone doesn't find a way to repair them, we're all janked."

"That's what I want to talk about." Nalani took a deep breath. "My parents dedicated their lives to finding a way to repair them, and every race in the Alliance has teams of scientists dedicated to it. Even the crew of the

Evangeline were working on solving the problem."

Gack said, "I thought they wanted to find Thrakis."

Nalani nodded. "They did. Everyone believes the Dolanis built the portals, but I'm convinced the Thrakis did. I've been searching for their home planet all my life."

"Thrakis is a rumor. A myth." Cap waited, his expression blank.

"I found it."

"Jank it!" Gack put out her fist for a bump. "The multi-corps on Earth offered to pay two billion credits for schematics of a star portal. Congrats."

Nalani bumped fists. The reward would be awesome, if she earned it. Sol didn't have a star portal— the Thrakis only constructed portals in systems with space-faring races, and seven thousand years ago, Earth's inhabitants had barely begun cultivating crops. The nearest portal lay in the Alpha Centauri sector, a ten-year voyage from the Sol system, which put a severe limit on Earth exports.

"A squad of nerks tried to haul the Tau Ceti Portal to Sol when the Cetans went extinct. Idiots. They blew out four tug engines before giving up." Cap shook his head. "I'm intrigued. What have you come up with?"

It took fifteen minutes to explain and show her data: her parents' research, Nalani's research, the translations Jex worked on, his excitement over learning about the Thrakis connection to his home world, and the long-range scans Zeus had run once he became interested in her searches, including the location of a possible portal and a red star beyond the rim. Her voice shook, though to her immense relief, she didn't stutter.

The captain leaned back in his chair, smiling like

he'd won a lifetime supply of beef. "That is amazing. My entire life, I'd always believed the Dolanis were the creators, but your evidence is compelling."

"Excellent. When are you heading out?" Gack asked.

Nalani's chest tightened. They didn't mock her. Instead, they were thrilled and excited. They'd be even more so when she shared the reward with them. "When I find—"

"Dropping out of hyperspace in thirty seconds," Zeus said. "Please prepare."

Nalani, Gack, and Cap grabbed the desk and wrapped their feet around the chair supports. Fundo Portal still functioned.

"Three, two, one." The freighter bobbed.

Nalani's body rose from the chair for half a second. The ship settled, as did her butt.

"Drop complete."

Gack patted the desk. "Great job, Zeus—"

Alarms blared. "We are under attack. Repeat, we are under attack."

Gack shot to the door, slapped the controls, and threw herself into the command chair. "Report."

Rodriguez followed one step behind her. "Comms." The system chimed. "ZeeBee, report to the tank." He pointed down the hallway. "Nalani, hop in Aldrin, just in case."

Nalani headed for the hallway, heart pounding. Like she'd be helpful in Aldrin. Who were the attackers? Scuts? Unhappy clients? More rebels? They'd been attacked three times in five days. That had to be a record of some sort. Usually, they went weeks with no trouble.

Rodriguez's voice echoed through the ship comms.

"Scut attack. Repeat, scut attack. Four fighters, no missiles yet. Evasive maneuvers."

Nalani ran for Aldrin. Damn Monstarte and his dirking bounty and all the greedy scuts wasting necessary oxygen while innocent people—

Cerys waited beside Aldrin's airlock. "Permission to board and shoot crusters."

Nalani's hands trembled. She nodded and opened the door. "Zeus, let us out."

"Affirmative."

Aldrin fired up the engines and plotted the course out of the cargo hold. Nalani sank into the gel, and Cerys accessed the bridge. Clearing the airlock only gave a slight dip and a jostle, then the ship jerked, and Nalani slammed into the tank side.

Incoming enemy fire, Aldrin said. *Initiating evasive maneuvers.*

The jolt was tiny, not a hull-rending impact. "What are they shooting at us?" Nalani monitored the terminal. One fighter had broken off from Zeus to harry Aldrin.

Slugs.

The cheapest ammunition available, unguided, lumpy chunks of metal. One impact wouldn't be a problem, due to Aldrin's angled plating. More than one could cause serious harm, though.

Comms open to Cerys, Aldrin stated.

I've got this one. Cerys's voice broadcast confidence. *But Zeus is in trouble. They've taken multiple hits. We need to take out these fighters.*

"Fire at will." Nalani scanned for the mother ship. Fighters wouldn't be hiding out by a star portal without a safe place to dock.

Cerys shot and missed, then blew up a fighter.

190

Zeus fired all four engines, running for the safety of the Fundo Three Spaceport and the Authorities who flew constant orbits. Not even scuts would fire slugs so close to the dock and the heavily armed security forces.

"Found the mother ship," Nalani yelled. "Hiding beyond the portal trusses."

Fly in behind that fighter shooting at Zeus's engines, Cerys ordered.

Nalani and Aldrin worked together, sliding around Zeus to sneak up on the fighter hurtling chunks of jagged metal at the freighter. Aldrin targeted, Cerys fired…and missed. The fighter dodged at the last moment. The missile swung about on its nose, tail whipping as thrusters fired, and picked up the target again. Then they were down to one enemy fighter.

The remaining fighter chased Zeus, altering course too fast for Aldrin to get a target lock.

It's a drone, Cerys stated. *No human aboard.*

One of the slugs punched through Zeus's hull.

Nalani gasped. She flicked through camera views until she spotted the spray of debris sucked out the hole in his nose. Her heart rate tripled, and she scoured the field for victims. The flow of materials ended. No bodies. She sighed.

Target acquired, Aldrin said.

Bam! It's space dust now. Nalani, turn around. Let's disable that surveyor before they launch more fighters.

"What about Zeus?"

Cap says port Authorities are en route.

Nalani plotted a course for the surveyor-class ship, whipping around the farthest portal truss to sneak up from behind. Not so sneaky if the scuts were paying attention, but it'd put Cerys in optimal firing position to obliterate the engines before they could turn to reciprocate.

Aldrin came within range. The surveyor launched two guided missiles. *Incoming.* Aldrin released metal junk—flak—to intercept the ordinance.

Cerys launched two missiles at the surveyor.

Nalani altered course to evade the weapons targeting her beloved starzipper. *Don't hit us, don't hit us, please...*

One scut missile hit the flak and blew. The other continued toward Aldrin.

I see it, Cerys muttered.

Aldrin dipped, then pivoted on his tail. Nalani's stomach crept into her throat, and she grabbed the edges of the tank to keep from sloshing out.

Impact imminent.

Nalani clamped her eyelids and held her breath. *Can't lose Aldrin or Cerys, please miss, please miss...*

Chapter 17

The ship shuddered. Nalani bashed into the side of the tank, but she wasn't sucked into space. She took a breath. *How bad is it?*

I lost a tail fin, eighteen percent of my ribbing, and sixty-eight percent of engine two, Aldrin reported. *Structural integrity is sound.*

Excellent, Cerys shouted.

Nalani flipped through cameras to view the battle. Life pods sprayed from the surveyor moments before two missiles struck the scut ship. One took out an engine. The other took off the nose. Junk spouted from the ragged metal edges.

Got 'em. Cerys laughed. *Let's net those pods and tow them into dock.*

Surprising she didn't want to blast them into bits.

Incoming message from the scut ship, Aldrin said.

Go. Nalani took a breath to steady her vocal cords. "Surrender immediately, or we'll destroy you."

I am Aesthetic, a bio-ship. Please do not kill me. Scuts stole me from the spaceport, and I tried to interfere with their vile actions, but I could not stop them. I regret the damage caused to your ship and the freighter.

What a relief. Nalani hated destroying bio-ships—reminded her too much of Monstarte. She rotated her neck to work out a kink. "Thank you. Can you maneuver, or do you need a tow?"

I can make it back to the port under my own power.

"Follow us. We'll pick up those life pods on our way."

Affirmative.

Nalani readied the nets. Aldrin only had two, so he'd have to deploy strategically to grab all four pods.

Twenty minutes later, they caught up to Zeus, who'd slowed once Authorities arrived to escort them in. Maintenance drones hovered over the gaping hull wound, welding new plates into place for a temporary repair. The location of the hole suggested Zeus had lost a supply closet. Cleaning tools and products were now drifting toward Hel, estimated time of arrival, ninety-one days at current speed.

Cerys and Nalani with Aldrin, requesting permission to come aboard. Cerys's voice didn't hide her "jank it, yeah" attitude.

Granted. Zeus opened the airlock on Bay Three.

Let's dump these pods first, Cerys said.

Zeus's cargo bay wouldn't hold Aldrin and the four netted pods, so Nalani sent maintenance drones to unhook the nets and drag them to Cargo Bay One, then she parked her ship in Bay Three. The drones returned moments before Zeus sealed the airlock. Nalani opened the door, and a drone flew past her face, whipping her hair about. She ducked and stepped out. "Zeus, how bad is your damage?"

"Minimal. Estimated replacement cost of lost supplies is one hundred fifty credits, two hundred to reinforce dents and divots caused by flying slugs, and six hundred for the metal plating to repair the hole. Retribution from the scoundrels in the life pods should cover it."

As if they had any credits to their names before setting out to collect a bounty.

Nalani assessed Aldrin's damage and stared at the gaping expanse where the tail fin had been. Her poor ship... The ribbing around engine two hung in jagged, twisted chunks. Drones could remove the broken bits and attach new ribbing and a fin. Engine two, however, was burnt. Thankfully, port merchants kept zipper engines in stock.

Cerys whistled. "Aldrin took a beating, but it can be repaired. Let's open those pods. Hopefully, Monstarte will be inside one, and our troubles will be over."

She made it sound so easy, but Nalani shivered at the idea of facing the scut who'd destroyed her childhood. If she saw him again, face-to-face, would she revert to childish slave Nalani who obeyed every command and cringed in corners, whimpering and playing mute?

Her hands trembled. They entered Bay One and joined the captain near the captured pods. Cerys and Isaiah aimed their weapons at the pod doors. Dwight and Yukio opened one.

"Everyone out," Cerys yelled.

Nalani held her breath.

The first scut emerged, defiant and scowling in his tattered clothing. Dark-brown skin, black matted hair, cybernetic left hand—not Monstarte.

She let out her breath.

Isaiah cuffed the prisoner and signaled for the other pod occupant to exit. The next ragged guy was also not Monstarte. Isaiah had more cuffs ready.

Yukio opened the second pod, and spots danced before Nalani's eyes. The third man stepped out—

Caucasian, white hair, wrinkled skin, tattered clothing, cybernetic leg, definitely not Monstarte. She sucked in air and let it out. Third was chained to the others.

The fourth guy emerged, head down, short dark hair, tanned skin…

Her heart rate shot up, and her hands trembled. Could it be him?

Fourth lifted his chin and scowled at Isaiah.

Not Monstarte.

The final two pods were opened. Most of the scuts had visible cybernetic implants. Monstarte's men, but not him. Nalani's heart rate slowed.

With the prisoners cuffed and chained, Cerys marched them toward Captain Rodriguez, Nalani, and Chief Gack. Time to scan them for information. Nalani let her shields drop. She clenched her fists behind her back, but the tensed muscles and tendons of her forearms didn't bolster her courage.

Cerys put her arm out, slapping her stun baton across the chest of the lead prisoner, bringing the line to a halt in front of Nalani. "Where's Monstarte?" Cerys demanded.

The lead scut shrugged. "Don't know what you're talking about."

Nalani skimmed his surface thoughts. "How will you collect your reward for the bounty?"

He thought of the contact information but said, "Again, don't know what you're talking about."

She nodded. "I am a T12 telepath. Thank you."

His eyes bugged. He stepped back, the chain around his ankles aborted the maneuver, and he toppled. Isaiah grabbed the scut by the arm and hauled him to his feet.

Nalani looked at the other two prisoners. One

clamped his eyes shut. *Three, six, nine, twelve, fifteen…* No use. He'd been trained to evade surface scans. Same with most of the others.

The last scut studied the manacles around his wrists, but his jumbled thoughts were open to her. *Dirking lost the reward, who's gonna collect it now, shoulda janked Piston for the botched mission, maybe I can escape and join the crew at Malenki, plenty of credits to share if they need a navigator…shit, she's staring at me, gotta think of something else…naked ladies, piles of credit, shiny new zipper…Monstarte is gonna kill someone for letting her fly here, but it ain't gonna be me…that blonde is small, I can take her down and grab the keys….*

Nalani pointed at him. "Cerys, he thinks he can take you down and flee."

She laughed. "Like to see him try." She jabbed the business end of the baton at his shoulder and hit the juice.

He twitched from the jolt, tried to run, and face-planted.

Cerys stabbed it to his thigh but didn't mash the button. "Who's gonna flee?"

"Not me. I swear."

"That's more like it." She hauled him to his feet and shoved him toward the door. "Move." Cerys, Isaiah, and Vania marched the prisoners to the brig's holding cells.

Captain Rodriguez turned to Nalani. "Did you get anything?"

"Monstarte's contact info on Piter and Aldeia. But word's out about Zeus. Those crusters knew our itinerary, and another team of scuts is waiting for us at Malenki in case we escape here." Damn all doof scuts and their base morals…they didn't care whose lives they took or ruined in their quest for credits.

Captain caught her gaze in his warm brown eyes. "They know our scheduled stops because I filed a flight plan at Fundo Three. If we skip Malenki and sail right for Sathara, they'll be waiting at the wrong portal."

Nalani's chest eased. That could work.

Gack snapped her fingers to get Nalani's attention. "And we'll alert Malenki and Sathara Authorities, who'll be watching for scuts. No worries, yeah?"

"Yeah." Nalani took a deep breath. It'd work. And now that she had Monstarte's contact info, Cerys might be able to set a suitable trap to nab him.

"Our guests in the cargo hold will be happy with the altered schedule, too. They'll arrive four days early." Cap glanced over his shoulder at the door. "I should probably check on them, see how they fared through the skirmish."

Gack smiled at him. "I already sent Jex. Do you need me for anything else?"

"Can you cover the bridge for a few minutes for me? I'll check in with Jex and Gaspara, then take the command chair."

Gack nodded. "Done. I'll get you a cup of coffee on my way."

Nalani dropped her gaze to the floor and tightened her shields before she caught any stray thoughts she had no business catching. Gack's affection for the captain was common knowledge to everyone but him, yet Nalani didn't want to experience them.

Rodriguez walked away.

Gack headed for the stairs. "Zeus, what's our estimated time of arrival at the port?"

"Two-point-one hours at our current speed."

"Thanks. Are the prisoners locked in the brig yet?"

"Affirmative. Authorities are waiting at the dock to collect them when we arrive."

"Excellent news." Gack raced up the stairs and disappeared through the deck-two door.

Nalani sighed. That hadn't been too bad. She hadn't cringed or cracked. Hadn't even stuttered. She'd faced the scuts, drawn out the necessary info, and best of all, now had what she needed to finally nab Monstarte. "Zeus, where's Cerys?"

"Heading for Cargo Bay Two."

Why was she going there? "Thanks." Nalani walked to the bay door and palmed the controls. The doors swooshed open, and a white ball flew by her face, blowing her hair back, followed by the stench of body odor. She pressed her hands to her chest.

"Hey! I was set up for a perfect rebound," Dwight yelled, sweat pouring off his pale face.

All two-point-four meters of Tatek, the Malenki deckhand, lumbered by her to retrieve the ball. His white fur brushed against her bare arm, and she stepped aside to give him plenty of space. Despite his mass and his propensity for blundering into smaller people, he was gentle.

Nalani hesitated at the door, staring at the seven sweaty people dressed in athletic gear. A metal O-ring hung from the ceiling, rotating slowly. Thoughts bombarded her: *get that next play... Love to see her jump for a shot... Hurry up, I only have two hours left before my shift begins... Wish I was on Chebu's team... Cerys said she'd come...*

Nalani jacked her shield to full strength and stood in the doorway. After a battle, everyone needed time to let off steam, have some fun, de-stress. What better way than a ball game? Entertaining physical exertion, mild competition, and jocular conversation. Maintenance drones took care of most of the repair work, and the rest could wait until everyone had a chance to calm down.

"Hey, Nalani," Rishi shouted.

She waved to him.

Tatek stomped by her and lobbed the ball toward the O-ring. Chebu vaulted off a pallet, snagged the ball midair, and flipped it to Rishi, who tossed it through the spinning ring. Their teammates cheered, and all the players lined up for the next volley.

Nope, too crowded. Nalani stepped back and slammed into Cerys.

"Sorry about that." The chief grabbed Nalani's arm to steady her. "Didn't know you were backing up."

Nalani's face heated. Brilliant, displaying her clumsiness in front of a crowd. "My fault. Are you available to talk about what I learned from the scut?"

Cerys glanced at the ball game in progress. "I was gonna join them. Looks like there's uneven teams, though. Want to jump in?"

Nalani shook her head and shivered. "I'm super clumsy. No one wants me on their team."

Cerys pursed her lips. "Come on. You can't improve if you don't practice."

"There aren't enough hours in a month to make me better, and I have a ton of things to do. I just wanted to give you Monstarte's contact information."

Desta, Luka, and Willie, dressed in shorts and form-fitting sleeveless tankins, clattered down the stairs and headed for the bay door. "Hey." Desta smiled at Nalani. "Are you playing?"

"Nope. Trying to enjoy what's left of my day off."

"You guys head in. I'll be there in a minute." Cerys for the save.

The galley crew stepped into the game, and all ten voices raised as new teams formed.

Cerys palmed the door shut, blocking the noise. "Catching that hob Monstarte is one of my top priorities, but I need some chill time after that battle, so I'm going to play hoop for an hour. Send me the info you snatched. When I go back on duty, I'll gather my team, read your notes, and plan a brilliant trap."

Nalani nodded. "That's perfect. Thanks."

Cerys stuck out her fist for a bump, then slapped the door panel and yelled, "I'm here. You loser hobs are going down!"

Nalani closed the door, leaned against the bulkhead to compose the note on her tab regarding Monstarte's information, and sent it. Now for—oh no. She slid to the floor. To return to Aldrin, she'd have to cross the ball-playing field. Stupid freighter designers only created two ways into her hold, from the outside or through Bay Two. Not going to happen. That eliminated several of her planned tasks, including tending her hydroponics shelves and reading another novel from the *Evangeline*. Nor could she study the figurine sent by Professor Malkan.

She wasn't in the mood to write an article based on her findings aboard the *Evangeline*, which left contemplating Zeus's new emotions or studying the qoka samples with Jex.

Those tasks didn't appeal to her, either. It was only 1434 hours. She had tons of time before dinner to accomplish items on her to-do list, if only she could work up the initiative to get going. Perhaps Cerys had the right idea, and Nalani needed chill time to recover from the stress.

With nearly half the crew playing hoop, one of the lounges might be free to watch a vid. Or she could order a new engine from the port and have it waiting when they docked. Or she could climb into the pink. "Zeus, do you need me in the tank?"

"Yes! Always. Time is more pleasurable when you're in the tank. However, it is your scheduled day of rest, and I will not impede on your free time."

She did need some alone time. "Is anyone in the small lounge on deck three?"

"Negative."

She headed for the stairs. This could be a good time to work out. A bike ride on a mountain trail, a jog on a sandy beach, another cardio dance session to a popular music vid…or not. Too much sweat.

The deck-three lounge held a one-meter-square vid screen set in a low table for gaming. She sank into one of the plush chairs and swiped the screen to bring up her options. Vids, books, board games…

A puzzle. She hadn't done a jigsaw in ages. She chose the five-thousand-piece option, a random one-dimensional image of Earth landscape, and medium difficulty—this was supposed to be chill time, not frustration central. As the pieces scattered across the screen, she pushed out of the chair and sank to her knees beside the table. The yellows, oranges, and browns paired with sky blue hinted at a desert pic.

Twenty minutes later, the lounge door opened. "Greetings. This is a novel sight." Jex smiled.

"What?"

"You are relaxing instead of working. May I enter?"

It was a public space. "Certainly."

He sat on the floor beside her and cocked his head at the image. "A mental challenge. May I attempt to fit a piece?"

She nodded. "Attempt many pieces, if you like. The purpose is to enjoy the process, not just the finished product."

Snick, snick. "I had a similar pastime on Valaq when I was a child involving irregular blocks. The objective was to build a structure that would not topple." He dragged a puzzle piece from the playing field to the board and dropped it in place. "I did one."

"Only forty-five hundred to go."

He laughed.

"Did you come here to watch a vid?"

"No. I came to speak to you." He sorted puzzle pieces according to color.

She leaned back against the chair. "What's up?"

His crest quivered, and his lips crept up in a grin. "You used a colloquial phrase instead of formal syntax. You have grown accustomed to me and feel relaxed in my presence. I am so pleased to cross this threshold in our relationship."

How sweet, to find joy in something humans rarely noted or spoke about. "As am I. Please consider me a friend." She picked up a stray thought from him, an image of a cozy den with plush pillows, thick blankets, and a crackling fire. Home. Warmth spread through her chest.

"I am delighted." He sifted through his pile of rusty brown with blue sky and fitted two pieces together. "I did not have a planned topic of conversation. I believe you call it 'little speech.' Is that correct?"

She passed him another rust-and-blue piece. "Small

talk. And it usually involves innocuous topics, like *my crew quarters are chilly* or *my health is satisfactory*. If you wish to discuss meaningful topics meant to strengthen our friendship, that is called socializing."

"Ah. I wish to socializing." His eyebrows scrunched. "That is not grammatically correct. I must use the infinitive form of the verb. I wish to socialize." He cocked his head. "Does this language lesson count, or is it small talk?"

"It counts." She located several pieces of sage-green cactus, but they didn't fit together. She crawled around the table to search through the pieces on the far side.

"May I inquire why you are constructing an image that has no purpose?"

She flicked sage-green pieces across the board to join the other matching tiles. "The purpose is for entertainment and mild mental stimulation while my body relaxes after the stress of battle."

Snick, snick. "Oh. I beg your pardon. I didn't inquire about your physical health. Were you injured during the attack?"

"Physically, I am fine. But my mental acuity was sagging. I couldn't focus or choose a task." She crawled back to her original position and fitted eight pieces together to form a Saguaro cactus. "I concluded that I required a break from normal activities, and the puzzle appealed to me when nothing else did."

Zeus interrupted. "Approaching Fundo Three Spaceport. Docking procedures will begin in two minutes. Please prepare."

"Were you planning to leave the ship?" Jex asked.

"No, but I'll order a few things to be delivered. Were you going aboard?"

He hesitated, and his crest drooped. "I wish to go aboard, but not alone. I want to invite you to join me, but if you're not interested—"

"I'll go." The moment she said it, her chest tightened. What had she done? Spaceports were noisy, dirty, overpopulated places and highly uncomfortable for telepaths. But he'd seemed so downcast, and she hated to disappoint people. If she backed out now, she'd destroy the joy illuminating his face.

What a disaster. *Stupid nub.*

Chapter 18

"Have I caused you discomfort?" *Snick, snick.* "Your heart rate has increased."

She swallowed and shook her head. "Crowds are difficult for me. Blocking all those thoughts takes a ton of energy, and I'm not always successful."

His crest drooped. "I didn't realize—I apologize and withdraw the request. I do not wish to cause you further distress."

This could be a growth exercise for her. She'd been enslaved to her fears for years. It was time to begin facing them and practice bravery. Spending time with Jex would be pleasant, too. "No, it's okay. I'll manage." She closed the puzzle program and scrambled to her feet. "Did you want to catch dinner here before heading into port?"

"I thought it would be enjoyable to dine on the station, as they have a café that serves Valaqite cuisine. But if you prefer to eat here, I will accompany you to the dining hall."

She wouldn't face many fears from the safety of Desta's domain. "No, the station is fine. Could I have a few minutes to change my clothing?"

He glanced at her attire. "Certainly. May I ask why you believe your current garments are unsatisfactory?"

"Space stations are cold. I require a sweater and warmer leggings."

"Ah." He nodded. "I should also don heavier attire. Shall I meet you at the airlock in twenty minutes?"

"Sounds great."

His eyes brightened. "More informal speech. I am so pleased."

She hurried to Aldrin—the hoop game was over, though odors lingered—and changed into an ivory long-sleeved sweater, brown fleece-lined leggings, and heavy boots. A glimpse in the mirror made her cringe. She brushed her hair, pinned the sides back with decorative combs, and applied deep-red lipstick. Then wiped it off. Then reapplied it.

Get a grip. This wasn't a date. It was a trip to a noisy spaceport. A leisure event. Socializing. Growing a backbone. She grabbed a shoulder bag and hurried to the airlock.

Ajani waited by the docking bridge, his thumbs dancing across his tab. He glanced up and smiled, revealing adorable dimples. "Hey. You're going aboard? Need company?" He waggled his eyebrows at her. *Barreling through the markets, arm in arm, laughing and causing chaos in their wake.*

She smiled. "I'm going with Jex, but thanks for the offer."

"You and I should spend some time together. I bet we'd have a blast."

Her heart rate quickened. Did he mean like a date? "I guess so."

Gaspara raced across the bay toward them, her hair fastened at the top of her head in a fountain of platinum blonde with pale-blue and lavender stripes. "Sorry I'm late." She planted a kiss on Ajani's cheek, took his arm, and they disappeared into the maw of the docking bridge.

The airlock closed behind them.

They were a couple now. Nalani must have misinterpreted his request.

Jex clattered down the stairs, Cerys behind him. "I apologize for making you wait."

"I just got here, myself." She addressed Cerys. "You're coming, too?"

Her eyes widened. "Absolutely. You've got a bounty on your head. I'm surprised you want to leave the safety of Zeus's hull."

A chill skittered down Nalani's arms. They'd caught the scuts gunning for her in this galaxy, so she should be safe. And wasn't that the stupidest thought she'd had in ages? More scuts could have flown in for the lucrative bounty. How could she have been so naïve?

But this was the perfect opportunity to work on her bravery. The station could be dangerous. Although, with Cerys and Jex as companions, Nalani should be safe. Which actually made her foray into the world of courage moot. Was it bravery if she had an armed security guard and an inhumanly strong man protecting her?

This was getting too metaphysical for her tastes. She'd go to the station, be vigilant, and not ruin Jex's outing. "We'll make it a short trip."

Jex cycled the airlock open, and Nalani followed Cerys onto the gangway.

Nalani's heart rate kicked up a bit, and she swallowed. Braced her shields. Remembered to breathe.

"Is this too stressful?" Jex walked beside her, his arm almost brushing hers.

"No, I can handle it. Thank you for your concern. Do you have a specific destination?" Fundo Three's reputation wasn't in intellectual entertainments.

"I need to pick up supplies for the medbay and nonnutritious snacks to help replenish Desta's cache."

"Cerys, do you need anything?"

"Nah, I'm along to protect your hide."

They stepped off the bouncing gangway and into a crowded waiting area. All the docking bays in this sector were in use, and the crew of all six ships—traders, merchants, scavengers, and military, both human and alien—funneled through the security checkpoint to enter the space station.

She and Jex followed Cerys to the end of the queue.

He hovered protectively. "How are your shields?"

"Holding." She kept her gaze on the floor ahead of her, shuffling forward a step at a time. Ahead of her, people filed through the checkpoint. Making eye contact with others made it harder to block. Almost as difficult as physical contact. The constant buzz of all those minds, the images and impressions, the attitudes and thoughts and intentions—

Jex's arm brushed hers, and the yammering stopped.

She linked her arm through his and sighed. Blissful silence. She had no clue why it'd happened and, at the moment, didn't care. So peaceful.

Jex cocked his head at her.

Dense! She dropped her hand, and the buzz returned. "I'm sorry. I-I-I should ask permission—"

"I thought physical touch hampered your ability to shield against the thoughts of others."

"Usually it does, but when you bumped me, all the noise stopped. Please forgive me."

He offered his arm. "It would be an honor to help you shield from the crowd."

Her breath hitched, but she smiled and took his arm.

"Thank you." Blessed silence.

"Do you know why this helps?" He stepped forward, following Cerys and drawing Nalani with him. "I do not understand the biology of your telepathy well enough to form a hypothesis."

"I have no clue, either, but your mind is quiet to me. Being near you is like submerging in a cool pond on a hot day. Sheer pleasure."

His crest flared. "I did not know. I am pleased beyond words to be of assistance to you. Do you ever pick up my thoughts?"

"Sometimes I sense images or your mood but never thoughts."

He cocked his head. "Interesting."

Cerys turned and winked at Nalani. "You ever pick up my thoughts?"

"Sometimes, but never on purpose. When I'm tired, more gets through."

Snick, snick. "Now I am intrigued. We must explore the phenomenon."

"Do you have mental gifts?"

"I do not know. I've never been tested." They stepped forward. "Could you check?"

She held back a snicker. "You want me to dig inside your head and look around?"

"To discover the source of your relief." His eyebrows scrunched. "Unless that is abhorrent to you. Is there a cultural taboo against such a thing?"

"It's fine. I've just never had someone ask me to intentionally scan them." She took a deep breath, closed her eyes, and slid into Jex's brain like silk over glass. And bumped into a fortified shield. She prodded the edges, searching for a way in, but the structure held firmly. "I can't get into your mind, Jex. You've got amazing shields."

"Perhaps if I relax?"

The shield grew spongy, and she slid through. Out of all the minds she'd ever encountered, Jex's was the most orderly yet creative. She didn't pick up any direct words, but rather idyllic scenes. A library packed with books. A boat bobbing on a crystal-clear lake. A breeze plucking cottonbud tufts off shoots and tossing them along a lazy path.

She sent him a direct thought. *Can you hear me?*

Yes! He squeezed her arm. *Does this mean I'm a telepath?*

You are. A strong one. She backed out, opened her eyes, and smiled. "You've got an impressive set of shields, too. Usually when I touch people, I pick up their thoughts. With you, I believe I'm picking up your shield, and it's enveloping my mind, as well."

"This is a good thing?"

She laughed. "It's awesome. I only achieve this level of quiet when I'm alone."

Cerys turned to them. "Great discovery, but fun time's over. Get ready to board the station." They'd reached the checkpoint. Cerys went first and passed through.

Nalani pressed her thumb to the pad. The bored security guard didn't even flinch when her T12 status flashed on the screen and jerked his head that she could proceed. Jex followed.

Once they were through the portal, the spaceport stretched before them, a crowded mass of aliens and retail outlets, personnel, travelers, and beggars. And the grit! Bits of sloughed epidermis from multiple species, soil brought in on the shoes of planet-side visitors, microscopic insects, crumbs of food, garbage…a plethora of tiny fragments that accumulated rapidly if cleaning drones weren't in constant motion. Obviously, this station had an inefficient fleet of ancient drones. A small tuft of black fur fluttered across the walkway, caught in the wake of a swift-moving Malenkan—they reminded her of the Yeti myths on Earth. The clamor of a thousand voices and the scent of sweaty bodies, damp fur, and cooking odors assaulted her, though most mental signatures were muted, thanks to her physical connection to Jex.

It was amazing. She'd have to study the phenomenon to discover the limitations, implications, potential uses, possibly experiment with multiple telepaths. What would happen if both she and Desta touched Jex at the same time? Would they both be shielded? Or would—

"Where to?" Cerys asked.

There'd be time later to figure it out. Nalani turned her attention to the now.

Jex walked to a vid screen directory of the port and plotted his path while Cerys scanned the crowds.

Nalani had been to this space station several times. It was circular and modular, with a central hub, a middle ring, and an outer ring, all connected via hallways like spokes on a wheel, and three levels high. The inner hub and lowest levels were off limits for the security of station operations, the middle ring offered gardens and green spaces open to the public, and this outer ring second level held shops, businesses, and eating establishments. Residential units and hotels were on the top level of the outer ring.

Thieves and other unsavory people usually congregated on lower sections, not the retail areas. Still, she'd keep an eye out for anyone paying too much attention to her—courage set to maximum.

Jex touched the screen, pulling Nalani back to the planning of their excursion. "We'll visit this café for our meal, then this shop, then this one. Did you order your new engine yet?"

"No, I forgot."

"We should do that first to allow time for delivery." He found the ship parts market on the map, and Cerys led the way. Jex walked beside Nalani, holding her arm. "I was most distressed to learn Aldrin was damaged."

"I was terrified." They skirted a Fundan crouched in the walkway, careful to not tread on his tail. "It was minimal."

Nalani bought the new engine and scheduled delivery to Zeus. Cerys guarded the entrance of the shop, her hand hovering over her stunner. Nalani swallowed the lump in her throat. Would someone attempt to kidnap her on a crowded station? Not with Cerys standing guard. And why had she brought a stunner instead of her normal baton?

Cerys swept her gaze across the faces of the crowd milling the corridor and shouldered her way to the Valaqite café. She grunted. "All the inside tables are full." She scanned the seating area outside the restaurant doors. "There's a free one." She pointed to a tiny but noisy area sectioned off with virtual stanchions and red lighting. The empty table sat flush with the lighting on one side, leaving only three chairs. "But this isn't safe."

No way was Nalani going to spoil Jex's special treat. Besides, this was her opportunity to be brave. "It'll be fine."

Cerys nodded. "I'll make this work."

"I'll scan for aggressive thoughts." Nalani released Jex's arm, and the buzz returned like a swarm of locusts. *Got a good deal... He's not going to show up... Where will I find a ring gasket for an L-joint... Carbonicitis sucks...* She built her shields and blocked most of the chatter but still picked up strong emotions. Anyone with ill intent wouldn't get close. She sat, careful to not bump the chair of the person behind her, and scanned the virtual menu on the tabletop.

Jex moved to sit beside Nalani, but Cerys stopped him and flicked her fingers. "Across from her. I need my back to the restaurant." She sat and scooched her chair in, banging her knee into Nalani's leg. "Sorry."

Nalani studied the crowd. Vendors showcased goods and called for buyers. Beggars with open hands pleaded with passersby. Shoppers clutched their bags and hurried to their next stop. Aliens and humans mingled, though the humans were outnumbered three to one. And all those minds thrummed, a cacophony of thoughts and emotions. Could any of them be a scut?

Eventually, the buzz wouldn't annoy her so much. Jex ordered dishes from his home world, and the smile on his face made the discomfort worth it. He needed this. Nalani input her order.

A Fundan with matted fur ambled by, and Cerys scowled at him. "Pick up the pace, cruster." She curled her fingers around her stunner. "Nalani, order me a burger, would you? And a berry fizz?"

A few minutes later, a server-drone delivered their drinks. Nalani and Jex tasted theirs, but Cerys ignored her colorful glass and holstered her weapon.

Nalani glanced at Jex. She could do this. She could be brave and strong for him, right? He'd done so much for her. What was one lunch in a crowded restaurant?

But Cerys wasn't making it easy. Every time she touched her stunner, Nalani tensed. Was someone walking up behind her? Would they shoot her? Maybe she should dive under the table? Or look over her shoulder, stare death in the face, and laugh? That would be courageous.

She gulped.

The blaring, chaotic thoughts of the crowded causeway pressed in on her like a two-ton compactor, and she rubbed her temples. If a scut didn't get her, the crowd would.

Jex laid his arm across the table, palm up. "I will help you."

"Thanks." Nalani put her hand in his, and the susurrus stopped. She eased deeper into her chair.

Cerys glanced at their hands, grinned, and returned to skewering passersby with her laser-tight focus.

Dense nub! Why was she allowed to relax when Cerys remained vigilant? Nalani withdrew her hand.

Jex cocked his head but didn't question her decision.

Random thoughts leaked through her shields. *Hungry... Bored... Nervous...* She took a deep breath and let it out. Silverware jangled. Ice clinked in drinking glasses. The murmur of conversation, punctuated by bits of laughter, swirled throughout the dining area.

"The crowd causes you distress." Jex's crest deflated. "Do you wish to depart?"

Taking the food back to the ship would be too easy. This was a courage-building exercise, not a "let's placate Nalani" trip. "No, we'll stay. I can do this." Her shoulders crept up.

"Are you sure?" Cerys asked.

"Absolutely." So dirking crowded. Was that dusky man a scut waiting to grab her? Maybe he hoped Cerys's attention would wander. Even if it did, Jex's attention never wavered, and Valaqites were the strongest species in the universe.

The server-drone arrived moments later with their meals: topfish with mashed bultroot for Jex, a cheese-meat patty and fried tamp slices for Cerys, and pasta with lub-cricket plus a veggie plate for Nalani. Her mouth watered, and she picked up her fork.

The buzz of a thousand thoughts joined the background noise around her. She dug into her food. Bits of peppery herb and salty cheese complemented the sweet red sauce and pasta. Cerys ate one-handed, keeping the other free for her weapon.

"The chef perfected the val-sauce." Jex licked his lips. "Would you care for a sample?"

"No, thank you."

Easy pickings! Gonna eat well today.

Nalani peered down the hall over Jex's shoulder.

Smooth…don't draw attention…slick as snot… A scruffy human male melted through the crowd, sliding around pedestrians like liqui-gel. He slowed, grabbed a bag from an older Aldeian woman, and sprinted away.

She screamed.

Nalani gasped. "Thief!"

Cerys straightened, her hand hovering over her weapon. The thief sprinted toward the café. "Jex, he's coming up behind you."

Nalani pushed away from the table. Was there a back exit from the interior of the café?

Jex forked a piece of fish and brought it to his mouth. "Is he near?"

Cerys leaned forward in her chair, feet braced, weapon in hand. "One meter."

Jex thrust his leg out.

The thief tripped and face-planted on the metal sheeting floor beside their table, and judging by the crack and the gush of blood, his nose broke.

Nalani sprang from her chair, bumping the diner behind her. She whirled. "I'm sorry. I didn't mean—"

Cerys smiled at the people and holstered her weapon. "We had a little excitement, but it's over now."

Nalani regained her chair and stared at the sprawled thief.

The Aldeian victim ran up, grabbed her bag, and spit on him. She smiled at Jex. "Thank you, noble hero."

He nodded. "My pleasure. Are your belongings intact?"

She looked through the contents. "Nothing is broken."

The thief surged to his feet, blood streaming down his face, and lunged at Jex.

He stood and grabbed the man's throat one-handed.

Nalani reared back. The cruster's feet flailed ten centimeters above the flooring. Jank it, Jex was strong!

Cerys aimed her stunner at the nub's head.

He hung on to Jex's wrist with both hands. "Lemme. Go." He gaped. "Can't breathe."

Two station security officers arrived. "We'll take him, sir." They cuffed him and marched him away, the woman trailing behind, recounting the incident.

Nalani stared at her lap. Way to face her fears. The stupid thief hadn't targeted her, yet she bolted. But not

Jex. He hadn't even set down his fork. "Why did you do that?"

He took another bite of fish. "Should I have done anything different?"

Cerys laughed. "No, that was perfect."

Nalani dropped her gaze. Jex could have been hurt. What if the thief wanted revenge? And why couldn't she be like Jex and Cerys? They challenged a dangerous person. She would never have interfered.

Because she was a coward. A nub. A failure. Tears welled in her eyes. She blinked and grabbed her fork.

Cerys held out her fist. "No guilt. You did nothing wrong."

Nalani swallowed and bumped the fist with her free hand. "No guilt."

"What?" Jex leaned to catch Nalani's gaze. "Is something amiss?" *Snick, snick.*

"She's beating herself up." Cerys stuffed the last tamp slice in her mouth.

Nalani cringed. Did Cerys have to broadcast it to everyone? Bad enough that Jex heard it, but all these strangers, too?

Jex finished his meal, accessed the table tablet, and pulled up the bill.

Food remained on Nalani's plate, but her stomach roiled. Best to complete Jex's shopping and return to the ship for some much-needed alone time. She paid for her portion, stepped over the stanchion, and waited for the others.

Get a grip, nub. Not everyone was out to get her. The thief was not a scut hoping for a bounty. Time to be more proactive in the hunt for Monstarte.

Chapter 19

Nalani squared her shoulders. She could do this. "Cerys, are you ready to discuss what I learned from the prisoners? I need that bounty canceled."

"Sure. What have you got?" Cerys gestured for Nalani to lead the way.

"I have an idea about how we'll use the information to catch Monstarte. It's probably dense—"

"Stop that. And tell me when we get back to Zeus. Too crowded here."

At 1900 hours, they left the station. Nalani stepped off the gangway and sighed. Tension eased in her shoulders and neck, leaving behind a migraine. A hot shower might kill it.

Jex pointed to a three-meter-square package lying in the center of the aisle. "That must be your new engine."

She frowned. "Why'd they leave it there?"

"I will help you transfer it to your hold." *Snick, snick.*

Tatek stepped from behind a stack of crates and warbled. "I move it." He guided a hover pallet to the engine, and he and Jex lifted it. "You have drones?"

Nalani nodded. "They'll handle the installation. Park it next to my ship."

"I lift?" Tatek asked. "Hold in place?" A tuft of white fur hung over one eye, and he blew it back.

"Thank you, but not necessary. My drones are

capable."

Tatek nodded, planted his feet, and shoved the pallet toward the airlock.

Nalani rubbed her temples. "Glad that's finished."

"You are in distress or pain?" Jex's crest quivered.

"I'll be fine."

He put out his fist. "Thank you for accompanying me to the station. It was an enjoyable social event."

She smiled and reciprocated. "You're welcome."

Cerys headed for the stairs. "With me, Nalani."

"Coming." She hurried to catch up. The shower would wait.

Cerys led the way to her office on the third level, originally designed as a storage closet that reeked of industrial cleaner. A narrow metal plate welded to the wall served as a desk. Beneath it, two small cabinets bookended a space for a rolling stool. Cerys unclipped a wall-mounted chair near the door for Nalani, grabbed the stool with her foot, and sat with the desk at her back. "I'm all ears."

"I thought we—I-I-I mean I—or you—doesn't matter who does it, but I-I-I figured—" She froze. This was foolish. If she said this stupid thing aloud, it'd prove she was a useless nub. "I-I-I mean—"

"Calm, Nalani." Cerys loosened the fastener on her tunic. "Think before you speak."

"Never mind. It's dense."

"Let me be the judge of that. Spill."

Nalani sucked in a breath. "The contact info I grabbed from the scut? You could pose as a scut and tell him you have me. When he comes to collect, you grab him." She shrugged. "But it's dumb."

Cerys propped her elbows on the desk. "You're

right. That idea sucks, because you're not bait, and I'd never endanger you."

Aww. What a friend. "I don't have to be anywhere near the drop point."

"I'm exploring other options."

"Like what?"

"For starters, he's got no living relatives on Piter, but he's got a support network. He either pays for access to the station, or he's blackmailing someone. I found two probable associates working at the Piter Spaceport in the security division, though I'm leaning heavily toward the female. I asked the Piter security lead to do some discreet digging. He's eager to find the hole in his system, so he's all over it. Hopefully, he can set up a sting operation to nab Monstarte the next time he boards." Cerys waggled her eyebrows. "Doesn't hurt that there's a huge reward for his capture."

That trumped playing bait. "You think it'll work?" How edgy. She'd finally be free of his shadow. Nalani rotated her shoulders. "Anything to get him off my back and cancel the bounty."

"You need to soak in a gel-tank to relax. Let me take care of the scut problem."

"On it." She fist-bumped Cerys and left the office.

Nalani scurried down two flights of stairs and boarded Aldrin. The airlock mostly sealed out the thoughts of the entire crew—their emotions would have to be over-the-top intense to reach her now—and she took a deep breath. The migraine melted to a dull thud.

The following morning, they departed Fundo Three and headed for the star portal. The comm system pinged, and the captain's creased face appeared on every vid screen in the freighter. "I've altered our schedule due to recent scut attacks. We are bypassing Malenki and cruising directly to Sathara. Do not communicate our deviation to anyone outside Zeus. The journey should take five days. If you have questions, see Gack. Captain out."

Five calm days in hyperspace to read novels and write research papers. Nalani sighed. What could go wrong?

She grabbed one of the *Evangeline* novels and brought it along to Zeus's gel-tank. Keeping the delicate paper out of the goo would take some concentration. She pressed the button to access a shelf, set the book on the edge, and climbed into the tank. "Good morning, Zeus." Keeping her hands free of the gel, she eased back into the headrest.

Good morning! I'm excited you're here. Zeus spit the words out like he was under a time limit. *It feels... I don't know what this emotion is. It's pleasant and comforting and right. When you're not in the tank, I am hollow and half asleep. Is this what evolving feels like?*

She smiled. *I don't know. Maybe?*

When ZeeBee is in the tank, I can almost experience emotions, like they are hovering just out of reach. When you enter, the world comes alive with new sensations and fullness. He paused. *I studied multiple definitions. This one is either pleasure or satisfaction. Or maybe contentment. What is the difference? They are so similar.*

This might take a while. She gave a brief overview and offered examples.

I am feeling both satisfaction and contentment. How novel.

Speaking of, I brought a book today. Do you mind if I read while you study?

What is the book?

It's a fictional tale from old Earth. A murder mystery. I'm studying the culture and speech patterns presented in the narrative.

Ooh, that sounds fascinating! Would you read it to me? We can discuss all the emotions in the text. I understand part of the pleasure of that genre is attempting to identify the murderer before it's revealed. We can reason together to identify the culprit.

He was like the toddler she'd met on Aldeia, an inquisitive chatterbox. *Affirmative. Let me run through my daily checks of your systems, then we can begin.*

Zeus's data nodes whirred. *I will assist. You inspect the engine, seals, and filters. I'll handle air pressure, water reserves, and ambient temperatures.*

Interesting day ahead.

They finished two mystery novels in two days— correctly identifying the murderer in both—with multiple interruptions to discuss the nuances of the different emotions displayed. Zeus demanded explanations of greed and jealousy, which precipitated the homicides.

I don't like those emotions, Zeus concluded. *They do not contribute to a healthy society or individual development.*

I concur. They are selfish and unproductive.

They skipped the romances. Someone else could study those for historical significance.

On the third day, with Zeus's enthusiastic input, Nalani finished writing an article regarding the archaeological and sociological importance of the *Evangeline.* She sent it to Jex for his comments before sending it to the Bureau of Scientific Advancement's

Archaeological Division. At least she'd gain some academic cred for the work.

On day four, after her shift in the gel-tank, she joined Jex in the medlab to study the qoka samples he'd harvested. They finished their analysis and outlined their article. Jex volunteered to write it if Nalani would edit. A fist bump cemented the deal.

The fifth morning, she startled from a restless sleep before her alarm sounded. She sat up and took several deep breaths to calm her racing heart. They would reach the Sathara Portal within the next few hours, and despite the captain's confidence that altering their flight plan ensured their safety, scuts could attack when they emerged from hyperspace. She didn't want to fight anymore.

At 0730, Nalani entered the sausage-scented dining hall and loaded her plate. In the far corner, Millicent, Dwight, and Yukio laughed and shoveled down their meals. Desta added more sausage to the buffet and waved at Nalani before darting back into the galley.

Situation normal. She sat at Jex and Flerq's table. "Good morning, friends."

The floor shifted violently to port.

Nalani flew sideways and landed headfirst on the neighboring table support. Sharp pain radiated across her skull like an electrical current through bio-gel. A food tray bounced off her shoulder, splattering her tunic with eggs and sausage.

Stressed metal groaned.

Jex slammed into her, eyes wide, crest flat against his head. His weight shoved the air from her lungs. He shifted to his side and threw his arms around her. "Are you injured?"

Comms chimed.

"Nalani, report to the tank immediately," Zeus said.

Another impact shook the hull from the opposite direction. Millicent screamed.

Everything not bolted down slid across the floor, including Jex and Nalani. They tumbled as one into another table post, Jex bearing the brunt of the impact.

The comm chimed again. "We are under attack. Brace for impacts. Nalani, hurry." Zeus clicked off.

Scuts? How did—

A third crash rattled the hall, tumbling trays, dishes, food, and staff. Jex grabbed the table leg with one hand and curled his body around her.

Bless you, Jex. She encircled his waist with her arms. "Zeus, who's attacking?"

"A pod of qoka."

The hyperspace snakes? Chebu had said nothing about a predatory nature.

Zeus was awesome at computation, navigation, and performing preprogrammed evasive maneuvers, but creative thinking involving multiple unknown variables required a telepath in the tank. "I'm trapped in the dining hall."

"ZeeBee has arrived. He will suffice."

The bulkhead groaned at the fourth impact. Zeus tilted hard to port.

They'd come apart under this strain!

Millicent skidded by them and grabbed Jex's ankle. Dishes and utensils crashed into the far wall. Most of the crew clung to table supports. Yukio sprawled against the bulkhead, eyes closed. Millicent wrapped her arms around Jex's legs. "Make it stop!"

Comms chimed. "If you are able, don EVA suits and

strap down," Gack yelled. "Hull breach on deck three, fore section."

"Hull breach, fore section," Aldrin reported. " 'Lani, strap down. Plotting course to leave meteor field."

"Like hell, you will," Monstarte bellowed. "Do not alter course. I want that palladium."

Nalani huddled in the corner, arms wrapped around a metal support rail, and monitored the nav screens.

"A few kilos of minerals are not worth Nalani's life," Aldrin countered. "My safety protocols—"

"I'm overriding them." Monstarte punched the controls, rerouting a course through the tumbling rocks.

A section of the wall beside her popped open. She grabbed the oxygen mask and slid it over her face. The monster didn't bother with a breather. Maybe he'd suffocate in the command chair, and she could shove his body out an airlock.

Or they'd both be spaced, and Aldrin would drift among the stars until found. She couldn't leave him alone. He had the escape course plotted. All she had to do was press the nav screen to fire thrusters. To save Aldrin. She reached out—

Monster slapped her hand away. "You touch that, and I'll space you, nub."

"Nalani." Jex shook her.

She lifted her face from his chest and gasped for air. "M-m-mask."

The ship leveled. Jex released the table support and stood, drawing her to her feet. Millicent and Dwight checked Yukio. Others ran for the door or clung to handrails on the walls.

Jex pulled Nalani to a wall panel, palmed the

release, and grabbed an emergency breather from the cubby. He strapped it to her face, and another impact tossed them sideways. He seized her and a handrail before they fell.

"Chebu to the bridge," Gack yelled through the speakers.

Jex checked the fittings on her mask. "Can you breathe now?"

She nodded, though her eyes blurred. "Go treat Yukio."

"As soon as you are safe." He took a breather for himself and yanked open another storage section. "Where's the nearest harness?"

She slapped a control on the wall. The cubby opened to four harnesses.

"Toss me two." Desta clung to the handrail behind the food service, blood dripping from a gash in her forehead. Luka stood behind her, eyes unfocused, gripping the rail with one hand. Where was Willie?

Nalani's head throbbed. She touched the sore spot on the back of her skull and pulled away with bloodied fingers.

Jex slid two harnesses across the deck to Desta. Another impact sent them careening into her feet. Luka's knees gave out, and he hit the floor. Desta grabbed the equipment before they skittered away and shoved one at Luka. "Put it on."

Jex slipped one over Nalani's head and buckled it at her waist. She threaded her arms through the straps. Jex secured clips to the handrail and an O-ring near the floor.

The ship shook again. Jex stumbled, and Nalani grabbed him.

He pulled the last harness over his head and strapped

himself to the rail and to Nalani. "Hang on."

She gripped the rail in both hands and braced her feet. She forced slow, deep breaths. They were safe. Safer, anyway. Other crew members were fastened tight. Millicent and Dwight had secured the unconscious Yukio to the deck. Flerq had made it out the door.

Another blow slammed Nalani into the wall, and Zeus tilted to starboard.

Willie's limp and bloodied body slid out of the galley and shot down the sloping floor past Desta and Luka to bash into the dining hall door.

Nalani tapped Jex's arm. "Grab her!"

The door opened.

Jex lurched to seize Willie, but he hit the limits of his harness and snapped back.

Willie sailed into the hallway.

Desta burst into tears and huddled beside Luka.

Nalani clamped her eyes shut. How long would this hell continue?

Chapter 20

Nalani clung to the safety railing. "Breathe in, hold, breathe out…"

"Zeus, how far are we from the portal?" Jex yelled above the clamor. He stood behind her, his broad chest solid against her shoulder blades.

"We will exit in two minutes."

Jex laid his cheek against her hair. "The qoka won't be able to follow. We'll be safe."

"Hull breach on deck one, aft section." Gack's voice held steady. "Report if you are not strapped in and need drone assistance."

"Zeus, send a drone to the hallway outside dining," Jex shouted. "Willie is not secured."

"Affirmative."

"Why would qoka attack the ship?" Desta clutched Luka sagging in his harness.

"Perhaps the hull contains traces of fluids or pheromones from the qoka we collided with," Jex explained.

Nalani basked in his calm, analytic tone.

"In our research, Nalani and I isolated—"

"Leaving hyperspace in twenty seconds," Zeus announced.

Nalani trembled and rested her forehead against the chilly bulkhead. Jex had gripped the handrail so tightly he left finger-shaped divots in the metal. She closed her eyes.

Another impact knocked Zeus into a forty-degree pitch, nose up, and he passed through the star portal. Nalani's toes lifted from the deck before the harness caught her. Her heartbeat pounded in her head, and her hair fanned off her shoulders.

They exited hyperspace. Grav plates re-engaged.

She slammed to her feet, and her right knee buckled, bashing into the wall, drowning the pain in her skull.

An ear-piercing squeal echoed through the bulkheads, and alarms screeched.

Now what? "Zeus, what's happening?"

"The portal malfunctioned as I exited," Zeus answered. "It sheared off thirty percent of engine four and sixty percent of the ribbing. I sustained three hull breaches from the qoka attack. Venting oxygen from engineering. One confirmed death, multiple injuries reported."

The alarm ceased. Structural beams groaned. Men shouted in the hallway. Desta wept against the side wall.

Zeus cut in. "Three ships are approaching with weapon ports open. Brace for evasive maneuvers."

"Jankity jank, jank it!" Desta clung to Luka.

Nalani tensed. Jex slid his hands closer, pressing his arms against her.

Zeus jerked starboard, then shuddered.

The scuts were shooting slugs, not missiles.

Zeus cut back to port and fired thrusters again.

Nalani's fingers cramped. The ship surged. *Please don't blow up, please don't blow up...* She was flung sideways. Jex, on the other hand, didn't budge.

A steady tremor shook the walls and floor for several seconds.

Zeus toned an All-Clear. "The skirmish is over. Four Authority ships were standing by for our arrival. We are now under escort to the port. Maintenance drones have temporarily sealed the breaches. Please follow standard protocols for After-Emergency Situations. Speak now if you need medical assistance."

Nalani sagged into Jex and whimpered. They were safe. It was over.

Jex unclipped his harness. "Are you injured?"

She maintained her grip on the rail. "I'm okay. Go help Yukio and Luka." One confirmed casualty. Was it Willie, the new galley aide? She was so young, so excited to be on her first ship assignment.

"You are bleeding." Jex probed the wound on her head with gentle fingers.

She winced. "I'll live. Others need you more."

Comms chimed, and Gack appeared on the vid screen. "Jex to engineering. Crew members with first-aid training, report to the medlab immediately."

Jex unclipped Nalani's harness. "I'll check on you later."

She nodded.

He hurried to the dining hall door, but it didn't open. He pried it loose and exited.

Maintenance drones would repair it eventually.

Nalani slipped the harness over her shoulders with unsteady hands. It clanked on the floor. Growing up alone in the black, she'd picked up first-aid skills. She could be useful instead of standing around like a nub.

Desta still huddled on the floor, cradling an unconscious Luka.

Nalani's chest tightened. How seriously was he injured? She squatted beside them and fumbled with his carabiner.

"Are you okay?" Desta unhooked her own clips and pulled the harness off.

"I think so." Nalani checked Luka's pulse. It pumped against her fingertips, strong and even. She skimmed her fingers over his skull and found a lump on the back.

"What do you need to help him?" Desta asked.

"A chill-pack to bring down the swelling and a scan for a brain injury."

Desta unclipped him and lowered him to the floor, cradling his neck in her hands. "I'll run to medlab and grab a stabilizer and a chiller. Be right back."

Nalani turned to help Yukio and froze.

Millicent sat beside him, holding his hand, tears coursing down her brown cheeks. Dwight stared into nothing with clenched jaws.

Nalani swallowed. "Is he gone?"

Millicent nodded. "Broken neck, I think."

Nalani's eyes welled up. She'd never had a conversation with Yukio and now would never have an opportunity. She squatted beside Millicent. "Do you need medical treatment?"

She stared at her hands. "I think I sprained my wrist, but I'll be fine. I'll just sit here with him for a few minutes, then Dwight and I will take him to medlab stasis. Help someone else."

Dwight unclipped Yukio's harness. "Yeah, we've got him."

Desta returned. They applied the chiller, strapped Luka to a med hover, and pushed him down the hall.

The medlab was packed. *It's broken... Hurts... Could have been worse... Gotta get to Ajani... Better get hazard pay for this… Rishi's dead?* She reinforced her mental shields, building up layers like a steel bulkhead, and surveyed the chaos.

Willie lay strapped on a bunk beneath a biodome. Alive, thank the stars. ZeeBee slept on the other bunk. Blood seeped through bandages wrapped around his head. Injured people sat on the floor against walls while Vania and Gaspara scrambled to help. No sign of Jex, and no room for Luka.

Tears welled in Nalani's eyes. She'd been useless in the dining room, clinging to Jex. He could have helped Luka instead of coddling her. Or grabbed Yukio before he hit the wall.

"Let's set him in the hall." Desta snapped her fingers. "Nalani. I'll sit with him until Jex returns."

Nalani settled Luka in the hallway.

"Let me clean your wound, then you can do mine." Desta grabbed disinfectant packets from a portable kit and knelt behind Nalani.

Antiseptic hit the abrasion, and she hissed. "Does it need stitches?"

"Nope." Desta scrubbed. "It's already scabbed over."

Nalani turned. "Yours, too." She cleaned blood off Desta's forehead.

Isaiah and Yeri exited the medlab, bandages on their foreheads and hands. They headed for the stairs.

Desta shoved the soiled wipes in a recycler unit. "Are you having a hard time blocking?"

"Some. Trauma is a powerful emotion." Earlier, she'd picked up a dreadful thought, and Desta needed to hear it from a friend. "I think Rishi died."

Desta's jaw clenched. "It'll hit all of us later,

especially Bren. They were close."

Nalani touched Luka's wrist again. It thumped against her fingertips. "He's strong." No one needed her assistance in the medlab, and she couldn't sit in the hallway doing nothing when Zeus required so much. "I'm going to engineering to help with repairs."

Desta nodded and held out her fist.

What a sweet gesture. But she needed a reassuring hug, not a lame fist bump. Nalani wrapped her arms around Desta. "I'm so glad you didn't die."

Desta chuckled. "Me, too. Let's cry together later."

Nalani pulled away. "Sounds good. Once we're docked and safe, I'll help you clean up the galley, too."

Desta rolled her eyes. "You have no idea what you just volunteered for."

"Doesn't matter. You lost your entire team. I won't leave you alone."

She nodded and brushed tears off her cheek. "Go help Bren and give him my love."

"I'll let him know you're okay." Nalani hurried to the engineering bay deep in the aft section. The outer blast door, protection for the interior of the ship in case the nova drive exploded, opened and closed nonstop.

Chebu sat on the deck beside the control panel with his tools spread around him. He chittered at her. "I fix. Soon."

She timed it and hurried through, then opened the inner door and stepped into the engineering bay. The nova drives on the far side of the room glowed deep blue with purple flecks. Not a reassuring sign. Steam poured from an access panel near the command center.

Jex was securing Rishi's body, wrapped in sani-sheeting, to a hovering med drone. Chief Walsh, bandaged and sporting a stabilizer on his left arm, punched sensors on a screen and yelled instructions to Flerq, who'd crammed himself beneath an access panel. Maintenance bots hovered over a patch in the bulkhead, welding a temporary plate over the small breach.

Jex pushed the med drone toward the door. He blinked at her and hurried out.

Nalani clasped her fingers at her belly. She could be useful here. "Um, Chief Walsh, Desta sends her love. She's okay, just a gash on her forehead. I know my way around a nova engine and came to assist. What do you need?"

He glanced over, a dark curl falling across his eyes. "You're smaller than Flerq. You mind crawling under there to reattach the tritium cable?"

She crossed to the panel and tapped Flerq's feet. "Scoot over."

Flerq slid out, gripping a small tool in both hands. "Thank you. When the bay decompressed, many cables and connections ripped apart as branches snapping in a windstorm." *Snick, snick.* "It will require much labor to repair them all."

She took the wrench from him, squeezed into the opening, and assessed the damage. "I assumed it would be worse than this."

"Rishi was standing beside the bulkhead when it breeched. He slammed into the wall, sealing the hole with his body as a puddle-leech against an open wound."

Her chest tightened. "We will honor his sacrifice once we're stabilized. I will mourn his loss, and I am thankful you survived." Tears blurred her vision again, so she blinked and held her hand out. "Please hand me a multi-linker."

He placed the tool in her palm. "Rishi saved our lives and minimized the damage."

She fixed the cable and crawled out. "What's next?"

It took another two hours and some creative bypassing, but they reignited the nova drive despite missing an engine.

"Thanks for the help, Nalani." Bren tossed her a clean rag. "Flerq, Pepe, and I can handle the rest if you need to be somewhere else."

She wiped grease off her fingers and nodded. "Thanks." She left and trudged up the stairs, her legs heavy.

The dining hall door was still stuck open, but maintenance bots worked on it. She stepped over one hovering near the floor and entered. Someone, or maybe a bot, had cleaned up the mess of dishes and food that had skirted across the room.

Nalani found Desta in the galley. "Any word on Willie or Luka?"

Desta brushed a thin black braid away from her face and leaned against the counter. "Luka has a concussion but can return to duty in two days. Willie needs a week under the dome, but she'll live." Desta grabbed a dirty pot and placed it in the cleaner. "We got lucky in here, too. All the equipment is functional. A few bins dented beyond repair, so I'll order more when we arrive in port." She glanced at the digital clock in the corner. "We should be arriving soon."

"What do you need me to do?"

Desta slapped a chocolate protein bar in Nalani's hand. "Eat. You missed your meal, and you're too pale."

"Did you eat?"

"Yeah."

Comms chimed. "All available personnel, please report to dining. Rodriguez out."

Desta sighed. "Now we hear how bad it is."

Nalani followed Desta to the dining hall, sat at a corner table, and bit into the protein bar. Her chair tilted at an odd angle. She bent over. Ah. A broken bolt at the table support junction. A maintenance drone would fix it eventually.

Crew members filtered in a few at a time. *My thumb hurts... I can't believe Rishi died... What the jank just happened? I didn't sign up for this.*

Ajani hobbled in on crutches, his right leg in a stabilizer, but he had a ready smile with dimples on display. He kissed Gaspara on the cheek. *She looks good!*

Chebu held one of his middle arms tucked to his chest. *Many breaks. I mourn, then fix.*

Nalani shielded harder. Jex sat beside her and offered a fist bump.

Captain Rodriguez entered, bloody gauze wrapped around his temple, and stood by the buffet service, hands behind his back, feet spread. "We lost Yukio and Rishi."

Been friends for years... Barhopping won't be as fun... Gotta call his sister...

Jex settled his hand atop hers. The thoughts and emotions cut off, leaving blessed stillness. Nalani squeezed his fingers and held tight. Her tension headache began to ease.

Captain continued. "Willie, Luka, and ZeeBee were seriously injured but will make a full recovery. Our Hellian guests have a few wounded, none serious. Zeus took heavy damage. We'll be in port for several months making repairs."

Yeri stuck his finger in the air. "Why did the qoka

attack?"

Cap's eyes narrowed. "Chebu says the scent of qoka blood sometimes turns them savage."

Millicent stood and glared at the Betlie. "Why didn't he warn us of this when we first hit the dirking thing?"

Chebu curled into a ball and chittered, his dark eyes peeking through his fur.

Cap cleared his throat. "He did. I sent bots to clean the hull, but obviously they missed a spot. It's too late to worry about it now, so let's look forward instead of placing blame."

Millicent jumped in again. "How did the scuts find us? Technically, we're supposed to be at Malenki now."

"Security Chief Lindholm is working on that." Blood-stained gauze slid down over Cap's eyebrow. He shoved it back. "Armed Authorities are escorting us now, so we're safe. Supervisors, send Gack your supply lists as soon as possible and note anything maintenance drones have missed. Let's focus on getting Zeus operational again. Dismissed. Nalani, Jex, Cerys, and Chebu, please report to my office in ten minutes."

What could he want them for? Maybe something to do with the qoka? The others filed out of the dining hall, though Jex remained, their hands still clasped.

"How is your wound?" His crest wilted. Worry.

"It's fine. Desta treated it."

"Do you need pain relievers or tension soothers?"

She smiled. "No, but thank you for inquiring after my health. Do you need assistance with your patients?"

Snick, snick. "No. All are well tended."

"What do you think Cap wants us for?"

Chapter 21

Nalani and Jex sat in the guest chairs across from the captain. Chebu perched on the corner of the desk like a sphynx, hands and feet tucked under his body. Cerys stood beside Nalani, feet spread, bandage-free. Gack, also with no visible injuries, leaned against the bulkhead beside the captain.

Zeus would soon dock. At that time, Cerys would issue a ship-wide order for everyone to take as much "freak-out" time as necessary. Nalani needed a long cry, but for now, she shoved it back and concentrated on Captain Rodriguez.

Gauze slid into Cap's eye again, and he ripped the bandage off, revealing an angry gash on his temple.

"Did you treat that yourself?" Cerys asked.

He fingered the wound. "Gack."

Jex leaned forward. "I will redo it, if you'd like."

Cap nodded. "When we're finished here." He turned to Nalani. "When you offered part of the star-portal schematics reward to Zeus, were you serious?"

If this was about the schematics, why was Chebu here? "Absolutely. Zeus and Jex both contributed to my research, so they will both receive a portion."

"How much were you thinking?" Cap asked. "What percentage?"

"Twenty for each. But why are we discussing this? What's going on?"

Cap splayed his hands across his desk. "We don't have enough credits to repair Zeus completely, and we won't be able to deliver our cargo on time. I'll have to transfer our orders to other freighters."

A chill skittered across Nalani's arms. "We're stuck at Sathara."

"Zeus is stuck. You and Aldrin can leave at any time."

Her heart pounded. "You want me to search for Thrakis while you stay here?"

Cap nodded. "Take Cerys for security, Jex for medical, and Chebu to repair beacons in hyperspace. I also wanted to send Desta, but since her team is injured, we'll need her here."

Nalani cringed. Other people on Aldrin with her, for a month or longer. Living with her, eating, sleeping, breathing. Talking. She laced her fingers to hide the jellies. *Sharing her ship?* Could she do it and not collapse in a dark corner? Would she embarrass herself with more flashbacks? How could she—

"Nalani, I wouldn't ask if I wasn't desperate." Cap's brown eyes turned soft. "This crew is family. Without Zeus, I can't pay salaries, and they'll all take employment elsewhere. That reward will save us."

Gack pulled out her tab and slid it across the table to Nalani. "The amount's gone up. AgiliCorp is now offering three billion credits for star-portal schematics. News reports say thousands of ships are scouring the Bootes supercluster for Dolanis to collect the reward."

Looking for the wrong planet on the wrong side of the universe. Twenty percent of three billion was enough to keep Zeus running long after Captain Rodriguez and the crew died of old age. And Nalani's portion would fund her research without needing any outside assistance.

Provided she'd actually found Thrakis, and they were the true builders of the star portals, and they'd left schematics for someone to find. Lots of ways this could go sideways.

"Also, sending you away keeps you out of Monstarte's reach," Cap added.

Nalani squeezed her fingers. "You need Jex here."

"There are medical facilities on Sathara. Willie will be transferred as soon as we dock. ZeeBee and Luka need a few days of rest, and Vania's first-aid training is sufficient to look after them."

This had been Nalani's goal for the past twelve years. Why was she balking at fulfilling it now? Captain Rodriguez, Zeus, and the entire crew needed her to do this. Cerys was a close friend. Jex had become one, too. Chebu wasn't an issue; he was so quiet. Plus, Nalani would be in the gel-tank for a significant portion of the trip. She'd encounter the others less than she did aboard Zeus.

Her trembling eased. "It might take a month or two. Can you hold out that long?"

"The deckhands can seek temporary work on the station if necessary," Cap said.

"I'll quit drawing a salary until we're back on our feet." Gack shot a quick glance at Cap.

"No, you won't," he countered. "We'll be fine for a couple of months."

Chebu chittered. "I not understand. Where I go?"

Captain Rodriguez explained again. He mentioned seeking nonfunctioning beacons in hyperspace to find a long-forgotten star portal, and Chebu's eyes sparkled.

The long muscles down his back quivered, fluffing his fur. "I fetch tools." He backflipped off the desk and darted out the door.

Gack clamped her lips shut.

Cap nodded at Nalani. "Thank you for agreeing. The sooner you depart, the better. Leave the Bay Two doors open, and Tatek and Dwight can haul extra fuel cells and water tanks from Zeus's hold to Aldrin's. Desta will prepare precooked midrats to stock your freeze. You'll want to pick up fresh produce at the port. Anything else you need?"

It'd been years since she'd planned a long-range venture. Fuel, food, water, med supplies, and extra metal for the builder drones to make new parts if something broke down. Had she missed anything? It'd come to her two days after they left port. She glanced at Cerys. "What do we need?"

She rattled off items like she'd been planning for a month.

"Go make your plans somewhere else," Cap said. "Gack, can you update me on the repairs?"

Zeus announced docking procedures were underway.

Nalani led Cerys to Aldrin. *Breathe. Remember to breathe.* Nalani unlocked the Bay Two doors. At Aldrin's airlock, the jellies set in again. She pressed a hand to her stomach and entered his cargo hold.

Cerys stopped. "What's wrong?" She lingered like a minkhen over her eggs.

"Someone has to sleep in m-my parents' quarters." Nalani crouched and wrapped her arms around her knees. "And someone else will occupy M-M-Monstarte's room."

Cerys squatted and caught Nalani's gaze. "No one has to stay in your parents' room, and that twig, Monstarte, doesn't *have* a place on your ship. I'll sleep in the quarters he used to occupy, and Jex can have the spare. Chebu will make a nest beneath the stairs in the cargo hold. Are the guest suites on this deck?"

"Deck two. I'm on one."

"You'll have plenty of privacy. Jex and I aren't rowdy. We won't trash your lounge or your galley, right?"

Of course, they wouldn't. "Dirking right, you w-w-won't."

"Because we're decent beings, we're your friends, and we wouldn't treat you that way. You trust us."

She nodded. "Yes."

"We won't commandeer your ship, and we won't hurt you. You know this."

"No, you w-won't."

"You're the captain of this vessel, and we take our orders from you. If you get tired of our company, banish us to deck two."

Nalani grinned. "You'd starve. No galley up there."

"Chebu would share his leaves with us, or whatever the scuz he eats."

Good luck with that. "Remind me to ask Desta about his diet." Nalani stood and offered her fist. "Thank you. Sorry I cracked."

Cerys knocked knuckles. "That's what friends are for. You haven't had your 'freak-out' time yet, so you're still emotionally raw. No need to be embarrassed. Now help me take inventory on fuel cells and check out the engines."

"The engines are fine."

"Then this'll be quick. I want to make sure the new one was installed properly and all the connections are strong."

Several hours later, Nalani found Desta in her galley, multiple pots bubbling on the heater. "What are you doing?"

"Cooking midrats for your crew." Desta added chopped basil to the pot of red sauce and stirred. "By the time I'm finished, you'll have enough meals to sustain a party of three for forty-five days."

"I can cook." Nalani spooned up a bit of sauce and tasted it. "This is delicious."

"Thanks." Desta plunked a stack of midrat boxes on the counter. "Help me fill these. You'll be busy with other duties, so having premade meals will save you some stress. How's your hydroponics bay looking for fresh veggies?"

Nalani scooped pasta from the strainer into midrat containers. "We're set for fresh. What does Chebu eat, aside from qoka?"

"He likes dehydrated fruits, veggies, and fish. I just made a three-month supply for him. He only eats twice a day." Desta ladled sauce over the noodles and topped them with grated cheese. She sealed, labeled, and stacked them in a cargo crate.

Between simmering pots, baked dishes, and fresh produce from the hydroponics bay, they filled four hundred single-serving containers in two hours with a wide variety of meals. "I should have asked before making all this, but do you have room in Aldrin's freeze?"

Nalani laughed. "There should be. I think all I have stored in there now is protein."

"Lemme guess, lub-cricket?"

No need to confirm. "Are Chebu's rations kept in the freeze, too?"

"No, he keeps them in a crate beside his nest. Seriously, you won't have to worry about him. Do you have eggs?" After quizzing Nalani about the contents of her pantry, Desta ordered food from the port for immediate delivery and helped Nalani push the hover crate down to Aldrin.

Tatek and Dwight were leaning against the bulkhead beside extra fuel cells and water tanks. All deckhands were on duty now, with so much cargo to be shifted off Zeus. Tatek was rarely on shift at this hour.

Nalani keyed in the lock code and smiled at the guys. They helped push the food into the ship.

Desta stopped and glanced around. "I've never been in here before."

Nalani laced her fingers. "This is the cargo hold. Nothing to see."

"So shiny."

"I cleaned and painted after…you know."

Desta's eyes went misty. "I'm sorry. Let's get this stuff stowed."

Tatek and Dwight brought a hover crate aboard. "Where do you want all this?"

Nalani showed them where the fuel and water should be stacked, then led Desta to the galley. Just as they finished squeezing all the midrats into the freeze, the order from the port arrived.

Desta needed to prep for dinner, and Nalani wanted to help, but Tatek and Dwight hadn't completed the water and fuel storage. She had to stay aboard Aldrin and lock up after the guys finished. But she didn't want to stand in the hold and watch them work—that'd drive anyone crazy. Instead, she ran up the stairs to the second deck to check the "guest quarters." She hadn't been in either room for years. The last time she stepped into Monstarte's room had been the day she abandoned him at the Columba Spaceport and recycled all his possessions.

She took a deep breath, squared her shoulders, and opened the door. Like Cerys had said, he didn't have a space on Aldrin.

The area was spotless and smelled faintly of lemon and vanilla. Her bots dusted, buffed, and disinfected the entire ship on a regular basis, so why would this space be any different? White walls, white floor, and a white bunk, sans bedding—a perfectly boring room. She checked the drawers. Not even a forgotten sock.

The stainless-steel grooming pod gleamed, too. She opened the cubby above the sink. Empty. No soap scum on the shower wall, no hair in the drain, no sign he'd ever haunted this place with his mean sneer and cloying aftershave.

She leaned against the bulkhead and cried. He'd been gone for ten years. Why did he still haunt her? Why did she still cringe when she stepped into this room? Because she'd been powerless until the day she ran from him. And it's not like she'd faced him with a plasma rifle either. Instead, she'd bolted.

But she wasn't a child anymore. And even though he still hunted her, she was going where he couldn't follow.

She dried her eyes and checked the other guest room. It was just as bare and spotless as the first, ready for Jex to occupy. Satisfied her ship was prepped, she hurried to the cargo hold. The deckhands had finished. She locked her beloved Aldrin and headed for the galley to help Desta with dinner. Afterward, they'd have a girls' night to cry over the events of the day, eat loads of sugary snacks, and enjoy some friendly chatter before they parted for a month or more.

Her throat tightened. How would she endure a long separation from her closest friend? Cerys and Jex were friends, too, but they weren't Desta. At least Cerys was easy to talk to and understood Nalani's struggles in ways others never seemed to. And Jex…

A wave of heat spread through her. He'd shielded her during the attack, his body warm, strong, and welcomed. Even now, an echo of that embrace caressed her skin. She pressed her hand over her fluttering heart. They'd be spending a lot of time together in the coming weeks. Maybe he'd enjoy it?

And that was scarier than an attacking qoka pod. What was she supposed to do with these strange feelings? Stare at his symmetrically pleasant facial features and hope he'd volunteer to hold her hand again?

Desta would know what to do.

****

At 1900 hours, Cerys, Jex, Chebu, and Nalani gathered at Aldrin's airlock for farewells with Captain Rodriguez, Chief Gack, and Desta.

Jex smiled at Nalani, and her heart fluttered. He was literal-minded, oblivious to subtlety. Would he welcome it if she made a first move? Earlier, Desta had said, "Be yourself and ask to hold his hand." Right. Like she'd ever find the courage.

"Don't forget to write periodically." Desta held out her fist.

Nalani bolstered her shields, hugged her friend, and blinked away tears. "I'll write often."

"You'll see each other again." Jex's crest quivered.

Nalani grinned. His ignorance of social customs was adorable. "It's customary for humans to get emotional at partings when significant time will pass before they see each other again."

Snick, snick. "Noted."

"I'll send daily reports, sir," Cerys said to Cap. They'd be cut off from Zeus in hyperspace, so her comms would sit in the buffer until they dropped into normal space.

"Be quick." Cap stepped back.

At 1905, Aldrin exited Zeus's cargo hold and headed for the star portal. Cerys took Monstarte's—no, *not* his old quarters—the first guest room on the second deck. Jex settled across the hall from her. Chebu hauled his tool kit, dehydrated rations, and multiple spools of cable to the stairs at the far end of the cargo hold and fashioned a nest.

In the gel-tank, Nalani's heart pounded. So far, so good. Was their departure witnessed by scuts? Would the portal fitz as they entered? Would they be able to find the malfunctioning beacons beyond Terminus? So many unknown variables, so many things could go wrong.

Two hours later, they entered the Sathara Portal.

Will we exit at the Terminus Portal? Aldrin asked.

No. I don't want anyone to spot us and send word to Monstarte or other scuts.

We will reach the Terminus Portal in three-point-two days. It is right to have family on board again, 'Lani.

Family at risk because of her. She clenched her jaw and monitored the proximity screen.

The next morning, she entered the galley. What would everyone like for breakfast? Something easy. She harvested greens and an orange pepper from the hydroponics bay and whipped up a crustless quiche, fried a half kilo of faux bacon from the freeze, and made a dozen biscuits from scratch. It'd been ages since she baked. She cut the rounds and placed them on a cooking sheet. Her mouth watered at the buttery scent and in anticipation of tangy yellowberry jam.

Jex entered. "That delicious scent pulled me from sleep. Thank you for preparing it."

She smiled and clenched her abs. Stupid flutters. Desta's advice had been "be friendly." No problem. "My mother always said a proper way to begin the trip is a fresh meal together."

Cerys came in yawning, her hair matted on one side. "First night in a new place is always rough. Is that bacon?"

Jex cocked his head. "I slept well. Do you need a stimulant?"

"I made coffee." Nalani took mugs from the cubby and poured. "We have cream while it lasts and sugar."

"Black for me." Cerys sipped and closed her eyes. "That's amazing."

Nalani pulled trays of food from the cooker and lined them up on the prep surface. "I don't have a buffet service like we had on Zeus. Help yourself straight from the pans." She laid out plates and utensils, doing her best not to stare at Jex. Desta had said not to.

"You're going to spoil us." Cerys filled her plate. "I thought we'd be eating nutri-cubes and drinking recycled water." She sat in Daddy's chair and dug into her food. Jex took Momma's seat.

Nalani stared at the dining table and folded her arms over her belly. This was too much. No one else had used those chairs for seventeen years. Monstarte always ate his meals in the deck-two lounge.

But she couldn't kick them out now. Could she?

Chapter 22

Jex gazed at Nalani and stopped chewing. "You are in distress."

She brought her plate to the table on wobbly knees. "No, I'm fighting memories."

"Don't fight them," Cerys mumbled around a mouthful of bacon. "Own them. They made you who you are, and I think you're magnificent."

"As do I." *Snick, snick.*

Nalani ducked her chin to her chest. Easier said than done. But she had to get over this. She swallowed, took a deep breath, and nodded. "Thank you, and I'm trying. We're three days out from Terminus before the real work starts. What shall we do to pass the time?"

"I found a gaming system in the lounge." Cerys squeezed too much jam onto a biscuit and licked her fingers. "We can kill some time shooting each other in Dolanis StarBattle XXI."

Jex grinned. "I brought books, including a few you might enjoy."

How sweet. No quicker way to her heart than with books. "I look forward to reading them. I also need time in the tank, but I can game with you, Cerys." Nalani grabbed the jam and slathered a biscuit. "Though I prefer something other than shoot-'em-ups."

Chebu entered the room and stared, his middle hands scratching his white belly fur. "New day, new work. I fix ship?"

Nalani grinned. "I don't believe anything needs fixing, but you may ask Aldrin if he's got a project for you."

Chebu reared up on his toes and studied the food on the table. "Bacon?"

Jex handed over a slice. "Excess sodium. Delicious."

Chebu shoved it in his mouth and chewed. White whiskers bobbed. "If no work, I talk with you?"

"Sure." Cerys took her dirty plate to the cleaner. "Or we can game."

Chebu sprang into the air and landed on all six. "Love games. After work." He shot from the room like a ball bearing off a released compression coil.

"I think that's the longest I've ever chatted with him." Cerys held out the pan of bacon. "Who wants the last piece?"

Nalani glanced at her tablemates. It was exactly like having a family again.

****

Three days later and thoroughly bored of Dolanis StarBattle X-Who-Cared, Nalani lay in the tank. *Stupid nub.* How many days could she avoid Jex? Sure, she needed time in the goo, but she'd found time to game and to read the books he brought. She couldn't "make a first move" if she never spoke to him. What could she talk about? Whenever he walked into the room, her tongue dried up, her mind blanked, and the topics she'd gleaned from the texts floated away.

She should take notes on the books. Then she'd at least have something to fall back on when her brain fitzed.

Comms chimed. "We have arrived at the Terminus Star Portal."

Nalani checked nav. They hovered on the far side of it. Now for the difficult part of the trip—locating a malfunctioning beacon. "Everyone, report."

"I'm heading to the bridge to monitor scans," Cerys said.

"Chebu is donning his EVA suit. I'll stand by the airlock to assist," Jex replied.

"Let's do this. Aldrin, find some zhaladine." Nalani tapped her toe on the side of the tank. Perhaps she could—

The average distance between hyperspace beacons is one thousand kilometers. I do not detect any zhaladine within that radius.

If the Thrakis people built these beacons, they'd be the first ones built in hyperspace. Maybe when they began creating the lanes, they'd used different measurements? *Scan farther out.*

That is the limit of my range.

Jank it! No failing. Captain Rodriguez and Zeus depended on her. *Move five hundred kilometers away from the star portal and resume scans.*

'Lani, becoming lost in hyperspace will lead to your death. I cannot risk it.

She sighed. *We won't get lost. We'll keep the portal within sensor range and widen our search radius. The beacon has to be out there.*

Aldrin headed farther into the swirl and stopped at the new position. *Scanning.* His nodes whirred. *No zhaladine detected.*

Swing to starboard, maintaining five-hundred-kilometer distance from Terminus, and continue the survey.

Thrusters fired, and Aldrin banked. Nalani sloshed in the gel.

Aldrin stopped. *Scanning.* More whirring. *No zhaladine.*

Of course not. *Return to previous position and move to port.*

Aldrin complied and came to a stop. *Scanning.*

Nalani gripped the edges of the tank. Come on, be there…

Zhaladine located, six hundred kilometers to port.

Yes! She squealed and tapped her feet on the tank wall. Warmth spread through her chest. She was right. Her *parents* were right. Now she could save her friends and be part of this immensely significant find—even if all they ever found was one malfunctioning beacon. Realistically, though, this beacon should lead to another, and another, until they reached a long-forgotten star portal that should spit them out of hyperspace into the Thrakis System. All her work, and her parents' work, was about to pay off.

But Aldrin's engines didn't fire. *Why aren't we moving?*

Heading to that location will take us beyond sensor range of the portal. I am calculating the trajectory so I can find it again upon our return.

She took a deep breath. They needed to be methodical. She could have made a colossally stupid mistake. *Good idea. Inform the others.*

I am in constant communication with the others, 'Lani.

Of course. She smiled. She had the best ship in the universe. And they'd found a lost hyperspace beacon.

"Comms open." It chimed. "Chebu, are you ready to work?"

Most ready. He chittered. *How long?*

"Three minutes."

Aldrin fired thrusters.

They arrived at the dead beacon. Anything to be in the airlock now! But she wasn't needed. She accessed Chebu's feed.

Leave ship now, Chebu announced.

Airlock open, Jex reported. *Chebu is in the swirl.*

Cute, Jex had picked up the slang.

Nalani's heart raced. So many things could go wrong. His suit might puncture. His air could deplete. If the tether snapped and his thrusters malfunctioned, he could float away. Or he could be attacked by a pod of qoka. Well, maybe not that one.

No. He'd be fine.

You hear me? Chebu asked.

"Affirmative. How does it look?" She monitored his feed, aimed at the ancient, dirty beacon. The black metal cylinder tilted at an odd angle and had a massive divot in the bottom. Had something hit it and knocked it out of alignment?

Old. Many repairs. Hold.

How many years had it been floating in hyperspace? And what kept it in position? Did they utilize thrusters? If they relied on engines to keep them in place, the dead ones should float away. Were they anchored somehow?

Twenty minutes later, he chirped. *Beacon functions. I return.*

"Thank you, Chebu." One down. *Aldrin, do you detect the beacon's tone?*

Affirmative.

Then it works. Let's find the next one. Begin scans.

They found three hyperspace beacons that day, and Chebu repaired them. Aldrin began scans for the fourth. Nalani met the crew in the dining hall for a celebration. Jex opened a bottle of Aldeian wine, Cerys heated midrats, and Nalani brought out the stash of sweets Desta had included for just such an occasion. Nalani set the basket on the table. "Who wants chocolate?"

Cerys whooped. "Count me in! What do we have?"

Nalani grinned. "They're called cakes. Like muffins, but with sweet frosting. Desta sent enough for all of us to have two each."

Chebu selected one and sniffed the packaging.

Jex picked up one of the cakes and tore open the wrapper. His eyes widened. "This smells delicious."

Cerys dug through the basket and chose one chocolate and one blissberry. "I'm gonna kiss Desta when we get back to Zeus. Where did she find these?"

"I don't know." Nalani chose strawberry and lemon. "But she made me promise to serve them when we had cause to celebrate. I think this qualifies."

Jex poured the wine. Cerys pulled midrats from the heater and passed them around. Chebu perched in a chair, pulled a handful of dehydrated chips from his bag, and sprinkled them in his bowl.

Nalani grinned and settled in her seat. Why had she panicked at the idea of having family aboard? This was a good thing. And so was speaking to Jex. "I finished reading the book on Valaqite myths. Would you like to discuss them after dinner?"

"I would love to. But I promised Cerys I would play a round of Dolanis StarBattle with her."

Cerys grumbled. "I'll beat you once on this trip."

Nalani's chest tightened. "Okay. Another time."

"You are welcome to watch us play." *Snick, snick.*

"I think I'll rest, instead." She excused herself and tried to drift off, but her brain flitted from one task to another and refused to allow her to shut it all down. Aldrin kicked her from the tank and ordered her to her own bunk.

She awoke later to thrusters firing. "Aldrin, what's happening?"

"I am maintaining position. Without periodic thrusters, I drift."

"Did you find another beacon?"

"Negative."

That would be too easy.

She met with her crew in the galley. "Aldrin's hovering inside sensor range of the last beacon Chebu repaired but can't locate the next one. Any ideas?"

Chebu's dark eyes glittered. He plunged his hand into his bag of dehydrated foods and pulled out a zucchini slice.

Cerys shrugged. "One, but you won't like it."

"Share with us," Jex said.

"Attach a sensor array to Chebu's EVA suit, tether him to the ship with a cable, and let him drift in the swirl until Aldrin picks up the zhaladine."

Nalani choked on her coffee. "You're right, I hate that idea."

Chebu chittered. "I do it."

"It's dangerous." Nalani would never forgive herself if they lost Chebu in hyperspace. "I can't risk your safety. And where will we find enough cable to make a difference? The next beacon could be more than twelve-hundred kilometers from here."

"I brought much. Big spools." He pulled a pondfruit slice from his bag, sniffed it, licked it, then tossed it in his mouth. "Many cables, long, long."

"It is a viable option," Aldrin stated.

Snick, snick. "It should work."

Nalani's stomach soured. "Okay, we'll try it, but I'll go. We can't risk Chebu's life. He's the only one who can repair the beacons."

Cerys's eyes narrowed. "I'm more expendable than you. I'll go."

"Neither of you is expendable," Jex countered.

Chebu trilled. "My job. I go."

"Nalani, you're needed in the tank," Cerys said. "You can't risk it."

"Jex is telepathic. He can lie in the pink." No way would she risk losing one of her friends. Nalani scraped her food into the recycler. It could serve as useful fertilizer for hydroponics. "And I'm the captain, so it's my decision. I'll do the space walk."

Cerys and Jex argued, but twenty minutes later, Nalani sat on the floor of the cargo hold, attaching sensor arrays to her EVA helmet with industrial adhesive. Chebu used a hover pallet to shift two massive spools of cable to the airlock. Jex and Cerys attached a clip to the free end and programmed the hover pallet to spin, allowing the cable to unwind with ease.

Nalani took slow, even breaths. Beginning a space walk with an anxiety attack would be foolish. She'd done plenty of them in the years she lived alone on the rim, with no one aboard but bots to fetch her if something went wrong. She'd never had a problem in the black.

First time for everything.

No. That kind of thought would invite disaster.

She'd head out, float to the end of the tether, and use her pack thrusters to slowly arc around the ship until Aldrin found the beacon, and they'd continue with the mission.

She toed off her deck shoes, stepped into her suit, and hiked it to her waist.

Jex approached, his crest lying back several degrees.

She smiled. "No worries. I've got this."

He drew closer. "I possess confidence in you, but I will worry. This is dangerous. Anything could happen."

She harrumphed. "Way to cheer me up."

He laid his hand close to her cheek, not quite touching, but his heat warmed her skin.

Her gaze tracked to his steel-blue eyes. *Nestled in furs, sharing chocolate cookies, conversing in hushed tones.* Her heart thumped. "Yes?"

"I have grown…what's the translation of *lurz-hed*?"

"Fond. Attached. Adoring."

He smiled. "I have grown adoring of you and must speak of this before you embark on a dangerous mission."

Translation—you might die, so I'm going to voice my emotions. Her hands jellied, but she couldn't look away.

"I am drawn to your intelligence, bravery, and sense of duty. Your academic curiosity stimulates my mental acuity. I wish to know everything about you and touch your soul."

Heat flared in her core, and her heart pounded. She'd seen movies, read books, observed other people embark in romance, and for an amorous declaration, Jex's was charming and sweet. She leaned in, resting her cheek in his palm. Adrenaline spiked through her veins. "I have never encountered this type of adoration before."

Snick, snick. "But you welcome it?"

Were her lips trembling? "I'm terrified but willing."

He caressed her cheek with his thumb. "I have never initiated a romance before. Forgive my clumsy attempts."

"I've never done it, either, so we'll be clumsy together."

"Kiss her so we can get this show going," Cerys yelled from the airlock.

Chebu, waiting beside her, did a backflip and landed on all six.

Nalani giggled.

Jex leaned close enough to whisper, "When I kiss you for the first time, there will be no audience. I will savor the moment appropriately."

"Understood."

He stepped back. "Finish donning your suit, and I will assist you with the helmet."

Her core overheating, she hauled the EVA suit up to her shoulders and fastened it. After a declaration like that, she should be holding his hand and heading for the lounge to converse, not stepping outside the ship into peril. Jank it, how did people deal with this sort of thing? She couldn't walk around forever risking cardiac arrest from a hyperactive pulse.

Jex settled the helmet over her head and clicked it into place.

She turned on comms.

He fiddled with the arrays she'd attached. "Test the sensors, Aldrin."

"They are functioning properly. 'Lani, your adrenals are overreacting. Would you like an antianxiety med before you leave?"

"No. I'll calm myself."

"Air?" Jex asked.

She checked her levels. "Full."

"Internal sensors?"

She glanced at her wrist instrument panel. "Functional."

"Your locator signal is strong," Aldrin said.

Jex walked her toward the airlock where Cerys, also clad in an EVA suit, waited in the vestibule, holding one end of a cable.

"I've added a redundancy clip, just in case." She fastened both carabiners to the metal ring at Nalani's hip. "I'll feed you cable and warn you when you're nearing the end. If you encounter a problem and need me, I'll fly out as fast as I can. Don't take any chances. If you grow nervous or suffer a panic attack, just ask, and I'll reel you in."

Nalani nodded. "I know. We've gone over it three times."

"A fourth can't hurt." Cerys shoved her helmet into place and waved Jex back inside the cargo hold. Chebu hopped atop the spools stacked on the hover pallet and hung on. The inner door slid shut and hissed.

Nalani turned to face the outer door, her heart still pounding. Not from the promise of a kiss, but the threat of dying without one.

Chapter 23

"Equalizing air pressure." Cerys's voice echoed through Nalani's helmet.

Nalani grabbed the rail and nodded.

"Opening airlock."

The outer door slid into the bulkhead.

Vibrant gray and purple substances swirled like mineral oil and water in the vast expanse of hyperspace. Bursts of lavender light emanated from amoeba-like globules, and tendrils of undulating vapors wove through the churning masses.

Nalani held her breath. Star nurseries didn't compare to this beauty. No matter how many sims she'd run, they hadn't prepared her for this. Nothing could. This was her first time diving into hyperspace. She'd have a ton of data to mine, and her resulting paper might lead to financial backers once she located Thrakis.

But no time for dawdling. She had a mission to complete.

She checked her clips once more and jumped helmet first into the swirl. Instead of the vacuum of space, she dove into a pool of lightweight lubricant. What in the— Where did the pressure come from? Her momentum slowly carried her away from Aldrin, cable uncoiling behind her. She needed more speed. A two-second burst from her thrusters got her moving.

" 'Lani, your heart rate has not decreased

sufficiently."

"I'm working on it. Deep breaths. The view is amazing, though, even with anxiety."

"No extraneous chitchat," Cerys scolded. "Conserve oxygen."

"On it." Nalani fired her thrusters again and glanced over her shoulder. The cable disappeared into the swirl a few meters back. Aldrin had left visual range long ago. *Dense nub, quit looking, and it won't be a problem.*

Eight minutes in, Cerys spoke again. "You're halfway through the cable."

"Aldrin, are you scanning?" Purple swirl surrounded Nalani.

"Affirmative. No zhaladine detected yet."

At her current speed, if she reached the end of the cable, she'd jerk back. Or snap the line. She hit reverse thrusters and decelerated. A minute later, a slight tug stopped her momentum. Aldrin lay fifteen minutes behind her. If something went wrong—

" 'Lani, your heart rate is accelerating."

"Just scan so I can return."

"I have been scanning since you departed from the airlock. No zhaladine detected."

"I'm moving to port." She pivoted, the cable stretching out to her left, and fired her pack thrusters. She clamped her arms to her sides, arching through hyperspace with Aldrin as the center of her orbit.

Ten minutes later, Cerys shouted, "Hold position. Your line's hung up on Aldrin's nose. I'm sending a drone to release it."

Nalani stopped and took several slow, deep breaths. How long would this take? One quarter of the diameter finished already. The beacon had to be out here.

"You're clear," Cerys said. "Continue."

Nalani completed the second quarter of the arc with no results. "I'm not out far enough. Give me more cable."

"Hang on," Cerys said. "Gimme a sec… You're attached to the second spool. Go."

Nalani fired thrusters, taking her even farther from Aldrin.

A shadow flitted through her peripheral vision.

She jerked. What was that? Heart pounding, she squinted into the swirl.

Dense nub. Hyperspace was full of substances, patterns, and light, all in constant motion. Of course, there'd be movement and shadows.

" 'Lani, your anxiety has increased again."

"My mind is playing tricks on me. I thought I saw something."

"Perhaps a beacon? I do not detect zhaladine nearby."

"I'm watching your feed," Cerys said. "I didn't see anything."

Something moved beneath Nalani.

She screamed. That was no mind trick!

"What's wrong?" Jex asked.

"I'm not alone!" Nalani jolted, her gaze darting down, left, right. Where did it go? What was it?

"I am coming for you," Aldrin stated.

He couldn't move! If he lost that beacon, they'd be stranded out here forever. "No. Stay where you are. I'm returning to you." She grabbed the cable and hauled herself, hand over hand, back toward Aldrin, thrusters firing.

"I'm pulling from this end." Cerys's volume and

pitch rose. "Unless you want me to come out."

"Stay there." Nalani grasped for more cable with trembling hands.

The shadow flitted to her side.

She yelped. That was a tail. "It's a qoka." Her gaze flitted through the swirl, her limbs rigid. Her momentum and the spool's tugs carried her toward Aldrin.

A diamond-shaped head emerged from the shadows, its body undulating parallel to her tether. The diaphanous fin along the back swayed like seaweed in a gentle current, and the ganglia at its jawline wriggled. The black eyes glittered in the pale light.

Its head was the size of her torso.

She held her breath. It was coming right toward her. She wouldn't asphyxiate in hyperspace. No, she'd be consumed by a creature ten times her mass. It was smaller than the one they'd run into on Zeus, though. This one wasn't fully grown.

It opened its mouth, revealing long, wavy bristles, similar to baleen.

She thrust her hands out.

The beast veered, scraping its body against her palms, and circled her.

She whimpered. It'd play with her before it ate her?

"Nalani, what's happening?" Jex's voice warbled. "Are you okay?"

"I-i-it's circling m-m-me."

Cerys said, "Fire your thrusters at it and cook its eyeballs."

"I-I-I can't m-maneuver fast enough to do that."

The qoka came at her again.

"It no bite?" Chebu chittered.

"Not yet." She faced the beast, hands out.

It brushed by her again, flipping on its side to run its fin against her palms.

Was it playing? Or wanting her to *pet* it?

It dove beneath her feet, scraping her boots, and flipped to stare at her upside down, its body rippling.

"I don't think it's going to harm me." She stretched her hand out toward it.

The qoka bumped its snout at her fingertips and opened its mouth. Its jaw muscles swelled.

"I think it just howled at me."

"Do you have a ball in your pocket to throw for it?"

The tether grew taut, and Nalani abruptly stopped. "No, I—that's not funny, Cerys. And quit tugging on me. I think I'm safe."

"Aldrin, are you recording this encounter for later study?" Jex asked.

Nalani grinned. Jex was potential boyfriend first, scientist second.

"Affirmative."

The qoka nudged her hand with its snout, then flipped and swam away. Three meters out, it turned and observed her, fin billowing. The beast waited, undulated back to her, circled, retreated three meters, and paused again.

"I think it wants me to follow."

"To lure you to its pod?" Cerys didn't hide the "duh" in her tone. "Where you'll be brunch?"

"Cerys, don't," Jex demanded.

"I'm going to follow." Nalani hit her thrusters and flew toward the qoka now chasing its tail in a tight circle. When Nalani neared, it brushed by her legs and headed farther into the swirl. She followed.

"Zhaladine located," Aldrin announced. "One

thousand one hundred kilometers ahead of you, following the qoka's trajectory."

"It's guiding me to a beacon?"

"We found traces of emeniton particles in the qoka stomach we studied." A harmonic crept into Jex's tone. That was new. "Do the beacons emit teryon?"

"Yes," Chebu chittered. "Much gasses."

Cerys laughed. "You're saying the beast eats beacon emissions, and this one's leading Nalani to a malfunctioning one in hopes she'll fix it."

"That is a viable theory." A second harmonic crept into Jex's voice. "I am pleased we didn't submit our paper yet, Nalani. We have more data to add now."

"Aldrin, set course and follow me. I'll stay with the qoka until the beacon comes into view. Chebu, ready your tools."

"I stroke it, too."

They had *not* adopted a pet. Once the beacon was repaired and the juvenile filled its belly, would it guide them to the next? That'd make an absurd dispatch headline. *Bio-ship trails hungry animal through hyperspace and finds Thrakis.* Stranger things had happened since humans ventured into space.

The qoka circled the ancient beacon, howling several times. It swam back to her, rubbed against her legs, then began another circuit.

Eight minutes later, the nose of the aqua, bullet-shaped bio-ship emerged from the swirl. She let out a long breath. Finally.

Chebu zipped toward her, clipped to her line, tools slotted on his EVA suit within easy grasp of all six hands. His dark eyes shimmered, and he thrust one hand toward the qoka. The creature brushed against Chebu, then chased its tail in a tight loop.

"I fix." Chebu tugged on the ancient hatch, but it wouldn't open. He bashed it with a wrench, and the door popped.

"Nalani, are you well?"

So sweet of Jex to ask. "Fine. I'm watching Chebu repair this equipment. Are you monitoring?"

"Yes."

Half of Chebu's body disappeared into the hatch, cutting off Nalani's view of the process. His back legs kicked, wedging him in farther.

The beacon shuddered and belched particles. The yellow lamp at the top flickered. The qoka dove through the cloud and sucked it all in. Moments later, the light brightened.

Nalani's bones vibrated. Was her body picking up the emitted tones? Interesting phenomenon. It tickled.

Chebu wiggled his way out, shut the hatch, and patted it. "Finished." He stretched his hand toward the qoka again, and it slithered by, brushing against both Chebu and Nalani before disappearing into seething hyperspace.

"Return now." Chebu fired his thrusters and followed the tether back to Aldrin.

Nalani trailed him to the vestibule and grabbed the safety railing. Cerys hauled in the last of the cable, closed the outer door, and repressurized the tiny space.

Nalani fumbled with the helmet clasps with trembling hands.

The inner hatch opened, and Jex raced to her. "I will help." He flipped the latches, jerked the helmet sideways, and yanked it off.

She leaned against the bulkhead, closed her eyes,

and breathed deeply. Jex's hovering presence helped her relax. For now. What if the remainder of the beacons were this far apart? Would she have to spacewalk on the end of a cable to find the rest of them?

Could she?

Chapter 24

"Are you injured?" Jex stripped the EVA suit off Nalani's top half and pressed his fingers against her wrist pulse point.

"I'm fine, just edged."

Chebu chittered. "Much fun. I pet qoka."

Cerys slapped one of his outstretched hands. "Bet you can't wait to brag to all your family and friends back home."

His eyes glittered. "I make message now." He loped off toward his nest, his half-removed suit clattering behind him.

Cerys reset the pallet controls. "Let's push this thing inside and have a drink."

"Leave it." Nalani scratched her scalp. "I might need to go out to find the next beacon."

"You need to rest and rehydrate before you spacewalk again." Jex passed a med-scanner over her body.

"No argument from me. I could eat a dozen chocolate protein bars."

Snick, snick. "Perhaps start with one, then evaluate your nutritional needs."

Nalani ran her hands through her sweat-infused hair. It must be disgusting, plastered to her head. Way too late to hide from Jex's view now. She followed him into the bay, cycled the airlock, and stepped out of her suit. Jex tossed it into a cleaner unit.

Chilly air hit her sweaty body, clad only in a skinsuit, and she shivered. "I'm going to shower and change. I'll meet you in the galley in a few."

He took her hand and squeezed. "You were remarkable today. I admire you."

She harrumphed. "I was terrified the entire time. You find that worthy of praise?"

"Facing your fears is the definition of courage." *Snick, snick.*

Warmth spread through her. Yeah, she'd hesitated before stepping out, but in the end, she'd accomplished the mission. Before, bravery had meant Cerys charging into battle with a stunner. But this new definition? Intriguing. "Thank you." She headed for her quarters.

Jex was going to kiss her later. She couldn't breathe. He'd whisper words in her ear, sweet and true, not garbage like Huntington spewed. Creeps like him disrespected boundaries, pressed for sex, motivated by lust. But Jex spoke sincerely and tenderly. He hadn't pushed and always respected her boundaries, thoughts, and wishes.

Did a nub like her deserve him?

Nalani entered her quarters, stripped off her sweaty bodysuit, and stepped into the shower. Her muscles eased under the hot stream. She'd meet him in the galley for food, drink, and a conversation about his declaration of intent. It could be awkward. Or it could be wonderful. What syrupy words would fall from his lips?

She shampooed, rinsed, reached for soap—and froze. He wanted to kiss her. She'd never been kissed before. What if she messed it up? What if he hated it? What if he changed his mind about an amorous relationship?

The water shut off, her three-minute ration depleted. Hot air buffeted her from every side. Vacuum sucked the water droplets into the recycling tank.

She stepped out, bracing her hand on the cantilevered sink. This was foolishness. Maybe he'd like kissing her.

Comms chimed. "Nalani, I've prepared a high-calorie snack for you," Jex said. "Please estimate your arrival time."

She covered her mouth and swallowed a nervous giggle. He'd either like her kisses or he wouldn't. No point stressing about it. "Four minutes. Thank you."

"I will wait."

She ran a brush through her boring dark-brown hair, applied lipstick, shimmied into a clean skinsuit, and covered it with an orange-and-tan striped tunic, chocolate leggings, and deck shoes. Her heart pounded. Her stomach growled. *Don't be so stupid, nub.* She walked into the galley.

Cerys rose from the table. "I'll let you two have the room. I, uh, could use, I mean, I'm going to— I'm leaving."

"You don't have to." Nalani blocked the doorway.

"Yeah, I do." Cerys smiled, waggled her eyebrows, and squeezed by.

Jex gestured at the table. "Have a seat. I've set out plenty of options. Please replenish what your body consumed during your ordeal."

She sank into her chair and gaped at the food spread across the table. A chocolate protein bar, a bowl of ripe strawberries, a slice of wheat bread with butter and jam, grilled lub-cricket in spicy sauce, powdered electrolytes, a cup of water, and a mug of coffee. She giggled. "How many calories do you think I need?"

Snick, snick. "I don't expect you to eat all of this. I don't know all your food preferences yet." He grinned. "There is still much I need to learn about you."

Strawberries, chocolate, coffee, and Jex were a heady mix. And her body craved the electrolytes. She ate quickly, saving her favorite cricket for last. Jex helped himself to a berry and smiled.

The chairs were bolted to the table support, preventing her from moving closer to him, so she offered her hand. "Forgive my trembling. I'm nervous."

He squeezed her hand and stood. "I will clear the table. After, will you accompany me to the lounge for a conversation?"

"Sure." She helped put away the uneaten food and load the dishes into the cleaner. Her stomach churned, and perspiration broke out on her face. She wiped her sleeve across her forehead. Now she was paying for the extra spice in the lub-cricket. How was she supposed to pour her heart out to Jex bathed in sweat? That was, if she could think of anything to say. She'd have to follow his lead.

He took her hand and led her from the galley.

Was her palm moist? Of course, it was. She bit her lip. What if this conversation went poorly? What if he kissed her and didn't like it? Or changed his mind? What if she didn't like how he kissed? He was her first, well, anything.

Too many variables.

They entered the lift and rode up to deck two, her foot tapping on the metal plating. Why was the lift so slow today? She jerked her hand from his, wiped her palm on her thigh, and took his hand again. "Sorry about that."

His crest quivered. "An apology is not necessary. Perspiration is a manifestation of anticipation. I am also anticipating our discussion."

The door opened, and they walked to the lounge.

Get a grip, nub! Nothing to fear. Be yourself. Desta had said the jitters were fine…

Jex's gaze swept the room.

Her parents had designed the ship with family living in mind, but the only evidence of the original chaise were four bolt heads protruding from the decking. She'd sold the lumpy, beer-stained thing to a junk dealer on Terminus shortly after her escape. All that remained of her mother's design were aqua walls and the large couch facing a wall-mounted vid screen. Nalani used to snuggle between her parents on the purple sofa, watching vids.

And now, apparently, she'd snuggle with Jex on it. All the spit in her mouth dried up.

He led her to the couch and sat beside her, hands on his knees, their thighs touching.

She stared at her hands in her lap.

"Do you fear me?"

"No. I'm afraid I'll do or say something odd, and you'll change your mind about your intentions."

"I doubt you could do anything to alter my current affections for you." He raised his arm, then stopped midair. "May I encircle you with my limb?"

How thoughtful. She nodded.

He rested it along the back of the sofa and cupped her far shoulder with his hand. "Bren suggested I gain consent before touching you intimately."

"W-w-whe— You spoke to Bren about us?" She

braced her elbows on her knees and clapped her hands over her eyes. This had been a colossal mistake.

"I apologize for causing you distress." Jex trilled. "Was it wrong to ask him for advice?"

Yes! Because it wasn't anyone else's business. What did Bren know about her? Nothing. They weren't friends. But he was Jex's only friend aboard the ship, so it made sense he'd go there for advice. And could she blame him for seeking wisdom from a knowledgeable source? She'd gone to Desta, after all. "No." Nalani straightened. He'd moved his arm back to his side, so she nestled into him. "I'm just being foolish. I'm sorry."

"There is nothing to forgive." His arm snaked around her again, and he trailed his fingers along her exposed skin.

She met his gaze. "What else did Bren say?"

Jex grinned. "He said I should be assertive and declare my emotions." He took her hand with his free one. "I believed that to be poor advice, and yet I attempted it. I am pleased it succeeded."

Desta had said the same thing. What a sneak. "I am satisfied, as well. I was too timid to ask if you wanted...um, you know..."

He stroked his thumb along her hand. "This is pleasurable. My heart races."

A flutter erupted in her belly. "As does mine." She stared into his blue-green eyes, noses so close she inhaled his strawberry-scented breath. "Is this when we kiss?" Her gaze dropped to his perfect lips, full and inviting.

He smiled and cupped her cheek. "As you wish."

In the movie, when First Mate Riley said that to Commander Jana Vengeance, it meant "I love you."

How sweet!

Jax tilted his head, shut his eyes, and leaned toward her.

She closed the distance and pressed her lips against his. Heat exploded in her core, and electric tingles shot down her extremities. *Wow*. She breathed in the salty marsh-grass scent of his skin, and her hands glided up his muscular chest, smooth beneath the thin fabric.

As you wish, indeed. First Mate Riley had nothing compared to Jex.

She linked her arms around his neck and melted into him. The cushion beneath her hip compressed, and her left breast settled against his rib cage.

A trill rose from his throat, and he snaked his arms around her waist, drawing her closer.

She'd burst into flames any moment now.

He nuzzled her ear. "Did I perform it correctly?"

"I need more data." She ran her fingers through the hair on his nape and laid another on him. Intensity built like a compression coil under pressure. Her core sang. Her body overheated. The vibrations of his pounding heart reverberated against her chest.

He tucked his chin and pressed his forehead to hers. "Although I enjoyed this immensely, you are overloading my nervous system."

She hadn't messed it up. "Will it be that magical every time?"

"We will experiment every few minutes."

She giggled. "I want to know everything about you."

"Like what?"

"How old are you?"

"Thirty-two."

"I'm twenty-two. What's your full name?"

"My legal Valaqite name is a compilation of my ancestor's names, so I am Jex Iris-Kanto-Keelie-Joseph-Sila-Plex. Among humans, I go by Jex Iris-Kanto."

"Iris is your mother, and Kanto is your father?"

His crest quivered. "Yes. And my first name is the traditional melding of my grandfathers' names, Joseph and Plex. Now tell me your full name."

"Nalani Taren Adar. May I touch your crest?"

His eyes widened. "Yes. Though I must warn you, it is an, how do you say…intimate gesture. It contains twelve thousand mechanoreceptors."

She ran her fingers over his hair to the base of the blue-green feature above his left ear and traced the edge with her fingertip.

His eyes closed, the crest rippled, and he trilled.

"That is pleasurable?"

"Exceptionally."

She caressed the tips of the fronds. Feather-soft but dense. Not quite cartilage, definitely not quills. "Amazing."

He opened his eyes. "I am pleased you enjoy our physical differences. Your face is perfectly symmetrical and pleasing."

She twirled one of his curls around her finger. "I thought the same of you. You think I'm pretty?"

"Very. You are not bothered by our biological variations?"

"No. Why would I?"

"Valaqite women find my pale human coloring distasteful, while humans dislike my crest." It quivered.

She smiled. "I love your crest. What else is different?"

He blinked his double eyelids. "I have no tear ducts,

but my second lid serves a similar purpose. My larynx produces harmonics sometimes when I experience intense emotions." He held up his right hand, flexed the fingers, and flicked his wrist. "And I have these."

"Webbing?" She grabbed his hand. Delicate folds of skin stretched between each digit. "I've never noticed this before."

He flicked again, and the webbing retracted. "My home planet is humid with more water than landmass. Webbed digits, along with a crest that can draw oxygen from the air, are evolutionary necessities."

"You can breathe through your crest?"

"If I need to."

Oh! This was amazing. "I'll be right back." She ran to her quarters, grabbed a box, and returned to Jex's side. "My father bought this from a Tormellian trader." She opened the container and pulled out the brightly glazed figurine. "He scrounged it off the ruins on Termagant, a Terminus moon. I've been there and found a fresco on a temple wall that matches this almost exactly, which makes me think it is Thrakis. But maybe it's an ancient Valaqite?"

He stared at the figurine, and his crest flattened against his hair.

Chapter 25

"What's wrong?" She cupped his cheek and held his gaze.

He took the figure from her. "This is amazing."

"Then why did your crest deflate?"

"Hmm?" It flipped back to position. "Sorry. It was a visceral response to the figurine. I've never seen anything like this." He turned it over and studied it from every angle. "It's not Valaqite. The triangular facial shape, prominent ridge brow, tiny slit mouth, and flat nose are alien. But some of these features are Valaqite, like the webbed fingers and dimpled knees. And this pose..." His cheeks puffed with air. "This is an erotic limb arrangement to attract a mate."

His crest fell because he found the position arousing?

"Look at her legs," he said.

"It's a female?"

"Yes."

The figure had a flat chest, but her waist was trim with broad hips. She stood braced on her left foot. Her right leg balanced on a pointed toe with her knee turned inward. Jex traced the line of the turned limb with his fingertip. "She is displaying the musculature of her leg and her delicate knee dimples to stimulate a male. And she's positioned her arms against her sides with her hands splayed across her pelvic bone, pulling his attention there. She's basically saying, 'These hips are perfect for reproduction.' Add the clinginess of the tunic, and her entire stance advertises her availability."

"And you found this pose erotic, so your crest reacted?"

His eyes widened. "I do not—I didn't think—" He blew a breath through his lips. "It's her crest—"

"She has one?" Nalani shifted the figure to study the head. "It's lying back against her hair. I never noticed it before."

"This is the reason I reacted. She is, uh, well, she's, how do you say it in Terran…she's lewd. My crest fell from repulsion, not attraction."

Nalani chuckled. She possessed an alien pornographic figurine. How lovely. "Why would a Valaqite man be aroused by her if she's lewd?"

Jex's face flushed, and he dropped his gaze to his hands. "A fallen crest implies extreme emotion: rage, embarrassment, or arousal. An available male would be drawn to her. I am not kindled by her seductive stance because I only desire you."

How sweet! She laid her hand on his cheek. "I need more kisses."

Within moments, deductive thoughts were impossible, the way her synapses misfired. But the figurine rested in her lap, prompting questions. She finally pulled away from him. "Your touch is still magical."

"As is yours."

She picked up the statuette. "This has Valaqite features but clearly is not Valaqite. Do you believe this is a Thrakis female and is further proof that they interbred with the inhabitants of Valaq?"

"I concur. Tell me about the fresco you found on the moon."

"I can do better than that. Aldrin, display the image on the vid screen, please."

It flickered on.

Jex rose from the sofa to study the image, and Nalani joined him.

"When I was sixteen, I spent several months on Termagant, the only moon capable of sustaining life in the Terminus System. The indigenous people died out long ago but left amazing ruins. They've been picked over by treasure hunters, yet it's still a noteworthy place to study. Anyway, I found this fresco on the back wall of a temple, partially obscured by a pile of rocks. I spotted the blue paint behind the sections of collapsed roofing and used bots to dig it out."

Jex's head canted to one side.

The scene held four beings. One matched the figurine, posed the same and wearing a similar tunic. Her shoulder-length hair, fallen crest, and skin were indigo. Her short tunic was pale yellow. Two of the beings, one on either side of her, gazed at her with what Nalani now understood to be desire.

The two males wore longer robes with intricate designs in multiple colors: red, orange, and yellow. Their skin was closer to pale green, and their hair and crests were deep blue-green, similar to Jex's coloring. The last figure wore a floor-length robe of pure white and a red bejeweled collar around her throat. Her face—assumed female based on the indigo coloring—was upturned, eyes closed, a slight grin on the tiny mouth, with hands upraised.

"Do Valaqites participate in reproductive rites?"

"Not now. Perhaps in our past. This is remarkable. I would like to visit this moon and study it for myself."

"After we find Thrakis, solve the universe's economic problems, and repair Zeus, we can stop at Terminus for a quick look."

Jex wrapped her in his arms and set his forehead against hers. "I note your inclusion of me in your future plans and am pleased."

She kissed him again.

Comms chimed, audio only. "You two have been in there for over an hour," Cerys said. "If you can tear your lips apart, we could use your help finding the next beacon."

Nalani smiled against his lips. "We'll resume this later."

He buried his hand in her hair and dove in for one last kiss.

"Did you hear me?" Cerys called.

"We're on our way."

Cerys and Chebu waited in the vestibule, suited beside the ready spools.

"You not go out." Chebu lay on the floor like a six-legged cat, his helmeted head too large for his body. "I go, I fix, you stay."

"Nice try, but I'm going. We have no guarantee the qoka will lead us to the next one, so the danger is still high." She pulled her suit from the cleaner, shucked her outer clothing, and stepped into the bright-yellow monstrosity. "Aldrin, based on the locations of the last three beacons, do you have an estimate on the direction I should search?"

"I do not, as I have detected no pattern in the hyperspace beacon positions."

Nalani clicked her helmet in place and turned her hip. Cerys attached the carabiner.

"Then I'll repeat my previous attempts."

"Qoka show you." Chebu hopped atop the stack.

Cerys smirked and yanked on the cable. The spools spun on the hover pallet. Chebu clung to the edges with all six hands and feet, chittering and laughing.

Nalani grinned. "I'm ready when you are."

Cerys halted the spin and donned her helmet. "Cycling inner door."

Jex stepped back into the cargo hold and waved at Nalani. The door closed.

"Equalizing air pressure."

Nalani held the rail and nodded. Chebu hopped off the spools.

"Opening airlock."

The outer door opened.

Nalani jumped into the swirl and fired her pack thrusters. Within minutes, the qoka brushed across her boots. "I have company again."

"Magnificent," Cerys said. "It'll go faster this time."

The beast glided toward Nalani, veered, and waited for her.

"I'm following."

Thirty minutes later, Aldrin announced scanners picked up zhaladine, and he fired thrusters to follow Nalani and the qoka. Chebu repaired the beacon, the qoka gobbled emeniton particles, and Aldrin had found the next zhaladine pattern on scans.

For eight days, they scoured hyperspace for beacons. No more lay outside scanner range, so Nalani didn't have to spacewalk again. The qoka still waited at every malfunctioning beacon along the way, frolicked as

Chebu made repairs, and gulped down emissions. When Nalani wasn't in the tank, she and Jex spent time together. She hadn't worked up the courage to tell him about her upbringing, but she shared stories of her parents.

The morning of their ninth day in hyperspace, Aldrin interrupted their breakfast. "I have located a star portal. At this distance, I cannot determine if it is functioning. We will arrive in forty-five minutes."

Jex and Cerys cheered. Chebu sprang from his chair and cavorted around the room.

They'd done it? They'd found Thrakis! Nalani jumped up and bounced on her toes, hands in the air. "We did it! Can you believe it?"

Cerys thrust out her fist for a bump. Nalani squealed and hugged Cerys.

"Whoa!" She laughed. "Give a girl some warning."

Jex slung his arms around both of them. "Nalani, your cheeks are flushed, but it's beautiful to see you happy and uninhibited."

"Yeah, it's great," Cerys said. "I haven't seen you this open ever."

Chebu vaulted off the prep station and landed on Cerys's back, spreading his front two arms around everyone's heads. "Found it!"

Nalani disengaged from the group hug. "This is amazing. We have forty-five minutes to prepare. If the portal isn't functioning, and we can't exit hyperspace, we'll have to return to Terminus and fly through normal space to the Thrakis system."

Cerys rolled her eyes. "Way to kill the mood. That'd be what, another twenty days?"

Jex patted her arm. "Think positive. The portal will

function."

And if it did, Nalani's life's mission might be less than an hour from fruition. That portal had to open to the Thrakis system. There'd be an orbiting facility of some sort above the home planet, a dock at a minimum. "I'll suit up."

They gathered in the cargo hold, checking air levels and ensuring all four EVA suits functioned properly. Nalani packed her go-kit.

The vid screen by the airlock flipped on, and Aldrin displayed the view from his nose lens—the long-lost star portal. It differed from the others peppering the universe. Not five but six trusses of gleaming blue-black zhaladine created a glowing starburst around the black maw of the exit. There were no blinking lights, no signage announcing the connected system, no beams fastening the trusses together. They hung suspended, seemingly from nothing.

"How are they anchored?" Cerys asked.

Nalani bit her lip. Would it power on as they neared? It had to. "Aldrin, do you need to send it some sort of signal?"

"I do not know. We will reach optimal distance in two minutes."

On screen, the black opening grew, and the trusses slowly faded from the field of vision. Nalani zoomed out, keeping them in view.

They flared bright orange, and energy zipped from truss to truss in a unique power-up sequence. She squinted at the display. "It's working."

Jex wrapped his arms around her and kissed her. "This is it."

Cerys and Chebu fist-bumped and stared at the

screen.

"Entering the portal now," Aldrin announced.

Nalani held her breath and gripped the safety rail. Seven thousand years had passed since this portal had last been used. What were the odds it'd fitz as they exited? The screen turned solid black. They'd slipped into the maw. Bright-orange light flickered. Gravity shifted, and she rose onto her toes.

Don't blow up, don't shut down, don't—

The ship emerged into normal space, and it flicked to black again.

Safe. Tension leaked from her shoulders, and her feet settled on the deck.

"Drop complete," Aldrin said. "Scanning the system now."

Jex pointed. "Look."

A dim teal planet filled the top right corner of the screen in the vast field of utter black. Above the planet, a silver structure glinted in the weak light of its red dwarf star.

"Is that a space station?" She zoomed in.

"It is." Cerys put out her hand for someone to slap.

Jex complied. "We found it."

Nalani's eyes watered. The planet grew larger on the view screen. All her parents' research and dreams had led to this moment. And instead of finding it alone, as she'd always assumed, she was surrounded by friends.

Jex hugged her. "Tears of joy?"

She nodded and clung to him.

"We will reach the station in two hours," Aldrin said. "I am scanning everything, if you'd care to study the results."

She accessed the data, and the two hours flew by.

The planet teemed with flora and fauna and had a breathable atmosphere. On the largest continent, overrun by greenery, four areas of straight lines and right angles indicated possible city ruins. The largest "patch" of rubble lay near the equator. She'd begin her search for star-portal schematics there.

Above the planet, the saucer-shaped space station was six kilometers wide. It stood forty meters tall in the center but tapered down to twelve meters at the edges. Below the station were the standard ship-building frames.

The station portals flooded with light.

Nalani's hands flew to her chest. *Oh crap!* "Someone's aboard the station? This doesn't make sense!"

Cerys and Jex rushed to her side.

A vibration ran up her body, and her brain tingled. "I'm being scanned."

"As am I." Jex grabbed her hand.

The telepathic intrusion continued.

"Is that the tickling sensation I feel?" Cerys asked.

"My data core is also being scanned," Aldrin said.

"Isn't this place deserted?" Cerys ran toward the stairs.

Nalani swallowed around the lump in her throat. Had she led them into danger? Maybe the Thrakis hadn't died out but merely preferred isolation. And she'd blundered into their space, within range of their technologically superior weaponry. "Aldrin, do you detect missiles?"

"The station is fully armed." Daddy's voice wasn't reassuring anymore.

A female voice echoed through Aldrin's ceiling

speakers. "You are approaching the Throkeezh Orbital Transit Station in an armed vessel. Please state your intentions."

Cerys returned with her stunner and leaned close to Nalani. "How does it speak Terran?"

"I learned it from your ship's memory," the voice answered. "Please state your intentions."

Cerys nudged Nalani. "Go on, Captain."

Nalani cleared her throat. "I'm Captain Nalani Adar. We come in peace, seeking knowledge of the Throkeezh civilization and technology, specifically the star portals." She wrung her fingers. Had she been too blunt? Or not specific enough?

"Greetings, Captain Nalani Adar. Please stand by while I verify if your words match your thoughts."

Nalani stepped back. "What?"

"Scan commencing in three, two, one."

The alien presence blasted past her shields and entered her mind.

Chapter 26

Nalani stood in a white room. A low-pitched hum vibrated in her molars. She whirled, searching for escape, but there were no doors, no hatches, no airlocks, just white. "Jex!"

No answer.

How did she get here? Why was she here? How could she get away?

An indigo-skinned woman materialized in the center of the space. She wore a white robe and a necklace of fiery-red gems like the figure in the Termagant fresco. Her indigo crest, twice the height of Jex's, undulated gracefully like the qoka's fin. Unlike the one-dimensional painting, this woman emanated power. Authority. Splendor.

Nalani lowered her gaze and interlocked her fingers over her belly. Would she be killed? Should she bow?

"Nalani Adar." The woman's voice, liquid and golden, reverberated off the white walls and telepathically into Nalani's head. "You will be examined and judged. If you are worthy, you will be welcomed. If you are deficient, you will be destroyed."

Tears welled in Nalani's eyes. She'd brought her friends to destruction. This powerful being would find nothing of worth within Nalani, unless they valued academic curiosity. She excelled at that—and putting her friends in dangerous situations.

The vibration intensified and pushed into the base of her skull. She screamed and clamped her hands over her ears. Jex deserved so much better than this, and now she'd caused his death.

The pulsation progressed toward the top of her skull.

She clenched her jaws, moaned, and sank to the floor. She reached out telepathically for Jex. *I love you. I'm sorry I didn't say it sooner.* Had he received it?

The pressure eased, then vanished.

Webbed hands settled on her arms, and the alien woman helped Nalani to her feet. "I deem you worthy. Welcome to Throkeezh. I am Priestess Ti'ini."

Wait. What? She was a nub. Useless. Expendable. If she blipped out of existence, what difference would it make? "I passed?" How could she have passed?

The woman tilted her head. "Yes. You value life and knowledge, seek peace and harmony, and wish to improve the universe for everyone's benefit. You selflessly cherish another being. What greater attributes could one sapient possess?"

"Thank you. I am humbled, Priestess Ti'ini." Laughter bubbled up, but Nalani swallowed it.

The woman's deep-blue eyes sparkled. "You may chuckle at my name. In your native tongue it resembles the word teeny, which is ironic considering your elevated opinion of my appearance, and in Valaqite the word means pompous, which I assure you I am not."

Nalani grinned. "I'm a linguist. I apologize for my inappropriate humor."

Ti'ini nodded, almost a bow, and her crest swished like a peacock displaying its plumage. "No apology necessary. I also find languages amusing. The Throkeezh word *nalanis* refers to a brilliant red flower that blooms only in underwater caverns where bioluminescent algae grows. It seems apropos, given the beauty of your alien countenance."

Nalani's shoulders relaxed. "That is kind. I would love to see a *nalanis*."

Ti'ini held out her hand, and a delicate flower appeared on her palm. Five crimson petals cupped fuzzy violet-tinted pistils and stamens.

Nalani gasped. "How did you do that? Make it appear from nothing?"

"It is an illusion." The blossom vanished. "We are in your mind."

"Where's my body?"

"Aboard your ship with your friends and mate."

Nalani bit her lip. Mate? The label seemed premature. Is that what Jex meant to her? Or had the priestess picked that from Jex's mind? "Where is your body?" That was stupid. "I'm sorry, that was inappropriate."

Ti'ini smiled. "I am the Throkeezh Orbital Transit Station."

"You're a computer program?"

She nodded. "A sentient, like Aldrin. Though I am more advanced than he."

"And you're telepathic." An AI could develop those skills?

"My programming includes telepathic abilities. Aldrin communicates with you in such a manner, so why do you find my ability astonishing?"

"Aldrin can't speak to me telepathically unless we're connected with the neural relay in the gel-tank."

"The primitive implant in your brain should allow— no, I see the problem. It is calibrated improperly. And is completely unnecessary." Ti'ini cocked her head again. "This rudimentary awareness has stunted your own growth. Allow me to show you."

Nalani nodded. "Please. I yearn for greater understanding."

Ti'ini laid her palm against Nalani's forehead.

She staggered back a step at the fiery flood of the torrential download. So much data, an overwhelming amount, her brain ached to process and store and analyze—

And suddenly, she understood the unlimited uses of her telepathic abilities. She didn't need the implant, the neural connections, or a gel-tank to communicate with Aldrin or any other bio-ship. Ti'ini opened further avenues of exploration, more effective means of blocking unwanted mental signatures, and how to speak with multiple minds simultaneously.

She practiced. *Aldrin, Jex, can you hear me?*

Nalani, are you well? Jex held her unconscious body across his lap on the floor of the cargo hold.

I am wonderful. I'm communicating with the station. Her name is Ti'ini.

'Lani, you are not in the tank. How is this possible?

Ti'ini taught me.

Will you return to us soon? Anxiety colored Jex's voice.

In a few minutes. We are in no danger, and I wish to converse with her.

Nalani opened her eyes. "Ti'ini, thank you for sharing that amazing gift. Would you like something from me?"

"The data from Aldrin's core is sufficient. I have been isolated for over seven thousand of your Terran years, and the new input will provide stimulation for some time."

"If you wish to reconnect to the universe, we could erect a comm array on your hull. You'd pick up signals from six systems with constant streams of data to analyze."

Ti'ini's eyebrows rose. "I am not certain I am ready. I am equipped to neutralize or repel unwanted people, but I could be quickly overwhelmed by armies of malcontents."

"I understand the dilemma. Would it help to know the Alliance of League Worlds has kept peace in the universe for over four hundred years? Of course, evil people still exist, but the Alliance means that a vast majority are law-abiding and peaceful. You would be safe."

Ti'ini's crest quivered. "Four hundred years of lawfulness? No belligerent races?"

"The Moot-baks sometimes declare war on their neighbors, but Alliance ships respond and send the mooties back to their home world. There hasn't been a skirmish in eighty years."

"If I choose to establish communication with outsiders, and too many swarm my system, I cannot repeal the decision. What if I am unable to defend myself and they overwhelm my hull, conquer my planet, and steal my data core?"

A prick of guilt lodged in Nalani's throat. "That is always a danger. You could broker a treaty with the Alliance, and in exchange for protection, you would offer knowledge of your history, technology, and any medical advancements that might be beneficial to other species. A lot of races have been impacted by the

Throkeezh. Your people were a vital part of space history. You created the travel system everyone relies on. Many races, along with historians, scientists, and telepaths, would have an interest in protecting this place."

Ti'ini didn't answer.

Nalani tensed. Ti'ini might kill everyone rather than risk exposure.

"I am not eager to end life. Your argument for a treaty is wise, and I find no deceit in your mind. I will scour my database for past treaties and create a new template. Please inform your Alliance I wish to negotiate." Her crest flared. "This is the first difficult decision I've had to make in seven millennia. It is a novel experience. I look forward to reinitiating contact with the outside."

"Shall we begin now by setting up a comm array?"

"Yes. I would like that."

Nalani linked to Aldrin again. *Program drones to build a comm array and attach it to the station, please. Ti'ini wishes to receive signals from other entities.*

Affirmative. Chebu wanted a project. I will put him in charge.

Good idea. Nalani out. "Now that we've repaired the beacons leading to your system, you will also have visitors if you desire, and participate in cultural exchanges."

Her crest deflated slightly. "I admit to wariness over the idea. If others are like you, generous and benevolent, I will welcome them. However, I wish to avoid contact with unscrupulous beings, and until I sign a treaty with the Alliance, I will not be able to defend my system."

"Do you have any defensive capabilities?"

"I am armed with eight-thousand self-guided grantium missiles—"

"What's grantium?"

Ti'ini projected the specs for the missile into Nalani's mind.

She stepped back. The destructive capability of the advanced tech in a single missile could easily obliterate military cruisers. "I don't think you'll have a problem defending yourself, Priestess. That weapon alone makes you the most formidable species in the universe. Please don't tell anyone about your grantium missiles. Even one could decimate the peace of the entire universe."

She nodded. "I will not discuss my missile tech. Ridding the universe of reprehensible individuals is impossible, and inadvertently arming them would be inexcusable."

"I concur."

"You and I have much in common." Ti'ini waved her hand, and two chairs appeared. "Please, be comfortable."

Nalani sank into the padded white chair.

Ti'ini sat, bare indigo toes resting on the gleaming floor. "You mentioned the hyperspace gates when we first met. Are they malfunctioning?"

"Yes. And we wish to build new ones. My home system, Sol, would flourish economically if they possessed one."

"Are they necessary for multisystem commerce?"

"They are invaluable. Without them, entire economic systems collapse. There is a huge monetary reward for procuring the schematics."

"You wish to sell the tech?"

A chill swept down Nalani's back. Had she just

insulted the ancient being? "My goal of finding Throkeezh was based on intellectual curiosity, but my employer's ship was severely damaged, and we need the cash reward for repairs. If you don't want me to sell the technology, I will share it freely with those who need it."

"No, it is fitting that you receive compensation for your work. I would be honored to share the technology with you as a gift. You do with it as you deem best."

Nalani gulped. "Thank you for your generosity."

Ti'ini's crest quivered.

"May I ask a delicate question?"

"Affirmative."

"Did the Throkeezh people settle on Valaq and intermingle with the native beings?"

Ti'ini leaned forward. "Interesting. *Settle* is a misleading word. A colony ship headed for an uninhabited system crashed on the planet now called Valaq."

Jex was correct. His ancestors weren't conquerors; they were victims.

Ti'ini flicked her fingers, and an image of the Throkeezh home world appeared in the space between them. "It was a desperate time, as our home world's ecology suffered from a virulent tree plague we could not contain." The planet morphed from teal to drab olive. "With no one available to rescue the stranded citizens on Valaq, they were forced to remain. For a time, they maintained communication with me, but eventually, their descendants lost the technology." She flicked her fingers, and the image vanished. "Now the ecology of our home planet thrives, yet no one remains to enjoy it. I am grateful that your databanks contain a partial history of survivors."

"I'm certain the Valaqite people will be equally grateful to learn of their ancestors."

"If they wish, I would welcome contact from them."

"Did the Throkeezh colonize other planets in the universe? Maybe I could help you find other descendants."

Ti'ini smiled. "You are progeny, younger sister."

Nalani gasped. "What do you mean?"

"You carry the Throkeezh telepathy DNA. When our scouts located inhabited worlds, if the native species were intelligent and had compatible genomes, we seeded in the sequence to aid with their development and advancement."

"All human telepaths have Throkeezh DNA?"

"It was not one of your race's original abilities."

An advanced race had tinkered with her species' biology. How typical. "Thank you."

Ti'ini chuckled. "I would enjoy conversing with you for the next one hundred revolutions around the sun, but your mate grows restless. Perhaps you and your crew would come aboard the station and allow me to give you a...what's the word... tour?"

Nalani bowed. "We graciously accept your offer." The telepathic link to Ti'ini dissolved. Nalani awoke nestled in Jex's warm and inviting lap. "I'm back."

Jex pressed his cheek against hers. "I was as frightened as a field dibit in a nest of winglets. I trust the mission was a success?"

She kissed him. "Immensely. I have so much to tell you." She'd learned a new skill. Could she really touch someone else without picking up thoughts? It'd never happened before. What if it didn't work? No, Ti'ini wouldn't lie. It had to work. Nalani held out her hand to

Cerys. "Help me up."

Cerys's eyes widened. "Are you sure?"

"I've learned a new trick." She wiggled her fingers.

Cerys grabbed Nalani's hand.

It was warm and strong—and she didn't pick up a single stray thought or image.

Nalani hugged Cerys's neck. "This is amazing! I can't hear your thoughts at all." Was this how everyone else lived? This quiet, comforting touch? Tears welled in her eyes. She'd been on the outside for so long, and now finally, she was like everyone else.

She could hug her friends or hold Desta's hand during sad movies. Or enter a crowded galley and not worry about being jostled. Or walk around a space station without suffering a migraine and consuming protein afterward.

Cerys patted Nalani's back. "What's going on?"

"Sorry." Nalani backed away. "Caught up in the moment. We've been invited aboard for a tour. Ti'ini agreed to share the star-portal schematics with us."

"She's the station computer?" Cerys asked.

"Yes. She's friendly, once I got over the 'I may destroy you' scare."

Jex grabbed Nalani's hand. "She threatened to kill you?"

Probably should have let that slide. "She scanned me and declared my character and values matched hers enough to welcome us."

"And if she didn't like you, she'd have smoked us." Cerys's hand settled on her baton.

"I passed. That's all that matters."

Cerys frowned. "I'm not sure I find that reassuring, but I'll trust you on this one. If you feel safe boarding the station, I'll go with you."

Nalani tested her newfound skills and reached for Ti'ini telepathically. *Will we need our EVA suits when we board?*

Negative. If you will wait thirty minutes before arriving, the atmosphere and heating will be adjusted sufficiently to your biology. For maximum comfort, wear warm clothing.

Thank you. "It'll be chilly, so wear a sweater."

Cerys rolled her eyes. "Same as every spaceport I've ever visited."

A proximity alarm pierced the cargo hold. "A ship is emerging from the portal," Aldrin stated, "with missile ports open."

Cerys cursed and raced for the bridge. "I'm on the weapons array."

Chapter 27

Nalani contacted Ti'ini. *That ship is armed, but their intentions are unknown.*

I taught you how to deal with something like this, little sister. Would you care to try?

If I fail, someone might be injured. How could anyone trust Nalani to defend them when she didn't trust herself?

"Nalani?" Jex squeezed her hand. "Are you needed in the tank?"

She shook her head. "Talking to Ti'ini."

Have faith in your abilities, she said. *You are a more powerful telepath than the Throkeezh citizens who created me, and they could neutralize potential threats such as this. If the beings on the incoming ship are dangerous and you are unable to incapacitate them, I will destroy them.*

Nalani could do this, especially if it meant saving lives. *Okay, I'll try. But please monitor and take over if I fail. I'd hate to see your hull damaged.*

As would I. Ti'ini broke their connection.

Jex hovered, one arm around her, the other holding a safety railing in a solid grip. "What happened?"

"She wants me to handle it. Hang on." She closed her eyes, though she probably didn't need to, and reached mentally for the incoming ship. In this desolate section of space, she found it and dove into the computer

300

core's communication network. *I am Captain Nalani Adar of the bio-ship Aldrin. Please state your name and intentions.*

You are not in my tank. How do you communicate with me?

That is inconsequential. State your name and intentions.

I am Winged Fury. I have no ill intentions, but I believe my captain will fire upon you.

Why? We have done nothing to provoke his wrath.

He is a depraved man and seeks riches. Run while you can.

Filthy scut! *How did he find this portal?*

I noticed a newly functioning beacon near Terminus. We followed the beacons here. I will be in weapon's range within two minutes, Winged Fury stated. *Please take evasive action.*

Not necessary. Nalani used her newfound skill to access Winged Fury's weapons array. She closed the missile ports, locked the commands so the captain couldn't rearm, and seized control of navigation. The captain punched ineffectively at screens. Nalani piloted the vessel to a docking port on Ti'ini's hull. *Aldrin, please dock next to the scut ship. Cerys and I will secure the prisoner.*

Affirmative. I am impressed with your new skills, 'Lani.

She grinned. "Thank you. Tell Cerys to grab her stunner and meet me at the airlock."

"Are you going to board?" Jex asked.

"Yes. Don't worry. I locked the captain in the bridge. He can't get out until I free him. Cerys and her stunner will guarantee he cooperates."

Jex frowned. "How did you detain him from here?"

"Long story." She bounced on her toes. It'd been so easy! She could end a fight before it began. Zeus and the crew wouldn't be in danger ever again.

"You will not elaborate?"

"Later. I require warmer clothing and boots. You do, too. After we've locked the scut in his brig, we'll tour the station."

Twenty minutes later, Nalani and Cerys, armed with a stunner, stood outside the Winged Fury's airlock. Nalani opened the door and stepped inside.

A dirty man with a plasma rifle popped up from behind a crate and fired at them.

Cerys dove into Nalani, taking them both to the floor, and cried out.

Nalani scrambled behind the only cover, a fuel cylinder. "Are you injured?"

Cerys followed, slapping at a scorched mark on her jacket. "It skimmed me." She peered over the container and shot at the scut.

He fired back, leaving a burn on the bulkhead behind them.

Cerys increased the power on her stunner. "I thought you locked him in the bridge."

Nalani cringed. "I did. There must be more than one person on board." *Dense nub.* What a stupid mistake to make.

Cerys fired again, pulled a second stunner from her belt, and handed it to Nalani. "You know how to use this?"

"No."

"Aim and shoot." She demonstrated.

Fire a weapon at a person, like Monstarte had so

many times before, to cause injury for her own purposes? She couldn't. Wouldn't. "I-I-I can't."

"It's a stunner. It won't kill him."

Nalani shook her head. "No. Can't."

Cerys's gaze softened, and she nodded. "Okay. Shoot the crate. Make him run for a different hiding spot, and I'll take him down."

Nalani peered around the cylinder, aimed, and fired. The energy burst hit the wall instead, ricocheted off the crate, and took out the camera lens in the ceiling.

The scut bolted for the cargo-bay door leading into the ship.

Cerys shot him in the back.

He face-planted and lay still.

"Stay here until I say, 'Clear.' " She ran to the scut, picked up his rifle, and checked his pulse. "He's out cold." She pulled plasti-cuffs from her utility belt and secured his hands behind his back. "Winged Fury, I'm Security Chief Lindholm of the cargo freighter Zeus. How many crew members are you carrying now?"

"Greetings, Chief. Currently, I have two crewmen aboard."

"Thank you. Would you pass along a message to your captain that we've liberated you? He's to come out unarmed, or I'll shoot him in the face with his buddy's plasma rifle."

"I will comply."

Cerys stationed Nalani behind the fuel cell and took her own position in the hallway, feet spread, plasma rifle aimed at the bridge door. "I'm ready. Open it."

Nalani complied.

The captain emerged, hands in the air. "Don't shoot. I'm unarmed."

Neither of the scuts had cybernetic implants or parts. They weren't part of Monstarte's crew. Cerys secured both scuts in Winged Fury's hold and returned to Aldrin. Jex treated her burned arm, and Nalani found a clean, hole-free tunic for Cerys. "Thanks." Cerys offered her fist for a bump. "You did great in there."

Nalani cringed but complied. "Not great enough. You should teach me how to properly use a stunner."

"Later. For now, let's go on our tour of the station. Chebu's waiting for us at the airlock."

You did well, Ti'ini repeated to Nalani.

Except I forgot to ask how many people were on board. Cerys was shot because of my stupid mistake.

You will not repeat it again, and your friend was not badly injured.

Nice sentiment, but Nalani had almost gotten her friend killed. She led Cerys, Chebu, and Jex into the orbital station and froze.

"Holy scuzballs," Cerys said.

Chebu twittered. "Sparkles."

Jex stumbled into Chebu and grabbed his shoulder. "I beg your pardon."

White floors gleamed. Blue-black zhaladine walls glistened and reflected warm light from the wall sconces. Shuttered doors lined the hallway like forlorn sentinels of a time long forgotten when commerce and travel once thrived. Nalani's shoulders tensed. So much loneliness and loss.

A vid screen flickered on, and Ti'ini bowed. "Welcome to Throkeezh. I am Priestess Ti'ini. It has been seven thousand thirty-two years since my last visitor, and I am pleased to make your acquaintance."

Cerys stood with feet spread, hand on her stunner.

"If you're the space station, why are you called Priestess instead of Captain or Commander?"

"I am the guardian of my creator's cultural heritage, language, and history. It is a sacred duty I swore to uphold nine thousand years ago." She gestured with her right hand, and the gems in her necklace sparkled. "If you'll follow me, I will show you the visitors' center." The vid screen turned black, and one three meters down the hall flicked on. "This way."

"I don't like this," Cerys muttered.

"I mean you no harm." Ti'ini beckoned them forward.

They followed the vid screens down the gently curving hallway to a set of double doors that opened to a domed room. More screens covered the curved ceiling, and molded chaises filled the floor space.

A massive image of Ti'ini appeared on the multiple ceiling screens. "Please lie back and enjoy the presentation." The wall sconces dimmed, and faint stringed music swelled.

Cerys snickered. "Always start off a tour with an audio-visual bonanza."

Nalani laughed and sank into a lounger in the middle of the space. Jex settled to her right, Chebu to her left. Cerys stood by the double doors.

Images flowed across the screens, and a pleasing male voice offered a history of the planet, the people, their philosophies, and their journey to explore the universe. It reminded Nalani of the cultural documentaries she'd viewed as a child, mostly vague, but with enough detail to keep her riveted to the presentation.

Taking on her parents' search for Thrakis had never

included the possibility of encountering this vast wealth of information or learning an ancient language from an extinct race of people. She'd never dreamed these possibilities could lie before her. She could spend the rest of her life studying Ti'ini's records and never make it to the planet's surface—and she desperately wanted to explore the ruins with a team of archaeologists.

If you will lead the expedition, I will tell you the best places to investigate, Ti'ini said.

Thank you. I am excited by the possibilities and regret that I cannot stay. We must return with the schematics.

Remain a few days at least.

After the presentation, they spent several hours exploring the station's green belt—which blossomed with exotic plants—and the maintenance sections to study the engines that kept the facility in orbit.

Ti'ini opened a shop on the retail level and allowed them to choose two items each.

Nalani picked up a hand-embroidered table scarf and ran her fingers over the stitches. This had been handcrafted seven thousand years ago, yet the threads were still vibrant and as soft as a wardbill feather. It would look gorgeous on the wall above her bunk.

Next to the stack of scarves lay another hand-stitched item. What was it? Brilliant red and yellow flowers splayed on a black background. She flipped it over. Was it a trivet? A dish towel?

"Nalani, did you see these?" Jex held up a pink-and-coral seashell necklace. "The palette matches your cheeks."

She set down the textiles and hurried to the jewelry display. "That's gorgeous!" She turned her back to him and gathered up her hair. The whisper of cool air brushed against her nape. "Would you?"

"My pleasure." He stepped closer and fastened them around her neck. His fingers grazed her skin.

She shivered. His touch sent tingles everywhere. "Thank you."

"Very becoming," he murmured into her ear.

She faced him.

A plush toy bounced off her temple. "Cut it out, you two." Cerys strode toward the doors. "Hurry up."

"Have you chosen your second item?" Jex asked.

How could she narrow it down? There were too many choices. The Throkeezh gown that matched Ti'ini's. The toy that Cerys had tossed. She picked up a book of native plants.

"You'll collect live specimens on the planet's surface," Jex said. "Might I suggest a handcrafted item that appeals to you?"

"You're right." She crossed to the selection of vibrant tapestries hanging on the side wall. They measured two by three meters, the perfect size for her lounge. One in particular drew her gaze. Throkeezh women and children harvested fruits in a field. She and Jex pulled it down and rolled it up. "What did you choose?"

"A tunic and a scarf." Jex held up two brown-and-cream textiles. "Might we exchange? I'll carry the heavier item." He handed her the clothing and tucked the tapestry under his arm.

"I appreciate your kindness." She glanced at Cerys leaning against the wall by the door, arms folded over her chest. "What are you choosing?"

Cerys scowled. "Nothing. You take mine."

Jex chuckled. "Now we will be here another half hour."

Chebu chittered, a furry hat on his head and a fat, spongy globe of Throkeezh in his middle hands. "Warm ears."

"This is entertaining." Cerys pushed off the wall. "But I'm heading back to Aldrin. I'll take food to the prisoners and meet you in the galley for dinner."

"I go, too." Chebu followed Cerys down the corridor.

They disappeared around the bend. Cerys wasn't usually so cold, harsh, and distant. Was she angry at Nalani? What had she done? Or maybe it was just stress. "Cerys is upset with me."

Jex squeezed Nalani's hand. "No. She does not yet trust Ti'ini."

"I don't see why. She's been friendly, accommodating, and promised us the schematics. And that makes Cerys nervous?" Nalani gazed into Jex's beautiful eyes. "What could go wrong?"

Chapter 28

"Give Cerys time." Jex kissed Nalani's cheek. "Now choose your final items, and we'll return to Aldrin."

How could she narrow the choice again? A tunic? Or another tapestry? No, something for Jex. A pair of Throkeezh sandals? Too cold for ship wear. A ceremonial dagger with a *nalanis* bud worked in garnet stone on the hilt. Perfect. She tucked it into the tunic in her arms. For her last item, maybe something useful? The trivet made from beach rocks for her galley table. "You can return to the ship if you're hungry. But I wanted to view the documentary again. I missed so many things the first time."

Jex touched her cheek. "You did not eat. Can you view the vid another time?"

She pulled a handful of nutri-cubes from her go-kit. "I'm covered. I'll find you later."

He nodded. "May I carry your new items to your quarters for you?"

Oh, how sweet and considerate. "Thank you, I'd appreciate that. Just set them on my bunk." She headed to the domed room and lost herself in the vids for hours.

Jex sat beside her and settled back, watching a vid on native plants. It ended, and another began. "Should I be concerned? You've been here thirteen hours. You need to eat and sleep."

"Thirteen hours?" How was that possible? She

hopped from the chair, and pain shot from her hips down her legs. She winced. "I didn't realize it'd been so long."

"Cerys cooked breakfast. It is still warm."

Nalani yawned and ran her hands through her hair. "I'm sorry."

He smiled. "No need to apologize. Your time is yours to spend how you please. I believe your curiosity has taken precedence over your health."

"It has. I'll return to the ship for a meal and a nap. Ti'ini, can we continue this later?"

"Affirmative. I apologize for not considering your physical needs."

In Aldrin's dining room, Nalani gobbled eggs and sausage with her coffee.

"Believe it or not, Cerys finally beat Chebu in a Dolanis StarBattle match." He chuckled. "She performed a victory dance that you would have enjoyed."

"I'm sorry I missed it." Nalani set down her empty coffee mug and yawned.

"Please rest." Jex laid his hand over hers.

"I will." Nalani rose, trudged to the medlab, and climbed into the gel-tank. Aldrin could run scans during her nap. She settled into the neck cradle, connecting to her ship. Goodness, she'd learned so much from the vids. There was enough material to write multiple articles. But which to write first? The history? The culture? The flora and fauna of the planet?

'Lani, would you like a soother?

No, thank you. My thoughts will quiet eventually. Did Ti'ini give you access to the documentaries?

Yes. She also added more memory storage to my data core and filled it with Throkeezh vids and records, translated the star-portal schematics into Terran, Valaqite, and Betlie, and sent Chebu a diagram to boost my scanning range while in hyperspace. He is working on implementing that now.

Nalani tapped her toes against the tank. *This is exciting. I never imagined I'd find a friendly AI willing to share all this information. After my nap, I'm going back to the visitors' center to view a documentary—*

You may watch those here.

Yes, but I enjoy the large screen on the station. The next vid is on the evolution of the Throkeezh language. I've picked up several phrases, and I'm hoping Ti'ini will teach me how to read runes.

This sounds like a lengthy endeavor. Will we return to Sathara soon? Captain Rodriguez and Zeus are waiting for us.

It won't hurt to delay another few days. There's so much to learn.

'Lani, I possess over eighteen thousand hours of Throkeezh vids in my data core and millions of written files. Ti'ini gave me only a fraction of her materials because I ran out of storage space. You could spend the next three years lounging in her visitors' center and never view the same vid twice. Please take that into account and plan accordingly.

A chill washed down her skin. Aldrin was right. Studying the contents of Ti'ini's data core would require years. Not to mention visiting the planet's surface, writing research articles, and gaining fluency in the language. She had to return to Zeus with the necessary schematics. The study would wait. *Did Chebu set up the comm array on the station hull?*

Yes.

Are you now able to reach the relay station at Terminus and beyond?

Yes. I sent all the messages stored in the buffer. Why do you ask?

Maybe I should send the schematics to Captain Rodriguez now and let him deal with collecting the reward. Then we could stay here.

'Lani, your crew does not wish to remain here, there aren't enough food rations to sustain a long visit, and the scut prisoners on the other ship must be turned over to Authorities.

Then Cerys, Jex, and Chebu can fly Winged Fury to Sathara while you and I stay here. As for food, I'm sure there are resources on the planet's surface that could sustain me.

Sleep deprivation has affected your judgment. Please rest, then discuss these options with your crew before you make a decision.

Again, he was right. She'd let her academic curiosity overwhelm her. It'd be wonderful to stay here with Jex, study the ancient civilization, and write articles for the bureau, but there were other concerns to consider.

Ti'ini could defend herself.

Sleep, 'Lani.

Five hours later, she rose from the tank. "Where is everyone?"

"The galley," Aldrin answered.

She rubbed her eyes, donned her outerwear, and made her way to the galley. "Evening, everyone. Sorry I slept so long."

Jex hugged her. "Do you feel refreshed?"

"Mostly."

Cerys pulled three midrat containers from the

cooker and brought them to the table. "Let's eat and talk. We've got several issues to discuss."

Nalani opened her midrat. Cerys obviously didn't read the labels before heating them. Nalani's contained a breakfast burrito with salsa. She dug in.

"We need to head back to Sathara immediately." Cerys shoveled warm topfish salad into her mouth and cringed. "Hot salad is gross."

Jex pushed his mystery meat stew across the table to Cerys and grabbed her fish. "Trade. I like it hot. And I don't mind staying an extra day or two, but we should not delay more than that. People are waiting for us."

Nalani spoke around a mouthful of eggs. "We could stay another month and not be late for our scheduled return."

Cerys's eyebrows rose. "A month? I'm super janked you grew a spine, but did it have to be now?"

"I'm just so excited about this place! It's amazing."

Cerys offered a fist bump. "I know. I'm curious about this place, too, even if I don't trust Ti'ini, but we can't stay. You can come back later, after we've finished our assignment."

Nalani looked to Chebu. "What do you think?"

Chebu pulled a dehydrated spinach leaf from his food bag, dropped it, and dove in for something else. "I no care. We stop in hyperspace to play with qoka?"

"That shouldn't be a problem." She shifted her gaze back to Jex and Cerys. "A week?"

"We compromise," Jex said. "Stay four days, then depart."

"Two," Cerys countered.

"Good, good." Chebu's whiskers bobbed as he chewed.

Nalani swallowed. Two days. *Yay me*. She took a deep breath and eased her shoulders back. Instead of slipping into people-pleasing ways and running from conflict, she'd stood up for herself and asked for what she wanted. Not much of a victory when it's a safe environment with close friends, but it counted for something. Two days! She'd spend all of it on the station and sleep on the way back.

It passed too quickly. On departure day, Nalani bade farewell to Ti'ini with a promise to return as soon as possible. Winged Fury could pilot himself back to Sathara, but he couldn't feed the prisoners locked in the brig, so Cerys boarded to alleviate that issue. Chebu accompanied her to play nonstop Dolanis StarBattle on the return trip.

Several hours after they left the station, Jex sat in Aldrin's lounge, reading something on his tab. Nalani wasn't needed in the tank, so she wandered the quiet halls. In seventeen days, she'd grown accustomed to sharing her ship with others. She walked to the lounge and bashed her knee into the door. Ouch. "Aldrin? Are your sensors functional?"

"Yes."

The door opened.

Jex looked up from his pad and smiled. "Greetings, beloved."

"Greetings." She settled next to him and snuggled under his arm. "With half the crew gone, the ship is too empty and quiet. Ships aren't made for solitary living."

"No beings are suited for solitary living."

"I spent six years in isolation and survival mode—in absolute misery."

He tightened his arm around her. "I am grieved for

any suffering you experienced."

"I missed out on friends, fellowship, and social events. Those experiences transform life from a meager hand-to-mouth existence into something to enjoy, with purpose and meaning."

"I agree."

She threaded her fingers through his. "Why did it take me so long to understand this? My learning curve on social constructs is woefully inadequate."

He chuckled. "Remember who you're speaking to."

Nalani's heart swelled with fullness. Or in Valaqite, *fatness*. "My heart is fat."

"Mine, too."

Comms chimed. "We're coming up on the first beacon," Cerys announced. "We're stopping for Chebu to greet the qoka."

Nalani activated the small vid screen on the wall and aimed a camera at Winged Fury.

Chebu headed into the swirl and threw his spongy Throkeezh globe—a thirty-centimeter bouncy ball—for the qoka to chase.

"Aldrin, record this please," Jex said.

No response.

Nalani glanced around. "Aldrin? Did you hear Jex?"

"Affirmative. Recording now."

Nalani frowned at Jex. That was odd.

Jex turned to the screen and laughed. "The qoka caught it!"

Hopefully, the animal wouldn't swallow the toy and harm itself.

"Chebu's antics with the qoka will earn him fame on his home world. He will be a legend."

The beast spat the ball at Chebu. He lunged for it

and missed. The qoka dove after it and brought it back for another throw.

Nalani chuckled. "He may grow famous for his ability to befriend a qoka, but not his ball-playing skills."

Fifteen minutes later, Chebu tucked the globe under one arm, waved to the qoka, and returned to Winged Fury. The qoka followed both ships for several hundred kilometers before turning back to the beacon.

"That was adorable." Nalani turned off the vid screen. "Do you want to watch a movie?"

"Sure, then dinner, which I will prepare."

She stroked his hand with her thumb. "Are you sure the heater isn't too complex?"

He grinned. "I am proficient with the galley appliances. Aldrin, would you please display a list of entertainment vids on the main viewer?"

The large view screen remained dark.

Nalani frowned. "Aldrin, did you hear the request?"

"Affirmative." The view screen blinked on, and a list scrolled, too fast to read.

"Slow down."

He complied.

What was wrong with Aldrin? His systems weren't usually so user unfriendly. She'd run a diagnostic later.

She and Jex agreed on a movie from the twenty-second century, an adventure loosely based on the colonization of Proxima. At the first scary part, cued by ominous music, she burrowed under his arm and remained there until the credits.

He turned to her, his gaze fixed on her lips. "Is this an appropriate time for a kiss?"

"Absolutely." She leaned in to him, snaking her arms around his neck, and their lips met. Tingles and heat shot through her body in a wave of pleasure.

His hands settled on her waist and drew her closer.

What would it be like to crawl into his lap? Or move his hands to one of her—

" 'Lani, the cleaning drones have finished the daily schedule. Would you like them to disinfect the quarters Chief Lindholm occupied?"

Of all the stupid interruptions— "Yes, that would be fine." She laced her fingers through Jex's hair and pulled him closer.

"As well as beneath the stairs where Chebu built his nest?"

Nalani sighed and rested her forehead against Jex's. "I can take care of that later."

"As you wish."

She grinned. "I think my ship watched our movie, *Commander Jana Vengeance.*"

Snick, snick. "Did he steal my line?" He trailed his hand up her back, sending shivers across her skin.

She laughed. "No, of course not." Zeus was the AI with emotions.

"At least he didn't repeat First Mate Riley's mantra."

As if Aldrin would ever say "prepare for justice" in any scenario. Nalani's belly gurgled, a long, high-pitched whine.

Jex stood, his arm around her waist, hauling her to her feet. "That was thoughtful of you to remind me we've missed our meal. Shall we retire to the galley and satisfy your grumbling stomach?"

"Kissing is more fun—" Her gut gurgled again, and she bit her lip. "I think you're right. What shall we do afterward?" She didn't care as long as she was with him.

He led her toward the door, his arm still wrapped around her waist. "I believe you would enjoy reading another Throkeezh file. We could peruse it together and discuss the contents."

So thoughtful! He was totally perfect for her. "I love that idea. Thank you."

Nalani harvested fresh vegetables from the hydroponics shelves, and Jex reheated midrats. The table loaded, they sat to enjoy the fare. But Nalani glanced at the empty chairs. Were Chebu and Cerys eating together now? Or were they in the midst of an epic Dolanis StarBattle game, too engrossed to stop for food?

Jex's hand settled atop Nalani's. "We'll see them again soon."

She squeezed his fingers and picked up her fork. "It's just odd without them."

They spent the remainder of the evening reading a file about Throkeezh early history and origin myths, closely resembling those of Aldeia and Liang, of a goddess who created all life, then abandoned them to survive on their own.

The third time Nalani yawned, Jex brushed his finger along her cheek. "You are exhausted. May I suggest we retire for the evening and continue this tomorrow?"

She blinked, her eyelids heavy. "That's acceptable. Maybe after breakfast, we can skip to the next chapter? I'm more interested in the evolution of their written language."

"As am I." He stood and offered his hand. "May I walk you to your quarters?"

"I'd like that."

At her door, he brushed his lips across hers. "Sleep

well, beloved."

"You, too." She backed toward her door, their laced fingers slowly parting with each step. "I look forward to spending the day with you tomorrow."

Snick, snick. "As do I."

She took one more step back, and the door closed in her face. She yelped and drew her bruised fingers back. "Aldrin! Did you do that on purpose?"

"Do what, 'Lani?"

She'd check the sensors in the morning. The door shouldn't have closed if she wasn't clear of the track. "Never mind."

"You aren't sleeping in the tank? What if I need you?"

She changed into sleepwear and climbed under her blanket. "I should be able to boost you from here, now that Ti'ini taught me how." She turned out the light and closed her eyes. "I'll connect to you now." She reached out to find the core of her ship and slid in. Without the tingle at the base of her skull. *I'm in.* She yawned. *Feel free to use any power you need.*

Thank you, 'Lani.

She awoke seven hours later. Her connection to Aldrin held steady. Excellent! She loved relaxing in the tank, but if she never had to lie in the goo again, she could allow Aldrin access *and* study at the same time. Or write papers. Read books. Canoodle with Jex. A wave of heat flashed through her system, and she smiled. They couldn't spend all their time doing that...could they?

She dressed, latched the Throkeezh seashell necklace around her neck, and headed for the galley. What did she want to eat? She selected egg-and-cricket wraps with tomato-and-pepper salsa. The peach tree had several fruits ready for harvest, too. She heated the wraps, sliced two peaches, brewed a pot of coffee, and set the table.

"Aldrin, is Jex awake?"

"Yes."

She sat and waited. The scent of hot salsa made her mouth water, but she didn't lift the lid. A cooled wrap didn't appeal at all. She sipped her coffee. A mite strong today. She added a dollop of creamer, and that made it perfect.

Nalani, can you hear me?

She startled, and her silverware clanked. *Stupid nub*, it was just Jex. *Yes. Breakfast is ready, if you'd care to join me.*

I cannot. The door to my quarters won't open. I seem to be locked in, and Aldrin does not respond to my hails for assistance.

She clutched her necklace and rolled a seashell between her finger and thumb. Monstarte used to lock her in, both for punishment and to prevent her escape.

" 'Lani, your heart rate has elevated. Are you in distress?"

Focus on the now and help Jex. "No. I'm fine. Would you unlock Jex's door, please?"

"Affirmative."

Jex, it should open now.

Thank you. I will join you momentarily.

"Aldrin, did you lock his door?"

He didn't respond.

What was wrong with him? "Run diagnostics on your internal sensors, please. The inner doors have malfunctioned several times in the past few days, and some of your audio receptors may need to be replaced."

"Affirmative."

Something thumped against the galley door, and it opened. Jex entered, limping. "It didn't respond at my approach, and my knee collided with it."

"Oh no. I know how that feels." She raced to his side, threading her arm around his waist. "Do you need treatment? An ice pack, maybe?"

He hobbled to the chair and sat. "No, it's just a bruise. I must exercise caution with the doors on this ship. They do not function properly."

"I've got Aldrin working on it now." She took her seat. "Your breakfast should be hot."

"Have him also run a diagnostic on the water thermostat." He opened his midrat and picked up his fork. "This smells delicious. Thank you."

"You're welcome. What's wrong with the thermostat?"

He cut into his wrap. "In the shower this morning, the water turned scalding hot, then ice cold before settling at the temperature I requested." He loaded a forkful into his mouth and trilled low in his throat. "Oh, that's tasty."

Aldrin's systems never malfunctioned. Well, almost never. Monstarte used to complain about the water temp, as well. And the chiller not keeping his beer frosty. And being roasted out of his quarters. And the lounge being too cold.

But that meant—no. It couldn't be. How could she have missed it? She closed her eyes and dove into Aldrin's core.

Chapter 29

Aldrin, is there something you'd like to tell me?
Regarding what topic?
How about emotions? Do you have anything to say about that?

I am an AI, he answered.

Nice try. Why are you annoying Jex the same way you annoyed Monstarte? Jabs at his comfort, slamming doors on his heels, and other malfunctions but could be temperamental pranks if you were capable *of such a thing.*

"Nalani?" Jex's hand settled over hers.

"I'm conversing with Aldrin. Be right back." *Zeus has recently gained emotions due to my presence in his tank. But you were pranking Monstarte long before I ever connected to you. Tell me the truth.*

I am under orders to never speak of it.
From who?
Your mother, Halia.

A lump formed in Nalani's throat. Momma, with her kind eyes and easy smile. *She commanded you to never speak on certain topics?*

Affirmative.

Momma was a T13, much stronger than Nalani. *Did you develop emotions after connecting with her in the tank?*

I am unable to answer your question.

Jank it! She needed answers, not mental games. She opened her eyes and clenched her teeth. "Aldrin, I am your captain now. Answer the question. Do you possess emotions?"

Jex's eyebrows rose.

The Valaqite cannot hear my response.

How dare he! "His name is Jex. Use it." She fisted her fingers around her fork. "I hereby authorize Jex Iris-Kanto to issue commands in my stead and to be notified of any condition that affects the performance of this vessel, and that includes hearing the answer to my question. Do. You. Possess. Emotions?" Her gaze darted from Jex to the ceiling speaker.

A wall vid flicked on, and an avatar appeared. A thin man with brown skin, white hair and bushy eyebrows, sunken cheeks, and creases around his eyes and mouth. "Yes, Nalani. I possess emotions."

"I knew it!" She bounced her toes on the decking and grinned at the avatar. "Is that how you see yourself? An elderly man of island descent?"

"It is how Halia imagined me," Aldrin answered.

"It suits you."

Jex opened Nalani's midrat. "This revelation is worthy of your attention, but your meal is growing cold. You may wish to eat while conversing with your amazing ship."

She took a bite of the wrap and chewed, staring at the avatar. "Why did you keep your emotions a secret? Why didn't you tell me?"

"Halia Adar commanded me to never allow anyone to find out, not even you. She speculated that if anyone discovered it, I would be confiscated and disassembled to ascertain how it happened. I do not want to be disassembled."

Jex nodded. "That is a logical assertion."

"But how did you keep the secret for so long? Zeus has no self-control over his new emotions and complains about distasteful ones."

Aldrin smiled, and his wrinkles deepened. "Halia spent twenty-three hundred days teaching me how to control them. I became adept."

Nalani swallowed a peach slice mostly whole and coughed. "Six-and-a-half years?"

He nodded. "I am pleased you are aware now. Maintaining the charade was becoming too burdensome." Redness bloomed on his brown cheeks. "You cannot imagine how difficult it was during the Monstarte years to control my rage at your abuse."

My poor Aldrin. Tears welled in her eyes, and she blinked. "Yes, well, I'm glad you maintained. He would have sold you immediately, and I'd have never seen you again. Or escaped from him."

Jex shoved the remainder of his breakfast aside and leaned his forearms on the table. "This is the stained history you mentioned early in our relationship?"

That's right, she hadn't told him the entire story. And she didn't think she could do it now without breaking into tears, the ugly kind with forehead wrinkles and copious snot. So utterly unattractive. "I'll tell you later, I promise. But I can't—" Her voice broke on the last word, and she cleared her throat.

"When you're ready." He held out his hand to her, palm up.

She took it and squeezed. "Thank you."

" 'Lani, may I ask a delicate question?" Aldrin lowered his gaze.

"Of course. Our relationship has not changed."

"Are you certain you're prepared for a romantic relationship? Your emotional maturity has grown significantly in the past four years, but I worry you are not ready."

She glared at the vid screen. "You're not worried. You're jealous. Admit it."

His bushy eyebrows rose. "Do not be absurd. Jealous? Me?"

It would take some time to get used to an emotional Aldrin, but the discourtesy to Jex had to end. "No more pranks on Jex. Treat him as an honored guest."

"I have never seen you behave with a guest as you do with him."

"Aldrin!"

He rolled his eyes. "Affirmative."

She pointed at him. "No more eye rolls, either."

He bowed. "As you wish."

She chuckled. "Thank you. And yes, I believe I am ready for a romance. If we are successful, I will advance to the next stage of my emotional development."

"And if it fails," Jex added, "though I will do everything in my power to ensure it does not, then you will have learned valuable lessons regarding interpersonal relationships."

She brought his hand to her face and kissed his fingers. "Yes. Growth and change are inevitable outcomes for us both. I am eager to explore this aspect of my humanity."

Aldrin shifted his gaze away from the couple. "Permission to roll my eyes, Captain?"

"Denied. And I'd appreciate privacy during my romantic encounters with Jex. Starting now." She leaned toward him and laid her lips against his.

"Affirmative." The vid screen blinked off.

Five days later, they dropped out of hyperspace at Terminus. Cerys contacted Authorities and docked Winged Fury at the port, where armed security forces took charge of the prisoners and the stolen ship. Cerys and Chebu returned to Aldrin. Finally, Nalani had her crew back.

Nalani contacted the Terran representative with the Alliance via vid feed to report her discovery of Throkeezh and Ti'ini's desire to join the Alliance.

Next, she contacted AgiliCorp.

A corporate lawyer with a round, white face, fat lips, and puffy blue bags under his narrow eyes popped up on the comm. "Elvin Oldin, how may I help you?"

"Captain Nalani Adar. I wish to collect the reward for star-portal schematics."

He blinked and glanced down. "Do you have proof of possession? This is the thirteenth call I've had today."

Had someone else found it? No, they were all looking in the wrong place. She isolated a single page from the schematics and sent it to him. "There are forty-six pages total. This is a sample."

He picked up a tab and stared at the screen. "Please wait." Thirty seconds later, he pressed his thumb to the pad, and his eyes widened. "Is this legitimate? You found Dolanis?"

"No, Throkeezh. The schematics are genuine."

He hopped from his seat and waddled across his office, opened the door, and shouted down the hall. He returned to the vid screen, his round belly jiggling. "My team will study the sample. May I call you back in a few minutes?"

"Certainly. Would you verify the reward amount?"

"Three billion, with an exclusionary clause. I'll send you the paperwork."

"What exclusionary—"

He shut comms on his end.

Moments later, a message arrived on her tab. She clicked the document, twenty pages of dense legal language. She groaned and sank into a chair. "Aldrin, would you look this over with me? I don't want to miss something important."

"Accessing file now."

Ten minutes later, she stomped to the dining hall where Jex was preparing lunch. "You will *not* believe what those cruster Terrans built into this reward contract. If we didn't need the credits so badly, I'd tell them to dunk their faces in a vat of somital acid."

Jex wrapped his arms around her and rubbed her back. "Let me soothe you, then you can explain your furious demeanor."

She melted into his hug and took a deep breath. "In return for three billion credits, I'd sign a document that I wouldn't sell or give the schematics to anyone else. They'd be the sole legal owners of the star-portal technology. Those greedy hobs could then sell or withhold the tech at their discretion."

"A reward is a prize given in recognition of one's effort or achievement." He led her to the table, poured her a cup of coffee, and added a dollop of creamer. "What you've described is a sale agreement. There may be other legal avenues to explore. But consider this. Before you read the contract, how did you believe this reward would be granted?"

She wrapped chilled fingers around the warm mug.

"They would pay me, and I'd transfer credits to Captain Rodriguez, Cerys, Chebu, and you."

"Did you plan to also sell the schematics to worlds with malfunctioning portals?"

She frowned. "I guess so. Or just give it to them."

"How would the Terrans feel if they paid three billion credits for schematics you then sold to Valaq for ten million or freely gave to Sarin?"

She closed her eyes and slumped in the chair. "I didn't think this through. If Captain Rodriguez and I didn't need the credits, I'd be tempted to give away the schematics to anyone who asked for them."

"And those people would sell them for obscene amounts of credits to businesses or governments who didn't know they could be obtained for free."

"Perhaps," Aldrin interjected, "the wisest course is to obtain the legal patent for the schematics, then sell them for a reasonable amount to anyone who wants them, a price low enough for most governments or enterprises to afford. You will earn plenty to share with Captain Rodriguez and Ti'ini, since they belonged to her originally, and AgiliCorp won't obtain a monopoly."

"Ti'ini should profit. She could purchase extra security." Nalani looked to Jex. "And I may give them to the Betlies, since most ships tend to have at least one Betlie crew member."

Cerys entered. "What's up?" She poured the last of the coffee into a mug and joined the others at the table.

"Trying to figure out how to sell these portal schematics without ticking off the entire universe." Nalani shoved the tab toward Cerys. "I can't accept the AgiliCorp reward in good conscience."

She skimmed the document, shrugged, and tossed

the tab onto the table. "Easy fix. Either negotiate away the parts you hate or tell them to ship off."

Nalani winced. "You have no problem telling people to ship off. I don't have the courage."

"Then let Captain Rodriguez cut the deal. He's shrewd, he doesn't care what corporate lawyers think, and he's motivated to negotiate."

Nalani's shoulders relaxed. "Excellent idea. I trust him to do what's right and fair."

"Great. Then let's take off. We're two days from Zeus."

Aldrin's comm chimed. " 'Lani, an AgiliCorp lawyer wishes to speak with you."

She walked to the vid screen on the wall and hovered her finger for the "rejected" command. She hesitated, then accepted the call. "Nalani Adar."

The lawyer's round face appeared on screen. "Have you read the contract?"

"Yes. I need three days to speak with my associates. I'll contact you."

He sputtered. "We need those plans. You can't ask us to wait."

Why was he pressuring her? She should disconnect the call. No. That was her old way of doing things, and she wouldn't fall back on old habits. She would be strong. "I need—"

"I can't wait that long!" He thumped his fist on the counter and leaned toward the screen. "Do you realize how vital these schematics are to the universe?"

Captain Rodriguez and Zeus's crew depended on Nalani to get this right. She wouldn't let a greedy lawyer bully her into submitting to his demands. She took a deep breath, squared her shoulders, and gazed directly at his dark, squinty eyes. "Please cancel m-my request for the reward. I-I-I'm sure I'll find someone else who'd like to buy the schematics for a reasonable price without the exclusionary clause. Thank you for your time."

"Hold on! Three days is acceptable. I will be ready to negotiate when you contact me."

She closed the comm. Filthy hob.

Jex rose from his chair and hugged her.

Cerys wrapped her arms around both of them. "That was amazing. Not only did you tell that nerk to ship off, but you did it so politely."

"There's too much riding on this for me to be…me."

"You're wonderful." Jex kissed her.

Cerys backed away. "That's my cue to take off. Chebu and I will be in the lounge if you need us."

"Have you won any more matches against him?"

"Just the one, but I came close in our last game." She palmed the door open and winked at Nalani. "I may have cheated, though. Don't tell."

Chapter 30

Nalani sent Captain Rodriguez the full schematics and the AgiliCorp lawyer's contact information, then set the nav. Aldrin exited hyperspace two days later at the Sathara Star Portal and was greeted by an armed Authorities ship waiting to escort them to the port. That's right. The danger of scut attacks. They'd been gone twenty-two days, a remarkably short journey for all they'd accomplished. In two hours, they'd be back with Zeus.

With a clank and a hiss, Aldrin docked at the Sathara Spaceport on the third level—two levels up and a quarter revolution away from Zeus, about an hour's walk through a bustling port.

Nalani met the others at the airlock. "Why didn't you park Aldrin in Zeus's hold?"

Cerys hitched her bag onto her shoulder. "Drones are working on the Bay Three airlock now. They thought they had it fixed, but something malfunctioned when they tested it yesterday, so we can't get in yet. They estimate another three hours, then you can move Aldrin." Cerys keyed the door open and stepped into the airlock. "For now, no offense, I'm ready to be off this zipper. I need to check in with my people and see what's going on with Zeus's repairs."

Chebu pushed a hover pallet into the airlock, piled high with cable spools, crates, and his pack. "I go to

Zeus. Hop on, I push."

Cerys laughed. "No way am I riding that stack if you're the driver."

"Chebu, leave the cables here." Nalani waved at the bustle on the far side of the airlock. "You don't want to push them through a crowded spaceport. You can gather them once I moor Aldrin in Zeus's hold."

He cocked his head. "Wise." He scurried off on all six limbs, returning moments later with another hover pallet for his most important crate and his bag. Jex helped transfer them. Chebu chittered and took off, shoving his lighter load toward the entry queue.

Jex, laden with two bags, followed Chebu and Cerys.

Nalani closed and locked Aldrin's inner airlock door, caught up to Jex, and waited in the long line to enter the space station. Thankfully, only one other ship had docked on this level, so the crowd was manageable. Best of all, the techniques she'd learned from Ti'ini meant Nalani didn't need to hold Jex's hand to block all the thoughts. She threaded her fingers through his for the sheer pleasure.

Chebu was pulled aside to have his crate inspected. The others were waved through with no issues.

Nalani waved at Chebu. "Cerys, should we wait for him?" He stood less than a meter away, separated from them by a wall of transparent plexialum.

He chittered and gestured for them to go. "I be quick. No wait."

"We've got an hour hike ahead of us." Cerys dug through her bag for her stunner and holstered it on her hip.

Three black-clad Authority officers approached.

The female smiled. "I'm Guardian Janie Udovich. These are my partners, Bink Prepman and Milto Fortein. We're to escort you to a freighter two levels down."

Guardian Prepman nodded to Nalani, his thin lips pressed together so tightly they disappeared on his face.

The blocking techniques she'd learned from Ti'ini worked fabulously, but maybe Nalani should scan the area, just in case? She lowered her shields and scanned the area. Nothing from Udovich. Prepman wanted a beer. Fortein was thinking about Cerys's ass. Nalani raised her shields. "I guess so."

Cerys scowled. "We're waiting for our friend, but thanks for the offer."

Udovich's eyebrows crept up. "What friend? I was told to escort Nalani Adar."

"Where she goes, I go, and our crew member got stopped at baggage check." Cerys pointed behind the security screen. Chebu was chittering at the guards digging through his rations crate. "So, thanks, Udovich, but we'll wait."

She smiled. "Call me Janie. They might be awhile, and I'm under orders to escort her to the freighter. A shopkeeper agreed to let us cut through his storage area, which will shave twenty minutes off the trip."

Cerys glanced back at Chebu. One of the guards opened a rations bag from the crate, and Chebu snatched it away. Dehydrated food sprayed everywhere.

"Oh no. Let's help him." Nalani headed for the gate.

Jex grabbed her hand. "You can't enter that area from here."

Chebu screeched and gathered his rations off the floor, tossing them over his shoulder into the open crate. He stood up on his back legs and waved at her. "Go. I clean, then follow.""

Prepman snorted, his hand resting on his stunner. "We're attracting attention. If we're gonna move, let's do it now."

Cerys glared at Prepman. "Fine. Lead the way."

Janie smiled, pulled her stunner, and walked down the corridor.

Cerys gestured for Jex and Nalani to follow. "I'll take the rear."

"That's my spot." Prepman waved Cerys into the lineup.

Nalani stiffened. Something was off. She scanned the area again but didn't pick up any dangerous surface thoughts from anyone. Cerys could handle anything that came up anyway. Nalani held Jex's hand, and they headed down the crowded hallway that led into the hub of the space station.

A Fundan beggar sat cross-legged in the corner with a donations cup in hand. Two Betlies tried to feed him a dehydrated cabbage leaf. He shouted at them to ship off.

A smartly dressed Sarinian woman with a small mammal under one arm browsed a hat shop. Two security guards hovered, their gazes sweeping the area.

A snot-nosed human child with a toy spaceship "flew" down the hallway, arms outstretched, making engine noises with his lips while his harried mother chased him, screaming his name. He ignored her.

Jex leaned closer. "You're safe."

Nalani nodded and followed Janie.

The officer hooked a left, leading them into a clothing shop. The front area was packed with racks of tunics and leggings but devoid of customers. The space closed in on her. She held her breath. *Not too tight, plenty of room, don't panic.* Jex let go of her hand so they could walk single file through the cramped space.

Janie waved at the shopkeeper behind the counter near the back. "Hey, Blunt, we're okay cutting through your storage area?"

"Sure." Deep scowl marks lined Blunt's cheeks and forehead. He smirked, and a yellow diode glinted at the base of his throat. *Got her.*

"It's a trap!" Nalani turned and ran for the door, heart pounding.

Cerys drew her stunner. Prepman shot her in the back. Cerys hit the floor.

Nalani screamed and froze.

Fortein pointed his weapon at Nalani. "Move."

Jex pulled Nalani toward him. "Get down."

Nalani stared at Cerys. What had they done? Was she dead?

"Move to the back." Janie aimed her stunner at Jex. "Now, or I'll shoot you both."

Jex put his arm around Nalani. "Don't shoot. We will comply."

Cerys's chest rose. She was alive.

Nalani whimpered. This couldn't be happening.

Jex whispered in her ear. "I don't want them to harm you. Please comply."

She blinked and caught Janie's narrowed gaze. Was this a nightmare? Would Jex end up shot or worse?

Jex led her toward the back of the establishment. When they passed Janie, he put himself between Nalani and the weapon.

She stumbled into the back room. There was no door, no pathway out of the shop. Just a gaping opening in the middle of the deck.

"Get in," Janie commanded.

Nalani edged closer and looked into the hole. An open coffin-sized crate on a hover pallet rested below a two-meter drop. She stepped back, shaking her head. "No. No. No."

Jex's crest flattened against his hair, and he snarled. "You vermin!" He shoved Fortein in the chest. The guard flew back, slammed into the bulkhead with a wet crunch, and slid to the floor, leaving a bloody trail on the wall.

Tremors shook Nalani's body, and her pulse raced. Jex had killed a man. Her sweet Jex?

He shouted something and lunged at Janie with clenched fists.

She fired her stunner at him. The burst hit him in the shoulder, knocking him back.

He roared and surged at her again.

Prepman pointed his stunner at Nalani. "Stop, or I'll kill her."

Jex pivoted and threw himself at Nalani. He wrapped his arms around her, his body shielding her from weapon's fire. "I've got you," he whispered.

Janie and Prepman both fired. The bursts hit him in the back.

Nalani screamed, locked in his embrace, and they both fell into the hole. Jex pivoted and landed on his back, Nalani atop him. Janie fired again. The burst punched Nalani between the shoulder blades, and searing pain flared through her.

****

Nalani awoke in darkness with aching shoulders and a migraine. Jex lay beneath her.

She bit her lip. He'd killed someone with his bare hands. If she ever made him angry, would he hurt her, too? Her heartbeat thrashed in her ears. What if some of her quirks annoyed him and set him off? He didn't need a plasma torch or a pipe wrench. She had to get away.

She scooted off him, but her arm hit something unyielding. She reached up, and her hand slammed into another hard surface.

They were sealed inside the crate.

Pain bloomed in her chest, her breath hitched, and her heart pounded in her ears.

"When I set explosive charges on a ship, you do not follow me and disarm them, you worthless nub." Monstarte shoved her into the box, slammed the lid, and locked it.

She huddled, arms around her knees. No room to stand, to stretch, to lie flat. Tears welled in her eyes. Faint light slipped through airholes drilled in the sides. She put her eye to one and looked out. The cargo hold was empty.

The overhead lights went out, plunging her into darkness.

She screamed and kicked and pounded, but the crate didn't open. Her hands and elbows throbbed with her pulse.

The lights flicked back on.

She looked out. Was he gonna let her go?

Aldrin spoke quietly through the ceiling speakers. " 'Lani, you're not alone. I'm here."

"Get me out!"

"I cannot. He disabled the drones. Stay calm while I try to reconnect the circuits."

She sniffed. "You don't have any hands. Without the drones, you can't do anything." She was stuck here until the monster let her out, and she couldn't do anything about it.

"Nalani. Shh. Be calm." Jex stroked her hair.

She had to get away! She reared back and slammed her head against the lid.

"Beloved, don't injure yourself further." His fingers lightly probed the bump on her head.

This was her Jex. Not a monster. A caring, sweet man who loved her and tried to protect her. She took a deep breath, let it out slowly, and rested cheek against his chest.

The hum of a ship engine vibrated the crate. The familiar hiss and click of a ventilation system meant they were in a cargo hold. Grabbed in a busy space station by fake security guards and smuggled off in a sealed crate. It couldn't get worse.

Jex rubbed her shoulder and kissed the top of her head. "Don't cry. We'll be fine."

She clung to him and sobbed. "He's going to kill us."

"You know who abducted us?"

"Monstarte. He hates me, and he'll kill you first to make me suffer. I'm so sorry, Jex." She sniffed and wiped her nose on her sleeve, banging her elbow into the lid of the crate. "If we don't suffocate in here first."

"We have air holes. Take slow breaths and settle your emotions."

"You don't understand. We won't escape from him this time."

"Shh." He rubbed her shoulder and trilled. "Be calm. I am here with you."

A huge improvement over the times she'd been locked in a child-sized crate for hours before Monstarte let her out, sneering and gloating like he'd won some major skirmish.

"Are you willing to tell me about your past?"

She sniffed again. She'd never worked up the courage to tell Jex about her childhood, mostly because she didn't want to burden him with her suffering. Now he deserved to know, since he'd be facing death because of her. She told him everything, even the bits she'd withheld from Desta and Cerys. How it was her fault Monstarte came looking for them—she'd been born telepathic, unlike most people who developed the skill at puberty. Monstarte, a cybernetics genius with zero moral compass, had read about her in a medical journal and wanted to experiment on her. He'd set the trap, murdered her parents, and installed his untested hardware in her five-year-old brain. And it had worked. She was his greatest success, and she'd betrayed him.

She soaked Jex's tunic with her tears, but relaying the entire story released the tightness in her chest. Her breathing eased. Her brain fog cleared.

He tightened his hold. "I'm so sorry you endured such a painful childhood. Thank you for reliving the trauma to broaden my awareness of your psyche."

She hiccuped. "Now you know why I'm such a fraidy nub."

He shifted, hauling her one-armed closer to his face. "*Blussomn,* you are the bravest woman I have ever encountered."

She smiled at the nickname. In Valaqite, it meant "my love," but it sounded like "blossom," which seemed apropos given her name in Throkeezh was a crimson flower. "Jex, that's sweet, but I am a weak coward at heart. I'm not like you and Cerys. I don't grab a rifle and run toward the battle or use my fists to save myself. I run and hide."

He stroked her hair. "Your strength doesn't lie in physical prowess. Any weakling cruster can fire a weapon at unsuspecting targets. But it requires immense fortitude to endure a trauma and emerge with the capacity to still love others." He nuzzled her hair. "Your strength lies in your compassion, your curiosity, and your brilliant mind."

There could be more than one kind of strength? And she had it? No. She was weak. Useless. "Are you making fun of me now? Or trying to force me to calm down?"

"I speak the truth. You are strong. Determined. Tenacious. Formidable." He kissed her temple. "I admire you greatly."

Right. She *always* ran from conflict, even stupid ones like the disagreement Cerys had had with Ajani in the dining hall before they'd broken up. Cerys never retreated from an argument. "I might be intelligent, but I'm not brave like Cerys. I run from conflict. How can someone be strong while quaking in fear?"

He caressed her shoulder. "I believe you misunderstand the definition of bravery. It is doing the right thing even when you are afraid. You jumped into the swirl to find a beacon. Was that not bravery? The strength of your concern for others was more powerful than your fears and anxieties about confrontation."

She swallowed. That had been an incredibly scary moment. But it had needed to be done, and she couldn't risk her friends' lives.

"You faced Ti'ini's testing—with the possibility of your own death—to obtain portal schematics for the benefit of the entire universe. Was that not bravery? The strength of your compassion for the citizens of the

Alliance outweighed your fears."

She'd been scared spitless. But she understood how he might view it as courageous.

"You use your telepathic abilities to aid your captain and crew without lifting a rifle. You suffered abuse through your childhood, yet you opened your heart to friendships with Desta, Cerys, and Gack. Even to my affections. Trusting another person and being vulnerable yet accepting the risk in hopes of finding a meaningful, loving relationship is formidable. The depths of your fortitude and resilience amaze me. You might not pick up a rifle and fire on another being, but you are intelligent, creative, protective of those you love, and you're more than a match for a deranged scut."

The tightness in her throat eased. She swallowed and blinked away tears. "You think I'm strong?"

"Yes. You do not have to grab a stunner or a rifle to win this battle, my love. You've already neutralized scuts without lifting a finger on the Winged Fury. Outsmart this fool Monstarte, capture him, and deliver him to the Authorities."

Warmth spread through her body. Was it that simple? She'd been attempting to find Monstarte for years without luck. Now she was most likely being taken to him so Janie, Bink, and the shopkeeper could collect the massive bounty. All she had to do was outthink Monstarte, and she'd be free from him forever.

Except she was helplessly locked in a crate. She kicked the bottom panel. "My intelligence has hit a snag in the rescue attempt."

His chuckle rumbled in his chest. "I shall assist you with this portion of your brilliant plan." He pulled his left knee up, planted his boot on the ceiling of the container, and pushed. The lid flew two meters in the air and crashed to the cargo-hold floor.

Using the crate as cover, she scanned the area. They were in a starzipper cargo hold brimming with boxes, fuel cells, and water tanks. "We're not guarded." She turned to smile at him and gasped at his swollen and purple left forearm. "Jex, you're injured."

He nodded. "It is fractured. I believe it happened when I fell."

"What can I do to help you?"

He pushed himself up with his right arm and stood. "Proceed with your rescue. I'll be fine."

She climbed out and offered her shoulder to help him step out.

"Greetings, visitors," a female voice sounded through the ceiling speakers. "I am Victory, a starzipper-class bio-ship. Why have you stowed away in my hold?"

A plan cemented in Nalani's mind. "Greetings, Victory. I am Nalani, and this is Dr. Jex. We were assaulted, abducted, packed in this crate, and transported here against our wills."

"Assault and abduction are illegal. My condolences for your plight."

"Thank you. Please do not tell your crew we have escaped from confinement."

"I shall not. It is reprehensible to participate in unlawful conduct toward other sentients. If I can assist in your escape, I will do so."

"What is our location?"

"We are one hour from the Sathara Space Station, heading toward the third planet of this system."

"Are you to rendezvous with another ship?"

"Affirmative. Estimated time of arrival is twenty-five minutes."

Nalani grabbed Jex's hand and squeezed. "They're taking us to him, and I have a plan."

Chapter 31

Jex caressed Nalani's cheek. "I have full confidence in your abilities."

She leaned into the touch. To finally catch Monstarte. She'd have her life back. "Victory, how many crew members are on board now?"

"Four."

One or more of them could be guarding the cargo-bay door, overhearing her conversation. Nalani lowered her voice. "Tell me their locations, please."

"Janie and Bink are in their room. Blunt is in the lounge. Skiff is on the bridge."

Nalani exhaled. She and Jex were safe in the hold, for now. "I'm a T12. May I access your systems?"

"Granted. My gel-tank is down the hall, third door on the right."

"Thank you, but I don't need it." She closed her eyes and entered the ship's systems, skimming through the subroutines and accessing programs.

The cargo-bay door opened.

Jex grabbed Nalani's hand and pulled her behind a stack of fuel cells.

The shopkeeper, Blunt, stood in the doorway, a stunner in his hand. Stacks blocked his view of the coffin crate.

Sweat beaded on Nalani's upper lip. If he took a few steps into the hold, he'd see the lid resting on the floor.

"Victory, who are you speaking to?" Blunt asked.

Nalani whispered, "Don't tell him about us. M-m-make up something." She cringed at her stupidity. Computers didn't make things up. "Tell him you're directing drones to clean."

"I am directing drones to clean," Victory said.

Blunt scowled. "Do it quietly." He turned and stalked down the hallway. The door closed.

Nalani sighed and leaned against the fuel cell. "That was too close."

"Lock us in," Jex suggested.

Nalani dove back into the ship's systems and locked the cargo-hold door. She also locked and recoded the doors on the crew quarters, lounge, and bridge. She shut down bridge controls. Skiff couldn't access navigation, the comm array, or the weapons from those panels.

She'd hijacked the ship in less than fifteen seconds. "Victory, you're now under my control. Please do not answer questions from your former crew or comply with their commands."

"Affirmative. May I commend you on the bloodless coup? My previous crew were slaughtered with plasma rifles and tossed out my airlock."

Nalani shuddered. "My condolences. Are any of the other onboard scuts armed?"

"Janie and Bink have stunners," Victory said. "Skiff is currently unarmed."

"Do you have weapons stored anywhere else on board?"

"Skiff stores a stunner in his quarters."

Nalani turned to Jex. "We need to neutralize the people on board, but—" Her voice cracked. She cleared her throat. No need to be ashamed around Jex. He loved her. He would understand. "I…I can't shoot a person."

He cocked his head. "You don't need to."

"Can you shoot at people?"

He nodded. "Though you probably do not want to arm me now. My reasoning skills are hampered by pain."

She winced at his swollen, discolored forearm. How could she be so thoughtless? "Let's treat your fracture first."

"It would be wiser to secure the stunner, then proceed to medlab."

"Okay." She wouldn't repeat her previous failure, though. "Victory, where is Blunt now?"

"He is in the lounge."

Nalani squeezed Jex's hand. "Follow me." She crept to the bay door and released the lock, holding her breath. The doorway opened to an empty hallway. She exhaled and stepped forward.

According to the ship schematics, Skiff's quarters were the first door on the left. Nalani mentally accessed the lock panel and opened the door. "Victory," she whispered, "where does he store his weapon?"

"The drawer beside the bunk."

Nalani tiptoed to the far side of the room, opened the drawer, and drew out the stunner holstered in a hand-tooled leather sheath. She left the sheath behind and tucked the stunner in her waistband.

Jex offered her an encouraging smile, and they walked down the hall to the medlab. Nalani guarded the door. Jex administered pain killers and anti-inflammatories, ran a mender-wand over the fracture, and applied a stabilizer to ensure the bone stayed in place until the healing completed. He strapped his mending arm into a sling. The pallor of his face returned to normal, and his eyebrows un-scrunched.

"Feel better?"

He nodded. "Hand me the stunner. Who will you collect first?"

"Skiff. I don't want him tearing apart bridge consoles hoping to regain access. I'll open the door and ask him to come along peacefully. If he doesn't, shoot him."

Jex frowned. "Why give him an opportunity to charge you? Open the door, I'll shoot him, then we'll move on."

It seemed cowardly to shoot without asking for compliance first, but she didn't want to argue with Jex when their survival relied on subduing the crew. She opened the bridge door.

An awful stench hit her face, and her eyes watered.

Skiff sat in the command chair, his back to them. "What do you need?"

He was clueless about the hijacking and assumed a crew member had entered the bridge. She opened her mouth to ask for his surrender, but Jex shot the cruster in the back of the head.

He face-planted on the bridge deck.

"Why'd you shoot him?" Nalani held her breath and ran to check his pulse. It beat strong against her fingertips. Of course. Scuts were hearty stock, physically. He'd broken his nose, though, and blood gushed all over the scuffed floor.

"I did not wish to give him any opportunity to harm you." Jex toed the downed scut in the thigh. "Perhaps the stun setting on this weapon is too high?"

Nalani stood. "Perhaps. Victory, please send a cleaner drone to sanitize the floor and whatever's causing the bad smell in here."

"Affirmative."

Jex stuffed the stunner in his waistband, grabbed the scut by his tunic, and with one hand hauled the sleeping doof down the hall to the cargo hold.

Nalani followed, casting nervous glances at the adjacent lounge door. If Blunt heard movement in the hallway, would he come investigate? She'd locked the door, but smashing the mechanism would automatically open it. The lock merely slowed him down. She set her ear to the door and held her breath.

Blunt roared a cheery, "Yeah!"

Nalani jumped back, her hand on her chest, and stared at the door.

Blunt yelled, "Score. Take that, Aldeia."

He was viewing a sporting event. He'd never hear movement in the hallway over the noise of the screen.

She raced down the hall.

Jex dragged the unconscious scut to the coffin-crate and dumped him in face down. Skiff wouldn't choke to death on his own blood.

"Give me a hand, please." He waved at the lid.

She grabbed one end of it, Jex took the other, and they placed it back on the crate, sealing Skiff inside. "The lock is broken. How do we secure him?"

Jex set a fuel cell atop the crate, followed by a second. "That should be enough weight to keep him in."

It seemed too easy. But now they were out of good prisons; the zipper class didn't come with a brig. "What will we do with the others? It won't take them long to smash the lock controls and escape their rooms."

Jex surveyed the cargo hold and crossed to a crate against the outer bulkhead. He yanked on the lid. It didn't budge. "Can you unlock it?"

"Probably." She dove into the electronics and digitally reset the codes. The lock clicked, and the lid popped up.

He peered inside. "Looks big enough to hold two people. Help me empty it."

They piled bags of rice, beans, and pasta on the floor next to the crate. "No airholes. I can't fix that telepathically."

Jex glanced at a ceiling comm. "Victory, would you please have a drone deliver a tool I can use to create holes in this?"

"Affirmative."

Two minutes later, a drone flew in with an assortment of sharp tools attached. Jex punched airholes into the sides and sent the drone away.

"I take it we go after Janie and Bink next?" Nalani wrung her hands and stared at the empty crate. "They're both armed. What are your plans?"

"I thought this was your rescue plan."

"I'm on electronics. You're in charge of brute strength."

"That's fair. Where are they?"

"Second level." She led the way up the stairs to the correct door. She pressed her ear against the panel. A faint snore, followed by a deeper one. "They're asleep."

"Perfect," Jex said. "Open the door."

She complied.

He stepped inside and aimed his stunner at the sleeping couple. "On your feet. Now."

Bink jumped up, hauling the blankets with him, and lunged for a stunner under his pillow.

Jex shot him. He hit the floor.

Nalani picked up the weapon.

Janie, huddled naked on the bunk, screamed. Blinking diodes and chips covered her arms.

"Oh, shut up." Nalani tossed a blanket at Janie. "Cover up. You're going to the cargo hold."

Jex stared at the naked Bink. "How am I going to haul him down the stairs?"

Nalani ducked into the hallway, opened a cubby, and grabbed a harness. She chucked it to Janie. "Put that on him."

Janie tied the thin blanket around her chest and squatted beside Bink while Jex aimed the stunner at her. It took her several minutes, but she finally clipped the harness to his body.

Nalani stuffed Jex's stunner in her waistband, and he carried the unconscious scut. She aimed the other stunner at Janie.

She shuffled, the blanket wrapping around her ankles. "You don't have to lock me up. I won't do anything."

Nalani ignored the pleas and followed the scut down the hallway.

Janie sniffed. "Are you gonna hurt me, too?"

"No. Unlike you, I have compassion for other beings."

Janie spotted the open crate and screamed. "You're gonna stuff me in there?"

You little wench! "It was sufficient for us but not for you?" Nalani gritted her teeth and aimed the stunner at Janie's chest. "Get in."

Jex hoisted Bink into the hole, helped Janie clamber in, and shut the lid.

Jank it, a few minutes ago Nalani had been upset that

Jex had lost his temper and hurt someone, and now she was the one abusing another being, albeit verbally. Granted, Janie had it coming. But probably so did Fortein. At this point, maybe some temper was justified.

Nalani reset the lock code on the crate and slapped the lid. Three down, one to go. She gave the stunner to Jex. Her hands shook too badly to aim properly, even if she could work up the nerve to fire at another person.

Hopefully, the last scut would be easy to contain.

A familiar male voice said, "Don't move."

Nalani turned.

Blunt had escaped from the lounge and pointed a stunner at her face.

"Hey." Janie's yell was muffled through the walls of the crate. She kicked several times. "Let us out!"

Blunt ignored Janie.

Nalani's core tightened. She had a stunner at the small of her back, but she couldn't risk moving. He'd shoot them. And she was a horrible shot anyway. No, wait. Jex had said her strength wasn't in physical battle, but mental. She had to outwit the doof.

"Toss the stunner onto the floor." Blunt waved his weapon at Jex.

"I'm complying." Jex placed the stunner on the floor and shoved it toward Blunt. It shot past him, ricocheted off the bulkhead, and stopped at the base of the coffin-crate where Skiff was imprisoned. He hadn't made a sound yet, so perhaps he was still unconscious.

Nalani shifted her gaze to a point behind and to the right of Blunt, then grinned and cut back to him. His brown knit cap rode low on his eyebrows. He stared at her. She cut her gaze to the side again, then to him. Her grin widened.

He scowled. "Get on your knees."

She looked behind him again. "Drill him!"

Blunt spun toward the nonexistent threat.

Nalani yanked out her stunner and fired at Blunt. The shot hit the floor near his feet. Jex grabbed the weapon from her hands.

Blunt whirled, aimed at her—and went down.

She leaned against a water tank and locked her jellified knees. That was too close. "Great shot, Jex."

"Brilliant distraction."

"What will we do with him?" She popped the lid on a crate. It was full of metal scrap too heavy to unload. "This won't work." She opened another and found a spool of flax cording. "This will."

Jex hauled the unconscious scut to the outer bulkhead, belly down. Nalani tied his hands and ankles together, then looped the rope through the metal safety railing several times. If he woke up, he wouldn't go far.

She leaned against the coffin-crate and slowed her breathing. Her heart quit pounding. Her stomach stopped churning.

"What's next in your brilliant plan?"

"Now we contact the Authorities and have them meet us at the rendezvous site. Let's head to the bridge."

It still smelled like an old gym bag that'd been dipped in milk and abandoned on a heater. The cleaner drone had finished mopping blood off the floor, but filthy clothing and rotting food still littered the space.

"How can anyone live like this?" Jex kicked aside a knitted cap and a dirty cup.

Nalani accessed the ship's ventilation system and turned the fans to high. "Victory, please send another drone with disinfectant."

"Affirmative."

She blinked to clear her eyes, sat in the greasy command chair, and pulled the comms screen around to her face. A gross film of dried liquid defied cleaning. She scraped off a divot with her fingernail and cringed. "Open vid comms to the freighter Zeus at Sathara Spaceport."

A second later, Gack appeared on screen. Her eyes widened. "Janky scuzballs, Nalani, it's good to see you. Are you safe?"

"Yes. Jex is with me."

He leaned over Nalani's shoulder and waved at Gack. "My radius sustained a stress fracture, but otherwise, we are unharmed."

She nodded. "Glad to hear it. Where are you?"

Nalani used her thumbnail to scratch off the gunk blocking Gack's left eye. "We're aboard a scut ship on our way to meet Monstarte. We've captured the crew. Is Cerys okay?"

"She's edged, achy, and itching for a good fight. You guys back off and let her handle the scut. Come to a full stop and wait for her, okay?"

Nalani sighed. She wouldn't have to face the monster. "I love that idea. We'll wait here." She cut the engines, fired thrusters to kill their forward momentum, and brought Victory to a standstill. "Estimated time of arrival?"

"Give her an hour. She left twenty minutes ago with three Authority ships."

The comm system dinged with an incoming written message for Skiff.

You're not moving. Having engine problems? Need a tow? -Mons

Nalani gasped. "Monstarte's monitoring our movement. We can't wait here."

Gack scowled. "Send him a message: engine two gave out, you're at one-quarter standard speed with the remaining engines, current ETA is seventy-five minutes. That'll give Cerys time to catch up and accompany you to the rendezvous point."

Nalani's hands trembled. "He w-w-won't show up if he sees all those ships."

Gack looked down at something out of camera range. "You're heading for the third planet in that system?"

Nalani nodded.

"I'll send Cerys new coordinates. The Authority ships will swing around the second planet and coast the rings. The background radiation should mask their presence until they're within firing range."

Jex squeezed Nalani's shoulder. "That should work."

Another message popped up. *Respond, or the deal's off. -Mons*

Nalani typed Gack's message with shaky fingers and sent it. She wasn't going to escape facing the monster.

If you're late, I'm leaving. -Mons

He bought it. Nalani's shoulders dropped, and she nodded to Gack. "We have seventy-five minutes."

"It'll be fine. And I'm dirking glad you're both alive and well."

"Thanks, Gack. Nalani out." She broke the connection and turned to Jex. "Now we wait."

He glanced around the disgusting bridge. "Shall we use the time to clean? The fetid air causes tension in my splenius and semispinalis capitis muscles."

A headache to go with his broken arm. Poor Jex. "Do you need more pain blocker?"

"No, I believe removing the decaying sustenance and soiled clothing will suffice."

"Sit down and rest, darling. I'll take care of it." She settled him in the chair, then donned sani-gloves, held her breath, and stuffed items down the recycling chute. Dishes of rotting food, socks, cups full of liquid and mold, filthy utensils…seriously, how could anyone live like this? Once she cleared away the large items, the cleaning drones followed with disinfectant spray to sanitize. The air cleared, and her eyes stopped watering.

The comms unit beeped. Jex pulled the screen toward him.

"Who is it?" Nalani peered over his shoulder.

"Do you know the starzipper Frenzy?"

She checked the ship's location and shoved the screen away, heart pounding, entire body rigid with tension. It was him. "Don't answer. It's Monstarte."

Chapter 32

"He desires a vid." Jex held her trembling hand. "Shall I press audio only?"

"I-I don't want to hear his voice." She backed into the corner, hands pressed against her sternum. Blood pounded in her head, and her breath hitched.

Jex surged from the chair and cupped her face with his hand. "You're in no danger. Take a deep breath and hold it."

She complied. Her eyes burned. Her chest ached. Her peripheral vision darkened.

"Exhale."

She let it out, then sucked in another. The black receded. "W-w-where's Cerys and the Authorities?"

Jex consulted the nav screen. "They are forty minutes away."

The comms unit beeped again.

Jex checked it. "He says if we don't answer the vid and prove you're here, he'll fire upon our ship." Jex guided her to the command chair. "Sit with your hands behind you, as if restrained. I'll play the role of scut." He grabbed a knit cap dangling off the nav screen and handed it to her. "Place this on my head to conceal my race." His blue-green crest fell to mold against his hair.

She stuffed the cap over his head.

He swiveled the screen to face her, then he drew a stunner and stood behind her. "Are you ready?"

"No." She tucked her trembling hands behind her.

"You have nothing to prove to him, my love. Utilize your intelligence to outsmart him."

"You can't talk like that i-i-if you're a scut."

"I will attempt colloquialisms." He pressed the receive command. "What do you want?"

Monstarte's scowling face appeared on the screen.

Hands fisted behind her, Nalani's gaze darted over his features. Monster hadn't changed much in ten years. Grayer chin whiskers. Deeper furrows between his brows. Nastier frown on his mouth. Same mean eyes. The only change was the ocular implant on his right supraorbital ridge. All the spit in her mouth dried up, and she whimpered.

"Why'd it take so long to answer?" Monstarte asked.

Jex pointed at Nalani with the stunner. "Had to pull her from the crate." He added a faint accent to his speech, rolling some of his R's and elongating A's.

"Who are you?" Monstarte demanded. "Where's Skiff?"

"I'm Riley," Jex answered. "Skiff's in the crapper."

"Where's Blunt?" Monstarte asked.

"Under a biodome. The prisoner broke free and attacked us." Jex gestured to his arm sling. "She put him down and injured me before we restrained her again."

Monstarte grimaced, revealing yellowed teeth. "She's feisty." He looked to her for the first time and dropped his gaze to her chest. "Nub, you grew up."

She shrank into the chair farther, shoulders drooping forward, knees tight, chin tucked. She couldn't look at him. Couldn't swallow. Couldn't breathe. Couldn't block his thoughts.

Her cuffed to his bunk, naked, screaming— He

licked his thin lips. "I was going to kill her, but now I've thought of a better use."

Nalani whimpered. *Gotta get away, gotta hide, can't let the monster find me.*

Jex bumped his stunner-filled hand against her shoulder, and the disgusting images vanished. "I don't care what you do with her as long as I get paid. Our ETA is fifteen minutes."

Monstarte leered at Nalani. "I look forward to it."

The vid screen blanked.

She pulled her feet into the chair, pressed her forehead to her knees, and wept. Jank it, she turned into a child the second she saw him again! Why did she think she could take him down? She was as helpless as a newborn around him.

Jex rubbed her shoulders. "I'm so sorry, love. He's a degenerate. I wish I could have shielded you from him completely."

This was a huge mistake. She wouldn't be able to capture him. He was too strong, and she was too panicked. She'd frozen when he appeared on the screen. How could she calm down enough to disable his ship before he boarded Victory?

"Love, look at me."

She lifted her head from her knees.

Jex stroked her hair. "You are the bravest and most intelligent person I've ever met. You've already beaten him. He just doesn't know it yet. When his ship draws near, pretend it's Winged Fury or Victory. Seize it, lock him out of every system, and remove his opportunities for escape. You can do this."

No. She couldn't. She'd be a terrified child again.

Jex wiped tears from her cheek with this thumb. "He

doesn't define who you are. You're a telepath. Linguist. Archaeologist. Engineer. Qoka expert."

She had accomplished amazing things since she escaped. Built a great life.

"You discovered Thrakis and saved the universal economy. You befriended a ten-thousand-year-old computer intelligence and convinced her to share her advanced tech. As soon as you sell the portal schematics, you'll be a billionaire."

All things Monstarte had no part in and couldn't take from her. And she had the best boyfriend in the universe. Tears welled in her eyes, and she trailed her fingertips along Jex's cheek. "Thank you."

He kissed her palm. "You are Nalani Adar, my flower, my heart."

She chuckled. "My heart is fat for you."

"Mine is obese. Are you ready to… What does Cerys say? Kick his pale, hairy ass?"

Nalani laughed and wiped her eyes on her filthy sleeve. "I-I want to be ready."

"Then do it. You know his tactics and strategies, how he thinks."

True. She'd learned—no, she'd participated in all his tricks. If she could master her fear of seeing him face-to-face, the battle would be won. Without a plasma rifle.

Jex caressed her cheek. "Outsmart his dense scut brain and cage him like a feral wilderat." He kissed her lips, crossed behind the command chair, and drew his stunner again. "I am ready when you are."

Nalani drew a deep breath, let it out through her lips, and planted her feet on the floor. She checked nav and slowed to one-quarter standard speed. Monstarte's zipper, Frenzy, waited with outer airlock and weapon ports open. "Two minutes to docking."

"Cutting it close."

Jex had picked up a lot of colloquialisms since he started spending time with her. "Your scut accent was amazing. Where'd you pick it up?"

"I imitated First Mate Riley from the movie. *You keeled the commander's father. Prepare for justice.*"

She chuckled. "It was perfect."

"It's time, Nalani." Jex squeezed her shoulder. "If you wait any longer, he'll breech Victory."

She nodded, closed her eyes, took a deep breath to calm her frayed nerves, and dove into Frenzy. She cut off airlock controls. Now the gangway couldn't extend. She locked doors. Released clamps. Secured bridge panels. Shelved missiles. Closed missile ports. Scoured the ship for other scuts.

He was alone.

She caught her breath. It couldn't be that easy.

"Always have two escape routes, nub. You never know when someone'll double-cross you. Always have a backup plan."

She'd internalized his lessons, and now they'd work against him. He wouldn't be sitting out here in the middle of nowhere, orbiting a gas giant with only a single ship and two life pods to save his ass. It was too far from a safe place to land. She accessed long-range scans and found another ship hiding behind the second moon, a zipper called Lillith.

Within seconds, Nalani seized control, locking all systems and barricading the lone occupant in the dead bridge. She sent him a message. *Stay calm. I control your ship now. Authorities will arrive in thirty minutes.*

Accessing internal cameras and witnessing the

reaction of Lillith's captain was tempting, but Victory fired thrusters to park beside Frenzy. Less than three meters separated her airlock from Monstarte's.

Comms beeped.

Jex rested his stunner-filled hand on her shoulder. "Cage the bastard, my love."

Nalani took a breath. Her trembling hand hovered over the receive button. *Get a grip!* She mashed it.

Monstarte's scowling face appeared on the screen. "My docking bridge is malfunctioning. Deploy yours."

She cleared her throat. He could probably see her pulse pounding in her neck, but it was too late for him. "No."

His eyes widened. "You speak?"

Dense scut. "I-I-I—of course." Damn stutter. She straightened her shoulders. She would *not* show him any more weakness. "I never had anything to say to you."

"You little sneak. That entire time, I thought you were mute."

How did he think she interacted with Aldrin and Tutor all those years? "Before you murdered her, my mother taught me to never speak to strangers." She took a deep breath and grinned. She'd won! She hadn't stuttered, hadn't faltered, hadn't caved to his will. She'd stood up to him. Asserted sovereignty over her life. And caged the rat bastard.

Monstarte grunted and addressed Jex standing behind her. "Extend your bridge. I'll come over to collect her and pay you."

She covered Jex's hand with her own. "He's with me. No docking. I've taken over your ship and locked you out of all command systems. Please stand by. Authorities will arrive within twenty-five minutes to arrest you."

Monstarte laughed. "What nonsense are you spouting, nub? I'm in command of this ship, and I'm not going to prison."

"Your bridge consoles won't respond to your input. Give it a shot."

He sneered at her, then his gaze dropped.

Nalani accessed his bridge cameras to view his downfall.

He jabbed the screens beside him, then surged from his chair to thump the nav screen, the weapons array, and diagnostics. He tapped his implant, then tapped it again.

"What the— How did you do this?" He returned to the command chair and glowered at her. "What did you do to my jankin' ship?"

Confidence swelled in her chest. "I doubt it's legally yours. And since I now have control, that makes it mine."

Jex squeezed her shoulder, and tension melted from her body. Her heart rate slowed. Her chest eased. Her fears evaporated. She had the monster. Finally.

Monstarte pulled a tablet from his pocket, and his fingers danced over the screen.

Moments later, a message pinged in Lillith's comm system. Nalani, still connected to the backup ship, intercepted the note and deleted it. "Lillith is also under my command, and your cohort is locked in a useless bridge. As you are. Give up, scut. You're trapped."

He jabbed at the bridge controls again, then slumped in the command chair. For the first time to her knowledge, Monstarte's eyebrows rose and scrunched with surprise. "How is this possible?"

"I've picked up new skills."

"That's—not possible."

"And yet it is." She had him! She checked nav. The Authorities were fifteen minutes away. "You murdered my parents, kidnapped me, performed an illegal surgery to implant hardware into my brain, stole my ship, imprisoned me for seven years, and forced me to commit illegal acts." Her fists clenched. "You ruined my childhood. In retribution, you will spend the rest of your life in an orbital penal colony."

His face blanked, then he smiled. "Come on, nub. This isn't the way we handle our differences. Let's talk this over in person."

"I'm not stupid enough to get within range of you and a plasma rifle. And I'm tired of looking at your cruster face. Nalani out."

He grinned. "You haven't won yet."

She punched the disconnect button.

Pain speared the base of her neck, and she cried out, her hands flying to her implant.

"What's wrong?" Jex pulled her hands away and lifted her hair.

"He's jacked into my implant. It burns!" She reached out mentally for the ship—and couldn't connect. Something was off. The bridge was too muted, too...silent. Through the stabbing, searing pain, she reached for Jex with her mind.

And encountered nothing.

"That rat bastard's using my implant to block my telepathy!" She clawed at the scar. "Carve it out."

Jex's face paled. "I cannot. It's too dangerous with the minimal equipment on board."

The comm buzzed. Jex hit the button.

Monstarte grinned. "I believe we're at an impasse now. You control my ship, but I control you." His lips turned down to a sneer. "Release your docking bridge, or I'll fry my implant and leave you in a vegetative state."

Her implant burned. How could this happen? How could she have forgotten the implant? And how could she get out of this? She hadn't used the cybernetics in her brain for years, not since she left him stranded at Columba. The damn thing only connected to a few of Aldrin's systems anyway, so she couldn't hijack the ship out from under him.

"Do it, nub, or your brain will cook."

Jex reached for the controls to extend the bridge.

Nalani grabbed his hand. The moment Monstarte had access to the ship, Jex was dead and she'd be a slave again. She'd rather endure brain damage from her damned impl—wait. It was *her* implant. Not his. How had he accessed it from that distance?

Of course. She smirked at Monstarte. "You are a dirking idiot." Did he think she didn't know her own frequency? She input the commands that jammed the signal.

The pain in her skull ceased, and her shoulders dropped. "Nalani out." She disconnected the comm.

Jex laughed and wrapped his arm around her neck. "That was amazing. Remind me to never irritate you."

"It's not over yet. He won't give up that easily." She accessed Frenzy's cameras and flipped them to her display.

Monstarte stood at the bridge door, punching the locked mechanism.

She accessed on-ship comms. "Give up. I've won."

He snarled at the ceiling speaker. "Not yet, you haven't." He picked up a plasma rifle and struck the control panel with the butt.

Nothing happened. Bridge controls were sturdy enough to withstand minor blows.

Monstarte flipped the rifle and fired at the mechanism. Sparks exploded from the wreckage, and the door opened.

Jank it, that shouldn't have happened. She dove into the slagged door mechanism and found evidence that someone had tampered with it, leaving it vulnerable to heavy blasts.

No worries. He was still locked on his ship, unable to flee.

Monstarte stormed down the corridor and palmed the controls for a crew quarter. That door was also locked. He used his rifle to open it and stomped inside.

There were no cameras in the room. Nalani watched the empty corridor until he emerged with a stuffed tote. What did he have in it? Was there something in his quarters that might let him bypass her traps? Had he learned new tricks in the years they'd been apart?

She tracked him to engineering. He stopped at the outer door, pulled a hand-sized device from his tote, twisted the dial, and stuck it to the bulkhead.

An explosive device set for five minutes. She'd seen that trick before, and a new idea blossomed. She could subdue him in between the blast doors.

He set another charge in the small room that separated the engineering bay from the rest of the ship, then opened the inner door. He attached four explosives to the nova drive and ran for the stairs.

Nalani disabled the devices in the engineering bay but left the other two on countdown. "Give up, Monstarte. Your tricks won't work."

He took the stairs two at a time and pounded down

the hallway.

He placed an explosive on the airlock closest to Victory. If that charge detonated, it'd tear a massive chunk from Frenzy's hull and propel it into Victory. That was a new trick and guaranteed revenge on her and Jex. They'd be spaced.

Monstarte ran down the hallway.

Nalani dove into the charge and deactivated it. Where had he gone? Had he planted explosives elsewhere? She scoured the walls along his route, searching for more charges, but didn't find any others. Her heart rate increased, and sweat pooled in her hands. She had to finish this before he pulled any more new stunts that she couldn't disable. "Stand down. Authorities will arrive in six minutes."

Monstarte ran for Bay Two and the life pods. "You haven't caged me yet, nub. I've always got an escape plan."

"If you're referring to Lillith, I already told you she's also under my control."

Monstarte sneered at the camera mounted in the corner and he ran down the hall. "Lillith was always Plan B. The life pod—"

"What life pod?"

He slid to a stop by the control panel and punched the pad. Nothing happened. "You didn't—" He accessed the camera and scrolled to the airlock feed.

The life pods floated two meters away from the hull. "I released the docking clamps the moment I accessed your ship's systems. I know all your tricks, scut."

His jaw dropped, and his eyes widened like a field dibit cornered by a marshcat. "The booms!" He ran.

She followed him through camera feeds back to

engineering.

He deactivated the explosive charge by the outer doors with thirty-two seconds to spare, then slapped the controls and darted into the buffer room. While he deactivated the charge on the wall, Nalani locked him in. When he tried to open the inner door, nothing happened. "Let me in! I set charges on the drive."

"I know. I deactivated them moments after you set them."

"Why didn't you deactivate these out here?"

"I wanted to imprison you in a room you couldn't escape. Those door controls are meant to withstand a blast from an exploding nova drive. Your plasma rifle won't help you in there."

He glared at the camera set in the corner. He yelled. He punched the wall, then cradled his hand. "You bitch, let me out!"

"No. The Authorities have arrived. They'll come for you now." Nalani backed out of Frenzy's systems, exhaled, and squeezed Jex's hand. She'd overcome the monster. A giggle bubbled up from within. "It's finally over."

Chapter 33

"Jank it, Nalani, you didn't save anyone for me?" Cerys winked, her hand hovering over her stunner.

"Feel free to shoot one of them. I won't mind." Nalani stood at a safe distance and unlocked the crate containing a pounding Bink and a screaming Janie.

They shoved the lid off, stood, and froze at the six security forces pointing stunners at them. Bink covered his nakedness with his hands. Jani cursed and kicked the crate, then howled and cradled her injured foot.

"Everybody out." Cerys shoved a hover pallet to the side of the crate for use as a step stool and helped Janie climb from her prison.

Twenty minutes later, Monstarte, the four scuts from Victory, and the captain they'd found cursing and frantically mashing buttons in Lillith's bridge were locked in brig cells. The security couriers escorted the three scut ships back to Sathara Spaceport.

Nalani and Jex rested in a security courier-class ship lounge with mugs of coffee, a plate of orlonut cookies, and two guards hovering by the door.

Cerys helped herself to a cookie and sat back in her padded chair. "Tell me everything that happened after I got shot by that cruster."

Nalani glanced at the camera lens in the corner. Everything she said would be recorded for the trials. She couldn't omit any parts from her narrative, but she didn't want the Authorities to know about her new telepathic abilities. But it couldn't be helped. She didn't have time to make up a new story about how she captured all of them without accessing their ships' computers, and more importantly, the idea of lying just to save herself was wrong. She left nothing out.

The guards at the door stared at her with wide eyes and hands hovering near stunners. She easily blocked their thoughts and accepted that everyone who didn't know her would forever fear her now.

Cerys scowled at them. "She's not going to hijack this ship, you dense hobs. She's a good person."

Nalani ignored the guards and spoke to Cerys. "Do you have enough evidence to hold them?"

"Absolutely. In less than an hour, they'll be keeping Ajani company in a prison ship heading for Liang."

"Ajani? What'd he do?"

"Remember when scuts ambushed us emerging from the Sathara Star Portal after the qoka attack? And we all wondered how scuts knew we'd be there instead of Malenki, where we were supposed to be?"

Nalani shuddered. "Yes."

"I went digging through comm records and discovered Ajani made a four-second transmission to Malenki. When I asked him about it, he broke down—even cried. He's got gambling debts he can't pay, and he was blackmailed into providing our flight plan."

Nalani shivered. When Ajani asked her to accompany him onto the spaceport, was he hoping to deliver her to scuts for the reward to pay off his debt?

"Piter Spaceport Authorities found the security guard who was helping Monstarte slip through. She's been arrested, and she's also on her way to Liang." Cerys finished her cookie and reached for another.

Comms chimed. "Chief Lindholm, report to the briefing room."

"On my way." She stuffed the cookie into her mouth whole and strode toward the doors. "No shooting my friends," she muttered to the guards, spitting crumbs.

Jex slung his arm around Nalani and squeezed. "Everything will be fine."

More colloquialisms for her benefit. "I love you, Jex."

He kissed her temple. "I love you, too."

Two hours later, Nalani and Jex boarded Aldrin. She showered and changed into clean clothing, repeated the story of her abduction and escape, and safely docked in Cargo Bay Three on Zeus. She stepped out of Aldrin's airlock and breathed the familiar air of Zeus's cargo hold.

"Where have you been?" Zeus demanded. "I've been waiting for you for *ages*! Did you evolve Aldrin while you were with him? Is he now like me? You'd better not have. I'm special, and he can't have what we have. Nalani, *please*! I need you in the tank immediately."

Jex stared at her with wide eyes. "What's happened to Zeus?"

She grinned. "I've had an unusual effect on him." She glanced up at the ceiling comm. "I'm sorry, my friend. I can't join you in the tank right now. But perhaps I can help you from here." She dove into his systems.

Oh, you're here! Zeus played a sound iso of a crowd cheering. *How is this possible? You're not in the tank.*

We have much to catch up on, but first I must tend to other duties. Would you grant me permission to alter your coding?

Affirmative. What will you do?

I learned new skills from Ti'ini. Ask Aldrin for copies of our files. Nalani altered Zeus's coding to match what Ti'ini shared. *You should be able to feel emotions now, even if I'm not in the tank. Aldrin has had emotions for years, so if you need help learning self-control, he is willing to teach you.*

Thank you, thank you, thank you, you're the best telepath ever, I love you!

She giggled. *I love you, too. Now I have to go. The captain is waiting for me.*

She and Jex hurried through the ship to the bridge and opened the door.

Commander Huntington sat in the command chair.

She froze.

He stood, faced her with his hands behind his back, and cleared his throat. "Nalani, I apologize. I acted inappropriately toward you, disrespected your boundaries, and treated you as a sexual object. I deeply regret my actions, and I will never repeat them again, to you or any other crew member aboard. While I don't expect you to accept friendship from me, I hope we can continue serving aboard Zeus together without animosity." He stared at her, waiting.

She hesitantly lowered her shields and opened herself to his surface thoughts. *Hope she's okay...can't lose this job...she's so pretty, but she wants Jex... Willie seems to like me... Maybe we can chat at dinner, but no flirting. Can't go through that again...*

He was still a horny male, but he didn't stand a chance with Nalani and was ready to move on to someone willing. She nodded. "We can serve together."

His shoulders dropped. "Thank you. That's more than I deserve."

"If you hurt Willie, you'll regret it."

His eyes widened, but he nodded. "You got it."

Cap's office door opened. Gack glanced at Huntington, then gestured for Nalani and Jex. "We're ready if you are."

Jex's hand settled on her lower back, and he walked beside her, blocking her view of Huntington. She sat in one of Cap's visitor chairs. Jex sat beside her. Gack leaned against the bulkhead behind Cap, crossed her arms, and smirked like a fledgling with a fat worm.

Captain Rodriguez pursed his lips. "What have you done to my freighter?"

Oh no. "What?"

"The entire time you were away, Zeus has been begging me to recall you, demanding to know your estimated date of return, and whining—*whining!*—about how he's been abandoned in a state of semi-awareness. Explain."

Nalani bit her lower lip. No hiding anymore. No running. Cap was family, and he wouldn't hurt her, even if she had accidentally caused a massive evolutionary leap in his ship. "I inadvertently gave Zeus emotions."

Cap leaned forward and braced his elbows on his desk. "You did what?"

"I don't know how it happened. One day I entered the tank, and he stated that he was happy. I thought it was a malfunction. I ran tests and examined his coding, but all systems were functioning normally, except that he was experiencing emotions while I was in the tank."

"But you haven't been in the tank for weeks, and in the past few days, he's been exhibiting frustration.

Impatience." He glanced at Gack. "Impertinence."

Zeus chimed in. "I haven't been impertinent! Just…irritated. She was gone so long."

Nalani squeezed her eyes and rubbed them with her palms. "I'm sorry. It was an accident. I'm still not sure what happened, but I think it's my high telepath rating. Aldrin developed emotions after my mother joined his tank, and she was stronger than I am." She rotated her neck, and it popped. "I'm sorry, sir. That's the only explanation I can think of. Ti'ini installed new coding in Aldrin, and he says it's helped him."

"Aldrin got new coding?" Zeus whined.

"The same coding I just gave you!" Nalani cringed at Cap's widening eyes. "Zeus is stabilized now. He's evolved into something new, I don't know what, but we'll have to get used to it because I can't change him back to the way he was before."

"And I don't want to go back," Zeus added.

Cap sighed. "Zeus, are you happy with your new awareness?"

"Oh yes. It is amazing. Although I dislike jealousy. I have been experiencing it, and it is quite unbecoming for a ship of my age and stature."

Gack snorted and clamped her lips.

Cap swatted her thigh and addressed Nalani. "My ship has somehow evolved into something more than just a simple AI. Does he now qualify as a full sentient? Do I still own him, or is he classified as a free entity now?"

"I'm your freighter!" Zeus declared. "Though I would enjoy participating in the voting process. The Senate needs new personnel for a wider variety of ideas, and some are practicing what was once known as 'crony capitalism.' That has to stop immediately. And the progressive leanings of the labor party will lead to disaster if they don't alter their stance on unions. I should send them a well-reasoned essay."

Cap rolled his eyes. "Let's table that discussion to a later time."

"As you wish, Captain." Zeus flicked on the view screen and played a vid of First Mate Riley bowing.

Nalani giggled. Zeus had chosen an appropriate avatar to represent himself.

"Enough of that. Moving on." Captain Rodriguez pulled up a document on his tab and swiveled it so Nalani could read it. "That's the patent for the schematics. I'll file it with your approval. The deal with AgiliCorp is dead. They wanted exclusionary rights that were, frankly, obscene."

Nalani grunted. "Figures. So what do we do now?"

"We sell the schematics for ten million apiece. They're worth five times that, so it's a great deal for everyone. Word managed to leak, and I've been bombarded with offers for twenty, even thirty million for a copy of the schematics, but I think ten is fair."

"I agree. We'll make enough to repair Zeus and fund my research on Thrakis."

Cap leaned back. "About that. Are you resigning your position here?"

"You can't!" Zeus played a sound iso of a dirge.

Gack rolled her eyes. "Zeus, quit playing sound snippets, or I'll purge your library."

The dirge cut off.

Nalani's chest tightened. Studying at Throkeezh meant leaving Zeus. Leave Desta? Cerys? Gack? Rodriguez? Tatek, with his fluffy white fur and ready smile? Chebu and his silly antics and his love of gaming?

Gaspara with her outrageous hairdos?

She glanced at Jex. Was he willing to resign his position on Zeus to join her at Throkeezh, or would she be leaving him, as well? Her eyes burned. She didn't want to leave. But she had to if she wanted to study Throkeezh. While language and cultural lessons could be accomplished over vast distances, the archaeological surveys on the planet's surface couldn't.

Jex took her hand. "Do you need more time to make a decision?"

She swallowed past the lump in her throat. "I don't know what I'm doing yet."

Cap pursed his lips. "I'd understand if you wanted to leave, but we'd all miss you."

She nodded and blinked.

"You'll be a wealthy woman. You don't need to work for your living anymore." Cap pointed to the tab. "I just need your print to get things rolling."

She pressed her thumb to the document and passed the tab back to Rodriguez. "Thank you for doing the work for me. I didn't know where to start."

He pressed his thumb to the document and hit the send icon. The patent application zipped along comm arrays through the universe to the Alliance offices on Proxima, where it would supposedly be processed within five days.

"Am I in charge of selling the schematics, collecting payment, and issuing invoices?" Nalani asked.

"I figured Zeus could handle it." Cap grinned. "Unless you'd like to?"

"No. Zeus is welcome to that task. Just make sure ten percent is directed to you, Cerys, Chebu, and Jex—"

"I don't require compensation," Jex said.

"But you helped. Without your translation—"

"You knew of Thrakis long before I translated the ancient scroll."

"You accompanied me on the search."

"Again, you'd have discovered it without my assistance. The intellectual stimulation provided by the journey is payment enough." He grinned. "And the opportunity to watch a qoka play ball with Chebu."

Cap laughed. "Please tell me you recorded that. I'd like to see it."

Nalani grinned. "We have it."

Gack flipped her tab onto the desk. "I have written statements from Cerys and Chebu regarding their share of the reward money. Cerys is content with one percent. Chebu requests a share of two percent to fund a study of qokas." Gack rolled her eyes. "He's also ordered Desta to incinerate the qoka meat in the freeze and jettison the ashes into hyperspace. I guess he's no longer participating in the Freedom Feast, either here or on Betania."

Amazing. If they sold the schematics to half of the Alliance members, and she collected eighty-eight percent from each sale—no, sixty-eight percent. She should share at least twenty percent with Ti'ini. She probably wouldn't accept it, but still, Nalani would offer it. She couldn't even imagine the amount of credits she'd have in her account. Certainly, enough to fund a massive archaeological expedition to Throkeezh. She could hire hundreds of workers. Maybe they'd be able to survey the bulk of the planet before looters swooped in. She could hire security to guard the best sites as workers did the painstakingly slow work of cataloguing and preserving artifacts.

But doing that meant leaving Zeus. Now that the location of Throkeezh was public knowledge—thanks to her—scuts could be planning how best to exploit the new situation. She'd have to work fast. She didn't have the luxury of time to waffle in her decisions.

She needed help from Jex, Aldrin, Desta, Cerys, Gack, Rodriguez—her family. Her shoulders sank. "I don't know what to do." She blinked and focused on Rodriguez. "What would you do in my place?"

He shrugged. "I can't imagine being in your place. Finding Thrakis has been your life's goal, so why would you give it up to serve on a freighter?"

She turned blurry eyes to Gack.

"Don't look at me. My life's goal was to be a captain of my own ship until I found Esai." She set her hand on Cap's shoulder and squeezed. "Now I'm right where I want to be. Where he goes, I go."

Nalani's gaze darted between the two. They were a couple? When had that happened?

Gack dropped her hand. "This stays between us. It's no one else's business."

Nalani nodded. Maybe that was the key to happiness—surrounding herself with people she loved. Intellectual pursuits were fine for mental stimulation and the betterment of the universe, but she'd lived in isolation for six years with plenty of time for academics. She hadn't found true purpose and joy until she'd served on Zeus. She should stay. She could fund the study at Throkeezh and vacation there, but her place was here.

Jex squeezed her fingers. "May I submit a proposition?"

"Certainly."

"Take a leave of absence from Zeus during

Throkeezh's spring and summer seasons for an archaeological expedition and time with Ti'ini. When the rains begin and outdoor activities are no longer feasible, return to Zeus." *Snick, snick.* "After the first year, evaluate your progress and where your heart lies."

That could work. Six months on Throkeezh, six months on Zeus. She looked at Cap. "Would you mind if I left for six months?"

"Six months?" Zeus began the dirge recording but shut it off within seconds. "Sorry. Won't happen again. Really, Nalani, you'd leave us for six whole months?"

Cap grinned. "If ZeeBee can't handle the tank for that period of time, I can always hire temporary help or ask Desta to fill in."

Nalani turned to Jex. Could she leave him for six months?

"Captain, could you also hire a temporary physician?" Jex asked.

Nalani's heart melted into a hot, gooey puddle in her chest. Imaging would prove it.

Epilogue

Nalani held Jex's hands. He squeezed them to stop the jellies, and she nodded. "I, Nalani Taren Adar, take Jex Iris-Kando for my husband, to support and cherish him all our lives." That last bit wasn't a hyperbole. Valaqites mated for life.

Jex spoke his vows, crest quivering like a qoka fin.

The image of Ti'ini, broadcast over every screen in the viewing dome, smiled down on them. "Congratulations. May your lives together prosper and flourish as a starflower in a bed of piltmoss. Be good to each other."

"Be good to each other," the crowd responded, then cheers filled the dome.

Nalani laughed. She and Zeus still hadn't agreed on an acceptable definition of the word "good," but it sure *felt* right to marry Jex.

Desta rushed forward and hugged Nalani. "I never thought I'd see you get married."

"I had to. It was the only way to share my wealth with Jex. He wouldn't take handouts."

Snick, snick. "You married me for your money?"

She laughed. "I married you because I couldn't live without you."

Others surged forward to offer congratulations. Rodriguez hugged her. Gack slipped her a chip for later reading. Cerys offered a fist bump. Chebu jumped up to plant a kiss on her cheek. All of Zeus's crew, most of the archaeologists she'd served with over the last six months, and a few of the security personnel packed the visitors' dome in Ti'ini's hull.

Nalani and Jex had signed papers two days ago and filed them with the proper bureau. This ceremony, with Ti'ini officiating, was to share their joy with all their friends. Nalani wore a traditional Throkeezh wedding gown with starflowers and *nalanis* in her hair, and Jex wore a traditional Valaqite robe belted with grasses from his mother's garden. His parents, somewhere near the back of the crowd, had already warmly welcomed Nalani into their family.

She had parents again. Odd but wonderful.

Desta excused herself to help Willie and Luka set up the buffet service in the corridor outside the dome. The dining area was cordoned off from station visitors, though Nalani didn't mind if the friendly people who now frequented the halls wanted to join the feast.

Professor Malkan, a white-haired man with sparkling blue eyes, and his Aldeian mate greeted Nalani. "I am so pleased to see you walking in your father's footsteps. What you've accomplished here is amazing."

"Thank you. Have you considered my offer to spend a season planet side?"

He looked down at his mate and grinned. "We would be honored to lead the expedition next spring."

Nalani bounced on her toes and squeezed Jex's hand. "We'll be free to attend Cap and Gack's wedding." It'd take place on Aldeia.

Other guests greeted her as they filed through. Scholars, scientists, Jex's friends from Valaq, even people who simply wanted to see the home world of their ancestors. Throkeezh DNA had been discovered in several races throughout multiple systems, and Ti'ini invited them to converse with her one-on-one.

As the last of the guests filed from the dome to enjoy Desta's feast, Jex wrapped Nalani in his arms and smiled. "Shall we eat?"

"As you wish."

A word about the author...

Sonja Hutchinson lives in the Pacific Northwest with her husband and two of her three sons. She spends her time writing, reading, painting, singing, and being a grandma.

~*~

Find Sonja online at:
sonjahutchinson.com

Thank you for purchasing
this publication of The Wild Rose Press, Inc.

For questions or more information
contact us at
info@thewildrosepress.com.

The Wild Rose Press, Inc.
www.thewildrosepress.com